SAL&GABI

BREAK THE UNIVERSE

SAL & GABI

BREAK THE UNIVERSE

CARLOS HERNANDEZ

RICK RIORDAN PRESENTS

 • **HYPERION**   LOS ANGELES   NEW YORK

Copyright © 2019 by Carlos Hernandez
Introduction copyright © 2019 by Rick Riordan

All rights reserved. Published by Disney • Hyperion, an imprint of Disney Book
Group. No part of this book may be reproduced or transmitted in any form or by
any means, electronic or mechanical, including photocopying, recording, or by
any information storage and retrieval system, without written permission from
the publisher. For information address Disney • Hyperion, 125 West End Avenue,
New York, New York 10023.

First Hardcover Edition, March 2019
First Paperback Edition, April 2020
10 9 8 7 6 5 4 3 2 1
FAC-025438-20052
Printed in the United States of America

This book is set in Bookman Old Style Pro/Monotype; Crillee Bold Italic Std/
International Typeface
Designed by Phil T. Buchanan
Art by Andrea Galecio
Lettering by Saskia Bueno

Library of Congress Cataloging-in-Publication Control Number for Hardcover
Edition: 2018021081
ISBN 978-1-368-02362-7
Visit www.DisneyBooks.com

SUSTAINABLE
FORESTRY
INITIATIVE
Certified Chain of Custody
Promoting Sustainable Forestry
www.sfiprogram.org
SFI-01054
The SFI label applies to the text stock

To Cynthia Hawkins.

In another universe, my dear, dear friend,
you are reading this book.

Sal and Gabi's Excellent Universe-Destroying Adventure

YOU KNOW HOW I can tell when a book is great?

When I can't even describe it to you without ruining the marvelous surprises. I mean . . . I could try to explain why Gabi's father is called Lightning Dad, or why Sal's teacher Dr. Doctorpants dresses like a gumball machine, or even why Sal's physicist father and his not-quite-human assistant, Bonita, are building a remembranation machine in the living room. But you'd never believe me. You'd accuse me of making up cacaseca. You *definitely* wouldn't believe me if I told you how that dead chicken got in Yasmany's locker.

Was it sleight of hand? Was it actual magic? Was it, oh, I don't know . . . something scarier? Something that might rip apart the universe and cause a cosmic mess so big even a super custodian like Mr. Milagros can't clean it up?

You'll just have to dive into the story and find out for yourself.

You're about to meet Sal Vidón. He's recently moved from Connecticut to Miami with his dad and American Stepmom because . . . well, let's just say things got complicated when Sal's mom, his *real* mom, changed from Mami Viva to Mami Muerta.

It's never easy to switch schools, even if Culeco Academy of the Arts seems much cooler than his old school. Sal gets to study for his dream job: becoming the world's greatest magician, while his classmates are dancers, musicians, actors, costume designers, and even a film director creating a cinematic masterpiece on the history of wedgies. Unfortunately, Sal's problems did not stop when he moved from Connecticut. He still has to monitor his diabetes with his own med kit and his emergency pack of Skittles. He's been to the principal's office every day for things that *totally* were not his fault. His classmates look at him strangely, like they're afraid he might be a brujo.

Then there's Gabi Reál—student council president and editor of the school paper—whom Sal either finds fascinating or wants to run away from at light speed. He's not sure yet. All he *does* know: Gabi is suspicious of Sal's deepest, darkest secrets. She is determined to find out more about this strange new kid who is able to pull impossible tricks. Can Sal and Gabi trust each other? They'll have to figure that out if they want to survive the year without, you know, ruining their reputations at school and wrecking the space-time continuum.

Welcome to Culeco Academy—a world only Carlos Hernandez could dream up! I can't reveal all its secrets, not without ruining the fun. But one thing I can promise you: After reading about Sal and Gabi's marvelous universe, you're going to want to move there!

1

THERE'S ALL SORTS of bad advice out there about how to deal with bullies. *Ignore them. Stand up to them. Tell a teacher, tell a parent, tell your dentist while he's jamming your teeth back into your face.*

The real way to deal with a bully is to stick a raw chicken in their locker.

I had my showdown with Yasmany Robles just three days after I had started my new life at Culeco Academy of the Arts, a magnet school in the middle of Miami. To get in, you had to have good grades, pass an interview, and either submit a portfolio (for painting or writing) or audition (for theater or music). You'd think all the effort someone has to go through to get into Culeco would've kept out bullies, but I guess not.

I guess there are just too many of them in the world. If your school only allowed in kids who'd never pick on anyone, you'd have an empty school.

Whatever. It's not like I hadn't learned how to handle bullies back in Connecticut.

On Wednesday, between fourth and fifth periods, I went to

the lockers, along with half a million other kids. I stowed my history book and grabbed math so I could do my homework during lunch, then opened my bag of magic tricks and put on my GOTCHA! stamp ring. We would be doing introductions in my eighth-period theater class, and I thought I could use it to demonstrate some sleight of hand. Magic is kind of my thing.

I had a minute before I needed to go, so I took out my diabetes bag and fished out my glucose meter. I thought I'd be all right until lunch, but I'd started to feel spacey and dreamy at the end of my last class. Blood sugar levels might be falling. Best to check now.

As I rummaged, I noticed the tall kid next to me struggling to get his locker open. He was as Cuban as they come: brown, built like a track-and-field champ, with a haircut so short you could see the bumpy skin of his scalp beneath what was left of his tiny curls. He'd wrestled with his combination lock yesterday, too, and never figured it out, so he'd had to carry a full backpack of books to his next class. I'd had trouble with my lock on the first day, until I'd figured out you have to squeeze it as you turn the dial.

And I'm a nice guy. So I said to him, "Hey, man. My lock sucks, too. The trick is to squeeze the top while—"

That's all I got out before he punched his locker. The whole hallway grew a little quieter.

Yasmany—I learned his name later, but why keep you in suspense?—slowly turned to look at me. He scanned me up and down, doing some tough-guy calculations to figure out if he could take me.

Apparently he thought he could, because he stepped up to

me fast, ferocious, chest out, arms wide. He'd been in a lot of fights, judging from his flat-as-a-shamrock nose.

"Just come back from safari, white boy?" he asked. "I mean, if you even *are* a boy."

Let's take a second to break down this insult.

The "safari" crack was because I had on canvas cargo pants and a cargo vest, each with four pockets brimming with gadgets and tricks of the trade. Pretty much all the clothes I own have tons of pockets. I'm ready to perform at any time. You never know when the world is going to need a little magic.

The "white boy" crack was because—I guess?—to him I looked white. Back when I lived in Connecticut, kids were telling me to "go back to brown town" all the time. But I was in Miami now: new place, new rules about skin color.

And the "if you are a boy"? I kept my hair pretty long. It gave me a place to hide stuff in the middle of a trick. And to this caveman's mind, calling someone a girl was an insult.

Whatever. I tried the *My Little Pony* approach to handling bullies. "Sorry. Just trying to help." And I started to walk away.

He body-blocked me. "*You?* Wanted to help *me*? Why would a sandwich like you think I'd need your help?"

Now I looked him in the eye. "Your locker's still locked, isn't it?"

I probably shouldn't have said anything. But he called me a sandwich. Some insults you can't let slide.

In response, he did what bullies do. He slapped my diabetes bag out of my hands.

It hit the ground with a glassy crunch. My stomach crunched right along with it.

That pack contained my insulin, my syringes, my blood-glucose meter, my sharps disposal container (for used needles), my Band-Aids, and a fun-size bag of Skittles. If he broke something important in that pack, I could be in real trouble.

I knelt down to pick it up, my hands shaking as they reached for the bag. I tried to relax. I closed my eyes, breathed slowly, and remembered what Papi had said to me after Mami died: *Fear is your body trying to tell your brain what to do. But the brain is the king of the body. It calls the shots.*

I opened my eyes slowly, the way the good guys in movies do when they've just figured out how to beat the villain. I noticed that the bright young scholars of Culeco Academy of the Arts had formed a ring around Yasmany and me. This crowd didn't seem as bloodthirsty as the ones in my last school had been. In Connecticut, kids hooted like in *Planet of the Apes* whenever a fight was about to start, jumping up and down and beating on each other in anticipation of someone getting wedgied back to the Stone Age. But these kids looked kind of grim and quiet, like this was some boring school assembly they had to attend.

Well, from my perspective, it didn't really matter whether they were enjoying themselves or not. They had me surrounded just the same. I was trapped.

Wait. No. That's an excuse, and I don't lie to myself. I could have pushed my way out of there if I'd wanted to. But now all eyes were on me. I had an audience. And I am a showman.

Yasmany stretched his fingers wide before he made two fists. "Time to die, little man. Stand up."

I stood all right. Got right in his face. "Time to die?" I asked.

"Time. To. Die," he repeated.

"Like the dead chicken in your locker?" I asked.

"What?"

See, that's the real secret of dealing with bullies: Change the game. You thought we were going to fistfight, Mr. Tough Guy, but—surprise!—suddenly we're talking about murdered poultry.

"The dead chicken in your locker," I said, explaining it to the crowd. "That's the real reason you didn't want to open it. You didn't want anybody to see your dead chicken so they wouldn't know you keep dead chickens in your locker. Because," I said, turning to face Yasmany again, "what kind of weirdo keeps dead chickens in his locker?"

"Stop saying 'dead chicken'!"

Everybody laughed. That probably would have sent Yasmany into a berserker rage if some girl hadn't shrieked, "Blood!" She was pointing at Yasmany's locker.

"What?" Yasmany asked again. He and everybody else looked at his locker, and yeah, there was watery pink blood leaking from it, the kind you find at the bottom of Styrofoam meat packages. Not a lot, but enough to drip from the bottom of the locker door and pool on the floor. And it only takes a tiny bit of blood to freak people all the way out.

Not me, though. I mean, I didn't know SANGRE DE POLLO was going to come dripping out of his locker, but it wasn't exactly a surprise, either. I could work with it.

"Open it," I said to Yasmany. "Unless you're too . . . *chicken.*"

If he hadn't been completely bewildered by what was happening, he would have gorilla-rushed me for sure. Instead, he walked over to his locker and tried to undo the lock. Two, four, seven yanks on it, each angrier than the last. Then he punched his locker door again and said, "I can't open the stupid thing! I keep trying, but I can't."

"Here. Let me."

He took a step back to let me through. But not without asking, "What? How you know my combo?"

His "combo" was still taped to the back of the lock. About as sharp as a bowling ball, this Yasmany.

I looked at him over my shoulder with spooky eyes and replied, "Fool! I am a magician. I can read your mind." Then I spun the dial with fast fingers, clock-, then counter-, then clockwise again. I tugged the lock open dramatically and, with a flourish, removed it.

"You want the honors?" I asked him, stepping aside with a gracious magician's bow.

Yasmany—bro had gone full autopilot by now—stepped forward and opened the locker door, every kid behind him on tiptoe, watching, waiting.

A whole raw chicken, like you get at the grocery store, with bumpy yellow skin and no head, flipped out of his locker, landed on its chicken butt, and went *splat.*

Kids scattered, screaming. Adults would be here any second. Yasmany did a 180 and looked around wildly. He didn't have eyes anymore: just fear. "I didn't put no dead chicken in my locker!" he yelled. "You gotta believe me!"

"I believe you," I said.

Of course I did. It was I who had put it in there, after all.

Abracadabra, chicken plucker.

2

"SALVADOR VIDÓN, HOW long have you been attending my school?" asked Principal Torres. I'd only been at Culeco for a few days, but I already knew three things about her: (1) she was a big woman, (2) she was a smart woman, and (3) most importantly, she was a principal. That meant she had zero tolerance for cacaseca.

"Cacaseca" is the word Miami talk-show hosts use instead of BS. It literally means "dry poop," but really it means "Dude, your poop is so played out. Don't try to play me with your played-out poop."

"Three days," I replied to Principal Torres, with exactly zero cacaseca in my voice.

"Three days," she repeated, letting her gaze drift around the room. Yasmany and I were sitting in tiny little plastic chairs in front of her desk, both of us doing our best not to move. Maybe then Principal Torres wouldn't see us. You know, like cavemen hiding from T. rexes.

No dice. Principal Torres's glasses suddenly caught the

light and locked on me like prison searchlights. "And how many times have I seen you in my office, Mr. Vidón?"

I paused before answering. The first time was on day one, because my doctor had told me to inform my principal about my diabetes and the special equipment I needed to manage it, like needles, because if you bring needles to school, everyone assumes you're a drug addict.

The second time (yesterday), Mr. Lynott, my PE teacher, had sent me to her office for eating candy. But what was I supposed to do—let myself pass out in the middle of the obstacle course? Principal Torres had said she would let Coach Lynott know I had special permission to pop the occasional Skittle.

And this time it was because of Yasmany. None of this was my fault.

But I didn't say any of that. Principal Torres, I already knew, didn't like excuses. So I kept my face neutral and said, "You have seen me three times."

"Do you think I see every child who attends this school once a day, every day of the school year?"

"No."

"That is exactly correct!" she said. Her smile could wilt flowers. "So why do you think I've had the great pleasure of enjoying your pleasant company in my office every day of the school year so far?"

I thought for a moment. Actually, I just made a face like I was thinking, for the sake of the performance. Then: "Because the students and faculty of Culeco have a lot to learn about how to make school safe for diabetics."

She blinked and kept blinking for a few seconds. "Huh," she said, sitting forward in her chair. "You know, I was all ready to tear into both of you. But honestly, Sal, you may be right. Culeco's still pretty new. We only opened five years ago, and we've been growing and changing the whole time." She shook her head to help her get back to her point. "We've never had a student with type-one diabetes before. I am going to have to instruct my whole staff on how to meet your needs. The students, too. I'll tell my science teachers to include a lesson or two on diabetes. We will do better for you, Mr. Vidón. I promise. And I apologize."

One of the quickest ways you can tell if an adult is quality people is if they'll apologize to a kid when they're wrong. Principal Torres was someone I could work with. "Thank you," I said.

She nodded before she turned her searchlights on Yasmany. (Not a hair moved, by the way. It was like her hairdo was made of Legos.) "I see I am going to have to make examples of a few people who don't know how to create a welcoming learning environment. Maybe then the school will get it through its thick collective head that *bullying will not be tolerated under any circumstances.*"

Man. Principal Torres wasn't even talking to me, but she made my guts flutter just the same.

"What did I tell you at the end of last year?" she said to him, parting her lips but not her teeth.

This was usually the point in the conversation when the bully starts denying everything, blaming the victim, changing the subject, etc. I was ready for this. I'd made two bullies cry in front of principals at my last school just by calmly sticking to the facts and being polite. Adults really like polite kids.

But Yasmany didn't behave like other bullies I'd known. He looked at his shoes. "I'm having a bad day," he told his ratty high-tops. A spattering of chicken blood decorated his right shoe's toe.

"No," said Principal Torres. "You *were* having a bad day. *Now* you're having the worst day of your young life. Because now I have to expel you."

What? "Wait!" I interjected. "It wasn't that big a deal, Principal Torres. He shouldn't get expelled just for knocking my med bag out of my hands."

She pushed her huge glasses up her face. "Unfortunately, Mr. Robles has a history at this school. Since the moment he got here, I have been bending over backward to try to give him a proper education. Do you remember, Mr. Robles, how I helped you to complete the paperwork last year so that you could attend this very special magnet school?"

Yasmany hunched over even more. "Yes."

"Do you remember, at the end of last year, after all the fights you got into and the problems you caused me, the little heart-to-heart we had, right here in this office?"

"Yes."

"And what did I tell you then, Mr. Robles?"

"That I was on probation."

"That you *were* on probation. One more altercation with another student and it would be a-di-os." She pronounced "adios" like an American, with three syllables. I wondered for a minute if she was a Latina who didn't know Spanish. But she cured me of that idea with her next sentence: "Y si no tienes ninguna defensa para ofrecer, te digo '¡Chao pesca'o!' ahora mismo."

My own Spanish is pretty okay, though I hadn't gotten to practice it much since Mami died. "¡Chao pesca'o!" basically means "See you later, alligator!" And "defensa" means "defense." She was asking him if he had anything to say in his defense. Or it would be bye-bye, Yasmany.

And, I mean, I clearly wasn't the first kid he'd bullied. Chacho was in big trouble.

"Yes," he said. He looked at the door, then back at Principal Torres. Then the door. Then Torres. "I will have a defense. In a minute."

Principal Torres cocked her head. She almost laughed but inhaled instead. "In a minute? Mr. Robles, the time is now. Speak now or forever hold your peace."

He didn't look up or raise his voice or anything. He just said, "I just need a second, Principal Torres. My lawyer is coming."

Now she did laugh. "Your lawyer?"

Her office door opened. In walked a very recognizable seventh grader, bringing in her own chair from the hallway and wearing a big smile on her face. I knew her, even though I'd only been at this school for a few days. It was Gabi Reál: student council president, editor of the school newspaper, and, apparently, Yasmany's lawyer.

"I came as fast as I could," she said. "So, what'd I miss?"

3

GABI PUT HER chair next to mine and sat down. Not next to her "client," as you might think she would. She offered her hand for a proper, businesslike shake.

"Hi there! My name is Gabrielle Reál, and I am your student council president, duly elected at the end of last year to serve all my fellow students. I want you to know that, even though right now I am serving as Yasmany's counsel, this in no way means I have anything against you. I am your advocate, too, and when you need representation someday, you will see how well I defend you from miscarriages of justice. What's your name?"

I just kind of blinked back at Gabi, trying to take her in.

It's a scientific fact that not all your body parts grow at the same rate, which may explain why Gabi's smile made up three-quarters of her lower face. I mean, she had a mouth like her mama was a shark and her daddy was shark food. It also probably looked bigger because Gabi was short. (Trust me, I don't mean that as a burn. I'm short, too. I'm just saying that three raccoons in a trench coat would be taller than she was.) Her skin was the color of the Pinewood Derby race car I made in shop class last year, after I'd brushed on two layers of stain. She had poofy black hair that she'd tried to control with Shaolin-monk barrettes. I'd never seen barrettes that looked like Shaolin monks before. They were fighting each other all over her head, and they kind of made me want to wear barrettes. She wore jeans, running shoes, and a T-shirt that said WELL-BEHAVED WOMEN SELDOM MAKE HISTORY. —LAUREL THATCHER ULRICH. Every fingernail on the hand she held out to me was painted a different color.

Sometimes the most honest response is the best. I shook her hand and said, "It's nice to meet you. My name is Sal Vidón. You seem like someone I can work with."

Gabi smiled, but she side-eyed me as we shook hands. I don't think she understood what I meant. Fine with me. As a magician, that's exactly how I want people to react.

"Ahem," said Principal Torres.

Gabi let go of my hand so she could get up and shake hands with Principal Torres. "I am so sorry, Principal Torres, I didn't mean to waste your time! I'm sorry for being late."

"Not sure how you could be late, since I didn't even know you were coming."

Principal Torres had the brutal timing of an insult comedienne—or a middle school principal.

"You . . . didn't know?" Gabi looked at Yasmany. "You didn't tell her I was coming?"

"Yes I did!" said Yasmany.

Principal Torres shook her head. "You said 'your lawyer' was coming, Yasmany. And while it's true that, one day, Gabi will graduate at the top of her law class, that won't be for a few years yet."

Gabi shook her head exactly the way Principal Torres had. "I don't understand why you make things so hard for yourself, Yasmany. When you texted me, I *told* you to tell Principal Torres I was coming." She turned back to Principal Torres. "You must think I just barged into your office uninvited. I am so sorry!"

"It's okay, Ms. Reál. Frankly, I'm glad you're here. I'm about two seconds away from having to expel Mr. Robles"—she talked over Gabi, who had started to interrupt her—"*but* I would love to be convinced that there's some way he can be allowed to stay. So convince me."

Gabi straightened up, squinted her eyes, and nodded, and all the Shaolin monks in her hair nodded along. "I will, Principal Torres. I am here to present vital evidence on the incident in question."

Principal Torres settled into her chair for a good listen. "What do you know, Gabi?"

"I have gathered testimony from eight students, Your Honor."

"'Principal Torres' will do nicely, thank you."

"Oh. Right. Principal Torres, I have eight witnesses willing to testify, under oath—"

"No one has to testify under oath. This isn't a trial."

"Okay. Ahem," said Gabi, clearing her throat. Clearly, she'd seen one too many *Law & Order* reruns. I almost laughed but swallowed it. Gabi collected herself and continued. "Those witnesses swear that Yasmany hasn't been able to open his locker since the first day of school. Which means Yasmany couldn't have put a chicken in there, even if he'd wanted to. In fact, the only person who has opened that lock so far this year is Salvador Vidón."

"Oh, ri-i-i-ight." Principal Torres turned her searchlight glasses back on me. "The health code violation and salmonella outbreak waiting to happen. We haven't gotten to that part yet, have we, Sal? Let's take a small detour from Yasmany's bullying—*which will not be tolerated under any circumstances*—and talk to our number one suspect. Now would be a very good time to fess up, Mr. Vidón. Because if you lie to me, by the time you get out of detention, your grandchildren are going to have to come pick you up from school. Did you put a raw chicken in Yasmany's locker?"

I felt my face go hot. The conversation had been going so well for me before Gabi showed up, but now? She'd managed to redirect Principal Torres's wrath toward me. And I *hate* it when wrath is directed toward me.

This would not do. That girl definitely needed to be managed.

Fine. It was nothing that a little more magic couldn't handle.

I sat back in my chair, closed my eyes, and relaxed.

4

YOU MIGHT THINK I would find it hard to relax just then. But I'm good at relaxing. Like, *really* good.

I can lean back into life like it's my favorite armchair. I can zone out so far that my body disappears. I'm like a sponge at the bottom of the ocean, just hanging, absorbing whatever comes my way. Nothing is ugly or beautiful, nothing is good or bad, nothing can hurt me or help me, nothing is anything. I just sit there while time floats on by without me.

When I lean back into life like that, it's like I can *hear* it. Life, so you know, sounds like the snoring that would rumble in your ear if you were resting on the belly of a sleeping giant.

And if you wait long enough, you'll be there when the giant wakes up, yawning and stretching.

The giant likes you, has been your friend since the day you were born. Will even do you favors, if you know how to ask.

I learned how to ask when my mami died five years ago. "I want my mami!" I cried.

"Pero ella se murió," said the giant. It's a Spanish-speaking giant, and very kind.

"Then I want my Mami Muerta," I sniffled.

And the giant took pity on me and helped me. And gave me way more than I bargained for.

Here in Principal Torres's office, I asked the giant to do me another solid. Then I opened my eyes.

"What chicken?" I asked Principal Torres.

Gabi, I saw out of the side of my eye, flicked her eyebrows at me, as if to say, *It's your funeral, buddy.*

Principal Torres bowed her head in disappointment before she answered. "I expected better from you, Mr. Vidón. I thought you were an honest young man."

"I am." And I really am. I only say things that are true. At the time. They might not *always* have been true, and they might not be true in the future, but they are true when I say them.

"Then explain to me why Mr. Milagros"—he was the school's chief custodian—"brought you and Yasmany here on account of a whole raw chicken that he had to clean up?"

"He fell for my illusion, just like everyone else," I said. "Did you know I am a magician?"

Yasmany shot up out of his chair and yelled, "He's a liar!" Between the words "a" and "liar" he added a word that students do not say in front of principals.

"Sit down, Yasmany!" yelled Gabi. "I told you to let me handle this!"

"Two weeks' detention!" said Principal Torres, pointing at him. I think she forgot she was going to expel him for bullying me.

"But he's lying, Principal Torres!" Yasmany said desperately. "There was a chicken! I can prove it!"

"Sit down," Gabi said through her teeth. She bolted over to him and tried to push him into his seat by the shoulders. "Sal's digging his own grave."

Yasmany looked at Gabi and almost laughed. "You're like a hamster," he said. "You can't move me."

"I am your student council president!" she said. "I order you to sit!"

He let her keep trying to push him down while he kicked his right leg onto Principal Torres's desk with the easy skill of a pro dancer. Which, since this was a performing arts school, probably meant he *was* a dancer and not a track champ like I had assumed earlier.

A bully ballerino. Interesting. There was more to this Yasmany than I had first thought.

"Check out the blood on my shoe," he said, pointing at it but glaring at me. "That's all the proof we need."

Gabi and Principal Torres came over to see for themselves. I finally got a good look at Principal Torres's red pantsuit, which looked like it had been co-designed by Hillary Clinton and Santa Claus.

I stayed where I was, since I already knew what would happen next.

"There's no blood on your shoe," said Principal Torres.

Gabi smacked her forehead and left her hand covering one eye. "Why do you insist on making things harder for yourself, Yasmany?"

Yasmany looked at his shoe, his mouth open. His face went through a cycle of fear expressions, like he was practicing to star in a horror movie. "But there *was*!" he yelled. "I'm not lying! There was blood on my shoe." He pointed at me accusingly. "You must have cleaned it off!"

"When?" I asked, innocent as apple pie.

The correct answer was "about thirty seconds ago," when I'd relaxed. But only I knew that. Nobody else could possibly think I'd had the opportunity to do anything to Yasmany's shoe. And questions can't be lies.

"Yas! Ma! Ny!" Gabi almost climbed on his back trying to get him into his seat again. When she got to the third syllable of his name, he finally allowed himself to be pushed down. He fell like deadweight, his foot dragging heavily off the desk.

Gabi straightened herself, patting down her hair and all its Shaolin monks, and turned to Principal Torres. "I don't know why Yasmany insists on sabotaging himself, Principal Torres. But I have eight witnesses, remember? And Mr. Milagros! He brought Yasmany and Sal here because he saw the chicken. Mr. Milagros wouldn't lie. I mean, I can administer a lie-detector test on him, but—"

"You are not giving anyone a lie-detector test!" Principal Torres said, working very hard not to raise her voice. Then, clearly curious, she added, "Wait. You have a lie detector?"

The way Gabi smiled and nodded was kind of scary.

Principal Torres looked tempted for a few seconds. What a principal could do if she always knew when her students were lying to her! But she shook off that dream and said, "We don't need a lie detector in this case. If Mr. Milagros says there's a chicken, there's a chicken."

"You should ask him again," I said.

Gabi buzzed her lips at me. "Getting desperate, Sal? You're

just trying to buy yourself time. Why would Mr. Milagros change his story?

"Trick's over now," I said, soft and low-key spooky.

Principal Torres lowered her head and looked at me over her glasses. She didn't need a lie detector. Her Ghost Rider stare could make any kid spill.

Any kid but me. For I am a showman. And I live by the magician's code: Never let them know how the trick is done.

Since she couldn't break me with her eyes, she went back behind her desk, sat down, and pressed a button on her phone. "Mr. Milagros," she said, "are you there?"

A second later, a crackly walkie-talkie voice with a thick Cuban accent said, "Para servirle."

"How is the chicken cleanup going?"

"¿Bueno?" he began, stretching the word out to three seconds. Usually, "bueno" means "good," but the way he said it then meant "welp." And that's all he said.

"Mr. Milagros, are you still there?"

"Para servirle."

Principal Torres massaged her forehead. "Me puede servir by telling me about the mess you had to clean up."

"¿Bueno?"

She waited five Mississippis, tapping each second out on the desk with her finger. Then, carefully controlling her voice, she asked, "What does 'bueno' mean?"

He sighed. "It's like this. I went back to the locker to clean it up. Made up a whole new bucket of cleaner for it, bien fuerte. Like, I could mop up a dead body with it, because basically that's what it was, a dead chicken body. If a student accidentally tripped and fell in my mop bucket, ooh, sería un desastre! It'd turn that kid into Kool-Aid."

"The chicken, Mr. Milagros. Did you clean it up?"

The walkie-talkie crackled as Mr. Milagros put his thoughts in order. "¿Bueno? I was going to. I was all ready to. But when I got to the lockers, no chicken."

The other three people in the office looked at me, a little stunned, a little scared, and yeah, I think, a little impressed.

"Do you mean someone took it?" asked Principal Torres. "Or maybe another custodian cleaned it up before you?"

"No one cleaned it before me!" he replied defensively. "As soon as I dropped off Yasmany and the new boy in your office, I headed straight back to make up the bucket of cleaner, then straight for the lockers. I'm ten times faster than anyone here. I'm like a greased pig!"

Gabi giggled. Which was unexpected; I wouldn't have taken her for a giggler. But American Stepmom is always telling me, "People are complex." This lawyer/shark/politician/journalist was also a giggler. Okay. Cool.

Principal Torres was the exact opposite of a giggler. "I appreciate the analogy, Mr. Milagros, but we're not talking about pigs. We're talking about chickens. If you didn't clean up the chicken, and no one else cleaned up the chicken, then what happened to the chicken?"

"¡Qué se yo!" he answered. "Puede ser que un diablo glotón vino y se lo voló. Este mundo está lleno de demonios que se pasan el día entero haciendo trampas y trucos."

"What'd he say? What'd he say?" Gabi asked Yasmany, sounding both worried and excited.

Since Yasmany was too busy staring at me like I'd just turned his mom into a rabbit, I translated for Gabi. "Mr. Milagros has no idea where the chicken could have gone. He thinks maybe a demon ate it off the school floor."

"Really?" she said, laughing nervously. "That's crazy-pants. He wasn't serious, right?"

I shrugged.

"Thank you, Mr. Milagros," said Principal Torres. "We will talk more later." She ended the call and then folded her hands on her desk. She stared at us so fiercely—each of us, one at a time—that if we were oranges, we would have juiced ourselves on the spot.

"Well," Principal Torres said finally, removing her glasses and wiping them with a hankie, "barring some supernatural explanation, I am going to have to conclude that there never really was a chicken, and that Sal is one heck of an illusionist."

"No!" said Yasmany, standing up and leaning on the desk. "It was there! Everybody saw it. *I* saw it. I heard it hit the ground. I got blood splashed on me."

Principal Torres stood up and leaned toward Yasmany. "There is no blood on you. Mr. Milagros says that there was no carcass to clean up. And if there's no chicken, I must acquit 'im. Sal, you are free to return to—"

But Gabi just couldn't keep her shark mouth shut.

5

"SAL INDUCED A PANIC with his trick," said Gabi. "He put dozens of students at risk with his, his . . . shenanigans!"

She sounded so outraged. I didn't even think you could be outraged and say the word "shenanigans." It's so . . . leprechauny.

"Hey!" I said to Gabi. "I thought you said you were my advocate, too?"

"Fair is fair," she sniffed. In that moment, I learned something important about Gabi Reál. That girl didn't like to lose.

"Well, Mr. Vidón," said Principal Torres, "you heard what Gabi said. Do you think it's in any way appropriate for you to induce mass hysteria in my school? People could have been trampled!"

"Oh no!" I replied, covering my mouth. "I never meant to hurt anybody! How many kids were trampled?"

Principal Torres blinked. "Well, no one. But you still can't go around causing disruptions."

I let my hand drop. "No, of course not, Principal Torres. I did not mean to delay the start of the next period. I am so sorry!"

Her mouth became as small as a cat's butthole. "You didn't delay the next period."

"Oh," I said, looking down again. "That doesn't seem like much of a disruption, then."

I peeked from the corner of my eye. Principal Torres smirked at me. It was an appreciative smirk. I'd read her right. She liked sarcasm.

But Gabi wasn't done with me yet. "Oh, no, nuh-uh, no way. You're not getting off so easily, Sal. Something's fishy here," she said, crossing her arms in thought. "Nobody could fool that many kids into believing a nonexistent chicken had fallen out of a locker."

I shrugged. "Fooling crowds is literally what magicians do for a living."

"Can't fool me," she said.

"Check your hand," I said.

Slowly, skeptically, Gabi uncrossed her arms and opened the hand I'd shaken earlier. She gasped.

Both Yasmany and Principal Torres craned their necks to see. And they gasped just as gaspily when they saw I had stamped Gabi's palm with the word GOTCHA! in black ink.

I showed them the top of my right hand and pointed at the silver ring on my middle finger. Then I flipped my hand over, revealing the stamp.

I hate showing people how my tricks work. But, you know. Desperate times. It was better than explaining the chicken.

"Whoa," said Yasmany.

"I never felt a thing," said Gabi.

"He's good," said Principal Torres. Then, seeming to decide

something, she stood. "All right, Mr. Vidón. You are free to go. And let's try really hard not to see each other tomorrow, okay?"

Time to get out of there before Gabi thought of any more ways to get me in trouble. I turned for the door.

"And as for you, Yasmany," said Principal Torres, "I laid down the law for you at the end of last year. This is your third strike. So I'm afraid I have no choice but to expel—"

"Principal Torres," I said, spinning on my heel and facing her.

"Yes, Sal?"

"Well, it's just that you kept correcting Gabi and telling her that this wasn't a trial. But now you're saying 'I laid down the law' and 'three strikes' like it is one."

"Hmm," she said. She leaned against her desk. "It is very interesting to me that you are now sticking up for a kid who bullied you not even an hour ago, Mr. Vidón. What exactly is it that you want?"

What *did* I want? Here was a chance for me to get rid of a kid who had attacked me for no reason. And he had a history of causing trouble, according to Principal Torres. I should have been happy Yasmany was about to be expelled.

Except Gabi, student council president and obviously one of the smartest kids in school, seemed to like him. And Principal Torres had bent over backward all last year to help him. And I'd bet fifty bucks he was a dancer who was good enough to get into Culeco. And I had a feeling that if he got kicked out now, he would never, ever, ever recover.

"Maybe you could give him another chance?" I asked.

"Yeah?" asked Principal Torres. "You think that's the best thing to do here?"

"I think it's a great idea!" piped Gabi. "This way, Yasmany could have a . . . a . . ." She struggled for a phrase, and then, when she remembered it, shot out of her chair like Patrick Henry. "*Teachable moment!* You *love* teachable moments! Well, now's your chance. Right here, right now, let's take a moment and give Yasmany here a proper teaching! Whaddaya say?"

Principal Torres squeezed the bridge of her nose. She was acting all put out, but I saw she was hiding a smile under her hand. "Laying it on pretty thick there, Gabi, no?"

Gabi took a bow. "Anything for my client. And anyway, you said you wanted to be convinced." Her smile was as big as a bear trap.

Shaking her head, Principal Torres said, "Okay, okay." She turned to Yasmany, and more gently than she'd spoken all day, she said, "You could learn a lot from Sal, Yasmany. Okay, Yasmany, you're not expelled. Instead, you're going to write me a five-page report on type-one diabetes, due by the end of the week."

"Awww," said Yasmany.

Gabi backhanded Yasmany's stomach—and hurt her hand. She danced around and tried to shake the pain out of her fingers. That cheered Yasmany up.

As Gabi winced, she asked Principal Torres, "Permission to help Yasmany with the report?"

"I would expect no less from you, Gabi. But I expect you, Yasmany, to do all the actual writing. Now, get out of my office, all three of you. And try to learn something in the rest of your classes today. That's what you're supposed to do in school, remember?"

6

I LEFT PRINCIPAL Torres's office first, and fast. My phone told me I only had nine minutes left in lunch period. Diabetics have to take meals very seriously. Bad things can happen to us if we don't.

Once I was out in the hallway again, I booked it for the nearest staircase. I had to go up two flights to my locker, where I'd be able to grab a bag of cashews and a cheese stick and a banana and Skittles—sweet, delicious Skittles, the world's most perfect food. Plus, I could switch out some magic props. Now that I'd used my GOTCHA! stamp on Gabi, I wanted to perform a different trick in my eighth-period theater class. By that time, everybody in school would have heard all about my ring. In middle school, rumors spread at the speed of texting—especially when Gabi Reál, editor of the school paper, was probably doing the texting.

Gabi, man. That girl was nothing but trouble.

"Hey, wait up, Sal!" someone yelled from behind me. It was her.

Give me a break.

I did not wait. I did the opposite of wait. I jogged toward the staircase.

When I looked over my shoulder, I saw her bounding toward me. Fighting monks gleamed in her bouncing, bushy hair.

I didn't think. I ran.

I took the stairs three at a time. Then, to shake Gabi, I took a right at the second-floor landing and ran down hall 2S. I slid and spun and dodged and juked around people like a running back.

I stopped in front of the clock on the wall: eight minutes left in the period. I gritted my teeth, lowered my head, and was about to run even faster for the staircase to the next floor.

But I noticed then that every kid in the hall had their back against the wall. They'd cleared the way for me. And they were all staring.

"What?" I asked them.

No one answered. But a voice from behind me, which sounded suspiciously like a student council president's, yelled, "Wait, Sal! I just want to apologize!"

I tore down the hallway of freaky kids and bounded up the stairs.

And fell.

Crack went my right knee on the edge of a step about three-quarters of the way up.

I almost yelled, but I swallowed it down. My eyes filled with water; I couldn't see clearly until I blinked. I sat on the stair and gripped my knee. It hurt like a mother.

"Oh my God!" Gabi rushed up and sat next to me. "Are you all right?"

The pain was starting to subside. But I didn't tell Gabi that. I massaged my patella and looked mournfully at the ceiling. "Diabetics don't heal like other people, you know. Even a small cut can lead to gangrene. And a smashed kneecap? They'll probably have to cut off the whole leg. Ah well," I said, now speaking directly to my leg, "we had a good run, old pal, didn't we?"

"Cacaseca."

I looked at her. Gabi's eyebrows sat flat on her forehead, her eyes slits, and her mouth a straight red scratch on her face. A classic *Your caca is so seca* expression. But she seemed a little worried, too. I could tell she didn't quite know what to think about me.

Which is just the way I like it. "Fine. Don't believe me," I said, sounding wounded. "But when you see me with a peg leg tomorrow, try not to join the other kids in making fun of me, okay? You've done enough."

She popped to her feet and punched her hips. "No one told you to run from me, chacho. And why did you, anyway? I just wanted to say I was sorry for how I acted in the principal's office. I got a little carried away."

"I ran because I didn't want to talk to you."

She could not believe those words had come out of my mouth. "But that makes no sense! Everyone wants to talk to me."

I laughed at, not with, her. "Are you from another planet?"

I jumped to my feet—which, since I really had hurt my knee, was probably not my smartest move. "You just spent the last half hour in the principal's office trying to get me in trouble, just to get your sapingo bully friend off the hook!"

Gabi was about to yell back, but instead she opened and closed her mouth a few times, like a guppie. Finally she asked, "What's 'sapingo'?"

Just as I suspected. Gabi might have a Cuban-sounding name, and she might live in Miami, but she didn't know much Spanish. Now, normally I wouldn't care. But I could see it in her face: She felt a little inferior because of it. And against someone like her, you had to use any advantage you could find.

So I was drippingly generous when I said to her, "'Sapingo' is a classic Cuban insult. It's basically how you tell the person whom you are insulting that they're about as smart as a day-old skid mark."

Gabi giggled. "That's nasty. You're nasty."

All of a sudden, I was giggling, too. Though I didn't want to. I was still pretty mad at how she'd tried to get me in trouble with Principal Torres. But Gabi had a laugh that made you laugh. She giggled some more. So I giggled more. Then she giggled harder, and I giggled back.

And then she got instantly serious. "Wait," she said. "Did you just use 'whom' correctly in a sentence?"

"Um, yeah," I answered slowly. And then I added, "Magicians have excellent grammar?"

She stared at me like she was trying to see my soul through my nostrils. "Who the heck *are* you, Sal Vidón?"

The warning bell for next period played over the intercoms. Great. No lunch, no props, and an aching knee.

That snapped the spell. I didn't have to pretend to be annoyed when I replied, "I am never telling you anything. I don't talk to reporters." I shook out my hair, turned up my nose, and, maybe exaggerating my limp a little, took the stairs up to my sixth-period Textile Arts class.

"You'll talk eventually!" Gabi yelled after me. "I'll make you talk!"

7

LIMPING FOR GABI'S benefit had slowed me down. So as soon as she couldn't see me, I had to sprint hard to be on time for class. I busted through the door of the Textile Arts classroom just as the bell sounded.

All the other kids must have ended their lunches early to get a head start on their work. They had already broken into their pace groups and were sewing, stitching, steaming, ironing, dyeing, felting, and/or modeling clothes like time was money.

It was one of the weird things I'd noticed on my first day at Culeco: The students arrived early. They stayed late. They hung out with teachers between periods to talk about what they'd covered in class. Basically, they *liked* school.

I liked how much they liked it. For once I wasn't a freak for liking school.

Another weird thing was how many boys there were in Textile Arts. For me, this was a required course for my future career as a famous illusionist. Magicians need custom costumes for their tricks and to look cool while performing. Back in Connecticut, I probably would've been the only boy in a sewing class, if they'd even offered one. And I probably would've gotten into a fistfight every day because of it.

But at Culeco, there were almost as many boys as girls studying Textile Arts. A lot of things were so much easier here.

The Textile Arts teacher was Dr. Doctorpants. That wasn't his real name—"Dr. Doctorpants's Cosplay Carnival" was the name of his mask-and-masquerade shop on Etsy, so that's what everyone called him. He always wore one of his costumes to class. Today, he was dressed up as a six-foot-tall bubble gum machine. The clear plastic dome he was wearing over his head held real gumballs up to his nose.

The pile of gumballs didn't muffle his voice, but it did shift as he spoke. "Right on time, Sal," he said, loud and clear. "But time's a-wasting! Time to get"—and to emphasize the dad joke, he dropped a coin into his costume's head, spun the key, caught the Venus-colored piece of gum that rolled out of the chute, and tossed it to me—"*on the ball!*"

I gave Dr. Doctorpants a wink and twin finger guns that meant *Good one, dude!* Then I popped the gum into my mouth and made my way to my pace group, Knitting for Beginners. It was the most basic pace group in the class, which was fine with me. I'd never taken Textile Arts before—because Connecticut. I had a lot to learn.

The other five kids in my pace group were laughing and working already, so I gathered up my knitting needles and yarn from yesterday (Dr. Doctorpants had already laid them out for me), sat cross-legged on the floor, and got down to business. I'd only been knitting for three days, but I liked it. There's a little part of my brain that enjoys doing a small task perfectly, and knitting is basically doing a small task perfectly ten thousand times in a row.

I was working on a red scarf—just about the last piece of clothing you'd ever need in Florida. But it was already giving me an idea for a new magic trick, where I'd hand the mark a scarf and let them unravel it entirely, until they were left holding a big ball of yarn. Then, presto-chango, I would turn it back into a knitted scarf right before their eyes!

But how? When you're making up a new magic trick, you have to figure out all the tiny details of how to make it work. Magic is basically doing a small task perfectly.

For this trick, I was thinking I'd need a mirror box, a classic magic prop about the size of a cat carrier. It looks like an empty box, and there's even a window to let people see inside it, but a mirror creates a seemingly invisible compartment the magician can hide things in. For my trick, I would put one scarf behind the mirror, and as the mark unraveled the other scarf, I'd stuff that yarn into the top of the box. The audience would be able to see the string the whole time through the window. Then I would reach up through the bottom of the box and slowly start to draw out the yarn—except it would appear to be reknitted into a scarf!

I'd have to pull out the unraveled yarn and the second scarf at the same time, and then palm the yarn and slip it in a pocket. Wait, no—that'd be way too much yarn to hide in my hand. Maybe I could disguise the string in the scarf itself? That would be the most natural thing to do, since I'd be pulling both of them out at the same time. But the trick would work best if

I could give the scarf back to the mark and let them inspect it, and I couldn't do that if the yarn was hidden in it.

I'd have to think about that some more. And I would have right then, if I hadn't noticed that no one around me was talking.

The first two days of class, my pace group had spent the whole class chatting. They'd talked so much, I had trouble concentrating on knitting. But everyone was nice and funny, and time flew by, so it was all good.

Today, all the other groups sounded like they were having a great time. But mine? Silence. Everyone was sitting cross-legged on the floor like I was, knitting away and working hard, and having, by the looks on their faces, zero fun doing it.

Hmm.

"Hey," I said to Gladis Machado, the girl sitting next to me. She'd been the funniest person in the pace group so far. "You're doing really good. You're almost halfway done with your scarf."

Gladis never looked up at me. "Thank you," she muttered. And then, holding her needles in one hand, she pulled an ojo turco necklace out from beneath her T-shirt and gave it a squeeze.

An ojo turco is a piece of blue glass with a blue eyeball painted on it. People wear them on necklaces and bracelets to protect them against the evil eye. Mami had one. Man, she was terrified of mal de ojo. She'd tell me stories about how a brujo could make you sick, make your cows give blood instead of milk, turn your hair white, make your teeth fall out of your mouth, age you fifty years in five seconds, all sorts of stuff.

Papi, who didn't believe in any of that, would wait until Mami left the room to tell me that her stories were just superstitions. And then, when he left the room, she'd come back in and tell me it was all 100 percent real.

And, I mean, Mami's ojo turco saved her life and mine when we had our car accident. But that's a story for another time.

Right then, I was busy noticing that Gladis was clutching her ojo turco just like Mami would whenever she needed a little extra protection against whatever curses life wanted to throw at her.

Suddenly, the kids who had gotten out of my way in the second-floor hallway and stared at me googly-eyed as I ran past made a lot more sense. Rumors had been spreading that I'd done black magic.

I pictured the horror that would have distorted my Mami Muerta's face if she'd thought for one second that I was a brujo. I needed to fix this, stat.

"What?" I said to Gladis, laughing a little. "You think I just gave you mal de ojo?"

She gasped as if I'd just accused her of committing murder in the ballroom with the candlestick. "How do you know about mal de ojo?"

That made no sense, and I let my face show it. "How could I do mal de ojo on you if I didn't know what it was?"

"No, I mean, I thought you would call it the evil eye. Aren't you American?"

I blinked. "Um, yeah. But my parents are Cuban." Which is mostly true—both my biological parents are.

"Oh," Gladis said, as if she didn't want to say any more.

Nice and slow and not at all angrily, because I don't get angry, I asked her once again, "So why'd you think I gave you mal de ojo?"

Gladis didn't look up from her knitting. But she was purling like there was no tomorrow.

"Because, Sal," said Juan Carlos Chaviano, Gladis's best friend. I'd gotten to know him a little over the past few days. Nice guy. He'd come to Culeco to study songwriting and was already three-quarters of the way to becoming the next Latin pop star. No matter what he said, he beamed at you like you were a camera that was broadcasting his smile to millions of fans.

I smiled back at him. "Because why, Juan Carlos?"

"Because," he said with a gleaming-teeth laugh, "you sacrificed a chicken in Yasmany Robles's locker. What else is she supposed to think? You're a brujo, chacho."

Welp. Worst-case scenario confirmed.

"I didn't sacrifice a chicken!" I said to Juan Carlos. "It was a magic trick!"

Juan Carlos shrugged, which meant *Sorry, man, nothing I can do for you.*

I felt my neck getting hot. "And anyway, there's no such thing as brujos!"

Gladis shook her head. She stopped knitting long enough to stare at me straight in the ojo when she said, "Can't fool me." She looked a little scared and a little defiant and a lot like she wished she could send me to the center of the Earth with her eyes.

It'd been a long time since I'd been around anyone that

superstitious. I'm pretty sure the last time it was Mami. It kind of stunned me.

So I kept my head down for the rest of the class. I needed time to think.

Seventh period was my PE class. Only at Culeco, they didn't call it PE, or phys ed, or gym. They called it Health Science and the Practice of Wellness. I guess the fancy name was to help make dodgeball sound like something smart people did.

The class was held in the multipurpose room on the second floor. It didn't look like a gym. It was bigger than average, with a tall ceiling and a hard, mean rug the color of sandpaper. At the start of class, everyone had to help lay big padded mats on the floor, and five minutes before class ended, we had to gather them up, lean them against a wall, and spray them down with nose-burning sanitizer. Probably the same stuff Mr. Milagros used to melt dead bodies.

Culeco was an arts school. Phys ed wasn't exactly the highest priority. You didn't even have to change into gym clothes if you didn't want to.

It definitely smelled like a gym, though—like socks made of cheese. And all the sanitizer spray did was add a blue-toilet-liquid stench on top of the cheese socks. But if there was one thing in the multipurpose room that made it feel like a *real* gym, it was the rock-climbing wall.

It stretched from floor to ceiling and was separated into green, yellow, and red zones, depending on how good a climber you were. So far in class, a lot of people had slammed the victory button at the top of the green part, which made a siren howl and a red light spin. A few people had reached yellow, with more sirens and lights. But no one had reached the top of red.

That's where I was going. I was getting to the top today. After my first two days of being defeated by the red zone, I had come up with a plan. The glory of making it all the way up would be mine.

And between Yasmany, Gabi, and the worrisome developments in Textile Arts, I could really use a little glory.

But as I headed to get in line for my turn on the climbing wall, Mr. Lynott intercepted me.

He looked like a brolic manatee wearing gym clothes—small head, big chest, and tiny from the waist down. He spread his arms and legs as wide as he could to block me.

"Um, Sal," he said, "maybe it's not such a good idea, you climbing. Maybe you should join the yoga pace group."

I was pretty sure of what was coming. I reminded myself that I do not get angry and played it straight. "Why?"

"You know. Because of your"—he leaned in to whisper—"condition?"

Oh.

Principal Torres must have had a talk with Mr. Lynott. On the first day, he'd spent all class busting my chops, and yesterday he'd sent me to the principal's office for eating Skittles. But now—after Principal Torres let him have it, I guessed—instead of acting like a drill sergeant, he was going to act like a chicken culeco for its only egg.

I actually did want to join the yoga pace group, eventu-- ally. Magicians need to be extremely flexible if they're going to escape from straitjackets and stuff. And after banging my knee on the stairs earlier, maybe climbing wasn't the best idea today. But the way Mr. Lynott whispered "condition" to me? Yeah, I didn't have time for cacaseca like that in my life.

So I made my eyes really big and asked, "Mr. Lynott, you're not denying me equal access to school activities based on my disability, are you?"

Mr. Lynott was a white dude. I mean white hair, white nose hair, white eyebrows, white Stonehenge teeth, white gym clothes, white sneakers, and a metal whistle hanging from a white string around his neck. This white dude's skin went from white to red as fast as a squid camouflaging itself. "What?! No! I would never do that! It's illegal to deny you access to all the same equipment as normal kids."

I had practiced looking like I was about to cry in front of a mirror for moments just like this one. "You mean I'm not a normal kid, Mr. Lynott?"

His face collapsed like a condemned building. "What?! No! That's not what I meant! You can do anything anyone else can! You're perfectly normal in your own unique way!" And then, trying to pretend he could still pull off the drill sergeant routine, he added, "Now, um, get on that wall and, er, show me what you got, Vidón!"

"Yes, sir!" I saluted, and headed for the wall.

Kids had lined up for the green and yellow zones, but it looked like everyone was sick of falling off the red zone. No line, no wait.

I belted myself into the climbing harness. Only when I was completely strapped in did I remember that I needed someone to spot me.

The harness was attached to a rope, which ran through a pulley on the ceiling about twenty feet up, and whoever was holding on to the other end of the rope would keep you from falling to your death when you slipped off the climbing wall. (Well, okay, there was an extra-thick pad at the bottom of the wall that probably would keep you from dying. But still.)

I admit it: I was afraid to ask anyone to spot me. The way the kids in the hallway had stared at me and the way Gladis had petted her ojo turco had me freaked. What if no one at Culeco wanted to spot a brujo?

"Whatcha waiting for, Vidón?" said Mr. Lynott from behind me. Then I did turn around. He had the rope tightly grasped in both hands. *He* was going to spot me.

Relief felt like cool water running down my back. "Nothing at all," I said, and made for the wall.

"You can do anything!" Mr. Lynott cheered. "Diabetics are number one!"

Well, he was trying. I started to climb.

The lower part of the red zone is only a little harder than the other zones. It was just missing a few footholds, compared to green and yellow. I made it halfway up the wall in no time.

The first tricky spot was where I'd fallen on the first day. You had to turn yourself upside down against the wall, like a cockroach changing directions. While upside down, you had to latch on to the two footholds above you with your feet. And then—this was the hard part—you had to bend your knees and arc your spine all the way back, like you were trying to stick your head up your own butt. You had to grab the single handhold above your feet, and, while holding on for dear life, flip right-side up again, and put your feet back into the footholds.

On the first day of school, I hadn't been able to make the flip. Yesterday, though, I'd managed to pull it off. When I did, the whole class broke into applause, and everybody had stopped what they were doing to see if I'd make it to the top.

But I'd fallen almost immediately. Feeling light-headed, I'd peeled off the wall. That's when I'd had some Skittles to level my blood sugar and Mr. Lynott had sent me to the principal's.

(Hadn't done a good job of eating today, either. Really had to take care of that soon.)

The thing is, I probably would have fallen yesterday, anyway. Because the next part of the wall is the real killer. There's only one hold to reach for, and it's more than five feet higher up. The only way to get there is to jump for it.

Which is stupid. The chance of you being able to jump high enough, slap at the wall, and grab the hold tight enough to support your entire body weight is practically zip. And even if you did manage to do all that, you still had to pull yourself up—with one arm—high enough to slap the victory button with the other hand. Complete and total cacaseca.

So last night over dinner, I'd told my padres about the climbing wall—showed them a picture I took and everything. The conversation got serious, fast. My papi's a physicist, so he got out paper and pencil and protractor and asked me to sketch the wall. After I did, he drew some lines and did some math that might as well have been magic formulas.

By the time he was done working his magic, he was pretty sure that wall had been designed to be impossible to conquer.

That made him angry. "Are they trying to discourage children? What's the point of putting up a climbing wall that's impossible to climb?"

"Well, then," said American Stepmom, "Sal will just have to do the impossible."

"Yeah," I said. "I'll just cheat."

Papi swallowed his lips and held up his index finger. "Um . . . Are you allowed to cheat?"

"Yes!" American Stepmom and I yelled at the same time. Then we high-fived.

So as a family, we came up with a way to get to the top of the red zone.

Now, as I stood on the two footholds, having already made the flip and looking up at the ridiculous jump I had to make, I pulled my secret weapon from a vest pocket: a plastic six-pack ring. Being extra sure I was balanced, I slipped my wrists through two holes on opposite sides and got ready to jump.

The idea was that I could catch the hold with the six-pack ring. I figured it could support my weight for at least a few seconds (one of the benefits of being on the smaller side) and buy me a few inches of reach as I jumped. It would also allow me to use the strength of both arms to pull me up, instead of just one. Then I could quickly free a hand and slap the victory button.

And best of all, maybe the kids on the ground wouldn't be able to see the clear plastic ring. I could tell them I did it with magic!

Which, I suddenly realized, seemed like a much better idea last night than it did today, before Gladis and Juan Carlos and who knew how many other kids thought I was a brujo.

I didn't look over my shoulder. I didn't have to. No one had applauded me for getting this far today, but I knew they were watching. If I made it to the top of the impossible red zone, my rep would be permanent. I would be a brujo forever.

Change of plan. I tucked the six-pack ring back into my pocket. A different kind of trick was called for today.

I leaped for the handhold above me, hard as I could. I slapped at the wall. I stretched my fingers as far as they would go.

Annnnnnd I didn't even get close. I fell.

Well, technically, I just swung in the air. I sagged in the harness like a depressed lobster, then punched my palm in fake anger. "So close!" I spat out as Mr. Lynott very carefully lowered me down.

"Not even," said Octavio Murillo. I didn't know what his specialty at Culeco was. If I had to guess, I'd say he was studying Being Really Freaking Tall for His Age. He was next in line for the red zone.

"Yes I was!" I retorted as my feet touched the ground. "Retorting" is what you do instead of replying when you know you're wrong.

He shook his head, sad for me. "Next time, better use your magic broom, mago."

"Mago" was . . . interesting. He'd called me a magic user. But he didn't say it like it scared him any. It was more like the way everybody makes fun of everybody in middle school—just hit 'em where they're weak. It was even kind of friendly, in a way.

So I unclasped the last buckle on the harness, walked up to Octavio, got under his nose, and said, "Mago, huh? Wanna see a magic trick?"

"Sure," he said.

"I can make a bird appear out of thin air," I said.

People in the green and yellow zone lines were watching, so I had to make it good. I started waving my hands around mysteriously. Nothing in my right hand, I showed Octavio, and nothing in my left. Then, after three great flourishes, I materialized from behind my hand . . . my middle finger.

"Tweet tweet," I said.

Octavio laughed, right along with everybody waiting in the lines. He could take a joke. Good to know some kids at Culeco could.

But I'd forgotten Mr. Lynott was right there. He blew his whistle. "Personal foul, Vidón! You're going . . ." Then he faltered.

I think he was going to finish that sentence with "straight to the principal's office." He'd caught me red-handed, or -fingered, or whatever. I had definitely just earned myself another heart-to-heart with Principal Torres. Not good at all.

But instead of a one-way ticket to Detentionville, Mr. Lynott said, "You're going . . . um . . . places, Sal! You're going places! Because being a diabetic will never get in the way of your dreams!"

The bell rang. As we headed for our next classes, Octavio, walking beside me, said, "Dude, I think you broke Lynott. What the 'seca was he talking about?"

My first impulse was to talk smack about Mr. Lynott, be funny, make Octavio laugh and therefore like me. But half a second's pause and I knew that's not how you treat people, especially not people who are trying to do better. "Lynott's all right," I said. "He's just never tangled with a mago before."

8

JUST ONE MORE class to get through, and then I could eat something before I keeled over. But it wasn't just any class. It was Intermediate Theater Workshop, and today we were all expected to put on a short display of our talent. Or "show-and-tell," as our teacher, Mrs. Waked, called it.

ITW was held in the prop room. I liked seeing all the past costumes and backdrops Culeco students had used in their performances. It made you feel like you were part of something bigger.

A lot of the props had been donated to Culeco by Mrs. Waked. She had collected a lifetime's worth of them from the movies, TV series, and commercials she'd been in. Scattered on shelves, hanging from coatracks, or resting in boxes and trunks, you could find wigs and hats, scarves and boas and sunglasses, crutches and umbrellas and a half-dozen trench coats. Lift a lid and you might find a talking toy parrot, a barking robot dachshund, and a sock-puppet butler that Mrs. Waked had voiced in six different Super Bowl ads. A bunch of "As Seen on TV!" products whose use no one could identify sat around like weird alien artifacts, daring someone to experiment with them. Makeup kits bigger than tool chests overflowed with all the fake noses, ears, teeth, and facial hair a middle school acting class could want.

It was BYO spirit gum, though. That stuff is expensive.

As I walked through the room (finally a few minutes early to a class), a bunch of the kids stood off by themselves, practicing for the show-and-tell we'd all be part of in a few minutes. It looked like several of them were going to perform monologues. And that meant you didn't want to sit in the front row. These were all *serious* actors dedicated to perfect pronunciation and crystal-clear enunciation. Every word that began with a "p" or a "t" would spray enough spit to put out a forest fire.

The singers do-re-mi'ed and mi-re-do'ed down again, and the musicians—saxophone, electric guitar, harmonica, a row of wineglasses, harp—practiced the toughest licks in their songs. Dancers rehearsed their moves deliberately, over and over, and it made me kind of wish that they always danced in slow motion. One girl had a puppet who apparently thought she was the stupidest person in the world. Adam Hoag wore a beret—that's how you knew he was a director—and sat watching his laptop screen while nervously going over the intro notes for his short film. Widelene Henrissaint, on the other hand, was the opposite of nervous. She ran through a kata with a bo staff, looking intense and very well trained and very Darth Maul–y. She was going to be tough competition. But I would beat her. As good as her kata was, it wasn't magic.

I'd had a chance to stop by my locker before class to grab the props I needed for my act: six pairs of handcuffs in all different colors. (Unfortunately, I'd been so excited about performing that I'd forgotten to grab my lunch, too—which wasn't a smart move for someone with a useless pancreas.) I'd been practicing a handcuff routine since I started my career as an illusionist, and at this point, I had it down to a science. I was going to blow some minds today.

And there was one mind I couldn't wait to explode into itty-bitty pieces: Gabi Reál's.

She hadn't made it to class yet. I admit that I wanted to catch a glimpse of her act before the period started. I had a feeling that, as good as kata girl's routine was, Gabi was my true rival. But there was no sign of her.

At the front of the room, Mrs. Waked, wearing a black velvet dress and a bustle that gave her a bumblebee butt, was arranging folding chairs in rows close to the stage. There were no desks in Intermediate Theater Workshop, just folding chairs. "No taking *notes* in this class!" Mrs. Waked had told us on the first day. "An actor *memorizes*."

She italicized words all the time when she talked. You could hear it.

"Want some help, Mrs. Waked?" I asked. You say her name "Wok-ed." I had emphasized both syllables in her name when I said it, and she noticed.

"Of *course*," she said, kind of laughing and kind of suspicious. "What a *nice* young man."

I worked for ten seconds setting up chairs before I said, "You let us mispronounce your name the whole first class. Everyone was calling you 'Mrs. Wāked, Mrs. Wāked!'"

She just kept on setting up chairs. But her face had like six layers of smiles.

"Why?" I pressed.

She set the last chair in place and looked at me straight on. "When I corrected you children on day two, it *'waked'* you all up, now, *didn't* it?"

I laughed. I guess it had.

"Class starts in *one* minute!" she announced to everyone. "*Please* to be *finding* your *seats*, pupils!"

"Mrs. Waked, may I go first today?" I asked. "I like to be the opening act of a show."

"*Well.* Far be it from *me* to *curtail* your enthusiasm. But I was hoping *you'd* go last, Sal."

"Why?"

She got close to me, squatted a little, and pulled up the sleeves of her black velvet dress. Nothing in her left hand, nothing in her right hand, and then: *plop!* A huge egg fell out of her dress and hit the floor like a cannonball.

She trapped it between her boots before it rolled away, then scooped it up and handed it to me. "I wanted to save the best for last. I *adore* magic!"

The egg was solid and heavy as all get-out. How in the name of pants had she been able to set up the chairs with this huge, heavy egg under her dress the whole time? And had she hidden the egg there just waiting for me to ask her the right question?

That was a great trick, and I told her so.

"That's *nothing. You* will do *better*," she replied. And on cue, the bell for class sounded.

Also on cue, Gabi entered the room. She was rolling in a computer and a projector on a stand. Chief custodian Mr.

Milagros followed her in. He was pushing a hospital gurney that held a weird-looking helmet resting on the pillow.

"I'm not late, am I?" asked Gabi.

"*Right* on time, m'lady," said Mrs. Waked. "¡Hola, Mr. Milagros!"

"Bueno," he said.

Gabi jogged her computer and projector up the ramp stage left and parked it there. Mr. Milagros rolled the gurney upstage center so it wouldn't be in the way of the performers who went before Gabi.

"Now, find seats, everyone. *Hurry, hurry!*" Mrs. Waked said. "This is my *favorite* class of the whole year. *Show*-and-*tell!*"

On the first day of class, Mrs. Waked had told us, "*All* of you are *geniuses*. Culeco only admits the *best*. Therefore, as your teacher, I have three jobs. *One*, to help you do your best work. *Two*, to help you do your best work more often. *Three*, to get out of the way while you do your best work. *Three* is my *favorite*, because it's like I am getting paid to sit around and watch great artists perform. It is the epitome of *decadence* and *laziness*. You will help me be lazy, won't you, dear children?"

We promised we would. And today, we were proving it.

The musicians rocked. I mean, they absolutely *shredded*—and if you've never seen someone shred on the xylophone, kid, you're missing out. The tragic soliloquies made it hard to breathe. On the lighter side, the funny acts cracked us up, especially ventriloquist girl. That puppet had me believing she really was stupid!

Widelene's bo-staff routine was even better than the

preview I'd seen. I seriously didn't know you could move a bo staff all around your body that fast. She was better than Darth Maul. She was like Darth Blender. Every time she yelled "Kiai!" everybody in the audience slid back in their chairs an inch. For her big finish, she did a 720 in the air and broke her stick over her knee. I think the whole class passed out for three seconds after that.

Once everyone recovered, Widelene got a standing O. She was definitely going to be tough to beat.

Even beret boy was better than I thought he'd be. He was still nervous when he got in front of the class, so I wasn't expecting much. "As an introduction to my work," he said, futzing with his laptop and the projector he was connecting to it, "I'm showing you today the trailer for a feature-length documentary-slash-philosophical-meditation on a topic that has defined me. It's called *Splitting the Adam*. It's about my relationship to wedgies."

I had never seen so many wedgies in a row. How he'd captured them on film was beyond me. Frame after frame showed poor Adam getting every single kind of underwear torture that evil schoolchildren had ever invented. All your old favorites were there—the Atomic, the Melvin, the Forklift, the Hammer Throw, and the Old Glory, which left Adam hanging by his undies from the school flagpole as the camera sadly panned away. But the trailer also featured a few I'd never heard of: the Perseus, where the bully rips the underwear all the way off and holds up the ripped briefs like the head of Medusa; the Tighty-Whitey Crotch Canoe, where two people work together to wedgie and melvin you at the same time (can I get an OUCH from the audience?); and—in the name of all that is holy, why?—the Double-Dutch, where the two people crotch-canoeing you swing your underwear like a jump rope and take you on a magic wedgie ride.

I think the whole class clenched their butt cheeks through the entire trailer. But we all knew quality when we saw it. Applause was muted but sincere.

Two performances to go: me, and the person who was going before me: Gabi.

As Gabi ran up to the stage, I noticed that she had changed T-shirts for her performance. This one was forest green, and the quote on it read "THERE IS NO GOD HIGHER THAN TRUTH."—MAHATMA GANDHI. She'd changed her barrettes, too. Instead of Shaolin monks, her head was now filled with what looked like huge eyeballs inside magnifying glasses.

Unlike Adam, Gabi stood at the lip of the stage like someone who'd never had stage fright in her entire life. "Hi, everyone!" she began cheerily. "We've seen some terrific performances today, haven't we?"

The crowd whooped and cheered. Clearly, Gabi had a lot of friends in the audience. That shouldn't have surprised me—obviously, she'd had enough friends to get elected student council president. But I admit, I was caught a little off guard.

"Music, theater, dance," she went on, "and every single one a great work of art. But I am here to switch things up a little. Instead of performing a work of art, I am going to demonstrate a work of cutting-edge science!"

Gabi signaled Mrs. Waked, who did something on her phone. Music started: the kind of happy-silly-spanky pop you'd expect to hear at the beginning of a cartoon for six-year-olds. Gabi jogged over to the cart with the projector and computer, rolled it to downstage center, plugged it in, and fired up both machines. The same big blank wall on which we'd cringed through *Splitting the Adam* now showed what kind of looked like a live heart monitor at the hospital. You know: A black background with a green blippy dot that jumps every time your heart beats? Only the green dot wasn't blipping at all right now. It was just hanging out in the center of the screen while, at the bottom, a digital readout of the current time scrolled by.

At the top of the screen, in blocky capital letters, were the words LIE DETECTOR! Just below the title were the words TRUE and PANTS ON FIRE! Each word had an empty black box next to it.

Gabi went upstage to grab the gurney and drag it over to downstage left. Once she'd set its brake, she faced her audience again and, smiling saber-toothily, said, "Until recently, lie detectors were pretty terrible. Polygraph tests were so unreliable, they were almost never usable as evidence in a court of law. The problem was that old polygraphs measured things like your heart rate and how sweaty you got. But a lot of people can lie without breaking a sweat. To make lie detection actually work, you have to go to the source of where lies come from: the brain."

Gabi picked up the weird helmet sitting on the gurney's pillow and slipped it over her head. It must have been wirelessly connected to the computer, because the green dot on the wall jumped up and down, leaving a trail of glowing scribbles behind it. "When you're telling the truth, you're using your memory, and this helmet knows it. For example: 'I had cereal and milk for breakfast today.'"

Next to the word TRUE on the screen, a green checkmark filled the box, and a *ding!* dinged.

Gabi strolled the stage with her hands behind her back. "If, on the other hand, you decide to lie, you have to use your imagination, and this helmet can detect that you're using the creative parts of your brain. For instance, 'I had hippopotamus burgers for breakfast.'"

Next to the words PANTS ON FIRE! the box filled with a red X and a buzzer went *blatt!*

Gabi sat down on the stage, took off the helmet, and let her feet dangle off the edge. "We're all here to study acting. If you want to be a great actor, you have to convince the audience that you're telling the truth. So my question to you, fellow classmates, is this: Can you defeat a lie detector that can read your mind?"

She shot to her feet and bent toward us, leering. "I will need a volunteer. Bwa-ha-ha."

So guess how many people volunteered to have Gabi read their brains and expose their lies to the whole world.

The answer—you're not going to believe this—is *everybody.* Well, everybody but me.

I mean, kids were waving their hands in the air, jumping out of their seats, yelling, "Pick me, pick me!" While I sat on my hands, everyone else in class was dying to have Gabi lie-detect them. Even Mrs. Waked had her hand up.

But Gabi's eyes were locked on just one person.

"Salvador Vidón! Thanks so much for volunteering. Let's give him a round of applause, folks!"

9

I'D DONE SOME reading about lie detectors. Magicians are obsessed with beating them. They'd come up with all sorts of tricks to fool them: bite your tongue, put a tack in your shoe, overreact to the easy questions, etc. But all the lie detectors I'd researched were the old-school kind. I didn't know a thing about Gabi's brain reader.

But what choice did I have? If I refused to be her guinea pig, everyone would assume I had something to hide. The brujo rumors about me would spread through school faster than lice.

So I bounded up to the stage, looking like a happy, stupid dupe who thinks having all his secrets exposed is the most fun thing in the world. I waved at the audience and, as they applauded, thought fast about how to confound the lie detector.

It took me only a few seconds to come up with three possible scenarios regarding the machine:

1. It really worked. If I didn't tell the truth, everyone would know.
2. It was fake, and Gabi was just having fun. It was just

a comedy act disguised as science. And if I didn't play
along, I'd look like a bad sport.

3. It was fake, but Gabi was going to pretend it was real.
   She was going to try to fool me into talking to her,
   because I had refused to talk to her before.

Whichever of the three was right, the audience couldn't
know for sure. Some people would believe it was real no matter
what, and some people wouldn't no matter what. But all of
them would be watching me, and judging me based on how I
reacted.

In other words, the only *real* lie detector onstage, the only
one people would really trust, was me.

Now I knew what to do. For I am a showman.

Gabi looked at the audience as she welcomed me onstage.
"Thank you so much for being my victim—I mean, *volunteer*,
Sal. I wasn't sure you would. I couldn't help but notice that you
were the only person in the entire class who didn't raise his
hand. Why is that, Sal?"

Man. Right out of the gate, and she was going for the
jugular.

All right, Gabi, wanna play rough? Let's go. "Because we
both knew you were going to call on me," I replied, more to the
audience than to her.

"Oh? And why is that, Sal?"

"Because I made a fool of you earlier today, in front of
Principal Torres. And that made you angry."

The audience oohed.

"I wasn't angry," she replied, and whether she flipped her hair because she felt irritated or because she thought it'd be funnier to look irritated, I couldn't tell.

So I pressed her. "You don't like to be fooled, do you, Gabi? You're dying to know how I do my tricks."

The audience oohed even more oohily.

I had to hand it to Gabi—she laughed, took my jabs in stride, and kept the show going. "So you're up here to tell me and the whole class how you pulled off your tricks? Isn't that, like, against the magician's code?"

"I am going to answer your questions," I replied. Then, stroking my chin, I added, "We'll see if your machine can sort truth from magic."

"This is great!" said Mrs. Waked over the applause. "Did you two plan this?"

"Music, Mrs. Waked!" said Gabi, giving her the hand signal repeatedly. It was the only sign she was losing her patience.

"Oh, right! Sorry, Gabi. Got caught up in the act!"

The same goofy music as before started to play through the speakers. Gabi whooshed over to me and made some dramatic hand gestures that meant she wanted me to lie down on the gurney. I did. Then, twirling like a ballerina the whole time, she made her way back to the helmet on the floor and picked it up. She did a mini interpretive dance with it, lifting it in the air as if it were Ye Olde Magic Helmet That the Prophecies Hath Foretold. Then she bounded over to me, half dancer, half clown. She raised my head with one hand, slipped the helmet on me, then gently guided my head back onto the pillow. Spinning again, she came to a stop downstage center, right next to the projector, exactly when the music ended.

I looked at the monitor. The green dot had started scribbling my brain waves on the screen.

"You're live, Sal," Gabi said, facing the audience. "Everything you say will be judged by the lie detector. Are you ready?"

"Do I have a choice?" I asked.

Because, see, a question can't be true or false. I wanted to find out if I could fool the machine with tricky wording.

The machine didn't respond.

"Please don't answer questions with questions, Sal," said Gabi, all smiles. "Are you ready?"

"Let's do it." Which is also not a true/false reply.

The machine, again, did nothing.

"Also, please actually answer the questions I ask you, Sal," Gabi said sweetly.

"Yeah, Sal," came a dude's voice from the audience.

"Stop trying to beat the machine," said a girl's.

Mrs. Waked prompted, "Yes-*and* . . ."

We actors are never supposed to say "no." We're supposed to build on whatever we're given.

Which, of course, Gabi knew. She was counting on the fact that I had to go along with her, no matter what. "Now, are you ready?" asked Gabi, smug as a sandwich.

I said, "No."

The green checkmark appeared with a *ding!* next to TRUE.

"Perfect!" said Gabi. "First question: Is your name Salvador Vidón?"

"Partially," I replied. *Ding!* went the truth.

"Will you please state your full name?"

"No. If you had the middle names Alberto Dorado—which mean *golden elf-boy*, by the way—you wouldn't share them, either!" Then, as if I hadn't meant to say all of that, I slapped my hand over my mouth.

Ding!

"Ha-ha-ha-ha-ha!" said everybody.

"Thank you for your honesty!" said Gabi, finally deciding to laugh along. "Next question: What color is the sky?"

I grabbed my chin. "Ooh. That's a tough one. It's blue a lot of the time, unless it's covered in clouds, which can be white or gray or almost black. But in the morning, or when the sun's setting, the sky can be yellow or orange or purple." The dot on the screen was jumping around like butter in a hot pan, scribbling all over the place. "And one time, just as the sun disappeared behind the sea, I could swear the sky turned a glorious green for, like, two seconds. I've never seen a green flash again, but I would like to. It looked like a sunset on a strange alien world. It was so beautiful."

"Very fine," said Mrs. Waked, tearing up and patting her chest. "Absolutely poetical, Sal."

Meanwhile, everyone watched to see what the machine would say. The green dot slowed and slowed until it returned to normal. The power indicator light on the computer showed the hard drive working hard to try to process my answer.

Finally, a *blatt!* sounded and a red X appeared next to PANTS ON FIRE!

"*How* is that false?" said Mrs. Waked. "It was *inspired*!"

Gabi nodded and shrugged, as if to say *Welp!* "He used his imagination. You're really enjoying this, aren't you, Sal?"

"Yes, I am," I replied.

Blatt! went the buzzer, and a red X indicated that my statement had set my PANTS ON FIRE! That got the biggest laugh so far.

"All right," Gabi said to the audience, rubbing her hands. "Here's the main event, the question I've been dying to ask you. How did you, Salvador Alberto Dorado Vidón, get a chicken into Yasmany Robles's locker earlier today?"

"Oh yes!" said Mrs. Waked, clapping. "That's been *all* the gossip in the teachers' lounge today. I cannot *wait* to hear your answer, Sal."

I smiled. *Well, here goes everything,* I thought. "I ripped a hole in the space-time continuum and borrowed a chicken from another universe."

The computer didn't have to think at all this time. *Ding!* it sang, and a check instantly filled the box next to TRUE.

"Wut?" asked Gabi.

I was in the mood to be helpful. "I said, I RIPPED A HOLE IN THE SPACE-TIME CONTINUUM AND BORROWED A CHICKEN FROM ANOTHER UNIVERSE."

Check-*ding!*

The audience tittered the way you do when you don't quite know how to react. People started whispering and murmuring to each other. Gabi, grumbling to herself, went over to the computer and started fiddling with it. "This isn't possible," she said loud enough for everyone to hear.

"Oh, but it is," I said, rising from the gurney and walking farther downstage with the same slow toe-first step I'd used back when I played Puck in a children's production of *A Midsummer Night's Dream*, speaking directly to the audience. "For we are not alone in the universe, my friends!" *Ding!* "There are countless other universes above and beneath our own, like pages in a book." *Ding!* "And it is my gift—and my curse—to see these other worlds"—*Ding!*—"and, if the circumstances require, to take the things I need and bring them here." *Ding!* "So when the Robles boy threatened me, and no one came to my aid in my hour of need—and yes, I see people in this room who were there, watching as Yasmany meant to beat me up, and you said or did nothing, for shame!" *Ding!* "In desperation, I searched the multiverse for a means of escape." *Ding!* "And then, I saw it—oh, that dear, delicious miracle that tastes so good with buffalo wing sauce." *Ding! Ding! Ding!* "I reached through the veil between universes"—*Ding!*—"and stole a chicken from another place and time"—*Ding!*—"and stuck it in Yasmany Robles's locker"— *Ding!*—"and was saved."

Ding!

The last *ding!* echoed over and over the room, quieter every time, so silent had everyone fallen.

Gabi walked downstage to stand right next to me. I kept facing the audience, smiling like a jester, but she looked at me when she asked, her voice thick with wonder, "Sal, what did you have for breakfast today?"

I pretended to think for a second, but I already knew my answer. "Hippopotamus burgers."

Blatt! went the computer. Because my PANTS were totally ON FIRE!

Mrs. Waked snorted louder than a lawn mower starting. A second later, the classroom exploded in laughter and even louder clapping. The class didn't stop whooping and yelling "Bravo!" until the bell sounded.

"Okay, my lovelies," said Mrs. Waked. "We'll *have* to save Sal's magic trick for tomorrow. Unless that *was* your performance, Sal? *Did* you and Gabi set this up together?"

I was about to answer truthfully, when Gabi slapped her hand over my mouth. "Yes, it was his performance, Mrs. Waked. He's pretty good for a new kid, isn't he?"

Mrs. Waked hugged herself. "You were both *incredible*. *What* timing! What *panache*! And, Sal, that soliloquy! Where in the *world* did you learn so much about parallel universes?"

Gabi removed her hand slowly from my mouth, but her eyes warned me against exposing her lie about our collaborating on the act. I was still wearing the helmet, after all. I blinked at Mrs. Waked and answered, "My papi's a calamity physicist."

The lie detector detected I told the truth.

"Splendid, just *splendid*," said Mrs. Waked, golf-clapping. "I have *absolutely* no idea what that means. Okay, well, *tomorrow*, my butterflies, we begin our unit on *acting with masks*. You're going to *love* it. It's my *favorite* class of the *entire year*! But for now, my *dear* geniuses, I must bid you adieu. *Class dismissed!*"

10

I HAD A FEW questions for Gabi Reál—like *Why did you just lie about us to Mrs. Waked?*—but they would have to wait. It had been *way* too long since I'd eaten. "We need to talk later," I whispered to her as we made our way through the crowd of our adoring fans.

Well, they definitely adored Gabi, anyway. They kind of looked at me like a mutt who'd snuck into the dog show and accidentally got second place.

"We do?" she trolled me, at full volume, no less. "About what?"

Whatever. Had to go. I was the first kid to bust through the doors of the prop room. I practically ran for my locker, where my emergency food stash awaited.

This time, as I dodged like a running back through the hallways, nobody pressed themselves against the walls and stared at me like I was going to eat them and their families. A few people snuck looks like I might munch on their cat or their annoying baby brother—but not their *whole* families.

It was progress. For now, I'd take it.

I sprang up the stairs to the third floor (yes, my knee was just fine, thanks for asking), sliding past the flood of people heading down. I reached the top and turned left for my locker.

And then instantly hid myself in the stairwell again.

There was exactly one kid left in hallway 3E: Yasmany Robles.

I peeked out to spy on him. The heavy, bulging duffel bag hanging off his shoulder looked like it had a dead elephant stuffed inside. While I watched, he tried twice to open the lock on his locker. Twice he failed, and twice he punched the locker door.

I winced both times. He hit the locker so hard. How was he not breaking fingers?

It didn't matter. What mattered was that a bad-tempered bully was getting angry. Not exactly the right time to show my face in hallway 3E. I turned around to head down the stairs again.

It's not like I'm afraid of him or anything, I explained to myself. *It's just that I'm afraid of him.*

I stopped one step down. *What did you just say, brain?*

Nothing, said my brain, slowly eating an imaginary sandwich.

I got defensive. *I've already handled him once today, brain. I can handle him again. And if he messes with me one more time, Principal Torres will expel him for sure.*

So why are you panicking?

Why did my brain suddenly sound like Gabi Reál?

I'm not panicking.

Don't lie to me, Sal. It demeans us both.

My brain was right. I was scared. And being scared *is not allowed.* No way was I going to let myself run, or even wait until Yasmany was gone before going to my locker. I needed to get to my locker right away. It was practically a medical emergency. That's how bullies win: They make you scared to live your life.

So I was going to walk past Yasmany Robles, take out my food, and eat it right there in front of him. I'd eat it nice and slow, really enjoy it. I'd offer Yasmany none of my Skittles, and if he asked for some, I'd tell him to get his own. Then I'd take out the books and stuff I needed for homework, close my locker, and leave. Slowly. Maybe I'd skip.

And if Yasmany dared to mess with me—well, I had six pairs of handcuffs on me that I hadn't gotten to use today. I'd truss him up like a calf at the rodeo and leave him in front of Principal Torres's door.

A deep breath for courage. Then I turned around and walked into the hallway. Past Yasmany. To my locker.

Yasmany pretended not to notice me. So I pretended not to notice him. So far, so good.

I dialed the combo into my lock, zip-zip-zip, and was about to pull it open, when I noticed that Yasmany had grabbed his lock. He was trying to copy me as fast as he could, which wasn't very fast: zip, ziiiipppp, and zizizpizzizppppip. Then he grabbed his lock the same way I was grabbing mine now, ready to pull it open.

But he'd done it wrong. He hadn't squeezed the top part the way I had told him to this morning, before he went full sandwich on me. *The kid doesn't listen,* I thought. *He must drive his teachers crazy.*

So I tried a little experiment.

I faked pulling on my lock and pretended I couldn't open it. And then I said, in my hear-me-in-the-back-row stage voice, "Oh, how stupid of me! I forgot to squeeze my lock while entering the combination. Now I will have to start all over again!"

I glanced over. Yasmany held his lock and stared up at the ceiling like he was minding his own business. He almost busted his neck straining not to look at me.

I spun the dial of my lock to reset it; Yasmany spun his. "And now," I said to the air, "for the secret trick that will allow me to open this lock: I will squeeze the shackle as I input the combination!" I squeezed it so hard my hand shook and, ever so slowly, started dialing. "Left twenty-three, right fourteen, left six."

The numbers I said didn't match the numbers I was dialing. I was inputting my own combination but saying *Yasmany's* combination. You know, to be extra helpful to him.

I flicked my eyes Yasmany's way to see how things were going. He was squeezing his lock! His fingers were white from the effort! Finally.

I watched him input his combination. He mouthed, *Left twenty-three, right fourteen, left six* as he did. If he realized how weird it was that I had said his combination out loud instead of my own, nothing in his body language let on.

Once he had the third number showing on the dial, I said, "And now, to open the lock!" I yanked on mine dramatically, and of course, it opened.

Yasmany yanked on his lock, too, just as dramatically as I had. And, wonder of wonders, his lock opened, too.

What happened next I was not expecting. Yasmany danced.

Well, first his fists shot up in the air. He woo-woo'ed while stepping away from his locker like he'd just won every medal in the Olympics. Then, letting his duffel bag slide off his arm, he spun on the ball of one foot so fast and so many times he could've drilled for oil. He exploded out of the spin into a jump, and the split he did in the air made me promise myself I'd never break a wishbone at Thanksgiving again. When he landed, he started popping and locking and plié-ing and jeté-ing like the fancy-pantsiest B-boy ever to hit the streets. He ended by spinning on his back like a turtle slapped by a hockey stick and tied off the move with a pilot freeze. You know, when you tangle your legs up and throw them in the air and hold the pose like you could stay like that forever and you wouldn't mind, no biggie, just chillin'?

He held the pilot freeze for so long I started to get uncomfortable. Were we done pretending we couldn't see each other? Should I, like, throw him a quarter or something?

A blink later, Yasmany rolled and did a kip-up and was standing again. "Oh [cussword], I gotta get to detention!" He wasn't looking at me when he spoke, and he didn't even glance my way as he clawed his duffel bag off the floor and ran down the stairs.

While leaving his locker unlocked.

Kid was a piece of work. I went over to his locker, shaking my head like an adult who was wondering what was wrong with kids these days. I had every intention of closing his lock for him.

But then I remembered that I'd made a chicken appear—and

then disappear—in his locker earlier today. I'd made a pretty big rip in the universe inside that locker. I wondered if it was still there.

Yasmany hadn't acted like he'd seen anything unusual, but he wouldn't have. He couldn't see the hole. I'd never met anyone else who could see them.

And maybe it had closed by now anyway. All the holes I'd made so far usually didn't last long. Most healed themselves within a few minutes—a few hours, tops. There was only that one time when a hole didn't close. My whole family had had to move out of our house in Connecticut because of all the weird stuff that kept emerging from another universe (PS: Unicorns are real, and they are just as unhousebroken as regular horses), but like I said, it was only that one time.

Still, better to be sure. I opened Yasmany's locker and looked inside.

Annnnnnnd snake eyes. The rip was still there.

The entire back of the locker had become a portal into another world. I could see across dimensions into a whole new reality. Who knew what bizarre aliens lived there, what strange lives they led, what mind-blowing powers and technology they had?

But I didn't see any strange and powerful aliens just then. No awesome futuristic gadgets, either. What I did see was a chicken-processing plant.

From where I was standing, I watched plucked poultry carcasses, hanging from their legs on a metal conveyor belt, zooming by at a thousand miles an hour.

I shoved my head into the locker for a better look. The portal

was high on the wall of the Chicken Plant from Dimension
X, because I had to look down to see the work floor. There,
employees wearing smocks and gloves and protective eyewear
and hairnets hung out along the conveyor belt at different sta-
tions. They pressed buttons and made check marks on clip-
boards and basically made sure the chickens flying by on the
conveyor belt kept on flying.

I pulled my head out of the locker for a think. The hole
wasn't gone yet. That was bad. Until a hole closed, there was
a risk that stuff I didn't intend to bring over from the other
universe would come through on its own. The bigger the hole,
the longer it lasted, and the higher the chance that something
would mosey out of it. Also, a bigger hole meant that a bigger
object, animal, or smelly unicorn could squeeze through.

This hole was not small. I'd dragged a chicken out of it and
then pushed a chicken back through. Oh, and I'd had to trade
Yasmany's bloody shoe for a clean one. This portal was going
to stick around for a while.

So I decided four things then and there:

1. No more dragging stuff either way through rips in the
   universe until this hole closes.
2. Keep an eye out for anything weird that might have
    already come through.
3. If something has come through, SEND IT BACK!
4. If you can't send it back . . . Um . . .

Well, okay, so I decided three things, and I really, really
hoped I wouldn't have to worry about a fourth.

I was about to close the locker, when I noticed what was actually *in* the locker. I mean, besides a wormhole to a different universe.

There was a big stack of books on the left, and stuck to the front of them was a sticky note that read TAKE THESE HOME! A small stack of books on the right had a sticky note on them that said LEAVE THESE HERE! And there was a note, folded in half, that had written on it READ ME!

Far be it from me to disobey an order. I took the note—two pages, front and back, written in big, bubbly letters—and read it.

Dear Yasmany,

I have taken the liberty of organizing your life for you, since you obviously need my help but don't have the good sense to ask for it.

Take the books on your left home with you and DO YOUR HOMEWORK! I can tell you from experience that it is easy and very interesting. You will love the Phoenicians as much as I did, promise! I wish I could take World History again.

I will quiz you on your homework tonight. And because I know you will ask: NO, YOU CANNOT COPY MY ANSWERS.

Once we have finished with your regular homework, I will help you get started with your essay on diabetes. I've done some preliminary research. It's a fascinating topic! The hardest

part of this assignment will be keeping it under
five pages.

To thank me for helping you with your homework
and essay, you can quiz me on my homework tonight
using the questions written on the other side of this
letter. All you have to do is read them to me.

Also, because boys can have trouble
understanding friendship, I will once again remind
you that I am not in love with you. I do love you, as
a friend, and I don't want to see your great talent
go to waste or your good heart fill with poison. I'm
going to make sure of it, even if it kills you.

I also need you to understand what a special
present you were given today by Sal Vidón. I don't
know if I could have convinced Principal Torres
to give you another chance. And, while I'm being
honest, that's partly because I kind of believe she
shouldn't have given you another chance. Yes, I
defended you to the best of my ability, just like I
said I would. But maybe I shouldn't have. You acted
like a bully, Yasmany. It's pretty unforgivable.

But, for whatever reason, Sal did forgive you.
Well, at least enough to speak up for you. He could
have walked out of the principal's office without
saying a word, and you could be looking for a new
school right now. But instead, he turned around and
asked Principal Torres to give you another chance.

Why? I'm not sure. Sal's very hard to read,

and he is pulling tricks all the time. I think all that
hocus-pocus magic stuff has gone to his head
a little.

But I know this much. He was kind to you for
no reason except that he wanted to be kind to you.
That means he's a good person. And thanks to him,
you got a second chance.

And you're not going to waste it—I will see to
that. You are going to start acting like the person you
are with me. You are never, ever again going to act
like you did today. Especially not to Sal. Or, I swear to
you, Yasmany Robles, THERE WILL BE A RECKONING.

That's a literary reference you won't get. You
need to read more. But don't worry about that for
now. For now, just DO YOUR HOMEWORK, and when I
call you tonight to go over it, pick up on the first ring.

I probably can't call before 8 p.m., because I'll
be visiting my brother in the hospital. It's his one-
month birthday, so we're throwing him a party. I
will try to call as close to 8 as I can. That should give
you plenty of time to DO YOUR HOMEWORK. Expect a
late night. We have a lot to do.

Your friend,
Gabrielle Reál

Student Council President
Editor in Chief, *The Rotten Egg*

"Love is the voice under all silences,
the hope which has no opposite in fear."
                                —e. e. cummings

I reread the letter twice, juicing it for info. Then I started to read it a third time, focusing especially on the parts about me.

"¿Bueno?" asked Mr. Milagros from behind me.

Have you ever spit out your entire skeleton, watch it do a dance in front of you, and then swallowed it back down after it dove into your throat headfirst, so it is upside down inside you and your hand bones are your feet bones and your feet bones are your hand bones and your skull is in your butt and you have a pelvis for brains?

Yeah, I hate being snuck up on, too.

Mr. Milagros calmly watched me freak out and collapse on the floor. He just leaned on his mop like he'd seen it a million times before. Yes, he had a mop, and a mop bucket full of soapy water with him. How the heck had I not heard him slopping up behind me? Either I'd been concentrating so hard on reading the letter that I'd turned off my ears, or Mr. Milagros can miraculously move without making a sound.

He offered me a hand. I took it and got up off the floor.

Before I could come up with even a poor excuse for opening another student's locker and reading the private correspondence I had found inside, Mr. Milagros said, "Me? I like a clean school. Todo limpiecito. When things are clean, it's easier to enjoy life. But when things are dirty, you feel wrong all over. No one likes to feel dirty, and no one"—and here he pointed at the ceiling with his mop handle, and for the first time, I noticed a security camera, a big black dome the size of a whale's eye staring at me—"likes to see dirty people doing dirty things. It's important to be clean, don't you think, Sal?"

I sighed. And nodded. And I handed him the note.

He put the note back in the locker with his not-holding-a-mop hand. He didn't seem to notice the rip in the fabric of the cosmos (no one ever had before, so that didn't surprise me). He just shut the locker door and squeezed the lock shut.

"¿Bueno?" he said, smiling, eyebrows flat.

I took that as a none-too-subtle cue and left for home.

11

WALKING HOME FROM school, I replayed the day in my head. It had not been a good one.

1. I'd gotten sent to the principal's office for almost being in a fight.
2. I'd been accused of being a brujo.
3. The red zone had defeated me. Granted, it was a strategic loss, since I didn't want to get labeled as a brujo. But a loss is a loss. I wanted payback.
4. I'd been publicly cross-examined by Gabi Reál and her lie detector.

On the other hand, I'd gotten sweet revenge by nailing my bit in Mrs. Waked's class. Gabi didn't know what hit her!

And she'd called me a good person in her note to Yasmany....

But, because of that, I'd had to leave school so quickly that not only had I forgotten to eat something, I hadn't even locked my own locker! And that was *after* I'd made fun of Yasmany in my head for doing the same thing.

Hopefully Mr. Milagros had noticed my open lock and shut it.

Good thing he hadn't sent me to Principal Torres for snooping. I'd gotten lucky. But sooner or later, luck runs out.

I needed to do better, be more in control. As I crossed the street, I swore to myself that I wouldn't do anything to get me sent to the principal's office for the rest of the year.

And then a car almost hit me.

Even though I was still pretty new to the area, I was quickly figuring out that Miami drivers like to spice up their boring car trips with tire-squealing blastoffs from red lights, *Tetris*-like lane changes, and exciting games of See How Close You Can Come to Running Over Pedestrians without Actually Hitting Them. Apparently, drivers get bonus points if the pedestrians die of heart attacks, so the sapingo who almost hit me did his best to scare me to death: a screeching stop, a blasting horn, tons of bilingual cursing.

I never even flinched. Not because I am very badass or anything. I was paralyzed. Classic deer-in-headlights syndrome.

When I turned slowly to look at the driver—like scarecrow-come-to-life slowly—he shut his trap and stopped honking. I think he saw how zombie I'd turned, how dead I looked. He quietly idled as I took a second in the middle of the road to compose myself. Then I finished crossing the street, and he cautiously drove off.

I was shaking and sweating even more than usual. The stupid Florida heat made near-fatal accidents feel even worse. I stumbled forward a little but quickly figured out I needed a sec. I leaned against a friendly neighborhood palm tree, took

deep breaths, and dreamed of all the Skittles I was going to eat
when I got home.

But the Skittles fantasy only lasted a few seconds. Pretty
soon my brain went on autopilot. Without asking me if I wanted
to remember—because no way did I want to—I watched the
movie playing in my mind of the car accident I was in with
Mami Muerta, back in Connecticut five years ago.

I started calling my mami Mami Muerta after she died. My
psychologist told me that was a defense mechanism. She'd said
it like it was a bad thing.

But, dude, my mami died. It's the worst thing that's ever
happened to me. I think finding ways to defend against how
terrible I feel when I remember she's gone is, like, pretty basic
survival. And anyway, it's not like I had a choice. She just
became Mami Muerta in my head like she'd been born with
that name.

But it hadn't always been her name. Back when the accident happened, she was still Mami Viva.

Like any good Cuban, Mami Viva hated it when the tem-
perature dipped below sixty-seven degrees. But freezing? She
could not understand that at all. Who would want to live anywhere where water turned as hard as rock and staying outside
too long could kill you? Not her, no way, no, señor!

But back then, Papi worked as a math dude for banks and
a physics dude for universities on the East Coast, from Boston
to New York to Washington, DC. We had to live somewhere
along that route, so Papi, who was always easygoing (he spent
all day breaking his brain against math formulas and didn't

have much fight left in him by the time he got home), let Mami Viva pick where she wanted to live.

Since she didn't like big cities, we settled in a small town in Connecticut, and Mami Viva, accepting her fate, added mittens to her wardrobe and hundreds of dollars to our heating bill, and learned to drive in the snow.

Kind of. She drove so slowly between November and March that, like the migration of birds and the shorter days, I came to associate winter with the nonstop blasting of car horns. For five months out of the year, we became the leaders of a noisy, grumpy traffic parade wherever we went. Mami would hunch so close to the steering wheel that her ojo turco would bounce against it every time she braked. And she braked a lot.

One day, Mami Viva picked me up from school so we could run some errands together. I vividly remember the merienda she brought me. "Merienda" means "snack time" in Spanish, and it is so important to Cubans it's almost religion. That day, she'd brought me cubes of guava paste and salty white cheese in a Ziploc bag, with a green plastic cocktail sword for stabbing them so my fingers wouldn't get sticky.

It was my favorite after-school snack. I am a maniac for cheese, and guava paste is probably the best kind of paste in the world. And I have always, always, always loved cocktail swords. Mami and I must have had a thousand cocktail-sword fights. She always let me kill her hand and win.

Mami Viva and I went to the bank, supermarket, post office, and somewhere else I can't remember right now. She always waited to run errands until I could go with her. Her English wasn't the best, so she counted on me to translate for her when she filled out forms, or wanted to understand food labels, or bargained with store managers. I learned how to sweet-talk grown-ups at the ripe old age of eight.

I got really good at it. My mami was counting on me, after all, and when you are in second grade and your Cuban mami's darling, you think your job in life is to be her hero. Also, adults encouraged me, laughing at my jokes and applauding my magic tricks, even though they sucked back then. They liked me, so I liked them.

The best part of being Mami Viva's hero was being rewarded like a hero. After our last errand—post office, I think—we headed back to the car in the early darkness of Connecticut in December. Before she opened the back door for me, she gave me one of her patented besuqueros. I guess the best way to translate that is "kissapalooza." She took my face in her hands and said, using pretty much all the English she knew, "Ay, jou're sush a goo' helper, ¡mi niño!" And then she rained down a storm of smackers all over my cheeks and forehead. She knew she could always crack me up that way. I was still giggling when she buckled me into my car seat. (I was such a small kid for my age I still had to ride in a car seat.)

She pulled out of the post office lot carefully, carefully, and inched onto the street. Pretty soon we were coasting along on a wooded two-lane road, the light snowfall making the darkness feel magical, quiet. No traffic behind us. We could ride easy.

Mami Viva had given me her phone to play with. But let's be honest: It was my phone more than hers, since she almost never used it. Whenever she did use it, she made a face like she was holding someone else's urine sample. I, on the other hand, loved her phone and took it from her every chance I got. I loaded it with games.

So there I was, playing *Poocha Lucha Libre 3*, the wrestling game featuring masked dogs that I still play today, when gravity went in four directions at the same time.

The phone launched itself out of my hands and flew sideways, breaking through the backseat window on the other side of the car. I must have watched it, rapt and in shock, even as I was violently thrown forward. While I was twisting left and up, I reached after the phone with all my might. Mami Viva had told me a million times how much trouble I would be in if I broke it.

Then my head snapped back like a tetherball. My body tried to fly apart, each limb in a different direction. My car seat's belts turned into iron bars that crushed my chest and waist and forced all the air out of my body. For a few seconds, I understood what life would be like as a boulder, never having oxygen inside you, never having to breathe.

It was peaceful. Interesting. Until I realized I was dying.

When I finally did suck in air, my lungs burned and grew heavy with pain. Inhaling felt like my ribs were stabbing my lungs.

I didn't realize we'd been spinning out of control until we stopped. We hit a guardrail hard enough to leave a car-shaped dent in it. It kept us from plunging off the road.

My eyes felt like they were floating outside of my head, hovering just in front of my face. I could still kind of see out of them, but they kept not cooperating, looking off in different directions like a gecko's. I could see, but I couldn't make sense of what I was seeing.

I heard Mami Viva yelling in raging-river Spanish, too fast to follow. A car door opened and slammed. A few seconds later—it must have been, but it felt a lot longer—my door opened, and Mami Viva unbuckled me, swept me up in her arms, and whispered in my ear, "I's okay, Sal. I's okay. Jou're safe now. Estop escreaming, my boy, my brave boy. Estop crying. I's okay. Mami's here. Jou're okay."

I remember her talking to me in English. But that's impossible. Her English wasn't that good back then. It *never* got that good before she died. I must have autotranslated her soothing words as she held me close.

And then . . . Then she started laughing.

It surprised me so much, I finally stopped howling.

"Why are you laughing?" I asked.

She had been crying, too, but now her wet face had become a mask of joy. "Because look!"

She held up her ojo turco to me. Half of it was still on the chain. Only half. The other half had broken off.

I couldn't understand why she was happy about her good luck charm breaking. But I couldn't speak. My brain still felt like lukewarm tapioca pudding.

"Don' jou see, my brave boy? It protected us! It save' us! Wha'ever brujería try to curse us, it didn' work! We're alive!" And, laughing, she lifted me up by the armpits and spun me around.

Looking back, that was a terrible idea. I could have had all sorts of broken bones, whiplash, a concussion—a million things wrong with me that spinning would have only made worse.

Luckily, I just had a few bruises striping my torso and waist. So her laughing and spinning did no harm. It fact, it fixed everything: It took the fear right out of me. I even tried smiling. Then giggling. Then she put me down and knelt on the ground, and we laughed in each other's faces because we were alive. And that moment seemed to last forever.

Forever ended a year later, when, thanks to something called diabetic ketoacidosis, Mami Viva became Mami Muerta.

I blinked. I was still leaning against the palm tree. I wasn't sure how much time had passed. My nails were digging into the tree's bark and I was sucking air like this was my first breath in the world.

Not good.

I stepped off the neighbor's grass and back onto the sidewalk. I needed to eat something, pronto. I ran wee-wee-wee all the way home.

PAPI AND AMERICAN STEPMOM had nicknamed our house the Coral Castle because it's this huge two-story rectangle that takes up half the block. The roof has these things called "crenellations," which, American Stepmom had informed me, is the word for the spaces between stones at the top of castle walls. Where archers shot arrows at invading enemies. "That's cool, right?" she'd asked.

Back when we were house-hunting over the summer, she'd tried to sell me on it harder than the real estate agent had, making it sound like our life here would be all kings and swords and dragons. "This will be our castle," she'd told me as we stood staring at it from the sidewalk, her arm on my shoulder.

"Our Coral Castle," Papi had added, coming up from behind to capture both of us in a gorilla-octopus-bear hug.

Coral. Yeah, right. The house was as pink as conjunctivitis. Weird, huge, ugly thing, that house.

I kind of liked it. Not because of any similarities to castles (because, hello, the thing looked more like the kind of nightmare fun house a serial killer would use as his secret hideout).

I liked it because I like weird things. Weird is the opposite of boring.

On the other hand, weird's also the opposite of home. The Coral Castle was interesting, but it wasn't comfortable. It wasn't family.

But it was where the Vidón refrigerator lived, and that's all I cared about at the moment. I turned my key in the lock, pressed the thumb latch on the door handle. The second I did, my whole body slumped. I had to catch myself to keep from crumpling right there on the welcome mat. I forced my knees and spine to be solid again.

Another rush of dizziness. But it wasn't low blood sugar this time. This felt like the same magnetic buzz I got when I relaxed.

The back of my neck felt hot. My skin cringed. I could just back away, call Papi or American Stepmom, wait for help . . .

But then I heard a woman's voice coming from behind the door. I knew that voice. It was singing.

In Spanish.

I didn't think. I just ran inside.

At about 7:30 p.m., I watched American Stepmom pull into the driveway in her tiny electric car. Kneeling on the couch, I studied her through the living room window as the last of the day's light foamed above the horizon like bubbles in a glass of soda. The night bugs sang with their whole bodies.

American Stepmom turned off her car. She had on the face of someone who had just spent ten hours herding hundreds of K–5 students since, as an assistant principal, that's exactly what she'd done all day. She took off her huge glasses, rubbed her eyes, and looked at her reflection in the rearview mirror. She blew a curl off of her face—she had big, wild hair that Papi said looked like the smoke trails fireworks leave behind—and said "Phew!"

I couldn't hear her, but I could read her lips. American Stepmom's favorite word is *Phew!* It can mean a hundred different things, but here it meant "The hard part's over. I'm home."

American Stepmom had just gotten the driver-side door cracked open when Papi pulled up next to her. Their cars looked like twins on the outside—two little eggs with wheels and headlights—but on the inside, they couldn't be more different. For instance, Papi's car didn't have a steering wheel. He just got in, told the car's computer where he wanted to go, and the vehicle would take him there. He spent every morning commute with the seat reclined, reading science papers that had more math in them than words. He spent the evening commute on his phone playing *Poocha Lucha Libre 5: Perro Sarnoso Edition*, the latest and greatest version of the game. We played against each other online a lot, but I hadn't gone on today after school; I'd been too busy cooking.

Only when Papi's car braked in the driveway and turned off its headlights and engine did Papi realize he had made it home. He looked up from his phone, blinking. He turned his head left and saw American Stepmom smiling at him from her car.

They got out of their cars at the same time. American Stepmom reached out her hand, and Papi wordlessly took it in his until, in the spreading darkness, their hands blended together, each of their fingers a current of dark water that swirled and intermingled with the others. The diamond in American Stepmom's engagement ring shone against their shadowy hands like a wishing star.

They walked up the short pathway to the front door with Papi's head on American Stepmom's shoulder. Still attached to each other, one of them unlocked the door; it didn't matter which, since tomorrow the other one would unlock it.

They had to separate to fit through the doorway, but they didn't really want to. Each invited the other to go first. This took a while; they were having fun. Eventually, Papi went first and American Stepmom wrapped her arms around his waist— barely, he's black-bear big—and they trained inside like a choo-choo of love.

Their love train screeched to a halt when they saw me standing in the middle of the living room. Just. Standing. There.

"Sal," said Papi, blinking. "What is it?"

American Stepmom lifted her head off Papi's back, nose twitching like a rabbit's. "Do you smell yucca, Gustavo?"

"And ropa vieja?" he ask-answered.

"And plantains?"

"And frijoles negros?"

They fell quiet. One of their phones buzzed, but neither of them reacted.

"Is she back, Sal?" asked American Stepmom.

I nodded.

Papi bit his fist.

American Stepmom, all business now, moved out from behind him and asked, "Sal, what did you do?"

I replied the way kids all over the world respond when their moms ask them that question. I shrugged.

On cue, Mami Muerta came into the living room, wearing a huge smile and one of American Stepmom's aprons. She announced, in Spanish, her arms open like a singer, that dinner was on the table. We needed to hurry up and go eat, but no! Go wash your hands first, you pigs. But before you go anywhere (this was to Papi), come give your beautiful wife a kiss. Or don't you love her anymore?

You can see how this put Papi in a difficult position. He looked from his wife to his other wife and finally, wildly, at me.

13

FACT: MAMI VIVA became Mami Muerta when I was eight.

Fact: Papi married American Stepmom when I was nine.

Fact: I figured out how to relax when I was ten.

Fact: I had relaxed Mami Muerta back from the dead five times since then. Six, including this one.

Fact: Mami Muerta went away every time. She and Papi and American Stepmom always ended up fighting. A couple times, it got ugly, and I almost didn't relax her away fast enough. Someone could have gotten hurt.

Fact: All I wanted was for me and all three of my parents to live together like one big happy weird family.

Fact: That was impossible.

Fact: A part of me that I had no control over kept ripping up the universe to bring Mami Muerta back to me anyway.

14

PAPI AND AMERICAN Stepmom stood speechless. Mami Muerta waited with her eyes closed and her cheek out and her lips puckered, expecting a kiss any second. Things were just about to go sideways. If I didn't act now, my plan would fall apart.

So I ran up to Mami and hugged her and said, "¡Estoy muriéndome de hambre, Mami! ¡Besos luego, comida ahora!"

I didn't have to use Spanish to tell her I was starving. This Mami Muerta understood English pretty well, unlike a lot of the previous Mami Muertas. But this English-speaking Mami still *preferred* Spanish, even if I was out of practice. I had discovered over the course of our afternoon of cooking together—as we chatted about all the small, stupid stuff of life—that nothing made her happier than to hear me say "sí" instead of "yes" and "te quiero" instead of "I love you."

It was so good to have Mami back. No, not back, not exactly. This Mami was different from the Mami I remembered. She spoke English, was thirty pounds heavier, and she wore shoes in the house, when the previous Mami always made everyone go barefoot to keep the carpets clean. But she smiled just how I remembered. She had the same chocolate-brown eyes as always. And she could still make me laugh out of control, like I was in second grade again. We had laughed all afternoon as we cooked.

Well, okay, some of my giddiness may have been due to low blood sugar. I was having too much fun with my mami—who used to be muerta, but who now was cooking up a storm and cracking jokes and bossing me around and telling me how to live my life and caring so much that I could see her heart over-flowing with love every time she looked at me—to worry about something as stupid as my diabetes. I'd be fine. And anyway, I needed to save up for all the carbs tonight. No *way* was I going to miss out on my mami's cooking.

"¡Comida ahora!" I repeated.

"Okay," Mami Muerta said in English, laughing and ruffling my hair. "Eat now. But," she said, looking at Papi the way a telenovela star makes eyes at her One True Love, "I expect besitos later. *Lots* of them."

As Mami Muerta and I walked into the dining room, our arms across each other's shoulders—she was short and I had grown, so we were exactly the same height—I looked at Papi and American Stepmom.

They were side by side as well, but not touching. They stood apart at a discreet, non-jealousy-provoking distance.

I mouthed to them, *Everything is under control! Just play along!*

They hesitated.

I couldn't blame them. All five of the other Mami Muertas had looked suspiciously at American Stepmom, wondering qué en el nombre de Dios Papi was doing with this . . . this . . . *americana* (I'm not going to repeat the not-so-nice adjectives some Mami Muertas added in front of *americana*).

Mami was a whole different person every time she came back. One Mami told me how she had competed on Cuba's track-and-field Olympic team; she had abs like a brick wall and arms like a Machamp. Another Mami, frantic, crying, had searched all over the house for my brother and sister (I don't have a brother and sister). So far, three of the Mamis had had diabetes; three, including the one who'd made this dinner, didn't. Two sold clothes in small Miami boutiques that didn't require English, one worked at the post office, another was a Catholic deacon, and the last one . . .

Man, the last one. The only thing all of them had in common so far was that they had picked a fight with my parents. I'd had to close my eyes and relax my mami away before something bad happened. But right before we moved from Connecticut, the one who appeared had gone from zero to maniac in under ten seconds. I'd wanted to make her go away, too, like I had the others, but it's really hard to relax when your Mami Muerta starts chucking shoes and silverware and vases at people you love. After she had run out of things to throw at my parents, she had hustled over to the wall and grabbed her and Papi's wedding picture.

The only reason the wedding picture was still up was because American Stepmom had wanted it there for my sake, so that I would always know that she wasn't trying to replace Mami Muerta. But it had been a mistake to keep it. After Mami

Muerta held it above her head triumphantly, she'd smashed the wedding picture on her knee.

Glass volcanoed up from the frame. Mami Muerta cut herself badly. Startled, suddenly afraid, she pressed her cotton dress to the gash in her knee, and it greedily drank her blood, turning from white to a spreading, growing red. I fainted.

When I woke up, Mami Muerta was gone. But everything she had broken in our family stayed broken.

The house had too many bad memories after that. So we moved to Florida.

It's okay! I mouthed over my shoulder to Papi and American Stepmom. *I got this!*

They looked at each other. Then they leaned in until their noses touched and had a two-second whispered debate. Lots of hands flailing and shoulders shrugging. Then a quick kiss for luck, the kind you see in movies before people go off to war.

I guess my side won, since they followed Mami Muerta and me single file into the dining room.

I know how upset they felt. But I also knew they'd be fine in a second. Because, let me tell you, there are very few things in life that can't be fixed by a Cuban feast. And that's what lay waiting for us in the dining room.

Our dark-stained table stretched as long as an airstrip (well, if mice flew jet fighters). American Stepmom had inherited it from her parents, which meant it had too much sentimental value for her to get rid of it. But it usually felt too big for our little family of three.

Now it looked just the right size to hold all the food on it.

In the center of the table, the pot of glorious brown-and-red ropa vieja—shredded meat in tomato sauce with peppers and cumin and onion and everything else in the world that smells good—burbled like the most delicious tar pit ever.

Around the ropa vieja, the side dishes formed a five-point star. There were:

1. A bowl of white rice the shape of the snowcap on a mountain;
2. A pot of black beans exhaling puffs of seasoned steam;
3. A plate with two kinds of plantains: half sweet and thick and syrupy, half salty and coated in olive oil;
4. A tray of baked yucca—crisp on the outside, soft on the inside—which had been turned blue-green by the loads of garlic heaped on it; and
5. A wooden pizza paddle serving up avocado halves. Each avocado brimmed over with a ladleful of hot bacalao, a tomatoey codfish soup that smelled like the kind of food you eat when you want to make your soul feel toasty and happy and warm.

"Phew!" said my breathless American Stepmom. Here, she meant *What a spread!*

Papi said nothing. His mouth was watering too much for him to speak.

"¡Vamo', vamo'!" said Mami Muerta. "¡Ante, que se enfrie!"

We obediently took our seats: Papi at the head of the table, with American Stepmom on one side and Mami Muerta on the other. I'd be sitting at the other end eventually, finally eating (I.

Was. Starving!), but I decided to play waiter first. All part of my plan. I grabbed the pitcher of water and filled glasses, starting with American Stepmom. "Some va-ter for ze mademoiselle?" I asked her, already pouring.

She ventriloquized, "Why isn't she trying to kill me?"

As I poured her water, I slipped a note onto her plate. Here's what it said:

> I told Mami that I started an Airbnb for a school project in business class. You're my first guest. Your name is Mrs. Scott. You're an architect from New York City. You're visiting Miami for your job. You're married, you don't have children, and on weekends you volunteer at the food kitchen at St. Gabriel's Catholic Church, which I made up, so I hope this Mami doesn't know how to google. But she can read English, so hide this note as soon as you understand it completely.

American Stepmom read the last line and panicked. She balled up the note, popped it in her mouth and chewed it up, and chugged her whole glass of water.

Well, that was one way to hide it. I refilled her glass.

Mami Muerta hadn't noticed. She'd been too busy piling Papi's plate with food.

Papi had always loved Mami Muerta's cooking. I mean, like bye-bye, brain, and hello, dinner! He grew happier and happier as Mami Muerta served him up a mountain of Cuban delights. He barely waited for her to set it down in front of him before he started throwing forkfuls of ropa vieja into his mouth like a farmer pitching hay.

Mami Muerta watched him eat, beaming. My time in the kitchen with her had taught me that one of this Mami Muerta's great joys in life was seeing people enjoy her food.

Remembering her hostly duties with a start, Mami Muerta walked over to American Stepmom and said, "Don't be shy, Mrs. Escott!" And before American Stepmom could do anything, Mami Muerta took her plate and quickly ladled it full of more food than any human could finish in three days.

"Thank you, Mrs. Vidón," American Stepmom said politely. And then, looking at the Mt. Everest of dinner on her plate, she added, "Phew, baby."

"Riquísimo," said Papi. And then, without turning his head, shoveling food into his mouth the whole while, he said to Mami Muerta, "Nadie puede cocinar como tú, Floramaria."

I hadn't heard Papi say a single word in Spanish for over a year. These days, even when he said "amigo" or "mañana" or "hasta la vista," he said them like an American. But now? It was like eating Cuban food had filled him with Cuban words.

As she returned to her seat, Mami Muerta put a hand on Papi's shoulder and, deliriously proud, said, "Cómo me encanta mirarte disfrutando de esta comida, mi amor. But just you wait. There's flan for dessert."

Papi froze, his fork floating in the air. And not because he loved flan. See, as long as he concentrated on the glorious meal in front of him, he could pretend everything else was fine. But as soon as she touched him, he was forced to remember that the woman who had made this most excellent dinner had died five years ago. His mouth and eyes and nostrils opened as wide as they could.

Uh-oh. Time for damage control.

"How about some music?" I asked. I scooted over as quickly as I could to Papi's vinyl collection and flipped on his turntable. The old-fashioned record player's arm moved itself into position; "Yiri Yiri Bon" started to play. In Spanish it sounds like "Jee-dee Jee-dee Boom!" It's all about how Cubans smoke cigars, drink coffee and sugarcane juice, dance, and have a good life. Mami Muerta, who'd just sat at her place, finally, immediately popped out of her seat again and started to dance.

Not all Mami Muertas have loved dancing, but this one sure did. She was getting down.

American Stepmom side-eyed Mami Muerta. Admiration? Definitely. But maybe jealousy, too. American Stepmom's idea of dancing amounted to clapping and jumping in place and looking around to make sure no one was laughing at her. As she watched Mami Muerta sway to the music, she said "Phew" snippily. This time it meant *How am I supposed to compete with that?*

She looked at Papi. His shock had faded away. He sat mesmerized by Mami Muerta's dancing, remembering good times.

When Mami Muerta finally noticed all of us staring at her, she laughed. "Do you know how to dance estilo cubano, Mrs. Escott?"

It took a second for American Stepmom to remember I had renamed her. "Oh, yes, my name is Mrs. Scott. Hi. Um, yes. No! I don't dance. Right?" She looked at me. "Nothing's ever been said about me dancing, right? Right. So, yes, I'm a terrible dancer."

"It's easy!" Mami Muerta shuffled over to American Stepmom and extended her hand. American Stepmom stared hard at it, then looked at me.

With an unsure smile, American Stepmom cautiously took Mami Muerta's hand. Mami Muerta, elated, whiplashed her out of her chair.

They stood about a foot apart and held only one hand. They waited a few beats, Mami Muerta counting with nods of her head. And then they started to dance.

American Stepmom watched Mami Muerta's feet and kind of stomp-copied her. Mami Muerta encouraged her with laughter and hooting and clapping. And Papi—how to even describe his face?—he looked thoughtful and wistful and confused and, for all that, strangely serene. It was a beautiful, impossible moment. Papi knew that, whatever else might be going on in his mind—and I am sure he was thinking about the physics that made Mami Muerta's visit possible—it was his duty to watch this miracle happen.

It's working! It's working! I thought. All my parents, together. I didn't know how I could keep this up. American Stepmom couldn't pretend she was renting a room from me forever. But I would figure something out. I had to. This was just what I wanted, this beautiful, happy, white-bright moment.

Whoa. Too bright, I suddenly realized. My peripheral vision grew painfully brilliant. That's when I remembered how long it had been since I'd eaten. I needed to get some food in me, now! Or—

I only finished that thought a few hours later. In the hospital.

15

WHEN I WOKE UP, I could tell by the smell—a little chemical, a little too cold, and a little like pee—that I was lying in a hospital bed. Before I opened my eyes, I decided to check in with my body.

My doctor in Connecticut had taught me a meditation to help me concentrate on my insides. I pretend my brain is a submarine. It unmoors itself from my skull, turns on its searchlights, cruises through my throat, and enters the underwater cave that is my chest cavity. Scientists inside the sub take notes as it stops to examine weird-looking organs. Next, it glides carefully into my right arm, going all the way past the wrist and lighting up each finger before turning around and doing the same to the left arm. It coasts down my legs and studies each toe. Then it's an easy ride back to the skull, where my brain docks itself again and submits its report about my body.

Nothing inside me hurt. That was the best news, since I could have cut myself or conked my head when I passed out. I didn't feel faint anymore, either, just groggy, like when you sleep for too long. My body sank into the bed like a garbage bag full of microwaved peanut butter.

Even with my eyes closed, I knew I had an IV tube in my right arm. They'd taken my vest off, but I still had on the T-shirt and cargo pants I'd worn all day. Good—I hate hospital gowns. Shoes were off, socks were on. Also good—for diabetics, socked foot is best foot. As a people, those of us who are pancreatically challenged have, well, ugly paws. We get calluses and corns and ulcers more easily than you norms. My pair already looked like overused chew toys, and I was still a kid. But sometimes we type-1 types have to have our toes and arches and heels and ankles amputated, so we're grateful when we get to keep them at all. You learn to love your beat-up feet, the same way homely dogs are cute.

They must have stabilized my blood sugar with the IV, but I still hadn't eaten real food in a long time. My stomach complained like a bubbling bog.

"Did you hear that?" asked American Stepmom. "Is Sal awake? Sal—"

"Don't wake him, mi vida," Papi whispered.

I made sleepy noises and shifted a little and then settled, as if I were actually asleep and not faking it so I could eavesdrop on them.

"Phew," said American Stepmom. That meant *I didn't wake him, and I would have felt really terrible if I had, and my poor son has it so tough, what a world.*

"No harm done," whispered Papi.

"Well," American Stepmom whispered back. But now her voice was totally different. She had gone from Loving Mother to

Assistant Principal of Doom in the space of a second. "Let's not minimize this. Plenty of harm was done. To us. By Sal."

"We told him not to bring her back," agreed Papi. "We made him promise."

"After your dead ex-wife wrecked our house in Connecticut."

We all three of us took a sec to remember that time when Mami Muerta stood bleeding in our house, a wet red circle spreading on her dress from the gash on her knee.

I wanted to tell them that I hadn't done it this time. Well, not on purpose. I hadn't called her. I didn't mean to almost get run over and have a flashback.

But I wanted to see where they were going with this. I snored.

"We've been too easy on him," said American Stepmom.

I could sense Papi nodding in agreement. "Walks all over us."

"Children need structure. I, more than anyone, should know this."

"It's my fault. I never discipline him. Ever since Floramaria died—"

"No, my darling. Who can blame you? Floramaria's death shook you both so terribly. You were completely heartbroken when we first met. Do you remember?"

Papi sounded like he was sad-smiling. "I was such a mess back then. Barely alive. What could you have possibly seen in me, mi amor?"

"A genius."

"Bah."

"A genius," she repeated, "who loves his son very much."

"Too much. I couldn't bring myself to say no to him once his mami died. 'You want ice cream for dinner? Sure, you're diabetic, but one time won't hurt, right?' Or, 'You want to stay up all night playing video games? Well, you only live once.'"

"What about me? I've made the classic stepmom mistake. I want Sal to love me so much that I say yes to everything. And now—"

"Now his dead mama makes us dinner."

American Stepmom must have shrugged. "Delicious food."

Papi smacked his belly like a conga drum and whisper-laughed. "Yeah. Too bad she disappeared and took all her food with her. Even what we'd already eaten, right out of our stomachs."

"It's probably for the best. Imagine eating like that every day. We'd weigh a thousand pounds apiece."

"And be happy."

They paused to think about all the good Cuban food Mami Muerta wouldn't get a chance to make for them now that she was gone.

"Sal's going to wake up hungry for sure," said American Stepmom.

"Should I find him some dinner?" Papi asked.

American Stepmom *tsk-tsk*ed. "Hospital food. No one deserves that."

"I could drive somewhere. Get him something."

"Let's wait until he wakes up. See what he wants."

"Before or after we punish him?"

"After."

They went quiet. My skin felt hot all over, boiling and wet, like I was a chicken getting fried. But I didn't move. They were right; they never punished me, even when we all knew I deserved it.

"She was really there," American Stepmom said a half minute later. "Your dead wife. In the flesh. I danced with her."

The room was so quiet I could hear Papi taking her hand. "Were you scared?"

"A little. But . . . curious, too. She's so different every time she appears. She was very nice this time."

Papi made an appreciative *hmph* sound. After a second he added, "You danced well."

"Shut up."

"No, I'm serious! You were learning. You were getting better."

American Stepmom play-smacked Papi before repeating, "Shut. Up!"

"What? It's true."

"It's . . . weird. This time, this appearance, I kind of . . . liked her. I liked her right away. The food she made, the way she welcomed me. Invited me to dance. Phew, baby. Is that more what she was like, when she was alive? Was that her real personality?"

"Real . . ." Papi said, his voice a million miles away. "Every time she visits, I always see parts of the Floramaria I knew. It's fascinating, from a scientific perspective. If there are infinite parallel universes, then the vast majority of them shouldn't have Floramarias at all, and those that do shouldn't have Floramarias I can recognize. But in *all* the Floramarias Sal has brought over, I've seen different aspects of the woman I married. It should be statistically impossible, unless Sal is somehow able to bring over Floramarias that most resemble his mami. But how could he do that? How can he do *any* of this? This is all exceedingly impossible."

Beep went the monitors, *drip* went the IV in my arm. Some machine exhaled the way people in movies sigh when they're in love. The hospital intercom said something in hospital code.

After a while, I heard American Stepmom scratch her scalp. "Is it time to check Sal for calamitrons, Gustavo?"

"Oh, right. Yes. Thank you," said Papi.

I heard Papi get up. There was some clanking and clattering. I opened my left eye a crack, just enough to be able to see a little through the cage of my eyelashes.

Papi was walking toward me with a device that looked like a black weed-whacker from the future. He turned it on.

"I'm alive!" the machine yelled happily.

"Shh!" said Papi. "Can you please be quiet for a change?"

"Oh, sure," the machine said sulkily, "I can just work like a slave for you, with no thoughts or opinions of my own, like I am some third-rate AI who doesn't even count as a—"

Papi turned it off. It took every ounce of my willpower not to laugh. After he looked at me for a few seconds and was satisfied I hadn't woken up, he turned the machine on again.

"I'm alive!" the machine barely whispered.

"Not another word," said Papi, "or I'll turn you off for the rest of the day."

He held the device up by its awkward handlebars, and a three-blade propeller, glowing ghost-blue and buzzing, spun as slow as a windmill beneath it. He swept the machine over the length of my body like he was beachcombing me. Then he sat back down with it. He and American Stepmom leaned close to look at a readout built into the handlebars.

The Metal Detector of Tomorrow chimed happily when it had finished its calculations and, in a loud robot voice, announced, "Zero calamitrons detected! Congratulations! Your universe isn't ending!"

"Turn that thing off!" American Stepmom yell-whispered.

"You were going to turn me off anyway," said the machine. "But you can't quench my spirit! I love to be alive!"

Papi switched it off. "Sorry, mi vida! Did we wake him?"

I closed my left eye all the way and smacked my lips. "It doesn't look like it," said American Stepmom. But she didn't sound all the way convinced, either. I'd have to be more careful. "Well, at least there are no calamitrons. Here, anyway."

"Which makes no sense." Papi started pacing; I cracked an eye again to watch him. "Sal was hanging out with Floramaria all day. He should have collected all sorts of calamitrons from her. Calamitrons love people."

American Stepmom rubbed her eyes when she said, "Especially us. Is this going to be Connecticut all over again? Are we going to have to move, Gustavo? We just got here!"

"We're not moving, mi vida. I'll fix everything. Starting tomorrow."

Something in the way Papi said that made my stomach burble.

American Stepmom had heard the edge in Papi's voice, too. "Gustavo, are you saying what I think you're saying? The remembranation machine? It's finished?"

Papi had the faraway look of an astronaut explaining what it's like to gaze out a space station window and see planet Earth rotating beneath you. "Lucy, mi amor, up to now, calamity physics has been helpless. We've known about calamitrons for more than a decade, but we've only been able to detect them for the last three years, thanks to these entropy sweepers."

He started petting the device. Its robot voice said, "Ahhhhh."

Papi jumped. "I thought I turned you off!"

"I'm a class-eight AI, señor. No human can turn me off if I want to be on!" said the sweeper.

Papi yanked its battery pack out of the handle, and it instantly lost all power.

"Why did you program that thing to be so sassy?" American Stepmom asked him. She was loving this as much as I was.

Papi shrugged. "Intelligent machines make for better science. What was I saying?"

"You were telling me about your shiny new remembranation machine."

"Oh yeah." Papi stood quickly, holding the entropy sweeper over his head like a battle-ax. "Tomorrow, mi vida, the game changes! We're getting a machine that will repair holes in the universe! Remembranate matter itself! Protect us from a potential universal catastrophe!"

Papi used to share everything about his work with me, but this was news to me. What did it mean? No more holes? No more visits from Mami?

I noticed I had stopped breathing. I thought it might be a good idea to start again. But slowly, so I wouldn't draw attention.

American Stepmom had been quiet for a while. She'd been thinking. I could hear the doubt coming off her, the way you can hear rain arriving. "Yeah? You've got it all figured out?"

Papi sat down heavily. The cushion on his chair wheezed. "Well, who knows, really? This is all brand-new, and in science, 'brand-new' usually means 'wrong.' But it's a start. With luck, we'll learn a lot about the barriers between universes—and, more importantly, what happens when you punch a hole in those barriers."

"When *Sal* punches holes in those barriers," American Stepmom corrected.

"Yes." Papi exhaled, and the air in the room felt as heavy as Jupiter's atmosphere, acidic gasses pressing down on us, getting into our lungs. Well, that's what it felt like to *me*, at least. I closed my eyes again.

"The elephant in the room," American Stepmom said with the precise pronunciation of a principal getting ready to punish a student, "is that we've been way too easy on Sal."

Papi's head sank like an anchor. "It's my fault. When his mami died, I didn't know what to say. So I told him, 'Mi niño, don't be sad! There are infinite universes out there where your mamita is alive, waiting for you!' I didn't think he'd, you know, actually be able to find her."

"And bring her back."

"And have her cook dinner."

After several loud ticks of the clock—just enough time to give herself a silent pep talk—American Stepmom answered with, "We've both made mistakes when it comes to Sal, Gustavo. But we have to do what's right for him. I know it's hard. But we told Sal he wasn't to bring Floramaria back anymore. We have to punish him for disobeying us."

Tick, tick, tock. "Okay," said Papi. Reluctantly.

"So what do you think?"

"Um . . . Ah . . . Well. What's traditional? Grounded for two weeks?"

"That . . . seems harsh."

"Yeah. One week?" But he immediately answered his own question. "We just moved here. It's not fair to keep him from making friends when he's the new kid. . . ."

"Yeah. What about no TV for a week?"

"He wouldn't miss it. It's not like when we were growing up, Lucy. Kids today just binge-watch a whole season in, like, half a day. It needs to be something he does all the time. Something he cares about." Papi snapped his fingers. "I've got it! What about no magic for a week? Now *that* he would miss."

Three dead seconds. Then: "Phew, baby. He'd certainly know we mean business."

"Too harsh?"

"No, I don't think so. I think it's just harsh enough, for a change."

"Okay. So it's agreed, then."

"When he wakes up, we present a united front."

"We will both walk up to his bed, holding hands."

"And we'll say, 'Sal—'"

"'For a whole week, you aren't allowed to do any mag—'"

"Hey, guys," I said, sitting up in bed, stretching sleepily.

My parents rushed to my bed so fast they forgot to hold hands. "How do you feel, mijo?" asked Papi.

"A little better," I said, and I gave each of them a worried look. "Is Mami still here?"

Both parents swallowed at the same time. American Stepmom answered, "No, Sal. She's gone."

I looked down and nodded. I could feel their desire to protect me radiating from them like heat from a Connecticut fireplace. That's when I looked up at them and asked, "Did she hurt anybody?"

Papi answered. "No. We're fine. Everything's fine."

"Thank goodness," I said, and I faked that I was getting sleepy again. I fluttered my eyelids shut. "I couldn't live with myself if I ever did anything to hurt either of you."

I opened one eye a crack. They both looked like they were about to cry.

"Are you going to punish me?" I asked, sinking into my pillow. "I didn't bring Mami on purpose this time. But it's still my fault. I know I deserve it."

"No," they replied at the same time. And then they looked at each other.

"Don't worry about that," Papi said.

"We're just glad you're okay," said American Stepmom.

"You just get some rest."

"We're going to stay here all night with you."

"Okay," I said. "I love you."

"I love you, son," they said together.

Look, I probably deserved some kind of punishment for a few things I'd done that day.

But a week without magic? Not gonna happen.

16

LATER THAT NIGHT, I woke up again. The clock on the wall read 10:37. As many lights as possible had been turned off, but in a hospital room, you're never fully in the dark. I sat up in bed, my eyes taking their time to adjust to the maple-syrup glow of the room. Monitors displayed eerie blue numbers, and green LEDs blipped on and off and on again. The whirs and sighs and beeps of the machines sounded like robots talking in their sleep.

I couldn't believe the day wasn't over yet. Seemed like I had been up forever. I probably should have rolled over and tried to go back to sleep.

But I was starving. Pretending to fall asleep had actually put me to sleep before Papi could score me some grub. I'd barely eaten all day.

Sometimes, when I get hungry enough, I daydream about just reaching into another universe and yoinking someone's chicken nuggets. *Mmm, chicken nuggets.* But it wouldn't work. Mami Muerta's meal had disappeared right out of my padres' stomachs because she had brought her own groceries with her from wherever she'd come from. In the same way, any food I swiped from a different universe would eventually vanish and leave me hungry all over again. Every time a hole closed, it took with it everything that had come through it: nuggets, Cuban feasts, formerly dead Mamis, everything.

And if a hole didn't close . . . Well, they usually closed, eventually. No need to dwell on that.

The point was, I needed grub, pronto. I could have woken the padres, but Papi and American Stepmom were snoring a restful duet in chairs at the foot of my bed. They'd had a long day, too.

I could handle this. I had a few bucks in my pocket, and I knew exactly where the closest vending machine was. I could be in and out before my parents snored a dozen times.

If you're wondering how I knew where the closest vending machine was, it's because I became a volunteer magician for the patients in the hospital within a week of our moving to Miami. When you're a magician, volunteering to perform at hospitals is a no-brainer. It gives me tons of practice (especially with up-close magic, which is the toughest kind, and also my favorite), a place to try out new tricks, and the most appreciative audience in the world: good people with rotten luck who are desperate for a little fun.

Plus, I have type-1 diabetes. Making friends with my local hospital is just smart.

A nurse must've taken out the IV after I'd fallen asleep again; all that was left in the crook of my elbow was a ball of cotton under a bandage. Nothing to stop me from foraging for some eats. So, gingerly, ninja-ly, I put my sock-silent feet on the floor one at a time, soft-footed it over to the door, and slipped through.

Hospital hallways are really bright: white walls, white ceiling, fluorescent lights whiter than white, and a white polished floor reflecting all that whiteness back up again. For a second I worried I was starting to pass out again.

I'd have to get past the nurses' station right after the elevators, because, well, all the nurses knew me, and they would probably try to make me eat some healthy cacaseca that tasted like pencil shavings. Or they'd stick another IV in my arm. And I was done with holes in my skin for the night.

As soon as I was past the elevators, I got down on all fours and started to crawl. Two nurses were working at the station: Ortiz and Calembe.

I knew them. They were all right. They were keeping themselves awake during the graveyard shift with high-speed Cuban gossip. It flew out of their mouths so fast I couldn't follow it, but it must have been really juicy, because they were laughing and having a good time. I'd been hoping they'd be sleepier, or out on rounds.

I snuck over to the desk, pressed my back against it, and waited for an idea to come. I didn't have a lot of props for magic tricks with me—my vest was back in my room—so I checked my cargo-pants pockets to see what I had to work with. Spare change, scarves, foam balls, poppers, six pairs of handcuffs from earlier, a finger guillotine, a deck of cards . . . Aha! This could work: a handheld alert siren I was supposed to set off if I needed help. It was totally impractical in real life—it's much faster to just yell "Help!"—but insurance had covered it, so I could find a use for it, sure. Like, say, distracting nurses.

Practice makes perfect. I silently went through the motions three times of how I was going to pull this off: (1) turn on siren, (2) chuck it down the side hallway, (3) run the other way, wet-cat fast.

I took a deep breath, pumped myself up. Then I set off the siren and threw it.

"¿Qué'eso?" said Calembe, who did that Cuban thing of smashing all the syllables in a sentence into one word. She made "What is that?" sound exactly like "Cheese?" in Spanish.

"¿Alarma?" asked Ortiz. Then she got up and added, "Extraño," probably because my siren didn't sound like any of the noises the hospital usually made. Believe me, with the amount of time I spent in hospitals, I knew them all.

A few seconds later, they both walked down the side hallway to investigate. I immediately crawl-galloped past the station and out of sight. I couldn't help but think that sometimes these things were just too easy.

"What in the name of bad ideas do you think you're doing, Chacumbele?"

Busted.

Whenever I'm doing a magic trick, there's always one person I can't fool.

One kid in the pediatrics ward will always spot me palming a coin. One judge at the talent show will always know exactly where to look. At Culeco, that person was clearly going to be

Gabi. And among the hospital staff, that person was Nurse Dulce Sotolongo.

I rose slowly, putting my hands on top of my head. "I give up. Don't shoot!"

She laughed as she walked up, grabbed my left wrist, and dragged me over to the hand-sanitizer dispenser on the wall. "Do you know how many germs there are on the floor of a hospital?"

"Like, six?" I said. "Oh, wait, that's way too low. Nineteen."

"Ha-ha," she said, right before she snorted. She seemed too young to be a nurse. She looked a lot like Mami Muerta does in her wedding photo: curvy, happy, black hair crashing like a waterfall over her shoulders. Maybe that's why we'd had this brother-sister mess-with-me-I'll-mess-with-you thing going from the moment we'd met. "Do I dare ask qué en el nombre de la alfombra you're doing on the floor?" she added.

With Nurse Sotolongo, honesty was the best policy. Usually. "I need food," I said.

"You didn't take out your IV just so you could get some Skittles, did you?" she asked, eyebrows raised.

I shook my head and crossed my heart.

She gave me cacaseca eyes, but I could see she was running through options in her mind.

Suddenly, an idea made her smile. "You like parties?"

I do, in fact. But I had a different question. "Isn't it a little late for a party in a hospital?"

"Not for this family. They get whatever they want. Follow me."

She led me past the waiting room, around the corner, down

another long hallway, and past another bank of elevators. As we approached the other waiting room on this floor, I heard a bunch of voices: Spanish and English, all ages, everyone laughing and talking at the same time. Papi calls that many Cubans partying together a "gallinero"—a chicken coop's worth of noisy, cheerful clucking.

It stopped me in my tracks. That much joy coming from a hospital waiting room is . . . unusual.

"This is the best family," Nurse Sotolongo said over her shoulder. "They'll probably adopt you before the night is over. Come on."

She entered the waiting room, and I, after taking a deep breath, walked in behind her. Seven people stood up from their chairs and cheered as we entered.

I mean *cheered.* They made me jump.

Before we could do anything, a woman exactly old enough to be Nurse Sotolongo's mami swooped over to a table filled with huge aluminum trays of Cuban pork, rice, beans, yucca, plantains, and a jumbo plastic bowl overflowing with packaged salad. In two seconds she had piled a paper plate so full I was sure it would collapse. She placed that plate in Nurse Sotolongo's hands and smeared a niña-buena kiss all over her cheek.

"Good, you're back!" said the Cuban mother. "Now you can eat!"

Poor Nurse Sotolongo. I knew that look on her face all too well. She wasn't hungry. My guess was that she had been at this party earlier and had been forced to python down enough food for three days. To a Cuban mother, it doesn't matter that you *have* eaten. That was *then*. Nurse Sotolongo had to eat *now*, or risk breaking this sweet mami's heart.

Sal to the rescue. "Hi!" I said to the Cuban mother, and stuck out my hand. "My name is Sal. Nurse Sotolongo said you wouldn't mind if I joined your party. Gosh, everything smells so good! I love Cuban food. And boy, am I starving!"

I had said the magic word: "starving." Say that to a Cuban mother sometime. I dare you.

The Cuban mother almost fainted. "Po! Bre! Ci! To!" she said, and literally took the plate out of Nurse Sotolongo's hands and placed it in mine.

"Hey!" said Nurse Sotolongo, suddenly jealous.

Cuban mother touched her face. "You don't mind, do you, mi niña? I'll go make you another plate right now. Double the size of the last one!"

"No, no!" said Nurse Sotolongo. "I . . . I'm being paged!" She wasn't, but she grabbed her pager and shook it herself as if it were buzzing. "See? I have to go."

"Oh, okay. But come back soon? We're going to cut the cake the second La Jefa gets back. She's just finishing up her homework in the cafeteria. She's heading up right now."

"I will," Nurse Sotolongo lied. She made mean eyes at me that meant *Cover for me, or else!* Then she turned back to Cuban Mom and asked her, "You'll watch over Chacumbele here?"

"Like he was my own." And she meant it. Nurse Sotolongo had been right—Cuban Mom was ready to adopt me on the spot.

Nurse Sotolongo left and the Cuban mother introduced me to the room: "Everybody! We have a new guest! This is Sal!"

"Hi, Sal!" said six adults at once. I raised my plate to them in greeting.

And then, from behind me, a shocked girl's voice asked, "Sal? What are you doing here?"

I looked over my shoulder to see the person the Cuban mother had called La Jefa, standing in the doorway with her mouth open. La Jefa couldn't believe that I was there. La Jefa was Gabi Reál.

There's no point in saying "Huh?" or "What?" or "What's going on?" when impossible things happen. It's better to just play along. So I smiled over my mountain of food and replied, "Hi, Gabi! I came to wish your brother a happy birthday!"

17

"HOW DID YOU know it's my brother's birthday?!" asked Gabi. I could almost see her head exploding. Very satisfying.

That's also when I noticed she had changed the barrettes in her hair *again*. Now they were colorful metal birthday cakes.

"Oh, good! You two know each other," said the Cuban mother.

"This is the kid I told you about, Mom!" Gabi said, pointing at me. "The one who caused all the trouble today? The one who made the chicken appear in Yasmany's locker? The one who fooled the most advanced lie detector in the world?" And when her mom wasn't getting it: "The brujo?"

"I'm not a brujo," I objected, maybe sounding a little too serious. So, to soften my tone, I added, "I'm a magician."

"Magician?" said the Cuban mother, somehow looking even more excited. "Cool!"

"I like magic," said the biggest, beardiest guy in the room.

"Ooh, me too," said an African American woman with black-and-gold braids piled like a vase on her head. She wore a doctor's smock. "Can you show us a trick, Sal?"

At first, Gabi had looked annoyed that her family was being

nice to me. But then, suddenly sly, she said, "Oh yeah. Sure he can. I bet he can make that whole plate of food disappear right before your eyes. Can't you, Sal?"

"You can?" asked Gabi's mom, wanting with all her heart to see that happen.

No, I couldn't. I had no idea how to make a trick like that work. I would have to design a whole act for it and practice it for weeks. The only way I could make it happen right now is if I tore a hole in the universe. And I'd done more than enough ripping for one day.

But still, I have a weakness for Cuban moms. So fine, Gabi. Challenge accepted.

I stepped into the center of the room and did a 360 on the ball of my socked right foot. The crowd oohed appreciatively. Gabi's mom almost lunged for me, scared I would drop the plate, but Gabi grabbed the back of her shirt.

"I can indeed," I said after the spin, in my deep performer's voice. "Watch in amazement as this plate goes from overflowing to empty right before your eyes."

I twirled the plastic fork like a magic wand, held it up in the air for two full seconds, and then . . . started eating. A nice big forkful of pork. I chewed dramatically, making *mmm-mm!* noises, surprised and wide-eyed. I swallowed theatrically, then took another bite.

"Um . . ." said Gabi's mom.

"What?" I asked, mouth full. "I said I would make it disappear. I didn't say how long it would take."

The room cracked up and applauded.

Gabi's mom steered me by the shoulders into an empty

chair by the table, right by the huge chocolate sheet cake. "Very funny. Now, you sit here and eat, and when you're done, there's cake for you." She turned her back to me and said to the rest of the room, "Okay, everybody, line up! Stop stuffing your faces and being so rude. Introduce yourself to Gabi's friend!" Spinning around to face me again, she thrust out her hand so fast it vibrated where it hung in the air. "Hello. My name is Reina Reál. I write an advice column called 'No es fácil.'"

"It's bilingual," said Gabi, beaming. "It's syndicated in eight countries."

I stuck my fork in the top of my food mountain like a flag so I could shake Ms. Reál's hand. "I'm Salvador Vidón. It is my distinct pleasure to meet you."

"Politeness is one of your tricks," said Gabi, moving from behind her mother. "But I told my parents about you. You aren't going to fool anyone here, chacho!"

"Don't be rude, Jefa," said Ms. Reál, putting a hand on Gabi's shoulder. "Sal is our guest."

A second later, Gabi extended her hand to me. But when I went to shake it, she yanked it away suddenly.

"Gotcha!" she said, and held up her hand so I could see the GOTCHA! stamp still imprinted on it.

I left my hand out there, floating in the air, and put on a wounded smile. "Yep. You sure got me. Feel better now?"

"Gabrielle Reál!" her mom exclaimed.

Gabi narrowed her eyes until only her black-claw eyelashes were visible. "I was just getting him back, Mom."

"You're already writing an article about him," said Ms. Reál. "Isn't that enough revenge?"

"Mom!"

I took the fork up again and enjoyed the one bite of salty, garlicky yucca I was going to allow myself. Yucca is delicious but, alas, loaded with carbs. "You're writing an article about me?" I asked with my mouth full.

Pro tip: Speaking with your mouth full is a good way to make yourself sound more innocent.

Gabi stuck out her chin and squared her body at me, the way you see heroes in movies face a firing squad. "Yes. What happened at Culeco today is the biggest story I have ever witnessed in all my year of reporting. The school newspaper has a responsibility to cover it."

I munched pork and, as casually as I could, asked, "Can I see it?"

"Sure," she replied. "Tomorrow. When everyone else does."

I paid attention to my food. "If it's about me, I have a right to see it now."

"Ha! You have zero right!"

"You don't have to be so confrontational, Jefa," said Ms. Reál.

"Actually, Mom, I do. Because it would be against journalistic ethics. You more than anyone else here should know that."

"What am I, yesterday's news?" said the man in line behind Gabi. He was medium in every way: medium height, medium build, skin tone right in the middle between white and black, and a medium amount of curls left on his middle-aged head. He wore casual-Friday pants and a tie that had as many digits of pi that could fit on it. "Weathermen are journalists, too."

Ms. Reál made her hands talk like puppets and mouthed,

Blah, blah, blah. But then she waved the man over. "Come here; introduce yourself, mi vida."

Gabi stepped aside, dodging the man's jousting-lance arm just in time. "Hi!" he said. "I'm Lightning Dad."

"I'm Sal," I replied. Then, after I had a second to think: "Um, Lightning Dad?"

"Don't you watch TV?"

"Not really."

"Oh," said Lightning Dad, deflated. But he recovered instantly, and, happy as a helium balloon, said, "I'm the chief meteorologist for the AhoraMismo News Network. Miami's most popular local news!"

"And Lightning Dad is your stage name?"

"What? Oh, no. That's just what the family calls me. Gabi has so many dads, you know. We need a way to tell us all apart."

My face must have done something when he said Gabi has so many dads. To explain what he meant, he pulled forward the next person in line—that big beardy dude who'd claimed he liked magic. "What's your name?" Lightning Dad asked him.

The man had been caught off guard by being yanked to the front of the line. So he blinked and guessed, "José?"

"No, your dad name!"

"Oh! Grizzly Dad'ums." He smiled like a well-fed bear and offered me his massive paw to shake. "I work for the American Heart Association."

After Grizzly Dad'ums came Cari-Dad, the black woman with the amazing braids. Yep, apparently women could be Gabi dads, too. Cari-Dad was a cardiologist, and she and Grizzly Dad'ums had been married for a while, years ago. They were divorced now. But you wouldn't know it by the way they laughed and loved on each other.

In fact, this was the most love-filled room I'd been in since . . . forever? I didn't have enough family for a family reunion, so I didn't know for sure, but my guess was that this was what family reunions felt like.

In the course of the next half hour, I also met:

1. Dada-ist, an artist originally from the Dominican Republic who had sculptures on display in the Miami Museum of Kinetic Art. He showed me a video of his work: mobiles made of shiny black tiles hanging from the ceiling on fishing lines. The tiles spun and swirled around slowly and, every once in a while, came together to become human faces. I liked his art a lot.

2. Daditarian, a second-gen Cuban American who had started a food co-op. He talked to me for fifteen minutes straight about how the world would be a better place if everyone ate bugs instead of cows. He pulled a bag of dried crickets out of his pocket (my guess is that he always had some dried bugs with him, the same way I always carried a trick or two) and asked me if I wanted to eat some. All the other dads made faces and said I didn't have to.

I ate some. They tasted exactly like Crunchy Cheetos. Plus, no carbs. Ten out of ten would eat cheesybugs again.

3. Dada-dada-dada-dada Dadman!, who exercised more

in a month than all the other dads put together
exercised in a year, because he worked as an actor all
over Florida, usually as whichever superhero happened
to be the most popular at the moment. He was the
most recent dad addition, and the most recent Cuban
immigrant in the family. He thought America was the
best country in the world.

"Confused yet?" asked Gabi.

She'd been watching me as I met each dad with the
sideways look of a hawk deciding if you're worth killing and
eating. I could tell that she'd had to defend her dads against
a disapproving world more than once. And she was more than
ready to defend them against me, right here, right now.

But she didn't have to worry. It was true I didn't know the
story behind why they all had introduced themselves as dads. I
was pretty sure they weren't all actually married to each other,
because that's illegal. So, okay, they were honorary dads. Cool.
It was clear they all loved each other as deeply as any family.
Ms. Reál was the mom, and these other people were dads,
and Gabi was the kid (and also La Jefa, lol), and everyone was
happy, and there was a huge chocolate sheet cake for dessert.
Love is all that matters.

So I said to Gabi, "What's confusing? You have a bunch of
papis. Awesome. I mean, I'm not sure how you can survive all
their dad jokes, but that's your business."

I didn't know it then, but that was the moment Gabi
became my friend for real. Months later, she told me the way
I had met her interesting, complicated family, pleasantly and

without judgment, and, especially, my dad-joke joke, made her think I was the most mature seventh grader she had ever met. Except for herself, of course.

Ms. Reál hugged me—she'd been standing beside me the whole time, too, making sure I kept eating between introductions—and said, "Lightning Dad's jokes are the worst. Watch out."

"I'm a meteorologist!" said Lightning Dad indignantly. "Bad jokes are my livelihood!"

"I am confused about one thing, however," I said.

"What's that?" asked Ms. Reál.

"Where's Gabi's brother? Isn't it his birthday?"

All the dads went quiet. Ms. Reál bit her bottom lip.

"You really want to know?" asked Gabi.

Given how everyone reacted, I did, now more than ever. "Yeah."

Gabi looked to her mom and dads, and everyone nodded approval. So she left the room, and I followed, and we went to see the most heartbreaking patient in the whole hospital.

18

I FOLLOWED GABI to the neonatal intensive care unit. I knew the way, too, but I let her lead. This was her show.

"Hi, Gabi," said Nurse Sotolongo, who was sitting at the reception desk. "What, is Chacumbele giving you trouble? You had to return him to me?"

Gabi, confused, laughed and asked, "What's a Chacumbele?"

"That's me," I said. "Chacumbele is this legendary hot guy in Cuba. All the ladies loved him. So Nurse Sotolongo is basically saying I'm hot."

Nurse Sotolongo laughed in that way that was mostly spraying spit. "You wish. Chacumbele got hacked to bits by the woman he cheated on. I call you Chacumbele because you play too much with fire."

"Stop the whole world," said Gabi. "How do you two know each other?"

"He probably puts in more hours here than I do with his magic shows. Got any new tricks for the kiddos, Sal?"

"Yep. Going to try one out in my next show. I call it the Flying Tarantula."

Nurse Sotolongo cringed. "Ew. Well, make sure I'm not around when you do it, okay? I hate spiders."

"Me too," said Gabi. And her voice sounded like she'd just drunk a six-pack of gasoline.

"Anyway," said Nurse Sotolongo, "Iggy was asleep when I checked on him, so don't wake him up, okay?"

"I'm always on my best behavior," I said, walking past her and into the NICU.

When I noticed Gabi hadn't joined me, I turned around. She was just standing there, gawking at me.

"You coming?" I encouraged.

Shaking her head to clear it, she waved thanks to Nurse Sotolongo and caught up with me, then passed me.

She was facing forward, marching ahead, when she said, "Salvador Alberto Dorado Vidón. I have never been surprised so many times in the same day by one person."

"Surprise is what I do," I said. Got a laugh out of her.

But then her mood changed. Never looking back, she said, in a quiet voice I didn't even know she had, "Look, Sal. This is serious. My brother is very, very sick. So no surprises. No tricks, no jokes, no magic. Or we don't go. Okay?"

We reached the door to the sterile-environment ward. Even after all the magic shows I had performed here at the NICU, I had never been inside. I'd always wanted to know what was going on in there.

Gabi cleared her throat. She was staring at me, arms crossed, waiting for an answer, blocking the door, tapping her foot, one eyebrow all the way up.

"Whatever you say," I replied. "No surprises."

The sterile-environment ward sounded like a machine exhaling. It felt a little colder than the rest of the hospital. Cameras looked down at us from the ceiling, which gave me a different kind of chill.

We entered, and Gabi shut the door behind us as fast as she could. All sound from outside was cut off.

Gabi walked me over to the hand sanitizer dispenser on the wall and caught a glop of it as it automatically fell into her hand. She rubbed her palms together like she was trying to start a fire with them. Then she grabbed a surgical mask from a plastic container and slipped it over her nose and mouth.

She flicked her eyebrows at me in that way that meant *What are you waiting for?* I sanitized my hands and put on a mask, too.

Besides the long waiting room Gabi and I were standing in now, the sterile-environment ward had four rooms, all with see-through walls. They looked like normal hospital rooms for kids, with beds and chairs and machines, cartoony wallpaper, and Playskool toys. The books, magazines, and little medical advice cards splayed over the nightstands were there to help the grown-ups pass the time while their kids fought for their lives.

Three rooms were unoccupied. The fourth had an incubator next to a bed. The incubator had armholes with built-in gloves so people could reach the very tiny person inside without popping the top.

In the center of the incubator lay the tiniest pair of footie pajamas I had ever seen, yellow and fluffy like a baby chick's feathers. It was hard to tell from here, but I was pretty sure those itty-bitty jammies had a baby inside them.

Gabi marched over to the fourth room's door with her hands in the air, her eyes as hard as a statue's. I walked with my hands in the air and followed her, as serious as a surgeon.

Gabi used her elbow to push down the door's handle and, walking backward, opened the door with her butt. She gestured with both raised hands for me to hurry up and come in. After I did, she closed the door with her foot.

We both peered down into the incubator.

"Sal," she said, "I would like you to meet my little brother, Ignacio Reál. Everybody calls him Iggy. He is thirty days old. Today is his one-month birthday."

Iggy lay asleep on his back. His eyes and mouth were thin, unbroken lines, with no eyelashes I could see. He had a fluffy yellow hat that matched his fluffy yellow footie pajamas. They were also handsie pajamas; the sleeves had no wrist holes. It looked like maybe he was making fists inside the sleeves.

He was so small. I had never seen a baby before, except on TV, and those babies were Christmas hams compared to this kiddo. He looked like a microwaved version of a TV baby, shrunken, wrinkled, and, judging by his flushed cheeks, hot to the touch. His face was a web of red veins. His mouth was covered with white stuff, like he had just eaten a powdered doughnut.

A wave of weakness shot through me. This baby looked like he could die at any second. He was so *small*. It was hard to tell if he was breathing, even. I wanted to tap the incubator to see if he would move, just to be sure he was okay.

I didn't, of course. Gabi would have killed me. And if she somehow failed, Nurse Sotolongo would have finished the job.

"You okay?" Gabi asked. Only then did I realize how long I'd been staring at Iggy with my mouth open.

"Yeah," I whispered back, and even I didn't believe me. He was *so* small. "What's on his mouth?"

Gabi stood on tiptoe for a better look. "It's either spit-up or thrush. I hope it's spit-up."

"What's thrush?"

"A yeast infection. People with weak immune systems get it."

"Iggy has a weak immune system?"

She nodded, just a little, looking away. It was one of those nods you use to keep yourself from crying.

Iggy stretched. He kicked with both legs together. He yawned. Then he went still.

I must have made a noise or something, because Gabi squeezed my shoulder, the way a coach comforts a pitcher who's just given up three runs. "Hey," she said. "It's okay. Iggy's doing all right. They're doing everything they can for him. That kid's so full of antibiotics right now, we could flush him down a toilet and he wouldn't get sick."

She laughed, which meant I could laugh, too. "Then why are we wearing masks and holding our hands in the air, Gabi?"

Her eyes were smiling. "I like masks. They help me get in character."

We both turned back to watch Iggy do nothing. After a while I asked, "Is there a cure?"

"Maybe," said Gabi. "They're 'exploring options.' Stem cells. Gene therapy. Bone marrow transplant."

"Are the odds good?"

Gabi looked at the ceiling camera as she answered. "Anytime someone says 'bone marrow transplant is an option for your infant,' the odds aren't great."

The room air purifier exhaled like a giant. I started. I felt jittery, paranoid, vaguely unhappy. The world felt like it was full of invisible enemies.

No, not "*like*." The world *is* full of invisible enemies. Like diabetes. I had to pay attention to sugar levels every day of my life. I had to poke my skin full of holes and stay on a strict diet and pump my veins full of insulin. Or else.

But that was nothing compared to tiny, tiny Iggy. Poor kid didn't even know he was alive yet. Or that he was already so sick. Why did the world allow newborns to enter the world with broken immune systems?

"So unfair," I said out loud, after a long time of only the room breathing.

"No one said life is fair," said Gabi, repeating what someone must have said to her once, trying to be helpful. It probably hadn't made her feel any better, either.

I made two fists. "It should be."

It took me a few seconds to realize Gabi was staring at me. "What?" I asked her. "It should be. I hate how unfair life is. Especially to kids." I couldn't look at her anymore, so I rested my hands on the incubator and looked at fluffy yellow Ignacio instead.

I could feel Gabi decide something just then. She bumped me a little out of her way with her hip and put her hand into one of the incubator's armholes. She wriggled her fingers until they were all the way inside the glove. "You do the other one," she said. Her eyes were full of thanks.

I'd been wanting to stick my arm in the incubator since I'd gotten here, so I didn't think twice. I slid my hand into the other built-in glove.

"Put your finger near his hand," Gabi told me. "Sometimes he'll grab it."

Nothing I'd experienced in my life so far made me as nervous as Gabi's suggestion that I put a finger, even one protected by a massive glove, anywhere near little Iggy. So I deflected. "I can't even see his hand, Gabi."

"It's at the end of his arm," she deadpanned. "That's where humans keep their hands."

"Ha-ha. Very funny." Okay, so deflection wasn't going to work. Perhaps a little honesty. "But, Gabi, really. It's . . . it's okay?"

With no sarcasm at all she said, "It's okay, Sal."

Right. I exhaled, then maneuvered the glove over to where I thought Ignacio's hand would be. Oh so carefully, I placed my pinkie finger on that spot on his sleeve.

Immediately, his little mittened hand grabbed my finger. He was stronger than he looked. But his hand was *so small.* This poor kiddo.

Gabi and I stood there for a long time. We just stood there and let the whole universe revolve around Ignacio's fist and my pinkie finger.

19

THE HOSPITAL CLOCK read 5:06 a.m. It was tomorrow. Finally.

Papi and American Stepmom were awake. The second they saw I was, too, they were all over me. They asked me how I felt. They said I could stay home from school. They said I *should* stay home from school. In fact, there was no question. I most definitely *was* staying home from school.

Believe me, after the Wednesday I'd had, that sounded great. I could see it now: sleeping in, squeezing in a couple hundred rounds of *Poocha Lucha Libre*, reading some Terry Pratchett—why didn't they assign his books in English class?— and working on my Flying Tarantula trick. It was only nine days before its debut. I needed to practice!

But all that fun would have to wait for the weekend. I had to go to school. No choice. I had to find out what Gabi's article in the school paper said about me.

I mean, even after she'd shared the life-and-death struggle her baby brother was going through, she still wouldn't give me one little hint about the story she had written. I'd done everything but beg her to tell me.

Okay, I *did* beg her. She wouldn't crack. In fact, I'm pretty sure she was enjoying watching me squirm. Still getting me back for the GOTCHA! stamp, I think. That girl could hold a grudge like a Disney witch.

So, in my hospital room at 5:07 in the morning, I did the unthinkable. I pleaded with the padres to let me go to school instead of staying home.

The padres kept saying, "No!" and I kept saying, "Please!" and they said, "No!" and I said, "Please!" and eventually American Stepmom winked at Papi and said to me, "Well, we'll see what the doctor says."

They thought the doctor was going to side with them, but—ha!—Nurse Sotolongo came in with him. When she heard the question, she responded like the big sister I never had: "What, is Chacumbele here trying to fake his way out of school?"

"No, no, certainly he can go to school," the doctor replied. He looked, I swear, exactly like a garden gnome come to life. He just needed the pointy hat and the creepy, gnomey grin. But alas, no hat, and judging from his frown lines, the last time this guy smiled people were still complaining about how bad mastodon farts stink.

Dr. Grumpgnome pressed the back of his hand to my forehead—why? I'd never had a fever—and said, "He'll be fine. Just take it easy today, okay, son?"

I couldn't help myself. Guy got under my skin.

I perked up like a child actor selling waffles on TV and said,

"Oh boy, will I, Doctor! I will make sure to care for my person, just like you would want me to if you were my father and I were your son, as you just implied by calling me son. Thank you so much for everything, Father—I mean, Doctor!"

I reached up and pulled his hand off my forehead and into a two-handed handshake. I mean, I was churning butter with his arm.

"Yes, ahem, well, you're welcome . . . young . . . man . . ." he said, struggling to free his hand. Three, four, five yanks, and—finally!—on the sixth, he pulled free. He shook his body out like a wet rooster and straightened the stethoscope around his neck.

Then he shot my parents a dirty look—one of those *Can't you control your child?* stares. "There's some discharge paperwork," he told them, like it was their fault or something. "Come with me." Then he waddled out of the room as fast as his lawn-gnome legs would take him.

The padres looked at each other, shrugged, and followed him out.

Once the door had shut itself, Nurse Sotolongo held out her hand and gave me mal de ojo. "Hand it over."

How in the name of extra-large pants did she always know where to look?

Huffing, I put the doctor's watch in her hand and said, "I was going to give it back to him."

"Yeah, well, now *I'm* going to give it back to him." But then her eyes got as thin as a fox's. "Later. If he's nice to me."

Oh, really? "Is he usually nice to you?" I asked.

She tilted her head and looked at the ceiling. "Could be nicer."

American Stepmom drove us home like the trunk of the car was on fire. We got there a little after 5:30 a.m., and all three of us had to be out the door again by seven.

The Coral Castle has like a billion bathrooms, which is great, but it has just one itty-bitty teeny-weeny water heater for the whole place. Even if you are the only one showering, you get about twenty-two seconds before the showerhead starts chucking icicles at you. And with three of us showering? We were about to start the next ice age.

But none of us was going to give up a chance to shower. All three of us were washing freaks. Papi's always been a germophobe, and American Stepmom is addicted to exactly two things in life: hot cocoa and squeaky-clean hair.

And me? I'm a teenager. If I don't shower, I smell like Swamp Thing.

So as soon as American Stepmom turned off the car, the three of us looked at each other in a shifty-eyed Wild West showdown. Then it was go time! We burst out of the car and raced for the bathrooms. First one in a shower would win twenty-two seconds of steamy bliss.

I lost. I cranked the hot-faucet knob as far as it would go and was fire-hosed in the chest by a blast of water so cold I instantly turned into a Ken doll.

I lathered and rinsed and, through chattering teeth, washed until I was pretty sure my pits wouldn't kill anybody at school that day. A few kids might get brain damage if I raised my hand, but I couldn't take the cold a second longer.

I got out, toweled off, and put on a bathrobe that was basically a rug with arm holes—a leftover from Connecticut that should have been way, way, way too hot for Miami. But I'm pretty sure just then it saved me from getting pneumonia.

I hugged and patted myself all the way to the kitchen, where I knew there'd be hot cocoa waiting. That had been the rule since we moved here: Whoever gets the morning hot shower has to make the espresso (for Papi) and hot cocoa (for American Stepmom and me). Papi, apparently, had won: He must have taken one of his patented two-minute submarine showers, then finished the job with a hand towel soaked in rubbing alcohol. He wiped himself down with 91 percent isopropyl alcohol like it was his cologne. As he stood in the kitchen in his own rug of a bathrobe, you could almost see the air wavering around him.

But he was holding out a mug of cocoa for me, so I wasn't complaining. "Thanks, Papi," I said, concentrating on keeping my hands from shaking as I cupped it. Twenty-seven grams of carbohydrates. I wouldn't be able to have any more carbs during breakfast.

"Ay, mijo, drink it fast, warm up, warm up!" he said. More to himself than to me he added, "We've got to get a new water heater in this house. You're going to give your whole family hypothermia one day."

I'd already chugged half my cocoa before I answered. "I kind of like the cold showers. They're exciting."

We both cocked our heads when we heard American

Stepmom charging down the stairs, slapping her arms and repeating, "The brain is the queen of the body! The brain is the queen of the body!" Papi grabbed her cocoa off the counter and held it out. She zoomed into the kitchen with small, fast steps, her bathrobe rippling like a sail, and snatched the mug out of Papi's hands. She poured it down her throat in great gulps.

"Phew, baby!" she said once the hot chocolate had warmed her up enough. "Nothing like a cold shower to remind you you're alive!"

Papi set his cup on the kitchen counter and enveloped American Stepmom. He hugged like an amoeba: full absorption. "I know a few other ways to remind you you're alive," he said to her.

They giggled into each other's faces, only the steamy cocoa mug between them preventing a full-blown, breakfast-ruining make-out session then and there. Then, at the same time, they remembered I was in the room. They turned to face me, looking guilty.

I smiled at them with lots of teeth. "Oh, don't mind *me*," I said in my best British accent. "I mean, you've done an absolutely 'orrible job of hiding your, um, shall we say, 'physical affection' from me up to now. All the emotional damage your public displays of affection could *possibly* do to me 'as been done a long time ago! So you just go ahead and snog like two vacuums in love, and I will stand 'ere and sip my cocoa and text my psychologist for another appointment. Right? Right. Right? Right."

"Don't you need to go get dressed for school?" asked American Stepmom.

"I do indeed." I took a long slurp of cocoa.

American Stepmom launched a kick at my smart-aleck butt—"Missed me, nyah nyah!"—and I took off for my room.

"Wait a second, Sal," Papi called. I stopped in my tracks. He had spoken softly, seriously. I came back into the kitchen, softly, seriously. "Yeah?"

He and American Stepmom looked at each other for courage, then walked a step toward me, holding hands. "We need a straight answer from you. A yes or no will do, but you can add any details you want. Did you bring your mami back on purpose?"

"No," I answered. It was the truth, which is maybe why I was worried they wouldn't believe me. So I took a minute to tell them about the hallucination I'd had on the way home after almost getting hit by a car.

Papi shook his fist in the air. "Miami drivers!" he raged.

He was convinced I had brought Mami on accident. But American Stepmom? Not so much. "Why do I get the feeling you're not telling us everything?" she asked me.

That would be because I haven't told you about a certain chicken in a certain bully's locker, I did not say out loud. What I did say out loud was "Hold on. You asked a question, and I answered it. So now I get to ask a question."

"Fair enough," said Papi. "Shoot."

I took a second to figure out the exact wording I wanted. "If your new machine can fix holes in the cosmic membrane, does that mean I don't have to worry about breaking the universe anymore?"

Both my parents looked at me like they were watching a

horror movie called *Sal Knows What You Talked about Last Night*. American Stepmom couldn't help but laugh. She ran behind me and gave me a squeeze. "I *knew* you were awake. You are such a *stinker*! You are so grounded!"

"No, I'm not! You have to answer my question."

Papi shrugged. "I have no idea if the remembranation machine will work. Maybe it will, maybe it won't. And until we know, the answer is you should be very worried about breaking the universe. You should definitely do everything in your power not to break the universe. Even one calamitron is too many, at least until we know more. Yes? ¿Comprendes? ¿Estamos de acuerdo?"

"Okay, okay," I said, shaking off American Stepmom and stalking to my room again. "I told you I didn't bring Mami back on purpose. What do you want from me?"

"They want you to stop," I said to myself in front of my bedroom mirror.

Look, I know I'm not perfect. I never said I was a saint. But I didn't bring Mami over on purpose this time. I'd told the padres the truth.

But not the whole truth. I put a big fat chicken in Yasmany's locker. Papi and American Stepmom would not be happy if they found that out. They'd say I should have known better.

And they were right. The hole in Yasmany's locker hadn't closed yet. What if it never closed?

But here's the thing. It *felt* like it would close. I don't know how I knew, but I knew, when I meditated on it, that it wouldn't be permanent. When I was diagnosed with diabetes, I had to learn quick how to listen to my body, understand it better than anyone, even my padres, and do what was best for me. I had to learn to trust my feelings.

Same thing. I was the one who could feel the fabric of the cosmos like a stage curtain in a pitch-black theater. I could feel it, and I could do things to it. Like open it.

Papi was being his usual logical self. But that "one calami-tron is too many" business? I knew he was . . . well, not exactly wrong. He just didn't fully understand it yet.

Neither did I. But the truth was somewhere inside me. I only needed to dig it out.

One step at a time. Today, I would go to school. I would have a nice, normal day, and everything would be fine. The hole in Yasmany's locker would be smaller. Maybe it would even be gone by the time I checked it. I needed to stay calm. Be in control.

I held a breath in front of the mirror, let it out slowly. Between my cargo pants, cargo vest, long-sleeved urban adventure shirt with sweat-wicking technology, and steampunk mad scientist's belt, today's outfit had even more pockets than yesterday's. Whenever I felt nervous, pockets always boosted my confidence. Because I could fill them with tricks.

So I went all-out Gandalf. I packed my clothes with bandannas and coins and dice and three decks of cards; putty, six mustaches, a bald cap, a Halloween makeup kit, and a pack of fake-blood capsules; six pairs of handcuffs again, in case I got to use them in Mrs. Waked's class; foam balls, balloons, snappers, and other party favors; a laser pointer and a metal telescoping pointer; a mini megaphone, a joy buzzer, two whoopee cushions, and my old reliable GOTCHA! stamp; a fake tarantula, four fake cockroaches, and a rubber rat with red LED eyes; a ball of twine and a ball of rubber bands; those hokey X-ray glasses that everyone knows don't work but are still great for misdirection; and a magic wand that turned into a bouquet of flowers.

Ah, flowers. Almost forgot. I pinned a white carnation the size of a curled, sleeping kitten to my cargo vest, then loaded it with disappearing ink. The perfect finishing touch.

In front of the mirror I made spooky magician's eyes and tried out a few *TA-DA!* poses. "Do your worst, multiverse," I told my reflection. "I'm ready for you."

Looking back, the mistake I made is clear. I'd forgotten how much Gabi Reál can mess with your life if you forget about her for even a second.

20

WHEN YOU WALK to Culeco, you can't see much of the school until you get past the tall brick wall that surrounds it.

From the sidewalk, I could only see Culeco's roof over the wall. And on the roof, standing proud, was a statue of the school mascot: an egg.

Not just any egg. A twenty-foot, sickly-looking green-brown egg. It wore yellow wrestling pants with flames running up the sides, a yellow scarf-mask, and a yellow superhero cape that flapped in the wind. It had noodly arms and gloved hands like a cartoon character. One fist rested on its hip (if eggs have hips) and the other held up the school's flagpole, making it look even more heroic. What didn't look quite so heroic was the huge crack that the egg had running down its left side. All the steam the school generated was funneled into and escaped out of the shell through that crack. That steam-spewing, cracked super-egg looked plenty rotten.

"Culeco" is a weird Spanish word. It can mean "proud" or "excited" or "gaga in love" or "nesting like a chicken" or, like, six other things. The only common thing in all the definitions is that if you're culeco, you're always a little out of your mind. So why would anyone call a school "Culeco"?

American Stepmom looked up the answer. Seven years ago, the forming committee had tried to generate interest and support by letting the public vote on names for the school. And the good people of Miami had done what folks everywhere do when they're asked to name something: They trolled the vote. "Culeco" got the most ballots by a landslide, even more than the swear words.

But instead of calling the contest off, the school embraced it. The school founders said, "We *are* crazy proud and crazy excited and gaga in love—with learning!" And the school's building used to be a poultry-processing plant, so even the chicken part of the meaning kind of worked. So, yeah. Troll or no troll, Culeco was the perfect name.

And that's why our mascot is basically a putrid Humpty Dumpty in a cape. Our motto is "Fiat Fetor," which is Latin for "Let there be stink." There are chicken and egg puns *everywhere*. Everything at Culeco is "egg-cellent" and "eggs-traordinary" and "egg-citing" and "eggs-quisite" and "eggs-treme, dude!" The first day of school, there were signs all over the place that read WELCOME BOCK-BOCK-BOCK! And carved into the stone above the main entrance is this:

WHY DID THE CHICKEN CROSS THE ROAD?
TO GET A GREAT EDVCATION AT CVLECO!

Yeah, pretty sandwich. But sometimes bad jokes are just another way for people to tell you they love you.

Culeco felt right. This wasn't your mama's namby-pamby art school. It had guts, and no cares about what people thought. It had laughed right back in the community's face, and now the community loved the school.

Everybody at Culeco is an artist. From day one, I'd been surrounded by actors and illustrators, sculptors and musicians, writers, performers, and makers of all stripes, doing whatever they loved doing best. They did it publicly and proudly. Literally out in Culeco's courtyard, even before school started.

Maybe my favorite thing about Culeco was the costumes. I mean, just about all the students seemed to dress up, one way or the other. Sometimes it was subtle, like Gabi's barrettes. But a lot of the time the cosplay was just plain incredible. Each day so far, as soon as I headed through the school gate, I'd been treated to a courtyard full of heroes and villains from every single novel or movie or comic book or video game you could think of (or at least that *I* could think of). I'd seen mechs made of so much actual machinery that they kind of actually *were* mechs. In the mix were some student originals, too, which looked as pro as anything you could stream or tube or watch on TV, except they were sharper, meaner, scarier, glitterier, over-the-toppier, and way too cool for the mainstream. Those were the best.

Yeah, yesterday had been brutal. But I knew as soon as I saw Culeco's schoolyard full of artists arting, ballerinas balleting, thespians thespianing, and cosplayers cosplaying, I'd be 100 percent again. The brick wall was like a curtain before a performance. Eager to start the show early, I picked up the pace, half ran to the gate, and jogged through.

And stopped dead.

Every kid in the courtyard—every caricature artist, mime, saxophone player, Broadway hopeful, alien smuggler, robot warrior, spandexed defender, and magical sailor from various planets and moons—stood around reading the school newspaper.

Like, hundreds of kids. In almost perfect silence. Sometimes they stood in groups of two or three, peeking over each other's shoulders. Occasionally someone giggled or whispered, but then they immediately fell silent again, reading and rereading the front-page news. Just the front page. No one was reading the inside of the paper.

Something ain't right with that thar picture, I thought Texas-ly. If you ever need a quick dose of courage, speak with a Texas accent. It really works!

No one seemed to notice me at first—they were too busy reading. But as I cat-footed up the walkway, doing everything I could not to be noticed, kids froze in place as I passed them. Some slowly lowered their papers to make staring at me easier. They still whispered to each other, but now they leaned together like tipping bowling pins and never took their eyes off me.

Gabi, I thought, glaring back at the mouth-breathers until one by one they looked away. I had to get a paper of my own and read what she'd written about me, stat.

When I turned forward to march into school to find a paper, Señorita Reál herself blocked my path. She'd come out of nowhere, and her patented shark smile was covering the entire lower half her face.

Clearly, she had snuck up with the idea of spooking me.

Not. Gonna. Happen. "May I help you?" I asked her like the snootiest British butler in the world.

Today her T-shirt read "PEOPLE CALL ME A FEMINIST WHENEVER I EXPRESS SENTIMENTS THAT DIFFERENTIATE ME FROM A DOOR MAT . . ."—REBECCA WEST, and her volcano-eruption hair—orange and yellow streaks today—was studded with dueling-sorceress barrettes. "I have a present for you!" she said. And she pulled from behind her back my very own copy of the school paper, the *Rotten Egg*.

I swiped it out of her hand, barely saying thanks, and snapped the front page tight. It was devoted to a single story with a one-word headline: "POULTRYGATE!"

"What does that mean, 'Poultrygate!'?" I asked. I instinctively knew you always had to say it with an exclamation point.

"You know," Gabi replied, smug as a sandwich. "Like Watergate? Gamergate? Cheetogate?" And when she saw I wasn't getting it: "It means 'scandal.' In this case—"

"A chicken falling out of a locker. Yeah, got it."

I had scanned half the article by that point. In "what represented the biggest mystery in Culeco's history," a whole chicken that "sources report was of the golden-fryer variety" fell out of "noted dancer Yasmany Robles's locker," landing in an "explosion of blood and chicken bits" and "generating unprecedented mayhem and confusion amongst the students of Culeco." They "ran screaming in all directions" creating "pandemonium in Culeco's sacred halls" and a "school-wide hysteria that lasted for the better part of fifth period."

"Exaggerate much?" I asked Gabi.

"'You must both 'inform' and 'entertain,'" Gabi said, making air quotes, a faraway look in her eyes. She reached over the top of the paper and jabbed at the article. "Read this part. You'll like it."

Her finger pecked at a paragraph in the center of the article that began "At the center of these inexplicable events stands a mysterious new student, Salvador Vidón." Apparently, I dress like "a nature-show host in training" who "only needs an Australian accent and a death wish to complete his outfit." Apparently, I use my "unnerving, mesmerizing eyes" to "stun and stupefy anyone foolish enough to return my gaze." "'It is he,'" I read out loud, "'who caused poultry to plunge precipitously from its perch and propagate a possible food-poisoning pandemic.'"

"I'm particularly proud of that passage," said Gabi, bouncing on the balls of her feet.

"This is a total hit job!" I didn't yell. I think yelling is a sign of weakness, because it shows a lack of control. I am always in control. I was just feeling very . . . *passionate* at the moment. "You saw for yourself, Gabi. There was no chicken. It was a trick."

Her eyebrows boinged up and down. "Keep reading!"

I did keep reading: aloud again. I mean, very loud. I might even have been yelling, only I don't yell. "'Perhaps, however, Vidón's greatest illusion lies not in making a chicken appear out of nowhere, but rather in making it disappear again. Neither the shrewd mind of our beloved Principal Torres' . . . Man, you are such a suck-up."

"Am not! She *is* shrewd!"

". . . 'nor the keen eyes of Mr. Milagros, Culeco's crack

custodian, could find any trace of raw poultry by the lockers. More shocking still in this age of camera phones is that not a single photo nor video was taken of the incident. It's almost as if there were a rich and powerful secret society using every resource at their disposal to hush this matter up.'"

"See? I told the whole truth."

"In the lying-est way possible! You're making it sound like some big conspiracy! Oh, and look at this! 'As of the publication of this article, Robles is awaiting punishment for his attempted bullying of Vidón, as Principal Torres, a moral lighthouse amid a sea of wayward ships' . . . Oh, come on! That is some chupamedia writing right there."

"You don't know what you're talking about. That is a beautiful metaphor." And then, a second later: "What's a 'chupamedia'?"

My eyes rose over the top of the paper like two angry moons. "It means 'brownnoser.' Literally, it means 'sock sucker.' That's you."

"I do not suck socks!" Her hair flattened a little, like the ears of a dog being scolded. She was getting flustered. Good.

I went on: "'. . . as Principal Torres, a moral lighthouse amid a sea of wayward ships, considers the facts of the case. The editors of the *Rotten Egg* only hope that she will show Robles mercy so that he can try to make amends for his unacceptable actions.' Right. 'The editors.' *You're* the editor, Gabi. You're just using the newspaper to cover for your friend, who also happens to be a repeat bully. You support bullies, Gabi."

"He can change," she said, her voice shaking, unsure. "Everyone deserves a second chance, right?"

"'And as for Vidón,'" I continued reading, flamboyant and sarcastic, almost dancing, "'what to make of him? Did he really pull off the greatest magic trick in Culeco history, fooling a hallway full of students, the finest custodial team in Florida, and the school administration with one mighty illusion? Or is there some greater power at work here? Perhaps Vidón's illusions aren't illusions at all, but actual magic: some power-ful, arcane spell that he used to conjure and then disappear a haunted, hoary hen. No one knows—yet. But the *Rotten Egg* is committed to pursuing this amazing story to its weird and spooky conclusion.'"

Gabi looked at me hopefully. "So now you get it, right? You see how much I helped you?"

I balled up the paper as viciously as I could. "You just called me a brujo in front of the entire school! Thanks to you, Gabi, everyone is now going to think I practice black magic."

Gabi's head shot back, like she was dodging a kick. "Nooo!" she said, holding the *o*. She was just beginning to realize what I'd known in an instant. She didn't believe in black magic, and I didn't believe in black magic. But a *lot* of people do believe in black magic. I'd learned that the hard way the day before in Textile Arts, and a long time ago from my mami.

She dropped her hands and held them out, pleading, "Sal, you're taking this all wrong. Sure, I got a little . . . creative, there in the end. But with a stroke of my pen, I have made you the most famous magician in all of Culeco."

"Oh yeah? How many other magicians are there in Culeco, Gabi?"

"Well, you're the only one."

I started to walk away.

She grabbed my arm. "But now everyone knows how powerful and mysterious you are! You defeated a bully with magic! Your reputation is set."

Yeah, my reputation was set, all right. I remembered all too well the big eyes Mami would shine at me when she told me the many ways a brujo could ruin your life. So yeah, people would be watching me now, but not they way they'd watch a showman, laughing and enjoying the performance. They'd watch me like I was a threat.

I was seething. The heat of my anger made my words evaporate before I could say anything. I tried to walk away again. I needed time to think.

Gabi clutched my arm even harder and said, "Hey! Don't be mad."

I really wished she hadn't touched me. She should've let me walk away. It would have given me a chance to calm down. Count to ten. Relax.

Instead, I shook free of her. "Mad? I'm not mad, Gabi! In fact, I want to thank you for all your *help*!" I smoothed out the newspaper ball against my right leg, then snapped it taut a few times for effect. The kids near us perked up; they could tell I was starting a magic trick.

While I made the paper into a large cone, I spun around to address my growing audience and said, "Behold the sun, good gentlefolk. It is the ultimate giver of gifts, for it gives everything on Earth the gift of life: humans, animals, and even—"

I stopped spinning in front of Gabi. *Pop!* A huge bouquet of silk carnations suddenly filled the newspaper cone.

"—flowers."

Ooh, aah, applause, applause! Gabi smiled, relaxed, touched her chest in a thank-you gesture. "That's so sweet, Sal!"

"Ah, but they smell even sweeter, m'lady."

I dipped the bouquet toward her for easy sniffing. She closed her eyes and brought her nose in for a mighty whiff.

And then I flicked a tarantula on her face.

21

THE HUGE CARNATION on my shirt was filled with disappearing ink. I could have tricked her into sniffing the flower and sprayed her with disappearing ink. The *whole purpose* of wearing a squirting flower filled with disappearing ink is to mildly embarrass someone without doing any lasting harm. Everything would have been so much better if I had.

But the anger I felt could not be quenched by mere disappearing ink. I was tarantula angry.

So look. I know some people are scared of spiders. That's why fake spiders exist: so people like me can mess with those people. Like Nurse Sotolongo. Part of the reason I was working up a Flying Tarantula trick was because I knew it would scare her bald. Or take Papi. He'll jump so high he'll smash into the ceiling if, for instance, you slip a fake spider onto his dinner plate, or you, just as an example, lob one over the shower curtain right after he shampoos so he can't keep his eyes open long enough to figure out whether it's real or rubber. And he gets me back, too—both he and American Stepmom. They hide around corners and in the kitchen pantry and in closets. I scream like a goat, every time. That's my weakness. I startle easily.

American Stepmom doesn't scare easy at all, but Vaseline in her bra really grosses her out, as does Vaseline on her steering wheel, and basically Vaseline anywhere. Papi and I go through a lot of Vaseline.

They're pranks. They're funny. And so I guess I thought that's how fear works. It lasts for a few seconds, then you laugh, then you plot revenge. Everyone has a good time.

I even knew Gabi was afraid of spiders. I mean, I kind of decided to flick a hairy spider at her *because* of the weird sound of her voice when I'd mentioned my Flying Tarantula act back at the hospital.

But I swear I didn't know that some people live in utter mind-erasing terror of spiders. People, as it turns out, like Gabi Reál.

The one I launched at her was the highest-quality novelty tarantula I have ever seen. It had been lovingly airbrushed tan and black, its hair felt velvety and genuine, and though it was actually too heavy for a tarantula (my fifth-grade class had kept one for almost a half year, until we snuggled it to death), its heft probably felt more convincing to people who'd never actually picked one up. Clearly, Gabi had never, ever, not even once picked up a tarantula in her entire life. So she had no way of knowing that the piece of silk-haired rubber that landed on her face weighed way too much to be real.

She pulled her head back and crossed her eyes for a second. Then, not freaking out, not having any kind of panic attack or anything, she smacked the thing off her mug without a care in the world. For a second, I thought my revenge had fallen flat.

She casually gazed down at the ground to see what she had slapped off her nose. There were maybe three or four seconds when she didn't understand what she was looking at. Slowly, her faced assembled itself into the dictionary definition of horror, one section at a time: first her pupils growing huge, then her forehead crumpling, then her nose scrunching, then her mouth gaping, then the scream repeating over and over, then her hands in the air, waving uselessly.

This was all good, I thought. She was scared. Got her. Ha-ha.

But her face changed again. The horror evolved into . . . what? Hopelessness. Agony. Knowing you're going to die, and the torture of knowing. It's hard to describe. She became so open, so purely afraid, that she didn't care who saw her ugly-cry. She fell back on her butt and scooted away from the spider with a kind of desperate, clumsy crab walk. (It's hard to crab-walk backward fast.) She kept falling and staggering to her feet again. Her clothes were getting dirty as she scraped along the walkway. A strap broke on her bookbag; it fell off her back. She howled the whole time. She screamed. She drooled.

The sun stopped in the sky. Nobody laughed or pointed or moved. Nobody thought this was funny.

Gabi slipped one last time and stayed on the ground, noticing finally that the tarantula hadn't so much as twitched a leg all that time. She stared at it, shaking still, a mouse in its hole, watching the cat.

"It's fake," I kind of whisper-laughed. "It's just a toy. It can't hurt you." I got under the tarantula with my toe and flipped it onto its back. Gabi flinched mightily, and so did half the schoolyard. But then, when Gabi saw it didn't wriggle or try to flip itself over, she leaned toward it. The underside had raised writing on it: FOOL ME ONCE NOVELTY CORP. MADE IN AMERICA.

"It's fake?" she asked, her terrified eyes reading the spider.

"Yes! It was just a joke, I swear!"

"Just a joke," she repeated. And once she'd digested my words, she regained her composure enough to bury her face in her hands and weep uncontrollably.

My peripheral vision informed me that kids were starting to move toward us. Some might have been coming over to console her; others, friends of hers who maybe wanted to fight me. But I couldn't tell who was which. My instincts told me to run.

So I did—right over to Gabi. I fell to my knees in front of her.

I locked my fingers together in a single fist of prayer and shook it at Gabi like a mighty maraca. I didn't think, I just let the words flow. "I am so sorry I am *so* sorry I had no idea you were *that* scared of spiders I mean I knew you were a little scared but I didn't know *anyone* was that scared of spiders I am the biggest jerk in the world I will make it up to you I'll do whatever you want I'm sorry please forgive me."

She didn't answer at first. I wasn't sure she had even heard me over her heaving, heartbreaking sobs. She hadn't removed her hands from her eyes, so she probably couldn't tell that new shadows were falling over the two of us. We found ourselves surrounded by a tight Stonehenge of kids tall enough to block the morning sun.

Gabi's crying petered off. She took deep, snotty breaths that rattled on the way in and on the way out. She nodded once, exhaling, like she had decided something. Then her hands flipped open like the doors of a cuckoo clock. Her face was a squished-clay version of itself.

"Sal. Vidón. You. Go. Too. Far."

"Never again," I said. "I am so sorry."

Gabi started to stand, and four different hands reached down to help her up. She straightened and smoothed herself over, wiped her eyes with the back of her hand, filled her lungs a few times. I looked at the other kids in the circle. They glared back, a jury of heroes and monsters and robots and even some plainclothes kids, all of whom thought I was a terrible person.

"Lots of people are a little scared of spiders," Gabi said with queenly composure. "You could not have known that I am an arachnophobe. I also recognize that I may have hurt your feelings with the story I wrote about you, which caused you to lash out. Mind you, I am not apologizing, as I believe too strongly in freedom of the press. But I understand that, in a moment of hurt feelings, you may have lashed out more than you had intended."

"Way more," I agreed.

She stood unsteadily. Her friends braced her up. "I am going to go to the bathroom to freshen up. I will accept your apology if you accompany me there and carry my bookbag. And if, on the way, you let me punch you on the arm seven or fifteen times."

When the jury heard Gabi would accept my apology, they backed off enough so that sunlight came flooding back into the circle. I hustled to pick up her bookbag by its one good strap, hustled back over to her, and rolled up a sleeve. When I was done, I saluted and said, "Ready for my punching, ma'am."

22

I WAITED FOR Gabi under a blue-and-white sign announcing that the bathroom was gender-neutral. It depicted a variety of people icons with these words underneath: WE DON'T CARE. JUST PEE NEATLY.

I wore my bookbag and hugged Gabi's to my chest, rocking on my heels, looking around, trying to be cool. But I had the after-adrenaline jitters. Every ten to twenty seconds, goose bumps would ride up my back like a motorcycle gang. I couldn't see my own face, of course, but from the inside it felt serious, quiet, thoughtful. I had that weak-in-the-knees feeling, only all over. I was so un-hungry I wasn't sure I still had a stomach. Maybe it had eaten itself.

I was so caught up with my body that I almost didn't see Yasmany turn the corner into the hallway. And head straight for me.

Thing is, I didn't care. I hadn't run from him yesterday, though I'd wanted to. From here on out I was never going to run from him, or any bully.

He passed by, pretending not to look at me, and then

stopped a few feet away to lean against the wall, putting his hands in his blue track pants. He wore a basketball tank top, a crucifix, and the same sneakers as yesterday. He looked straight ahead. So did I.

"Class in twenty minutes," he said.

I blinked. Not the opener I had expected. *So, okay, let's see where this goes,* I thought. I said, "Yep," and hit the *p* so hard it was its own syllable.

"I went to detention yesterday. They help you with your I-have-to-write-a-paper-on-diabetes, thanks to you."

Thanks to me, dude? Did you learn nothing? Whatever. I wasn't going to engage. I just said, "You're welcome."

He looked like he was counting the number of tiles in the ceiling. "I'm learning a lot."

Why was he telling me this? What was he even doing here? *Easy, Sal. Stay calm. One-word answers.* "Terrific," I said.

"Yeah." He faced me. "You really have diabetes?"

I swallowed down all the WTFs threatening to shoot like bullets out of my mouth and just said, "Yeah. I really, really do."

"That sucks."

"I appreciate your concern."

A tumbleweed rolled down the entire length of the hallway.

"I saw what happened out there with you and Gabi," he said after a while, quietly, and to his shoes.

Okay. Now we were getting somewhere. But again, I just played it cool. Specifically, I snorted. "You and the whole maldita school."

He made a face. "My mom says 'maldito.' That's, like, an old-lady word."

"Well, I say it. So it's also a Sal Vidón word."

He jammed his hands in his pockets and shook his head. "You just give feero zucks what people think about you, don't you?"

Feero zucks. I'd have to remember that one. "What makes you say that?"

"I mean"—and he turned to face me now, taking his hands out of his pockets and spreading them in a gesture of pleading confusion—"back there with Gabi. You knew everyone was watching you. But you still got on your knees and said you were sorry. On your knees. In front of the whole school. How'd you do it?"

I couldn't help smiling a little, but I was genuinely confused, too. "What do you mean, 'how'? I just did it."

"I mean . . ." And he had to stop for a sec to search for what he meant. "I mean, how did you not care what everybody thought? Everyone's talking out there."

I blinked like a cat at him. "What are they saying? That I'm a brujo?"

"No. Everyone thinks you like Gabi."

I sighed with relief. "Oh. Good. That's all they're saying? That's fine. I do like Gabi."

Yasmany's head almost fell off his neck. "Yo, chacho!"

"Ohhh," I answered. I really am a little slow sometimes. "I don't *like* like Gabi. I mean, I just met her yesterday."

Now he looked at me like I'd just held out a used tissue

that I wanted him to eat. "Here you are, hugging her bookbag like it's your baby, and you gonna tell me you don't like her?"

"A second ago you couldn't believe I liked her."

"No, I couldn't believe you *admitted* you liked her."

"If I liked her, why wouldn't I admit it?"

He frowned. "Because."

This was getting fun now. "Because why?" I asked innocently.

"Because," he clarified. Then he coughed. A few seconds later, he came clean. "Because you're a guy, chacho. And guys don't . . . don't—"

"Tell the truth?" I finished helpfully.

"Naw, it's not lying. It's . . ." And when he couldn't find a way to end his thought, he gestured to me to finish it for him.

Sure, why not? "Express their feelings?"

"Yeah. Like, yeah, kind of. I mean, they do some. But not, like . . ." And again, he held out his hands for help.

"But you just said I'm a guy."

"Yeah. So?"

"So if I'm a guy, and I got on my knees to say sorry to someone for scaring them half to death, that means that it's something guys sometimes do. Or at least one guy. This guy." For emphasis, I used both thumbs to indicate me.

"I know. That's what I'm saying."

I couldn't help laughing. "I have *no idea* what you're saying!"

"I'm saying it was . . . it was so *decent* what you did."

The second he said the word "decent," my whole body responded. Relief lit my brain like a gas stove igniting. I felt pins and needles in my shoulders and knees. I pushed off from the wall and for a few ticks enjoyed the feeling of being more alive than before. I had done a decent thing, apologizing to Gabi. It was so decent that Yasmany, even with his fists-first approach to life, could tell it was decent.

So okay, Yasmany. I'll be even more decent. I'll tell you how I did it. The whole truth. "I didn't let my brain talk me out of it. I did the right thing before I could make up excuses." And then I realized something about myself. Not a good thing. "I make up excuses. I got to work on that. I mean, we're performers, you and me. Our whole life is making ourselves look good. But this time? What I did was too terrible. I had to make it right, no matter how bad it made me look. As fast as I could."

"You're doing a pretty good job," said Gabi from behind me.

"Ha!" said Yasmany, clapping and cracking up. "Busted!"

I mean, did he really think I'd be embarrassed now, after what I had just told him? Chacho needed to learn how to listen. I turned around to Gabi—all the sorceresses in her hair had been straightened and looked ready to go back to dueling—and said, "I am super sorry. Really."

"So make it up to me." She grinned, taking her bookbag back from me.

"How?"

She'd thought this whole thing through in the bathroom, I could tell. "Let me interview you for the next issue of the *Rotten Egg*. It's what my readers will want to read about, in my ongoing coverage of Poultrygate! And you can share your side of the story. You can set the record straight. We both win."

That . . . actually made sense. So I put out my hand to her. "Deal."

She shook my hand once, very formally. "Done and done. When should we do the interview? It should be right away. Reporters have deadlines, you know. How about after school? I want to record you, so somewhere private, where there won't be a lot of noise."

"Well, I live fifteen minutes away."

"We'll walk there after school. Perfect."

"You're going to his *house*?!" asked Yasmany, as shocked as any abuela watching her telenovelas. He tsk-tsked and added, "You two *so* like each other."

We both rotated our heads to face him, like two owls who had no time for his nonsense. "Sal is"—Gabi looked at me before she finished the thought, smiling—"a friend. The fastest friend I have ever made, in fact."

"Same," I agreed.

"Friends don't hold hands for ten minutes," said Yasmany.

We had never let go of our handshake. But we did now— our hands shot apart like same-side magnets. "We were sealing a deal!" Gabi protested.

"That's how adults interact with each other," I added. Was it getting hot in here?

"Look," said Yasmany, smiling like a mob boss, "I ain't gonna tell anyone your little secret." Gabi and I started protesting again, but he talked over us. "For now."

Gabi slit her eyes. "There's nothing to tell."

"That's not what I saw." And then he made kissy faces.

That's when Gabi attacked Yasmany.

Don't worry, it was all play-fighting. Gabi jumped on Yasmany's back (and Yasmany helped her get up there) so that she could, and I quote, "pound it into your thick skull that I don't like Sal, except as a friend." She immediately turned around to assure me that I shouldn't feel bad that she didn't *like* like me, because "being my friend carries with it all sorts of benefits."

"Benefits?!" Yasmany asked. "You're friends with *benefits*?!"

Rawr! roared Gabi. She pulled Yasmany's ears, noogied him fast enough to start a fire, and gave him the sickest, wettest willy I have ever seen in my life. Seriously, I gagged. I'm gagging right now, remembering it.

After each little torture, she'd ask him, "Do I like Sal?"

And he'd reply, running down the hallway, holding her legs to make sure she didn't fall, "Yes, you love him, he is your boyfriend, he brings you roses, you bought your wedding dress, what are you naming your baby?!"

I'd be lying if I said I didn't feel a teensy bit jealous. Not because I wanted Gabi to give me wet willies or anything. *Blech.* I wanted to jump all over them and play-fight and laugh and have fun, too. You know. I was the new kid.

But Gabi and I had just declared our friendship, like, five seconds ago. And I wasn't even sure what Yasmany was to me. It was too soon for name-calling, play-fighting, running, and jumping. Maybe that would happen, with enough time.

But for now, I had my dignity. I stopped following after them like a puppy and took the long way to my locker. The first bell would sound any minute, and I was determined to be a perfect student today.

"Great to see you, Sal," said Principal Torres, wiping her glasses clean. "You made it more than half the school day before you got sent to my office. Is that a new record for you?"

"On Tuesday I made it until seventh period," I replied, shrinking in the orange plastic seat in front of her desk. "It's only sixth period now."

"Oh, but Tuesday wasn't your fault," she said, her eyes huge with sarcastic sympathy. She inspected her glasses, then put them back on and pushed them up her nose in a way that made me feel even more in trouble. "Neither was Monday, and neither was Wednesday. I can't wait to hear how it wasn't your fault today, either."

I sighed. "Today *was* my fault."

Principal Torres tilted her head. Clearly, she hadn't been expecting me to admit guilt. "Yeah?"

"Yeah."

"You're taking responsibility?"

"Yeah."

"Well," she said, considering. "Do you want to say anything in your defense?"

I thought about that. "If I defend myself, will that sound like I'm making excuses? I don't want to make excuses."

She nodded, rubbing her chin in consideration. "I appreciate the question. I appreciate you taking responsibility. But it's not excuses. It's just giving me all the information I need to give you a fair punishment."

Making sure to look and sound hangdog sorry, I said, "Then in my defense, Principal Torres, I was trying to be nice."

"Nice?!" Principal Torres stood up and leaned over her desk. Ain't gonna lie: I flinched. "You nearly scared Gladis to death!"

I shrugged. "The road to heart attacks is paved with good intentions."

23

AFTER NEARLY SCARING Gabi to death and having to beg her for forgiveness, my day had gotten much better—at least before sixth period. In English, we started reading an old-timey play where a guy makes a deal with the devil to get magic powers. Couldn't wait to find out how it ended. Math had us working on geometric proofs, which had become my new favorite math. In science, I found out that three hundred million years ago on Earth, there was only one huge continent called Pangea, and that in another three hundred million years, all the continents might float back together and form a new Pangea. I really want to be around to see that happen. In American history, we were studying all the nations that existed in North America before Columbus came. I left that class with my head full of names, places, myths, legends, and the music our teacher played: flutes and hide drums and a high, jumping voice that sang words I didn't understand but sounded like the most impor-tant thing in the world. It gave me the same sense of wonder I felt when I relaxed and could see into alternate realities. And bonus: no universe-breaking required!

And then, lunch! I actually got to eat lunch! It was delicious, and life was beautiful.

And then, sixth period.

I was the first student to make it to Textile Arts, ten minutes early. Dr. Doctorpants, who was dressed as a Jigglypuff for the day, set me up at my pace group's table so I could get a jump on my scarf.

The other students arrived one by one. They seemed friendlier. Juan Carlos told a funny story about lying about his age and almost getting a part in a shaving commercial. So far, so good.

Then, a minute after the bell had rung, Gladis Machado showed up.

I kept on knitting, but I watched her, side-eyed. She went up to Dr. Doctorpants and got on her tiptoes to whisper something into his jiggly ear. He jiggly-shrugged, and then jiggly-pointed to a corner of the room. Gladis didn't look at anybody in our pace group, not even her buddy Juan Carlos, when she swooped in to scoop up her knitting and stomped off to the corner. There, she got on a stool and proceeded to angry-knit.

It had to be me she was avoiding. And that made me feel a little sick. She was that scared of me.

I needed to be sure. "What's with Gladis?" I asked casually.

Juan Carlos, who, I noticed, had a mustache that looked like someone had killed a few mosquitoes on his upper lip, laughed. "Don't you read the paper, Sal? You're a brujo, chacho!"

It was the exact same line as yesterday, but the pace group gave him a few chuckles for free because, well, when Juan Carlos told a joke, you wanted to laugh.

But I was too busy feeling terrible to laugh along. I couldn't risk looking at Gladis anymore, because if she caught me, she'd think I was giving her more mal de ojo. Only a few hours ago I'd thrown a tarantula at my student council president and scared her out of her mind. I just wanted to go up to Gladis and say, "Look, really, you don't have to be frightened of me. I'm not a brujo. I can just reach across universes and pull out chickens. It's science!"

Yeah. Gonna take a wild guess and say that that probably would have made things worse.

Even when I'm feeling miserable, I am a showman. I sighed loudly and turned my eyes heavenward. "I wish I could convince Gladis I'm not a brujo."

Aventura Rios shook her head, wearing a thin smile.

She was new to our circle; she used to be in the advanced cosplay pace group, so I wasn't sure what she was doing here. She was brown and big-haired and the kind of thin that gave Cuban mamis nightmares.

And the scarf she was making? It was so complicated and beautiful and twisty and decorated with dips and whorls that I could hardly believe it existed, even when I was looking straight at it. It was like math done in yarn.

"Nee, nee, nee," said Aventura, smiling. "Don't worry about Gladis. She is an idiot. She's like a Pop-Tart: You know how they look good, and then, when they jump out of the toaster, you, like, smell them, and you're thinking, 'This gone be good!' But the second you bite into it you want to vomit and half-chewed Pop-Tart is falling out your mouth and you're like, 'Why did I think that would be good?'"

I blinked really fast, couldn't help smiling. "Well. *That's* a description."

"A disgusting description," said Juan Carlos. He actually looked slightly queasy.

"Easy there, chacho," said Aventura, taking a brief break from her knitting to grab Juan Carlos's shoulder sincerely. "I'm not saying you can't like your personal little Pop-Tart. I am just saying that Pop-Tarts that believe in brujería are idiots. But if you don't care about that, you go right ahead and enjoy all the Pop-Tarts you want."

Juan Carlos was clearly having trouble following Aventura's speech. That's what happens when you let your smile do all your thinking for you. "I don't eat Pop-Tarts," he said, smiling unsurely. "An actor has to watch his figure."

The group laughed, though I'm not sure everyone was laughing at the same thing. I, however, was feeling much better about everything. "So, Aventura," I said, "you saw the *Rotten Egg* article about me, right?"

"Uh-huh," she answered. She could knit so fast. It was hypnotizing, watching her.

"It basically called me a brujo. You don't believe it?"

"That would be"—she paused for effect—"ah-no."

"How come?"

She lay her knitting on her lap to count on her fingers. "One, because there's no such thing. Two, because *I* have a bruja abuela."

Juan Carlos laughed the loudest. "But, Aventura, how can both be true?"

"Because, Juan Carlos, she *thinks* she's a bruja, and she

acts like a bruja, and she is legit *scary*. Like, you go into her house, which is, like, basically just a kitchen and a bed and no light, and the door shuts behind you, and you smell the greasy soup that's probably some kid being cooked for dinner, and you're like, 'This is how every horror movie starts.'"

"I do eat children," I said defensively.

"Nee, nee, nee."

"What's 'nee, nee, nee'?"

"It's 'no, no, no,' plus 'stop fronting.' It's really useful. People are fronting *all the time*. Oh my God, people, just be real, okay? So much cacaseca coming out of people's mouths."

The more she talked, the more I liked Aventura.

"I still wish I could just, like, explain to her I'm not a brujo," I said. "That way she wouldn't have to be scared."

She started knitting again. A soft black web grew out of her hands as she spoke. "Gladis hurt your feelings. I get it. But you have more friends than you know. Lots of people in this school like it when a kid acts decent."

Oh. *Decent*. She must have seen me on my knees this morning. Which was both a little embarrassing and a huge relief right about now.

"So what should I do? Apologize?"

"You don't need Gladis," Aventura said. "Just ignore her."

Of course, the second someone says "Ignore her," the first thing you do is look at her. I shot a quick glance at Gladis.

Big mistake.

Gladis got up, threw her knitting down on her stool, and, clutching the ojo turco around her neck, stomped over to Dr. Doctorpants. She whispered furiously at him.

As she stomped back to her stool, Dr. Doctorpants jiggly-waddled over to me. "Um, Sal. Do me a favor? Don't look at Gladis anymore."

"Dr. Doctorpants," said Aventura, "I've been sitting with Sal the whole time. He didn't do anything. Gladis is out of line."

"It's okay," I said, and moved to a seat where I had my back to Gladis.

"Thanks, Sal," said Dr. Doctorpants, jiggling away with a wave.

"Hard to ignore people when they come after you," I said to Aventura.

Aventura was fuming. "So unfair." She chewed. And somehow, her fury made her knit even more interesting patterns into her scarf. That thing had become its own little microverse at this point. No matter where you looked, your eyes dove in, wanting to see more.

"The best revenge is to do great work," she said after a second, cooling down, her needles flying. Watching her knit, I almost believed her.

But I didn't want revenge. I wanted to be decent. If people liked it when I just got on my knees to ask for forgiveness, just wait until they saw *this* apology. It was going to be spectacular!

I relaxed.

Now I just needed to find the perfect . . . Just needed to have a look around the multiverse for . . . Got to be a universe around here with the perfect . . . Hey, is that *me*?!

It *was* me. I was looking into a universe that had a classroom just like mine. In this one, Dr. Doctorpants was dressed as Amethyst from *Steven Universe*. All the same students were there: There was an Aventura and a Juan Carlos and a Gladis. And the Gladis was sitting right next to a Sal.

I mean, it made sense. Multiple universes, multiple Sals, just like there were multiple versions of Mami Muerta. No surprises there.

What was surprising was that this universe's Sal was looking *right back at me.*

Whoa, I thought.

"Hola," said that Sal, pronouncing the *h.*

It took me a second to realize he hadn't moved his lips.

Hm. I relaxed and imagined talking with my forehead instead of my mouth. *Can you hear me?* I thoughtsaid toward him.

And I guess he did, because he replied, *Yeah, spada. You're pretty good. It took me a long time to make my forehead talk. So. You're here for a reason. What is it?*

Um . . . I thought/replied. And then, to clear everything up, I added, *Um . . .*

This Sal nodded at me the way I nod when I do random squads online and get paired with noobs—half-resigned, half-determined to have fun anyway. *The multiverse knows what it's doing. It always seems to lead you just where you need to go. So what do you need, spada?*

I didn't know what "spada" meant. I was guessing it was that universe's slang for chacho.

My friend is scared of mal de ojo, I thoughtsaid. *I came looking for a way to help her.*

That Sal bent over laughing, tenting his hands over his mouth. When other people around him noticed, he immediately played it cool again. But then he looked at me sideways and thoughtsaid, *Dude, you are going to love this.*

He tapped Gladis on the shoulder, who had been sitting next to him without a worry in the world. She turned to him and smiled. It didn't take me two seconds to figure out they were friends in this universe. She seemed happier, too. Like a totally different person.

Sal, almost whispering to her, judging by how close they were, seemed to be asking her for something. She looked vaguely in my direction, but I don't think she could see me. And then, with a big smile, she took the scarf she'd been knitting off the needles and handed it to Sal.

Sal stretched it out for me so I could see it. It was *an ojo turco scarf,* with a big blue eye and everything. No way any mal de ojo was going to get past that thing!

We just need to switch this for your Gladis's scarf, Sal thoughtsaid. *Can you do that without ripping?*

I leaned in closer. *Ripping the scarf?*

No, you sandwich. Ripping the universe.

Well, at least they used "sandwich" in that universe, too. Made me feel a little better.

I guess I took too long to forehead-splain to him that, no, actually, every time I try to bring anything in from another universe, I rip a hole bigger than a Saint Bernard trying to squeeze through a cat door.

He shook his head. *No worries, spada. This one's on me.*

And then—How? No, seriously, tell me how?—he brought the ojo turco scarf over to where my Gladis was sullenly knitting by herself and presto-chango-switcheroo! Now, sitting there on Gladis's needles like she'd been knitting it all class long was the ojo turco scarf.

My vision of the other universe was starting to fade. I could just make out the Sal from there handing his Gladis the scarf he'd taken from my Gladis before I was completely, unrelaxingly brought back to my universe by my Gladis's scream.

"My magic trick scared Gladis," I told Principal Torres.

"¿No me diga?" said Principal Torres. "That girl's at the nurse right now. She's frightened out of her mind."

"I was trying to help."

"Sal, according to your own account, you were across the room, with your back to Gladis. Yet without moving a muscle, you switched the scarf Gladis was knitting for a totally different one."

"I know! It was a great trick, right?"

That's when Principal Torres laid the ojo turco scarf across her desk. "You had to know how she was going to react to it, Sal."

"But I didn't, Principal Torres. I really thought she was going to love the trick. I mean, who doesn't love magic?"

"A lot of people," she deadpanned.

But I kept on plunging ahead. "And the scarf! I thought she would really love the scarf. Because, see, it has the eyeball thing on it! It will protect her from black magic!"

That earned me a look. A long, long look. "Do you think I am stupid, Sal?"

Uh-oh. It's never good when an adult says that. "No, ma'am."

Principal Torres started to pace around the room, hands behind her back. "Let's review the facts, here. To pull off this stunt, you had to come to school with that scarf and had to set up everything before sixth period. You must have been planning this trick since at least yesterday. That's premeditation, Sal."

Well, there she was wrong. Not her fault: How could she know that I'd just relaxed my way around the multiverse and found a nice little world where another Sal was willing to help a spada out? Well, I couldn't tell her the truth. She'd never believe it.

So how about the biggest lie I could think of?

"It's true," I said to Principal Torres, bowing my head and wringing my hands. "I've been plotting my terrible revenge against Gladis since yesterday, when she first accused me of giving her the evil eye. I felt attacked. Embarrassed. Misunderstood. So I let those feelings turn me into a . . . a villain! A monster! A regular Rasputin! Oh, what evil glee I felt, knitting that scarf! How can you ever forgive me?"

I know I was laying it on thick. That was supposed to be part of the charm.

Smiling and fluttering her lashes like she really had been charmed, Principal Torres said, "Oh, I think two days' detention should earn my forgiveness."

"What?"

See, because I'd never had detention before. I thought she'd let me off with a warning.

"Today and tomorrow," she said, sweet as honey. "Your assignment is to write an apology to Gladis. And it'd better be good. Do you think you can write an actual apology, Mr. Vidón? Something from the heart?"

How could I apologize for crimes I had not committed? There'd been no premeditation! I really was trying to help.

But okay, I felt genuinely sorry for Gladis. I was sorry she ended up in the nurse's office. *That* I could apologize for—from the heart.

Wait, the heart? There it was, thumping in my chest, brainlessly beating, stupid as a stress ball. It didn't care a thing about what I did or who I hurt or how much of a jerk I had been today. It just kept on pumping.

Writing from the heart wasn't the answer, not if I honestly wanted to say sorry. "I'll do better than that, Principal Torres. I'll write a letter straight from the stomach."

Her outburst of laughter almost made her glasses fly off her nose. But then—she was a smart one, my principal—she sat down in her chair and said, "If your apology makes your stomach feel better, Sal, you'll have written a very fine letter. Have it done by tomorrow, okay?"

I got up to leave. "I will. Thank you. Sorry again. Good-bye. See you later. Have a nice day. Hope all is well. Best wishes."

"One more thing, Sal," said Principal Torres.

I literally had one foot out the door. I stopped midstep and looked at her, bracing for the worst.

"If you happen to see a student in detention who needs help with a paper on, say, diabetes, perhaps you could lend him a hand? I daresay you're the school's foremost expert on the subject."

"Happy to," I replied. And then I vamoosed.

24

I MISSED MOST of seventh period talking to Principal Torres. Conquering the red wall would have to wait for tomorrow. And I felt so bad about getting detention that I almost forgot to enjoy Intermediate Theater Workshop.

Luckily, Mrs. Waked had brought in her collection of masks from all over the world—fancy and expensive-looking, full of colors and feathers and costume jewels and empty eyes. We spent the whole class trying them on and coming up with characters based on them.

Mine was a beautiful goat mask. Because it had real horns and real fur and looked like it cost a fortune, I took really good care of it and tried not to move around too much.

Which was the wrong thing to do. "Sal," said Mrs. Waked, "goats are *brilliant* and *ornery*. They like to hop around, head-butt people, scale mountains, and eat homework. Now I ask you, *are* you a goat, or are you *merely* a child in a goat mask?"

Then she pointed at her solar plexus with both hands and nodded encouragingly.

I didn't need to be told twice: I got on all fours and rammed her in the gut (super gently, of course—this was acting class). She did a pratfall and shot an egg out of her dress, then applauded me from the floor. "Excellent. You were *marvelous*! Now, go forth, billy goat, and be gruff about it!"

I had excellent goat fun for the rest of the class, perching on chairs, chewing pages out of people's notebooks. It was impossible not to feel better.

Until the bell rang. Detention time. Ugh.

"Hey!" said Gabi, running up to me. She was wearing a shark mask that had a bloody leg sticking out of the mouth. "Don't forget! We're doing your interview now. Are you ready to go? Come on! Oh, wait, I have to go to my locker and—"

"I have detention," I said glumly.

She pulled off the mask. Her actual smile was every bit as sharky. "Yeah, I know."

"How do you know?" I asked, but I knew it was a stupid question as soon as it came out of my mouth.

And I got the exact answer I thought I would. "I know everything that happens at Culeco. I'm the editor—"

"Of the *Rotten Egg*, yes, I know. So why'd you ask if I was ready to go if you knew I was going to detention?"

"Because I'm going with you."

I suddenly felt a little better, in that misery-loves-company way. "Oh, you got detention, too? What a shame. What'd you do?"

"I didn't *earn* detention. What, you think I'm some kind of hoodlum or something? I just like it."

I crossed my arms. "I'm not a hoodlum." And then my brain

caught up with the rest of what she had said. "Wait. Did you say you *like* detention?"

She looked at me with genuine pity. "Oh, you really don't know? C'mon, Sal. Follow La Jefa. I'm going to show you one of the coolest things about Culeco."

Gabi led and I followed.

Detention was on the third floor, in the Library and Technology Commons. I hadn't actually been to the library yet. The Coral Castle is so full of books, I basically live in a library. And, I mean, it was only the fourth day of school.

"Welcome to detention!" said Gabi, as if it were a carnival.

She held one of the glass double doors open, and I entered the library, ready for the worst.

Detention *was* a carnival.

The bookshelves, which were futuristic-looking white carts as tall as walls, had been all pushed to the sides of the room. That left space for the, what, like, fifteen big round tables. Board games were spread out on some of them—maps with tons of wood bits covering them. That made me drool a little. Other tables were carpeted by card games, mostly the Poocha Lucha Libre Collectible Card Game, which I hadn't learned to play yet and really wanted to. One table had become a workstation for the advanced cosplay pace group from my Textile Arts class, where it looked like they were building some kind of turtle-squid-grizzly-tiger straight out of cheesy Japanese live-action kid shows. I saw Aventura there; she gave me a friendly wave, and I waved back. Five different tables had signs up advertising their club meetings. Four tables announced their book clubs, and the Fantasy and Science Fiction Book Club was reading *A Wrinkle in Time*, which is one of my all-time favorites. Kids at another table were busy building combat robots. They had an open space behind them where they could drive their robots around and test them and beat on other robots. I've always loved watching combat-robots shows, but I never thought I could make a robot myself—it'd be too hard. But now, seeing that there was a club at school where other kids did this for fun, it suddenly seemed possible. That's a good feeling.

Behind a glass wall at the back of the commons, looking like a zoo habitat, a soundproof study room with two long tables caged up the detention kids. Several teachers and librarians roamed around or sat next to students as they worked on their homework or whatever detention punishment they had to finish. Every once in a while, kids would rest their cheeks on their hands and look at all the fun everyone else in the library was having before they sighed and got back to work. Those poor schmucks.

"That's where you have to go," said Gabi, pointing to the soundproof room. "C'mon."

Reluctantly, I did a death-row shuffle past the gamers and the makers and the readers, and followed Gabi to the door to detention. Again, she opened it for me. In I went.

"¡Hola!" a man greeted me. He looked like a leprechaun reporter from the 1920s—green jacket, yellow vest, paisley tie, white shirt, brown tweed pants, and boots with way more buckles than were humanly needed. His hair shot up like a black flame. "I'm Daniel Miranda Rivero. I'm the chief learning coordinator. You must be new to Culeco. What's your name?" He put out his hand for me to shake.

I very politely went to shake his hand, when Gabi, yelling a slow-motion "Noooo!" jumped between us. She turned my hand over, checking for my GOTCHA! stamp, no doubt. When she didn't find it, she straightened her hair and said, "Okay. Carry on."

I shook Daniel's hand. "I'm Sal Vidón."

"So," Daniel asked me, looking sly, "whatcha in for?"

I put my left hand in my pocket and shrugged. "Scaring Gladis Machado to death."

"Oh, you're the magician! Principal Torres told me about you."

"Really?" I scratched my head, tried to sound casual. "What'd she say?"

"She told me to watch you with both eyes."

"Three, if you have them," Gabi added, dry as moondust.

"Won't help." I smiled. "Check your hand."

Daniel checked the hand we shook. I could tell he was hoping I'd done something. But he had to say, "I don't see any-thing" after searching.

"Not you, Daniel. Gabi."

The look of horror on Gabi's face was everything. The howls she let out after she saw I'd stamped GOTCHA! on her palm were like music. "No! No! How? No! That is *not* how it works! No! When could you possibly have— Arrgh!" she said, stomping and flailing her arms, her hair tossing the sorceresses around like a tornado.

I wish I could have watched her little tantrum from outside the study room. I bet it looked especially funny without sound.

Detention was great.

I mean, zapping Gabi got it off to a great start. But what was cool was how Daniel ran it. Kids could go in and out whenever they wanted to. Sometimes they'd go outside to the commons, join a game, or talk to friends, or watch combat robots kill each other for a while. And then they'd come back and pick up wherever they'd left off. The teachers in the room assisted everyone who needed it and left them alone when they didn't. Other kids who didn't have detention were there just to help their friends get done sooner. The mood was light and jokey and easy and not like detention at all.

It's funny. When I saw the room for the first time, I'd thought the kids were trapped in there like zoo animals. I'd assumed they were miserable, but that was just because I was feeling salty and didn't want to be in detention. Now that I'd seen it from the inside, I had a whole different perspective.

Emotion literally changes your eyesight. I would have to remember that.

While I worked on my apology to Gladis, Gabi toured the room, glad-handing teachers and helping other students with their homework. She completed her circle of the room just as I finished my letter.

I gave it to her to read. But when her eyes started scanning it, I added, "Can you read it out loud? I want to hear if it sounds good."

Gabi's eyebrows touched her hairline. "Are you sure? Isn't this, like, private?"

I don't think Gabi had noticed Yasmany coming into the detention room just then. But I sure had. I'd seen him coming the second he walked into the commons. "I'm sure, Gabi," I said.

Gabi gave me one of those *it's-your-life* tilts of the head and then read the letter out loud.

Dear Gladis,

I started studying magic when my mami died. It was a way for me to cope with the pain and try to take back control of my life. I didn't know at first how happy magic can make people.

That's why I love performing tricks now. I love to see people's eyes fill with wonder. I love it when they ask, "How did you do that?" I think the best thing I do with my time is go to the hospital and perform for sick children. It's because of the joy I see in their eyes that I know I have learned how to take the tragedy of my mami's death and turn it into something good.

But today, I misused magic. Instead of using it to make people happy, I made you feel afraid with it. That goes against everything magic is for. And the worst part of all is, if my mami were alive today, she would be disappointed in me. That's almost more than I can take.

I am sorry for the trick I played on you today. I will never play another trick on you again. I won't ask for your forgiveness, but I hope you will forgive me anyway. If you can't, I understand. I will just leave you alone and be sorry that I did something mean to you that you can't get past, and try to learn from it.

Sincerely,
Sal Vidón

Gabi read it beautifully. I knew she would. The whole room had stopped to listen to her, even Yasmany, who had pretended not to listen. Too school for cool.

When she reached the end, Gabi slapped the letter against her legs and looked at me with a wishy-washy smile that I knew could turn into an ugly cry any second. "That was a very good apology, Sal," she said.

"I'll say," said Daniel, smiling softly. "Where'd you learn to write from the heart like that?"

"Not the heart," I said, patting my belly. "From the stomach."

25

FOR THE REST of detention, Gabi and Daniel and I helped Yasmany finish his paper. He and Gabi had already started it, so Gabi pulled it up on her laptop and made Yasmany sit in front of it. Daniel found books and docs on diabetes that we all scoured for information. I was the resident expert and shared how I managed it day to day. I also checked my blood sugar right there, so Yasmany could see how it was done. Dude almost fainted.

Yasmany, man. His main contribution to his own paper was to say things like, "What?" or "Really?" or "Nuh-uh," or "[cussword that expressed sympathy but also relief that he wasn't type one]" whenever he learned something new about diabetes. I'm not sure he even knew he had a pancreas at the start of detention. But he sure as heck knew by the end of it. So mission accomplished, I guess?

By the time we were halfway done with the paper, detention had been over for half an hour. Yasmany ran off as soon as he noticed the time: dance practice again.

What was weird was that basically everyone else was still there. I mean, not just the detention kids, but the gamers and makers and cosplayers and readers, too. Everyone was just hanging out at school.

"I know," said Daniel, reading my mind. "No one wants to leave. It's a strange and beautiful sight, don't you think, Sal?"

"Speaking of leaving," I replied, "I still have one more day of detention, but I finished my apology. Do I have to come back tomorrow?"

"Yes."

"But what I am supposed to do?"

Daniel gestured widely with his hands, encompassing all the possibilities the commons offered. "Anything you want!"

"What if what I want is not to come?"

Daniel looked at me like I'd just told him his dog had run away. "You don't want to come to detention?"

"No, no," I answered. "I love detention. I'll definitely be here tomorrow."

Man. Never thought those words would come out of my mouth.

Gabi grabbed the back of my cargo vest. "You. Me. Interview. Now!" she said, and pretty much dragged me out of the library.

I needed to put stuff away, so we headed for my locker, just around the corner from the library commons. To get to my locker, we had to pass Yasmany's. Gabi headed straight for his, and started working the dial of the lock.

"Hey, you better not," I said. "I got in trouble with Mr. Milagros yesterday for doing that."

Gabi turned on me like a tiger. "Aha! That's how you knew it was Iggy's birthday! You read the note I put in Yasmany's locker, didn't you?"

I swear, I have never been busted so many times in one week. Was I losing my touch or something?

All I could think to do was shrug and say, "Sorry."

"Wel-l-l-l," she said, drawing out the *l*'s, "I've been known to peek at other people's letters when I probably shouldn't have. A folded note is very hard to resist. Apology accepted."

Gabi, I was noticing, was a very forgiving person. I've noticed that sometimes smart people aren't. They're more interested in being right, being on top, and they think that means crushing the competition with their huge brains. But Gabi didn't need to put others down to raise herself up. Interesting.

"Thank you," I said.

"You're welcome." She curtsied.

"So, what are you planning to do in Yasmany's locker?"

She opened the lock and held on to it as she answered, "The same thing I do every day: nag him like the mama he wishes he had. Mr. Milagros knows what I'm doing. So does Principal Torres. They know I'm just trying to help him get his act together."

"Okay, cool, cool. Don't let me stop you."

"I wasn't going to." She opened the door, but then side-eyed me. "Why are you staring?"

"What? I'm not staring."

I was too staring. I wanted to see if the hole in the universe, there in the back of Yasmany's locker, had closed itself. I didn't think it had—I was pretty sure I could still feel it, like a breeze through a car window—but I wanted to see if it had at least gotten any smaller.

"Don't you have to put stuff in your locker?" asked Gabi, clearly waiting for me to get lost.

Whatever. I went to my locker, dumped some books in there, and was contemplating which trick props to keep in there and which to take home, when Gabi said, with a voice like a fake Discovery Channel ghost hunter who realizes—too late!—that the house is actually haunted, "What is that what is that what is that what is that what is that?"

I looked over. Gabi was on her butt crabwalking backward for the second time today, this time away from the lockers.

Thoroughly trained on not being a jerk since this morning, I ran to the locker and investigated. It was mostly empty, just a couple of thin books left. "What, there a spider in there? I'll kill it for you."

When Gabi didn't answer right away, I turned to face her. She paused mid-crabwalk, her face as stunned-looking as a bowling ball. "You don't see them, Sal? The chickens? The flying chickens?"

"Oh, those," I said, rolling my eyes. "Yeah, stupid hole doesn't want to close. It's a lot smaller now, thank goodness, but—" I stopped talking. Now it was my turn to have bowling-ball face. "Wait, Gabi. You can see the hole in the universe?"

"'*Hole in the universe*'?! What do you mean 'hole in the universe'?!"

I reached out a hand to her, the way I would a scared dog, so it could sniff me and know I was a friend. "It was there yesterday, too. Why didn't you see it then, when you put the note in Yasmany's locker?"

She took my hand, and together we carefully got her on her feet. "I was busy. There were a lot of books in the way yesterday. I am short, okay?"

"Hey, no judgment. I'm short, too."

She moved past me to look inside the locker again, on tiptoes. Chicken bodies just kept zipping on by. "You weren't lying yesterday. You didn't beat the lie detector. . . . You were telling the truth."

"Yeah. Where'd you get that thing, anyway?"

"One of my dads hooked me up. Stop changing the subject. You're telling me I am looking at an actual doorway to a parallel universe."

"Yeah."

"A parallel universe full of chickens."

"All you can eat."

She faced me, shaking her head. "I'm a vegetarian. Ew."

I couldn't help but laugh. "Fine! Don't eat the extradimensional chicken. That's not exactly the point right now."

She stood beside me, both of us facing the locker, watching the conveyor belt carry chickens away. "What *is* the point, Sal?"

"The point is, you're the only other person I've ever met who could see a rip. My papi can't, and he studies these things for a living. American Stepmom can't, Yasmany can't, Mr. Milagros can't. That means you're like me," And to myself I added, *Yes! There's finally someone else like me.*

She turned to me, looking low-key scared. "Is that a good thing?"

She had me there. "Beats me. But it makes me wonder what else you can do."

"What do you mean, 'do'?"

I walked over to the locker, moved the books out of the way, and then, on tiptoe, reached my hand through the locker until

I was spanking the chickens on the conveyor belt. "I mean, like, do this."

I turned back to the locker and threw myself halfway into it, hands forward, almost like a dive.

I heard Gabi squeal behind me. "I'll save you, Sal!" she whooped. By the time I had plucked a chicken off the conveyor belt, she was holding both my legs, and a second later, she yanked me out of the locker. We both fell sprawling to the floor.

She sat up, looked at me, and then saw what I was cradling in my hands. "Sal, is that—"

"Extradimensional poultry? Yep."

We got ourselves up from the floor. Gabi never took her eyes off the chicken, never quite shut her mouth all the way. I decided to experiment. I threw the chicken in the air and caught it, like a basketball. Her eyes went up and down with each throw.

This was kind of fun. It gave me an idea. "Hey, think fast!" I said as I no-look-passed the chicken to Gabi.

She caught it, then immediately started hot-potatoing it. "Ew! Ew! I just told you two seconds ago I'm a vegetarian!"

She might have kept on yelling at me, except just then an angry woman's head poked out of the locker.

"Ah!" screamed Gabi.

"Ah!" screamed Sal. It scared me so much, I felt like I was out of my body watching myself being scared.

The woman was middle-aged and wore big safety goggles, a protective paper mask, and a hairnet. She looked kind of exactly like Principal Torres.

She scanned the room quickly before locking her gaze on the bird carcass. "¡Ey!" she yelled.

"¡Ey!" is a very special Cuban expletive. I'm not even sure how you spell it. It's not the kind of word you write down. Also, it's hard to translate into English, because it can mean a lot of things. But this time it meant something like "What's going on here? Oh, you think you can make a fool of me? How about I rip out your heart and stick it in your ear so you can hear yourself die?"

Gabi, now cradling the chicken like it was her baby, asked the lady, "Who are you?"

The lady, being a full-grown woman, looked like a human cannonball stuffed into an itty-bitty cannon. She had to wriggle and fight to get even one of her hands out of the opening in the back of the locker. When she did, she shook her fist at us. "¡Devuélveme ese pollo, o vamos a tener un problema tremendo!"

"What's she saying?" Gabi asked me.

"She's demanding the return of her chicken."

"¡No le tengo miedo a nadie!" said the squirming, struggling lady, trying and failing to bring her other arm forward. "¡Ser humano o demonio, no me importa! ¿Creen que me pueden robar sin consecuencia? Voy a mandarlos al infierno con tres patadas en sus nalgas infernales."

I stood there listening, fascinated. I hadn't heard Spanish that angry since the last time one of the Mami Muertas had lost her chill. It felt kind of like home.

"Sal!" elbowed Gabi. "What'd she say?"

"She thinks we're evil spirits, or devils, or something. She says she is going to kick us in the butt three times and send us back to hell."

"Exactly three times? That's very specific."

"If she ever figures out how to pull herself all the way through the locker, I imagine she will kick our butts a lot more than three times."

Gabi nodded in comprehension. I mean, I have no idea what she thought she comprehended from this situation, but she obviously didn't think freaking out would help anything. Instead, she steadied herself, tossed her hair, then walked forward, holding the chicken out to the woman like Rafiki holding Simba. "Sorry, mujer. Mucho sorry. Like, tres patadas sorry."

The lady eyed Gabi suspiciously as she approached. No doubt she thought Gabi was speaking in tongues to her, the way she was butchering Spanish. But the lady's voice was softer when she answered, "Los jefes nos cobran a nosotros por cada pollo que se desaparece. Ya somos pobres. Por favor, tenga compasión, diablita bonita. No los robe más."

"She's saying," I translated, "that the bosses make the workers pay for any chickens that go missing. She's saying they're poor already. She asked us not to steal from them anymore. Also, she thinks we're devil spawn."

Even though I was looking at the back of her head, I could tell Gabi smiled. "No más robos," she promised the woman. "Somos angels."

Gabi's terrible Spanish was working. The woman laughed. "Júralo, si eres tan ángel."

"Los dos se lo prometemos, señora," I replied.

The lady's eyes volleyed between Gabi and me, and her smile landed somewhere between doubtful and trusting.

"Bueno, si me están diciendo la verdad, voy a rezar por ust-
edes. Si Dios quiere, quizás pueden subir al cielo y vivir con
los ángeles. Pero tienen que ser espíritus buenos y ayudar a
los vivos, empezando ahora mismo. ¿Entienden? ¿Pueden ser
espíritus buenos?"

"Sí," I answered.

Gabi quickly added her own, "¡Tres patadas sí!"

With one last *I-mean-business* stare at each of us, the
lady grabbed the chicken with her one free hand. Then she
shimmied, struggled, shrugged, slid, shook, and finally shoved
herself back into the hole, and was gone.

I felt both relieved and worried. The hole in the locker was
now bigger than I'd ever seen it. And before this it had almost
closed all the way! Sometimes I don't make good decisions.

Gabi, however, felt a little differently. She slammed the
locker door closed and leaned against it. She looked flushed,
exhilarated, ready to run a marathon. "Did you see that?"

"Um, yeah. I was right here with you the whole time?"

"Sal! That was the most amazing thing in the history of
amazing things."

"It's definitely up there."

"How in the *world* did you do that? *Wait!*" she said suddenly,
running over to cover my mouth with her hand. "Don't answer
that. Let me get my phone out. I want to record every word of
this. I don't want to miss a thing!"

26

IT WAS NINETY DEGREES outside—ten thousand with humidity. Florida in August, man. Kill a Connecticut boy faster than you can say "sunstroke."

At first, Gabi wanted to start the interview right there at Yasmany's locker. But then she said she wanted time to process everything she'd seen—and to wash the raw chicken juice off her hands. I said okay; we could talk once we got to the Coral Castle.

But she couldn't wait that long. About ten seconds after we'd left the school grounds, she asked, "So, you really are a brujo?" She used that TV-reporter voice that makes everything sound like the scoop of the century. Also, she looked completely, annoyingly, unbothered by the heat: no pit stains, no forehead sweat, no flushed cheeks, no nothing. The metal sorceress barrettes in her hair took turns blinding me. Also, she stuck her phone too close to my mouth to record my answer.

I eased her hand away from my face and, loud enough to be heard over the rumbling traffic, replied, "No."

"No?" But she didn't say that into the phone, so she

brought the speaker to her mouth and repeated, with even more panache, "No?!"

"No." I smiled. Sometimes, smiles are masks.

She harrumphed off the record, and then, struggling to be professional, followed up into her phone. "So let me get this straight, Sal. Despite the fact that you confessed to ripping a hole in the universe, despite the fact that you put your arms through solid metal and concrete to pull a chicken out of who-knows-where, *and* despite the fact that a weird lady popped out of the locker to get her chicken back, you maintain that you do not possess supernatural powers. Is that correct?"

That's not what I said. But instead of correcting her, I deflected. "I didn't take you for the superstitious type, Gabi. There's no such thing as brujería."

Gabi went suddenly quiet, switching her recording app off and watching her feet walk for a while. "I am *not* superstitious," she said finally, more to herself than to me. "I am *skeptical.* I require evidence to support my opinions. But I have to admit, after what I've seen today, I believe in brujería! I mean"—and, suddenly remembering her job, she started recording again, glaring at me—"how else do you explain what happened today, Sal? It has to be brujería. You have to be a brujo. Do you deny it?"

Man, how do people walk around in Miami? I felt like I was being digested inside a dragon's stomach. "I'm not a brujo, okay?" I snapped. "I don't like that word. I swear, if you call me that again, we're done."

"Hey, take it easy! The whole reason I'm doing this is to give you a chance to share your side of the story."

"If you hadn't printed your story in the *Rotten Egg*, I wouldn't need to give an interview in the first place."

Now it was Gabi's turn to get overheated. "So you think you can tear open the universe and pull chickens out of thin air and everyone's going to be like, 'Oh, that's fine. It's impossible and unexplainable and as scary as spiders, but we'll just pretend nothing happened and go on with our lives'? No, no, no, no, no. Right here, right now, you tell me how you made a real live person come out of that locker, Sal."

She shoved her phone so close to my mouth I could have kissed the screen just by stretching my lips. So I did.

"Ew!" she said, and wiped her screen on the leg of her jeans. "Look, bub, you can try to distract me all you want"—she took hand sanitizer out of her pack, squeezed a fat drop onto her screen, and scrubbed it with her finger—"but I am going to keep asking you until you answer me." She wiped her phone against her leg again to remove the excess alcohol. "So you might as well come clean." She examined her screen, seemed satisfied that she'd killed whatever cooties I had put on it, then raised it close to my mouth to record my response—but this time, not quite close enough for me to make out with it again. "Spill it."

I wasn't spilling anything. I wasn't going to take orders from Gabi Reál.

I inhaled deeply, ready to lay into her good and proper, but she grabbed the back of my shirt. We had arrived at a crosswalk, where the Red Hand of Doom on the light was telling us to wait, and she had kept me from walking into traffic and getting run over.

That was nice of her, saving my life and all. I really had to do a better job crossing streets.

So when I pressed the call button on the traffic light, I gave her a more truthful answer than I thought I would. My voice was mostly wind when I said to Gabi, "Maybe I don't know, either."

She thought for a moment, then decided I was full of it. "What do you mean you don't know? You *have* to know! You did it. You made the hole."

"Sometimes you can do things without knowing how you do them."

"Don't change the subject, Sal. A mechanic can't just fix an engine without knowing how the engine works. I can't go home tonight and be like, 'Oops, I accidentally finished all my geometry homework!' I have to study first and learn how to solve the problems. Even babies have to learn to walk. You have to know what you're doing to do anything."

Hmm. She was a good debater. I stuck my hands in my cargo-pants pockets and thought about what she'd said.

The crosswalk signal changed from Red Hand of Doom to Glowing White Dude. Gabi made a big show of looking both ways, like she was teaching me. It was a little annoying. We crossed the street in silence.

All around us, Little Havana sponsored a music-free dance party. Car engines drumrolled, and car horns trumpeted, and the people outside the corner store we were approaching slapped dominoes on their folding table hard enough to make their tiny paper cups of espresso jump. A mami coming toward us mother-ducked her three small children—stumbling and amazed by the world, babbling musical nonsense—across the street. A viejo loitering against a cross-signal pole, wearing a white guayabera with only one button fastened and sucking noisily from his cigar, was thinking the deepest thoughts in the world. Life is so complicated because it's just so massive. Truth seemed so small to me then: like tickets you hand out to people before a carnival ride. Life was so much bigger than truth. It was *real.*

"Well?" said Gabi.

"I'm still thinking," I answered. "Let's cross the street. Then we take the next right on Fifteenth."

This street was mostly residential, if a little sketchy. But even in rougher neighborhoods, Miami has a crazy amount of trees compared to Connecticut, and they're huge and prehistoric-looking. It's like there's this thin layer of asphalt covering the city, but just beneath it, there's a raging jungle raring to burst through, plants and trees ready to gush out of the ground in explosions of leaf and bark and flower.

"I don't know how a tree makes fruit," I replied, slowly, reading the idea in my head as it occurred to me, "but I can still eat fruit."

"You have to know that it's okay to eat the fruit, or it might be poison," she countered, fast as a swordfighter. "You still have to know stuff."

"No, you don't, Gabi!" I said triumphantly. "Some hungry cave dude took a risk one day and ate the fruit."

"Or cave dudette."

"Whatever. They didn't know what was going to happen.

They just tried it. And sometimes it turned out to be a delicious apple, and sometimes it turned out to be poisonous berries. But they couldn't know in advance. They just had to chew and swallow and see what happened."

She thought about that for eight steps, as the heat rising off the sidewalk made the whole world waver before our eyes. Finally, she nodded, deciding something. "So, what you did with the locker, it's like eating mystery fruit?"

I shrugged. "Maybe? I'm still figuring things out. Oh, we take a left here."

As we turned the corner down my street, Gabi said, "Let's just be really clear for the readers at home. So there are things you can control and things you can't. Which is which? List them."

Man. Easy for her to ask.

One good thing about Florida's infinite flora is that you can find shade pretty much whenever you need it. A tree in a neighbor's yard had a canopy that stretched over the sidewalk, so I took a seat underneath it. Gabi sat next to me, tipping the phone's mic near me.

"Help me figure it out," I said. "You could see past the back of the locker. I've never met anyone else who could. How did *you* do it? What, are you a bruja or something?" *There. That'll teach her.*

Or not. "You bet I am. I'm the brujaest bruja that ever turned a prince into a toad." When she was done laughing, she added, "But I get your point. I don't know how I could see it. I just could."

"Exactly."

A thought was coming to her. She ruffled her hair with her free hand, and her barrettes sparkled. "Okay, Sal. So don't explain. Show me."

"What, right here?"

She got up and spun around, her arms wide. "Right here, right now, Sal. Do your thing. Make a hole in the universe. But talk me through it. What you're thinking, what you're feeling, everything. We'll figure it out together."

I looked around. There were a few people outside, tending their yards, chatting with friends on phones, filling the air with happy Spanglish. That made me nervous about "doing my thing" out in public. But no one would understand what was happening. I was pretty sure no one else would even be able to see what Gabi and I would see. In a way, this "thing" was the opposite of magic. There was no spectacle to it, no pizzazz, no booms or puffs of smoke or anything to say "Ta-da!" about. *Nothing to see here, folks. Move along.*

I stood, took a breath, let it out. "I use meditation techniques that I learned from my psychologist," I told Gabi. I closed my eyes and kept talking. "Right now, I'm picturing a screened-in porch. I'm imagining myself poking a hole in the screen with my finger."

"I've done that before," said Gabi. "Every kid in Florida has, I bet. I got in big trouble for it, too."

I literally held up a finger, pushed it through the imaginary screen, and pulled it out again. I opened my eyes. "Okay, Gabi. Look and relax at the same time. Can you see the hole I made?"

Gabi stared at the spot where I had just poked my finger in the air. Her eyebrows got all bent up.

"Remember to relax," I said.

She exhaled. Her eyebrows straightened themselves. "I see it! I see it! It looks like a little blurry spot."

I stepped back and bowed. "Have a peek through, m'lady."

She stood on her toes and raised an eye to the blurry spot. Then she jammed her whole face into it.

I yelped, but she couldn't hear me, because her ears were somewhere else. For a few seconds it looked like she had no head—her neck just ended. When she popped her head back out again, she was smiling.

"That is so cool! That house over there," Gabi said, pointing to the tan stucco two-story across the street, "is orange when you look at it through the hole."

I nodded. "It's like us, but a different version of us. And there are, like, a trillion different versions."

"Sal!" She started skipping, hopping, racing around me, a dog on a walk in love with life. "Do you know what this means? *You just made a peephole into a whole different universe!* This is just . . . I don't even know what this is, but it's the greatest thing!"

Half my mouth smiled and half didn't. I started walking home again, and Gabi, maybe sensing she'd said something wrong, got in step with me and let us walk quietly for a minute. Each individual beam of sunlight felt like a separate hot spear sinking into my face.

"I keep bringing back my dead mami," I said finally.

"Whoa, what?" she saidasked.

"I don't mean to. Well, I used to do it on purpose. But a few days ago, it just happened. I didn't even do it. Well, it had to be me who did it. But I didn't mean to."

"You brought back your dead mom? Like, from another universe?"

"Yeah. For a little bit. It was kind of nice, actually. But she's gone again."

"Oh." Gabi started walking again. "I'm . . . sorry?"

"Me too." I have to admit, it felt good to talk about it with someone. The sunlight didn't hurt as much anymore. "You know, for someone who was accusing me of brujería a few minutes ago, you're taking all this surprisingly well."

She shrugged. "One of my dads is a scientist."

"Did he help you with your lie detector?"

She nodded. "That dad's a *she*. She's always talking about stuff like this. But even so, Sal, you have to admit, what you do, it really is like brujería. No one is supposed to be able to see other universes, or pull chickens out of them."

"Or dead mamis," I agreed.

"Yeah."

Any other time, I would have shut up at this point. But Gabi could see holes. She really understood me, better than anyone else. I couldn't stop talking. "I don't know what I'm doing. It's a little scary, maybe." I took a breath. "Maybe I need a little help."

Gabi locked onto me with her full attention. And I am here to tell you, looking at her when she's locked onto you like that is like staring at the sun. "I'll help you, Sal Vidón. I will help you get control of this. I swear it. We'll do it together."

I believed her. You know how good it feels when a leg that's fallen asleep starts to wake up? That was my whole body.

I stopped walking. "This is my house." I gestured toward the Coral Castle.

"Whoa," she said. "It's hideous. I love it."

Couldn't have said it better myself.

Gabi, now sounding a little suspicious, asked me, "But why's there a moving truck in your driveway? I thought you moved in over the summer."

"We did," I said. I had no idea what that truck was doing there. It was an unmarked gray eighteen-wheeler that had no business that I knew of at the Coral Castle. "Something's not right."

I stepped slowly up the walkway toward the front door. Gabi followed. The window shades were pulled; I couldn't see anything inside. I took out my keys and started to unlock the door. On the other side of the door, a bunch of voices started talking at the same time.

"What the—?"

"Oh God, it's late! We're behind schedule!"

"We gotta hide the—!"

"Stall them! Stall them!"

I don't know about you, but that sounded like a burglary in progress to me. Gabi and I traded looks.

"Who's in your house?" she asked.

"I don't know," I said.

"What do we do? Should we call your parents? Or the police?"

"Nope" was my only answer. And, ready to chuck whoever had broken into my house into another universe, I threw open the front door.

27

I MEAN, I TRIED to throw the door open. But the criminals in my house had set the chain lock.

From my sleeve I drew my magic wand, the one I'd turned into flowers for Gabi that morning. I slipped my arm through the gap in the door and used the wand to unlatch the chain. A second later, I flung the door open and charged inside. Gabi, running in behind me, had her phone out, video-recording our entrance. The reporter in her smelled a scoop.

The couch, love seat, easy chair, coffee table, and entertainment center had vanished from the living room. Replacing all of them, and taking up even more space than they had, was the hugest black computer I had ever seen.

There were more people in the room than I could count quickly. They were frozen in place by our entrance. Some of them had opened the walls to install fiber optics and electrical wires, which bulged out of the new holes. Computer programmers, all in ironic T-shirts and jeans, were swarming all over the black computer. One lady in a black skirt suit wore a virtual reality headset and, judging by the gestures she made, was programming in four dimensions. She was the only one who kept working now that Gabi and I had busted up the party. Everyone else stared back at us like cornered cats.

Especially Papi.

He stood in the center of the room, where he had been directing all the action. He looked at me, guilt lighting up his eyes, and said, "Hi, son! Um, how was school?"

The woman in the skirt suit, finally realizing something weird was going on, pulled off the VR headset. There was something very . . . unblinking about her. She looked at me with bland curiosity. And then she looked at Gabi.

"Dad?" I asked.

"Dad?" Gabi asked.

"Um, Gabi?" I said, pointing my wand at Papi. "That's *my* dad."

She stopped recording, lowered her phone. "Yeah, the dude in the Hawaiian shirt. Figured. But the woman next to him is *my* dad. Her name is Dad: The Final Frontier. She's my scientist dad. The one I was telling you about?"

"How many dads do you have, Gabi?!"

She shook her head. "If you only knew."

"This is your daughter?" Papi asked the woman. He was coming out of his daze.

The woman nodded, then ambled up to Gabi. Her legs—well, they looked like legs. She had thighs and knees and ankles and feet in her shoes. But she moved like a toddler who was still learning how to walk. Like, a little too fast, and then almost falling over when she stopped.

The woman bent down and hugged Gabi. Her smile

snapped into place. And then her face snapped into a puzzled expression. She moved between expressions really quickly. "Gabi, honey, what in the world are you doing here?"

"What in the world are you doing in my house, person I have never met before?" I asked her back.

She didn't seem hurt by my tone. She looked like she had never been hurt by anyone's tone in her entire life. Instead, she tilted her head at me and said, "Hello, Sal. My name is Bonita. I am here because I work for your father. We are installing this remembranation machine in your living room."

"Yeah. I noticed."

"We're setting up camp," said Papi, stepping up next to Bonita. He gave me his classic *Quit the cacaseca* eyes. "*Something* happened here last night. Perhaps you remember?"

I wasn't going to give him anything for free. "Perhaps."

He snorted. "Yeah, well, we're bringing in the heavy equipment to fix it."

"Looks like you had to do a little"—I looked around—"*remodeling*, too."

Papi, peering around the room also, flapped his shirt to cool himself down. "Ah, yes. The machine is a little bigger than I thought. We couldn't get it up the steps. I was going to put it upstairs, you know, where it wouldn't be in anybody's way."

"But it didn't fit. So now it's in the living room."

"That is correct."

"American Stepmom is going to kill you."

"Yes," Papi said, inflating his cheeks. "Yes, she is." And then, resigning himself to his death, he clapped his hands. "So, who wants ice cream?"

In the kitchen, Papi and I got to work. He pulled two unopened containers of rocky road from the freezer while I set out an assembly line of fifteen bowls. I ran the scoop under hot water, then started dumping snowman-size balls of ice cream into the bowls. Papi, meanwhile, produced three huge boxes of bonbons from behind a tile in the kitchen wall—which he thought was his secret hiding place, and which I totally knew was his secret hiding place—and studded the ice cream with them.

"Our guests are going to faint when they see these sundaes!" said Papi. He loved throwing parties and serving over-the-top desserts, and he didn't get to do either very often, poor guy. One, he was always working, and when he wasn't working, he was trying to grow his brains back, because his job had used them all up. Two, his stupid son was diabetic, and he was too nice a guy to torture his kid by eating Willy Wonka sundaes when his kid couldn't enjoy them, too. Those quarts of ice cream would have lasted our family a month and a half under normal circumstances.

But now Papi would get to use them up in one sitting, to entertain guests in his house. He couldn't have been happier.

And that meant it was the perfect time to bring up what was bothering me.

"So," I said. "Even one calamitron is too much?"

"Yep-p," Papi answered, barely paying attention. Most of his thinking was devoted to the exact placement of bonbons.

The next part was hard to ask. "So does that mean that I'm a danger to the universe?"

"What?" He dropped a bonbon on the counter.

"It's just, I didn't mean to bring a mami this time. My brain

brought her over without me. And if I can't control this . . . thing
I can do, I might—"

"Think fast!" said Papi. He had walked to the pantry and
pulled out a jar of peanut butter, which he now underhanded
to me. I caught it. I knew what he wanted and started spooning
peanut butter into a microwave-safe bowl. Microwaved peanut
butter is an awesome ice cream topping.

As I watched the peanut butter melt down to gooey
goodness, Papi said, "I miss your mami as much as you do,
you know."

Um, what? Then I said, "Um, what?"

He leaned against the counter. "It's true. Probably even
more. I mean, I knew her longer. I married her. I loved her. I
love her still."

The peanut butter started to boil at the edges. In a few seconds, it would burn. But I let it keep on cooking and spinning
and bubbling.

"Her death is the worst thing that's ever happened to either
of us," he went on, moving around the kitchen now, bustling,
grabbing sprinkles and toppings from cabinets and drawers. "I
thought my life was over when she died. Even talking about it
now, I can make myself relive some of that pain. I thought it
would kill me, you know. Literally stop my heart. Oh, bad days.
Those were bad days. You know what kept me going, mijo?"

"What?"

"You."

I stopped the microwave but left the peanut butter inside
to cool. "I know."

He put his two huge hands on my shoulders. "When I heard

about this job in Miami, your stepmom and I jumped at the chance. You know why, mijo? Because we thought I might be able to help you. Here, I could be on the cutting edge of calamity physics. Work with some of the best minds in the world to figure out what it is, exactly, that you can do. Because what you can do, mijo"—and he gave my shoulders a big squeeze—"science says is impossible."

I took out the peanut butter. It wasn't burned, but a little had crisped on the edges. Perfect, in other words. I put it on the counter, stirred it with a spoon, grabbed the bowl again, turned around, and handed it to Papi. "Science doesn't know what it's talking about," I said.

Papi made the apology face. "It doesn't until it does. It's my job to learn about calamitrons. And once I figure them out, I'll tell everybody the truth about them, whatever it is. Then I'll use that knowledge to fix anything that needs fixing." He took a big whiff of hot peanut butter. "Ah. That's the good stuff."

"And that's what the machine in the living room's for?" I asked. "Fixing . . . 'things'?"

Papi headed over to the bowls and started spooning peanut butter over the ice cream. "We have to move fast now, mijo. The ice cream will turn to soup!"

I ran to the fridge and grabbed two cans of whipped cream, then got behind Papi. As he spooned peanut butter over the bonbons, I squirted on mountaintops of whipped cream. We were quick and efficient, like circus performers.

"Theoretically, yes," Papi said, finally, as we worked. "But it's like I said yesterday. We don't know enough yet. I mean, we don't even have a full understanding of what a calamitron is."

"They're the particles that destroy the universe, right? What else do you need to know?"

Papi slowed down. He couldn't work as fast when he was thinking. "See, that's the thing, Sal: Calamitrons don't destroy anything. They're *evidence* of destruction. Specifically, they're the particles that get released when the membrane of the universe is damaged." Papi stopped moving for a second to look at the ceiling and figure out the next part. "Imagine a window. Some kid throws a baseball through it. All the pieces of glass that explode out of the windowpane? Those are the calamitrons."

I gave the last bowl extra whipped cream. "So when you find a lot of calamitrons, you're worried, because it means someone broke a window in the universe."

"Exactly."

"Huh. Skittles?" I asked, pulling out a king-size bag from pretty much nowhere.

Papi blinked. "Mijo, your sleight of hand is getting good! And, um, yeah, Skittles!"

I started pouring Skittles onto the whipped cream. They sunk into those white mounds like multicolored meteors. Then Papi got behind me in the assembly line and stuck sparklers in each bowl of ice cream, one by one. Yes, we're the kind of family that buys enough fireworks during the Fourth of July to last the whole year.

"I'm scared," I said, not looking up, working steadily, doing my job.

"I know," he said. "But there's good news, too. You can fix the universe."

I faced him, and the next handful of Skittles was for me. Papi gave me a look that meant *Should you have done that? What's your sugar at?* And I gave him a look back that meant *Don't change the subject. You just said something super important that I need you to explain, and when I get stressed I like the occasional Skittle, okay?*

"Last night," he began, "you sent Floramaria away, just as you fainted. She vanished like the *Enterprise* was beaming her up, just as she was lunging to catch you. And back in Connecticut, when that other Floramaria went berserk, you sent her away, too. That's twice that you sent someone back to their original universes. Did you do that with your other Mamis, too?"

This conversation was making me sad. "Yes. When they got too unhappy, I sent them back. They always got unhappy."

"¡Exactamente!" he said, a little too boisterously. He urged me to keep dropping Skittles as he explained. "See, Sal, the holes, they can heal in time. Like a cut on your skin. But you can't pick the scab, right, or else it won't heal, and it might leave a scar. And sometimes something really terrible happens. Like, someone loses a finger. But you know"—and he started to get pretty excited by his own explanation now—"when someone loses a finger these days, doctors can sew it on again. They just have to put the finger back where it belongs, right? And then they have to give the body time to heal, right? The cosmic membrane can heal if all the pieces—the calamitrons—are back where they belong."

As I finished raining Skittles on the last sundae, I thought about relaxing in Principal Torres's office to get rid of the chicken evidence, even the blood on Yasmany's shoe. "And you think I can do that, Papi?"

He speared the last sparklers into the sundae. "You've done it before, with your mami. We just have to figure out *how* you did it. That's why we can't lose hope. We have to be guapo! A scientist has to be smart, sure, but at the bottom of it all, scientists need enough courage to explore how weird and wonderful the multiverse really is. It's scary wandering into the unknown . . . without . . . a . . ."

Papi was patting his pockets down, searching for his lighter.

Which I had lifted from him as soon as he broke out the sparklers. It was one of those nice metal lighters with a flip-top lid, which he used to smoke the one cigar a month he allows himself. I lit it with a flourish. "A light to guide you?"

Papi laughed and rubbed his forehead. "Exactly. Well, go ahead, then. Light the sparklers. Guao, kid, you are a scary-good pickpocket."

I did, moving down the line. Every sparkler looked like a new, brilliant idea, and together they made a whole parade of inspiration.

"So you're saying I need to be smart," I said as more and more sparks flew around our kitchen. "And being smart means thinking twice, moving slowly, and being sure before I act, right?"

"Exactamente."

"But you're also saying I should be brave, which I think means, like, trusting myself, being confident, and not letting fear get in my way."

"Sí, señor."

The last sparkler lit, I turned to Papi and flipped his fancy lighter shut. "But they're opposites. How can I do both at the same time?"

"A good question," he said, pacing with his hands behind his back. "Let's use our present situation to think about it. Right now, we could have a big philosophical discussion about when to think and when to act, and the ice cream will turn into rocky road puddles in their bowls, and our guests will be sad. Or we can talk later and serve ice cream now and everybody will be happy. Do you think there's a clear answer here?"

"Let's go make our guests happy," I said. I moved to gather the bowls onto one of the carrying trays we'd set out.

Papi patted my back and started filling his own tray with bowls. "Good choice. The key is to make your best move in the moment."

Everyone agreed that this was the most spectacular bowl of ice cream they'd ever had.

But I wouldn't know. I was eating beef jerky. Diabetes sucks.

There they sat around the dining room table, shoveling gobs of sundae goodness into their mouths like they'd never tasted food before, too busy eating like No-Face from *Spirited Away* to carry on a civilized conversation. Gabi, who was sitting across the table from me, had already sucked hers down and was now working on Dad: The Final Frontier's.

Dad: The Final Frontier hadn't eaten even a spoonful. She sat at the table holding a sparkler in each hand, looking at

Gabi like nothing made her happier in the world than watching her daughter hork down dessert while she waved fireworks in the air.

"Bonita," I said. She snapped her head around and smiled at me. Well, it was more like she lifted her upper lip like a curtain and showed me her top teeth. "Don't you like ice cream?"

"I can't eat it," she said, without complaining. I recognized the tone. It's the same one I use whenever I talk about diabetes.

"Oh. Are you lactose intolerant?"

I had learned about lactose intolerance over the summer, and now I was kind of eager to meet someone who was.

I noticed that Bonita was still smiling at me. Like, her face had never stopped smiling. Never moved—until it suddenly did. Suddenly she was looking at the ceiling and touching a finger to her chin. "What an interesting question, Sal. Hm. I suppose I am. I suppose I cannot tolerate lactose at all! Ha-ha-ha!"

Her weird laugh creeped me out. But even weirder, everyone else at the table laughed, too. I was the only one not in on the joke. I hated that feeling.

"What's so funny?" I asked.

"Sorry, Sal," said Bonita. "It's just that I'm a robot, and therefore can't eat ice cream. Or any food, for that matter."

I stopped chewing down on jerky. "Ha-ha. Yeah, whatever."

"No, really," said Gabi. "Dad's a Robot American."

"That's not accurate," said Bonita. "I'm not currently an American citizen, though I hope to be one day."

"That's only because we're behind the times," Gabi said between spoonfuls of sundae. "Robots can get citizenship in Saudi Arabia."

"Several other countries, too," added Papi. He was smiling at me but watching me carefully, too. Wondering how I was going to react. "South Korea started giving class-nine AIs full citizenship last year."

"And France did just last month," added one of Papi's physicist flunkies at the other end of the table. But nobody had asked him.

"You all are full of it," I said. And I tore off a chunk of dried cow meat, chomping on it defiantly.

Bonita got up from her seat, wobble-walked around Papi (who was at the head of the table), and stood next to me. "I don't have a heartbeat," she said, smiling. She stuck out her wrist. "There's no pulse. Try to find one."

I most certainly did not want to take her pulse. "So? People with artificial hearts don't have heartbeats. Or maybe you have a prosthetic hand. I grew up in hospitals, Bonita. You can't fool me that easy."

"My skin is artificial. All over. Touch it."

"Maybe you needed skin grafts. Were you in a fire?"

"She wasn't in a fire, Sal!" yelled Gabi. "She. Is. A. Robot!"

"Bonita, if you're a robot, prove it. Take off your head and throw it across the room."

Bonita looked at me horrified. "I can't do that. That would kill me."

I folded my arms. "Exactly."

"Part of the requirement for class-nine sentience is that the AI has to be mortal," said one of the computer nerds at the other end of the table. But nobody had asked her.

Bonita   made   the   exact   same   look-at-the-ceiling,

finger-on-her-chin expression she'd made before. "Okay. Let's try this, Sal. I can't move my tongue. It's just a piece of painted silicon at the bottom of my mouth. I don't use my tongue and lips to form words. See how my jaw moves, but the lips don't? Surely that must prove it."

"I've met, like, six people with artificial voice boxes. They just use a speaker in their throats to talk."

"He's got you there, Bonita," said Papi. "Maybe you are human after all."

That got a big reaction around the table. Gabi stopped pigging out on ice cream long enough to clap. "She is human! She's a human being robot!"

"You're not helping, Dr. Vidón," Bonita replied. Pretty snappily, too, for a robot.

"Yeah," I pressed, "and if you're a robot, why did Papi bring you a bowl of ice cream? He would have known you couldn't eat it."

"I have no idea. That *was* strange. Why did you bring me ice cream, Dr. Vidón?"

Papi tented his hands. "By accident. I just did a quick count in my head: sixteen people in the room, so I told Sal to put out sixteen bowls of ice cream."

"He did," I agreed slowly. "I subtracted one for myself, because I knew I shouldn't have any. Papi forgets I am diabetic all the time."

"And I forgot you weren't human, Bonita. I think of you as just another person. I'd give you ice cream like everyone else if I could."

"That is so sweet!" said Gabi. "Sal, I love your dad!"

"That is very sweet indeed," said Bonita. She wobbled over to Papi and stuck out her hand. "Thank you for that compliment, Dr. Vidón."

Papi surprised me with the gentleness and respect he used to shake Bonita's hand. "Anytime, my friend."

I slow-clapped. "Very touching. But you aren't fooling me. I am a magician. I know all about long cons. There is no way you are a robot. You are *way* too human."

"Sal, stop being so thick-headed," said Gabi. "My dad is a robot!"

"How can a robot be a dad? You all just admitted Bonita can't even be an American."

Papi shrugged like he was saying, *Good point.*

"I know how I can prove it," said Bonita, walking up to me. "Sal, look at—"

But she was interrupted by someone's cell going off.

"Pardon me a moment," said Bonita to me. "I've received a text. It's marked urgent. Do you mind if I read it?"

"No," I said.

She didn't take out a phone or look at a watch or anything. She just kind of looked a little higher in the air, and her eyes moved like she was reading. A second later, her face snapped into a new expression: horror and sadness.

"Oh no," she said. She was right; her lips didn't move when she spoke. "Gabi. Quickly, get your things. We have to leave immediately for the hospital."

"The hospital?!" said Gabi. She dropped her spoon in the bowl and hopped out of her chair. "Iggy?"

And this is the moment when I believed that Bonita was

a robot for real. She started crying. Her tears looked totally human; whoever had made her had done a perfect job on her tear ducts. But she didn't look ashamed, or try to hide her grief, or be brave in front of everybody. She just honestly let everyone know that she was scared and shaken. I've never met a human who could be as truthful as she looked just then.

"Yes," said Bonita. "It's Iggy. He's taken a turn for the worse. We have to go."

28

NO ONE SAID much of anything as Gabi and her dad-droid gathered their things. They moved quickly, waved good-bye (neither of them could really speak), and walked outside. Soon, a car picked them up, and they were gone.

None of the rest of Papi's work buddies felt like having any more ice cream. They left soon after. Papi and I found ourselves sitting alone in the dining room with a lot of dirty ice cream bowls and a lot of burned-out sparklers.

Papi, feeling as miserable as I did, assessed the table of dirty bowls. "Let's wash these later."

"Excellent idea," I agreed.

We got up and walked into the disaster area that the living room had become. The big black computer had generated a lot of heat by then, making the living room, like, ten degrees hotter than the rest of the house.

"It's not so bad, is it?"

I rubbed my forehead. "Dude. American Stepmom's gonna wedgie you *in two*." I pictured in my mind a brand-new kind of wedgie: the Reverse Guillotine. I'd have to tell Adam Hoag about it tomorrow. Maybe he'd interview me for his documentary!

I swear I saw Papi's butt cheeks clench. "You're right. Better break out the big guns for this one."

And that's what we did. We picked American Stepmom up from work—"Surprise! We're taking you out to dinner! Isn't that nice?"—and ate at Chocolatón, a restaurant where basically everything was—you guessed it—chocolate. It was American Stepmom's favorite place to eat in the entire world. She had chicken mole with chocolate bacon and chocolate jalapeño poppers on the side, and a chocolate malt to drink. I almost went into diabetic shock just watching her eat.

After a glucose check and a little math, I had egg-white crepes with pepperoni and tomato sauce. Papi had a glass of water. He was still full from the ice cream social.

We had fun. We joked, we laughed, we heard about all the gross things elementary school kids do in a principal's office and we gagged. Well, I gagged. Elementary school kids are gross.

And then, right when American Stepmom's dessert came—a personal fountain of melted chocolate with strawberries and marshmallows to dip into it—Papi told her that they had installed the remembranation machine in the living room.

"You got it up and running already?" asked American Stepmom, around a mouthful of marshmallows. "That was fast!"

"Yes," said Papi, scared to say the next sentence. "But we still have a little . . . um . . . cleanup to do."

American Stepmom stopped chewing. She knew that guilty tone of voice.

She side-eyed him so hard, I'm surprised he didn't fly out of his chair. "How much cleanup?"

"You're gonna wedgie him in two," I said.

American Stepmom did not, in fact, cut Papi in half with his underwear. I think he might have preferred that.

When we arrived home and stepped inside, she swallowed her anger down one gulp at a time. When she finally did speak, she expressed, very slowly, and with a lot of "Phew, babies!" thrown in, that she was "very disappointed" that Papi would leave "the shared space of the living room" in "such a state of disrepair" that "it was unusable by anybody but him and his coworkers."

"We have this huge house," she said, "and we're not even using half of it. Why'd you put the machine here?"

"It's the only place it would fit," Papi replied, looking like a dog that had been caught drinking out of the toilet. "I wanted to install it on the second floor, but we couldn't get that monster through the hallway."

"I see," sniffed American Stepmom. "So we can't entertain in the living room, we can't watch TV or play games in the living room, we can't read or take a nap in the living room, because you decided our living room isn't a living room anymore, it's a transdimensional remembranation room, and there isn't any room for living anymore."

"Now, Lucy, I didn't think—"

"You can say that again."

Ouch.

"Sal," Papi said to me, "would you excuse your mother and me?"

"Please don't fight," I said. I didn't mean for it to come out so squeaky.

American Stepmom softened her posture. She smiled at me. "Hey, kiddo. Your papi and I love each other very much. We can disagree without being cruel or unreasonable."

"I think we both agree I messed up," said Papi, hugging American Stepmom from behind. She squeezed his big, shaggy arm. Eyes closed, she let her head sink into his bicep as he apologized. "I'm sorry, mi vida. I was in such a hurry to install the machine and stop—"

He interrupted himself. But I knew the end of that sentence: *stop Sal from bringing Mami Muerta back ever again.*

"It's getting late," said American Stepmom, "and we have school and work tomorrow. Maybe it's best if we all got ready for bed."

"Yes," said Papi. "Let's all get ready for bed."

But they didn't move. They stood there, Papi hugging American Stepmom, watching me until I shut the door to the bathroom.

"Don't fight!" I yelled from behind the bathroom door. "I'll be listening!"

My alarm went off at 1:00 a.m. I checked my fasting glucose— yep, still diabetic—then rubbed the dreams out of my eyes and cat-walked to the living room.

The remembranation machine was so black it was like a hole in the world. It was a blackness that ate space. It took up half the living room with nothingness.

Well, until you got to its front, where its screen shone with blue-gray light. It displayed a 3-D blueprint of the first floor of the Coral Castle, like Google Earth, except it was my house. A VR headset hung on a hook. A touch pad and keyboard were just sitting there, dying to be used.

I didn't know how to operate the remembranation machine, but what I did know is that adults used it all day long. And adults suck at computers. A kid like me could probably work it better than they could.

I tried the touch pad, and, yep, in three seconds I figured out how to pan through the house and rotate the camera and basically see the Coral Castle from any angle. Candy from a baby.

At the bottom of the monitor, the graphical user interface read **CALAMITRON COUNT: 679**. I guessed that the silver dots of light, hovering all over the monitor like fairies in the forest, were calamitrons.

I used the machine to scan the first floor. There were a few random drops sprinkled throughout the living room, the kitchen, and the dining room—little puddles where several drops clustered together. But most of the drops were pooled into human-size silhouettes, silvery shadows in the shape of a woman. A woman exactly the shape of my latest Mami Muerta.

In all, there were five silver shadows in the Coral Castle, all in different poses. There was the silver shadow of Mami Muerta in the kitchen, in front of the stove. She looked like she might be stirring a pot there, but no utensils were drawn in silver dots, since the machine only detected calamitrons. A river of particles whooshed over to the next Mami Muerta, who appeared to be walking into the dining room with her hand on someone's shoulder. That must have been when she and I had led Papi and American Stepmom to dinner. The last three shadows, all connected by gleaming, sparkling currents of calamitrons, were in the dining room. There she was, serving Papi's plate—you couldn't see the plate or Papi, but I remembered her posture exactly. There she was, dancing with American Stepmom, her leg kicked up. And the last one was blurry, but I think she was running with her hands outstretched toward the place where I'd been standing when I passed out. That must have been the last thing she was doing before she disappeared. Papi had said she was trying to catch me when I started to faint. There was the evidence.

This Mami, she loved me. We'd gotten along so well, all afternoon. And she had danced with American Stepmom! As I stared at this ghostly afterimage of her, I couldn't help but think that maybe she was the one, the perfect mami to join my family and make all my dreams come true.

Except she'd brought 679 calamitrons with her.

I felt sweat rising out of my skin in tiny beads. How many calamitrons were too many? Was it five million? Five thousand? *Five?*

Okay, Sal, I thought. *Take it easy. Relax.*

No wait! Don't relax! That's how you started all this trouble in the first place!

So I tensed up instead.

I hadn't destroyed the universe yet. So maybe a few calamitrons were okay. I mean, what's a few calamitrons among friends, right?

Wrong. It wasn't smart and it wasn't brave to keep calamitrons around. Mami was already gone; there was no point in keeping the calamitrons she'd left behind. The answer here was clear: Get rid of them.

But part of me didn't want to. I liked the idea that some of Mami's particles were still floating around in our house. She wasn't all the way gone. I never wanted Mami to be all the way gone. The opposite—I wanted her all the way back.

And anyway, could I actually get rid of them? Papi had said that he thought I could send anything from another universe back, and that would begin the healing process for holes. But I'd already returned Mami, the same way I'd sent back Yasmany's chicken, and her calamitrons remained. Maybe they needed a little help going back to where they belonged. To reattach a finger, you need a surgeon. Maybe I needed to be the calamitron surgeon.

OR! We had the remembranation machine! I could fix this *right now*.

I buried my love of Mami deep inside so I could think clearly again. My fingers started flying over the remembranation machine's keyboard, like the blurry hands of a hacker character in the movies. In no time I found the command to **INITIATE GENERAL CALAMITRON PURGE**. It asked me **ARE YOU SURE YOU WANT TO PURGE ALL CALAMITRONS IN RANGE? (RANGE = 5KM FROM EPICENTER)**

In smaller letters beneath that question was the message **(YEAH, YOU PROBABLY DO.)**

So I moved the cursor to the button that said **YES** and—

"I wouldn't do that if I were you," said American Stepmom from behind me.

I jumped so high I fist-bumped Uranus before I crashed

back to Earth and landed flat on my back in my living room.

American Stepmom pretended to be all worried about me, but she couldn't help but laugh. And hey, I would've laughed if I was her.

She reached out a hand to help me up. "I appreciate you wanting to make amends for your actions, Sal. You're worried that you've inadvertently done something bad by bringing back your mami, and you want to undo the damage."

"I just wanted to see how it worked," I said, taking her hand.

She smiled, half-laughing, half-sad. "This is your Papi's equipment. It's his experiment. He gets to decide when and how to run it."

"Okay, I get it. No more touchie the machine," I said when I was back on my feet. "I'll make it up to him. And you."

Surprise changed her face. "Oh yeah? How?"

I gestured all around us. "I can help clean up this mess. You know Papi will take a hundred years to get around to it."

She thought about it for a second, then stuck out her hand. "Deal."

We shook.

American Stepmom put a hand on my shoulder. "You know what? I could use a cup of cocoa. Want to join me?"

I looked at her with one eye. "Didn't you, like, eat four thousand pounds of chocolate for dinner?"

She shooed my words away with all her fingers. "That was then, kid. You in or you out?"

Sugar-free cocoa is pretty much the best thing to drink that has "sugar-free" in its name. No marshmallows, no whipped cream, and made with water instead of milk: Altogether, that sounds like *three strikes, yer out.* But at least it's chocolatey enough to cover the taste of whatever weird chemicals they use instead of sugar to sweeten it. And American Stepmom put a cinnamon stick in it, and a little squirt of pure vanilla, and 100 percent cocoa dust (which is actually a little bitter, but in a good way), and a soft peppermint candy that was also sugar-free, stuck on the end of a cocktail sword.

It was the greatest cup of cocoa in the world. She knows how much I love cocktail swords. She knows pretty much everything about me.

American Stepmom had been the vice principal in my elementary school back in Connecticut. I liked her when I first met her. She was nice, easy to talk to, really funny. Her husband had died a few years ago, so we could relate to each other. I thought Papi might like her, too. And Papi was so sad. So sad.

That's why I kept getting myself sent to the vice principal's office. I mean, not to brag, but I'm pretty sure no one in the history of the world has ever tricked their fifth-grade teacher into sitting on a whoopee cushion more often than I did. Never got detention for it, either. See, my vice principal thought I might be acting out because I was depressed over the loss of my mami.

So Papi had to keep coming into school to talk with my vice principal and me. They found reasons to keep talking even after I stopped playing pranks on my teacher. And then one day, the summer I graduated from elementary school, my former vice principal made breakfast for Papi and me—well, she poured cereal, but she also whipped me up some cocoa with a peppermint candy on a cocktail sword—and asked if I thought it would be okay if she joined my family, because she loved Papi and she loved me, and, no, she would never try to replace my mami, but maybe, if I could find room enough in my heart, she could be my American stepmom?

"American Stepmom," I'd repeated, taking the sword out of my hot chocolate and popping the peppermint in my mouth. "I like the sound of that."

"You've had a tough couple of days, haven't you," said American Stepmom, studying her cocoa as if she could read the future in it.

I made the ¯_(ツ)_/¯ face. "You could say that."

She put her mug down hard on the counter, stomped over to me, and hugged me from behind like I'd just come back from the war. "You're my hero, you know that?"

I was struggling to keep my cocoa from spilling as she rag-dolled me around. "What? Why? All I do is cause trouble."

She sucked in breath like I'd cursed in front of her. Then she came around to face me, bent over so we were eye-to-eye, and held my shoulders. "Sal Vidón, listen to me. You've suffered so much, and you're so brave, and so very clever. You are a magnificent young man. You hear me? You're just trying to figure things out. All of us are. Everyone you know is trying to figure out how life works. But I'll tell you a secret, Sal. No one knows. I mean, if I could do what you do, and I thought there was even a chance I could bring my mama back, don't you think I would have done exactly the same things you have?"

The tears in her eyes made them seem bigger. And look,

I'm thirteen. The Teenager Code for Acting Cool required me to feel embarrassed by what American Stepmom had said. But I didn't. It was just us in the kitchen, and she was such a good mom, and I'd have to be an idiot not to know it. So, as honestly as I could, I said to her, "I know you wouldn't have. Because you always know the right thing to say and the right thing to do. At least Papi messes up sometimes. But you? You're perfect."

She ducked her head and laughed. When she looked up again, she wasn't crying anymore. "Are you *kidding* me? I mess up fifty times a minute, and that's on a good day. But what you learn as you grow up is that everybody needs help. The sooner you ask the people you love to lend you a hand, the easier life becomes. Really, that's it; that's the secret. Trust in the people who love you. We can all figure it out together."

"Yeah?"

"Yeah. Now, is there anything you want to talk about?" And I could see in her eyes that she was steeling herself for it. She wanted to be a good mom to me, so if I wanted to talk about my dead mami yet again, she'd be there for it, even though every time we did, she got a little weepy and sneezy, like I just pulled a hair out of her nose.

But I surprised even myself when I asked, "What's the best way I can help Iggy?"

29

"WHO'S IGGY?" ASKED American Stepmom.

Oh, right. There was no way she could have known about him. So that took a while to explain. I basically had to catch American Stepmom up on the last two days of my life (minus the stuff she already knew, and the stuff she didn't need to know).

Once I'd finished, I thought we'd get right into brainstorming ideas to help Iggy. Instead, she said, "So. Gabi Reál."

And her face was all fox meets chicken.

"Yeah. So?" I answered, shaking the last dregs of cocoa into my mouth.

"She sounds like an interesting person." Oh, if eyebrows could talk.

All right. Let's go. "She is an interesting person, Mother."

"The sort of person you might want to, oh, I don't know, get to know better?"

I made wide eyes at her. "Oh yes, Mother. Why, she's the fastest friend I've ever made, Mother."

"Oh. That's great," she said, in that way that meant *That's not quite what I meant.* "Friends are great. Aren't friends great?"

"Friendship is magic," I agreed.

"And sometimes, you know," she continued, fishing for chocolate bits in the bottom of her mug with her fingernail, "the right friend can become even more than a friend." Her eyes flipped to me.

Time for gg. "Are you implying that you want Gabi Reál to be my girlfriend? Because I don't think I'm ready for dating. What with all the universe breaking and all, I've got a lot on my plate."

She looked shocked and hurt (she was neither, the big faker). "I'm not implying anything," she said, scrambling. "You don't want romance, you don't have to have romance. You get to be whatever gender you want and love whoever you want. Or just have lots of friends—whatever! It's up to you. You can always adopt to give me the grandkids I require."

"We were talking about Iggy?"

"Oh yeah, Iggy." She took our mugs to the sink and rinsed them. "Well, the best thing you can do is support the family. Why don't you text Gabi and ask her?" She looked over her shoulder at me. "Oh, unless you don't have her number."

"No, I have it," I said, taking out my phone.

"Has her phone number," she said, placing the mugs in the dishwasher and definitely not sneaking looks at me.

"Stop trolling. What should I say?"

"Just tell her you're really sorry about her brother, and you want to help. And, oh," she said, walking up to me, "this is serious: Make sure she knows you mean it as a friend. Girls have to be careful, you know."

"Trust me, Gabi can take care of herself," I said, and pressed send.

"Good job," said American Stepmom, leaning against the same piece of counter I·was. "Now, what do you say we get some sleep? School tomorrow, for both of us."

"Shouldn't we wait to see if she writes back?"

American Stepmom patted my shoulder. "Darling, it's really late. I'm sure Gabi Reál has been asleep for the past—"

My text tone is the sound in *Poocha Lucha Libre* when you dominate your opponent so bad you become their master and can make them do dog tricks. "Yesss, master!" my phone said with a slobbering voice.

I showed my screen to American Stepmom. "Told you," I said.

"Yesss, master!" my phone said again.

And again.

And then fifty-six more times.

American Stepmom watched, completely hypnotized, as Gabi machine-gunned text after text at us. My arm started shaking from holding up my phone up to her for so long.

When I was pretty sure it was over—oh, wait, no, there went sixty—when I was pretty sure it was over, I asked American Stepmom, "So, what did Gabi say?"

She blinked like she'd just learned how. "Phew, baby. It's a long story."

Iggy, Gabi had texted, had "suffered an episode" that "left the Reál clan in a state of poignant despair" all night long. Only Gabi's mom "could enjoy the privilege of keeping vigil at the side of the incubator" this late after visiting hours, which was "one of the myriad indignities I and my fathers are forced to endure." They "held their collective breath" every time a doctor or nurse entered the room, only to be told that "Ignacio's condition had neither improved nor deteriorated since the initial incident."

My heart is rent in two, like an abandoned valentine, read text 64. Four more texts had come in while I read them. Text 65 was the only emoji she'd used during her entire text storm: a broken heart.

"Your girlfriend is quite the writer," said American Stepmom. She could see how the news about Ignacio was hitting me, and she was trying to lighten the mood.

I turned and smiled at her: no teeth, stretched lips, and shaking my head. "Dude, I play online. Can't tilt me."

"Seriously, though, Sal," she said, not too seriously, but actually completely seriously, "if you want, I'll drive you over to the hospital right now. Oh, no—you'll have to wait for visiting hours."

"No, I don't. The Reáls are practically running that hospital. They throw parties all night long in the waiting room. I'm sure I could visit them now. I could put on a magic show for them. Make them feel better."

She hadn't been expecting that answer. But American Stepmom wasn't someone who backtracked once she offered you something. "Well, okay. Ask Gabi what she thinks."

But Gabi stiff-upper-lipped me.

What a generous, selfless offer, kind Sal! she texted back. **You are a true, if still relatively new, friend. I would gladly accept the solace of your company in this dark hour if I weren't in need of**

an even bigger favor from you. It seems I will be unable to attend school today. Therefore, I need you to collect notes from all the classes I will miss. Momentarily, I will send you an annotated list of the students whose notes you must copy for me. Some of them are more thorough than others, and all leave a great deal to be desired, alas. But I must make do. If you will kindly deliver the notes and homework assignments to me after school today, you will be doing me the greatest favor possible.

Over the next several minutes, Gabi texted me psychology reports of all the people she wanted mè to get notes from.

Gladis Machado, according to Gabi, responded best to bribery—a pack of my Skittles would work perfectly on her.

Gladis Machado. The ojo turco girl. Great.

I didn't know the second person Gabi wanted notes from. Her name was Teresita Tómas, and, according to Gabi, she needed to be strong-armed a little. If, for example, I implied that she might lose her gossip column in the *Rotten Egg*, her notes for math and the History of Technology would be, and I quote, "impeccable."

Gabi had three separate classes with Aventura Rios, and apparently she was the smartest note taker of the bunch, but she had handwriting "like a San Francisco earthquake." Aventura, Gabi decided, would "simply have to write more neatly for me." If she didn't, I was asked to tell her that Gabi might put off running the "Valedictory Notes" article she was planning to write about her. Aventura really wanted that article; she was going to use it to bolster her application to a costume-making summer program in Italy. **She'll play ball**, Gabi ended, as sweetly as a mob boss.

And, oh, if I would "be so kind" as to go over the lesson in our Intermediate Theater Workshop with Gabi in the hospital that evening, she would be "ever so grateful."

"Phew, baby!" said American Stepmom, reading over my shoulder again. "That kid's a shark. Are you sure you want her as your girlfriend?"

I rolled my eyes at her. "Get good, Mom," I said, and went to bed.

30

SOMETIMES, THERE'S NOTHING more expressive than Spanish. Take "madrugada," the word for "so stupid early it's still dark outside." It's one of those words that seem to mean more than a dictionary can tell you. It sounds like the word Merlin would use to turn his enemy's teeth into worms.

The madrugada is my time. It's when I feel the most magical. And I was going to need all the magic I could find to succeed in today's mission: close the hole in Yasmany's locker. If I could.

So when my alarm went off at stupid-early o'clock, even though I hadn't gotten much sleep the last two days, I felt full of power and potential. I showered, did all the pokey-bleedy-beep-you're-fine stuff, microwaved breakfast, mathed out the rest of my food for the day, loaded my pockets with tricks, and put on a very special ball cap (see below).

On the way out the door, I grabbed one more little item: the entropy sweeper Papi had used to scan me when I was in the hospital.

I wouldn't have taken the device if it hadn't begged me.

I didn't even see it at first. I just heard it moaning "Woe is I. Woe is I!" over and over.

I had the front door open already, but I closed it and followed the sound of the sweeper's wailing. I found it behind the couch and under a blanket.

I pulled it out, leaned it against the wall, and peeked under the blanket. "You okay there, entropy-sweeper dude?"

"No, I am not okay!" it snapped. "What part of 'Woe is I!' was unclear to you?"

"Well, now that you mention it, isn't it supposed to be 'Woe is me'?"

It laughed triumphantly. "No! The correct grammar is 'Woe is I'! Shakespeare got it wrong in that little speech of his. Therefore, I am smarter than Shakespeare."

"Riiight," I said, dropping the blanket. "Well, good luck with that."

"No! Wait! Don't leave!"

Reluctantly, I turned back around. "Dude, I have to get to school."

"Yes, but I'm going to be so lonely! Now that your papi has his stupid *remembranation machine*, he doesn't need his loyal old entropy sweeper anymore. He threw me behind a couch! He's gonna recycle me, kid! Cut me up for spare parts! You've got to save me!"

I walked back over to it and removed the blanket. "Papi wouldn't do that. You're lying." And then, doubting myself, I asked, "Can a class-eight artificial intelligence lie?"

"Oh yeah, sure. I lie all the time. I'm lying right now."

My brain short-circuited a little. "But if you're lying about lying . . . But if you're telling the truth about lying . . ."

"I just blew your mind, didn't I, kid? Bwa-ha-ha!"

This thing was trouble. I should have just walked away. But the fact was, it could really help me with my plan. And if Papi had left it under a blanket behind the couch, he probably wouldn't be using it anytime soon.

So I grabbed the weed whacker from the garage, stuck it behind the couch, put the blanket over it, and took off for school with the number one mobile calamitron detector in the world before the parents' bedroom door had even cracked open.

Out on the sidewalk, I asked the entropy sweeper, "Do you want me to turn you off until we get to school?"

"I treat the on/off switch as more of a suggestion," it said.

That's when I noticed that the switch was already set to OFF.

Yeah. I yanked the battery out of the handle then and there, and Mr. Class-Eight AI went to sleep for a while.

I had to solve three problems to pull off this mission:

1. Get inside Culeco
2. Beat the cameras, so I didn't get recorded
3. Distract Mr. Milagros

If the doors were locked, I'd have to find another way to get in. But I was sure I could. I am the Master Magician, Salvador Vidón!

The real trick was getting inside undetected. The cameras looking down from the ceiling would nail me if I wasn't prepared.

Of course I had a plan to beat them, which in this case came in the form of the single ugliest hat in the multiverse. It was made of reflective rainbow material, and on the front it said WHAT'S THE BRIGHT IDEA? That's because it was also studded all over with like fifty LED lights.

The moment I saw it in the bargain bin in a dollar store—and, dude, if you make it into the bargain bin in a dollar store, you know nobody wants you—I knew I had to have it. (You should've seen the look American Stepmom gave me when I asked for an advance on my allowance so I could buy such a hideous thing.) Because, see, all those LEDs bouncing off that reflective rainbow material would blind a surveillance camera. The light would overwhelm the lens, and all people would be able to see on the video would be this huge glowing shape moving around.

I turned on my hat—I think I was legit brighter than the peeking sun in that moment—and then tried the front door to Culeco. It was unlocked.

I opened the door and walked in. Two problems solved, one to go.

Of course, Mr. Milagros was going to be the hardest problem of all. But, once again, I had a plan.

I, disguised in rainbow light, burglar-stepped over to the administration office, which was close to the front doors. It also wasn't locked. Culeco seemed to be a weirdly trusting school.

Once inside, I tiptoed over to the office manager's desk. Judging from it, Mr. Zacto was more OCD than I was. Both his inbox and outbox trays had zero papers in them. He had a calendar almost as big as the desktop, and he had jotted notes on it in a beautiful cursive script, like a Founding Father's handwriting. The fountain pen he used, complete with white plume, stood proudly in the back right corner of the desk.

On the front right corner, Mr. Zacto had squared his phone so that it looked like it had been custom made to fit in that spot. The phone was why I was there.

I had to be careful not to move a thing on the desk. Dude would know. I took a clown-size hanky out of my pocket, held it with my thumb and finger, and used it to pick up the receiver. There was still plenty of clown hanky left to cover the part you speak into, which I did, and still more clown hanky I could use to press the appropriate button on the phone's speed dial.

I could see from the carefully labeled phone that the top button was for reaching Mr. Milagros. This guy had the janitor in the number one speed-dial spot. Mr. Zacto? Yeah, definitely a clean freak.

The phone rang just once before he picked up. "¿Bueno?" he greeted.

I *knew* he would be at school already! My favorite custodian back in Connecticut was the same way. He basically lived at school, saw everything, knew everyone. Nicest guy you could ever meet, too, just like Mr. Milagros. They were two of a kind.

It's harder to play tricks on people you like if you can never let them in on the joke. You have to stick to tricks that definitely won't hurt them or make them feel bad. So, in terms of classic Sal Vidón pranks, this one would be pretty mild. But all that mattered was that it worked.

Time to find out if it would. "Mr. Milagros," I said.

"Buenos días, jefa. Llegó tempranito esta mañana. ¿Mucho trabajo?"

And see, he said all that because he thought I was Principal Torres.

I'm pretty good at voices, but it also helped that I was doing this over the phone, and that the only person Mr. Milagros would be expecting to hear from this early, calling from the office, would be Principal Torres. Just like emotions change your eyesight, people hear what they expect to hear.

"Mr. Milagros," I repeated, "have you had a chance to look at the all-gender bathrooms on the first floor this morning?" I delivered the line with the same tone Principal Torres used on students in her office—the tone that meant *I already know you're guilty, but I want to see if you're going to lie to my face.*

I literally heard Mr. Milagros sit up straight. "No, jefa."

I exhaled into the phone like a bull about to charge. "Well, then, perhaps before anyone else has occasion to visit them, you could bring the very cleanest mop in the school, and a very large bucket filled to the *brim* with powerful chemicals, and you could make sure they are just a little bit cleaner than they are right now? What do you think?"

There were a few seconds of silence. This was a man who took pride in his work. Filth was the enemy, and he would defeat it no matter what. I could almost hear him powering up. I could almost hear his eyes narrowing, his warrior's smile spreading over his face.

"Para servirle," he said, two octaves down from his normal voice. And then he hung up.

I hadn't lied to Mr. Milagros. I had just asked him if he'd check the bathrooms, and if he thought it'd be a good idea to make them a little cleaner. A *very* mild prank. Not even a prank, really. More of a recommendation.

It'd take him a few minutes to prepare his bucket, and if I knew the man, he'd spend every last second up until the first bell scrubbing the first-floor bathrooms. They'd be gleaming by the time he was done. And in the meantime, I could experiment on Yasmany's locker without getting caught. Everybody wins.

But I had to move quickly. I left everything exactly the way I'd found it on Mr. Zacto's desk, then, careful not to bang the entropy sweeper against anything, I quietly lunge-walked out of administration and up two flights of stairs. It wasn't a minute before I was face-to-face once again with Yasmany's locker.

I set the alarm on my smartwatch to go off twenty minutes before school started. Then I took a breath, exhaled an "okay," popped in the sweeper's battery pack, and turned it on.

"I'm alive!" it said.

I looked around for anyone who might have heard it blurting. No one. But still.

"Shhh!" I said.

"Silent mode activated," the entropy sweeper said. It sounded disappointed.

"I said, 'shhh!'"

"I know. And I was acknowledging that I had heard you and was complying with your request."

I let go of one of the handlebars to wipe my own forehead. "You can't answer me and be silent at the same time, you stupid machine!"

"But if I don't answer, that could mean I hadn't understood your command and was not ready to comply. The only way you could know for sure that I was ready to start being quiet is if I *told* you I was going to—"

I pulled the battery pack. Why did everything need a brain these days?

I counted to five, then pushed the batteries back into the slot in the handle.

No whining AI, which was good. But no noises at all. No lights. No readout on the handlebars. Had I broken it or something?

"Oh no," I said, and gave the sweeper a little shake. "Why aren't you working?"

The lights came on. "Oh, I'm working," said the AI, loud and triumphant. "But you couldn't tell, could you? Because I wasn't responding. See? Perhaps now, rude human, you understand my point!"

I didn't have time to fight with an AI. More importantly, I needed it to be my friend so it wouldn't narc me out to Papi once I returned it. Time to change tactics. "Entropy sweeper, I need your help. You are my only hope."

"I am here to serve!" the sweeper said happily. It started cycling through colors with joy.

I started talking fast, hoping it wouldn't interrupt me anymore. "I need to conduct a silent scan of this hallway. What's the best way for us to do that?"

"Hm," said the AI. "I think"—and now, thank everything, it was whispering—"perhaps we should communicate through color?"

"That sounds smart!" I said encouragingly.

Oh, the AI liked that. It started whispering a mile a minute. "Great! So, red means 'no,' green means 'yes,' yellow means 'maybe,' blue means 'I'm still working on it,' orange means 'thank you,' indigo means 'no thank you,' chartreuse means 'Are you insane? Pedro Martinez is the greatest pitcher ever. From 1999 to 2003, he outperformed—'"

"Perfect," I whisper-rupted. Man, this was the most opinionated entropy sweeper I'd ever met! "When can we start?"

"Right away!" said the AI. And then, without another word, it turned blue all along its edges. It was working on it. Finally.

I raised the entropy sweeper so its propellers could get a good, long taste of Yasmany's locker. After several seconds, I whispered, "Any calamitrons?"

The machine turned even bluer all over. It was thinking. Blue, it pulsed. Blue. Blue. Blue.

Then green.

Stay calm, Sal. "How many?" I asked it.

"Oh no!" the sweeper burst out. "We forgot to assign numbers to any colors. Okay, teal is 'one,' puce is 'two,' ochre is 'three,' magenta is 'four,' gamboge is—"

"Or maybe," I intruded, "you could just display the number on the screen on your handlebars?"

"Oh yes!" the AI said happily. "Good idea. You're all right, human."

"Thanks, entropy sweeper."

It cycled through colors like a chameleon in love and displayed the number of calamitrons in the hallway: thirty-seven.

"Thirty-seven," I repeated to help me think. If I could somehow fit the remembranation monitor in this hallway, I would be able to see the calamitrons on its screen. But the entropy sweeper's screen could barely display emojis. I knew there were calamitrons here, but that's all. And knowing that much only made me feel scared and uneasy. It didn't really help anything.

"You okay, buddy?" asked the sweeper, using its lowest volume setting. "Your pulse is rising."

"Yeah," I answered. I tried to be nice about it. It wasn't the sweeper's fault that the hole I'd ripped in the fabric of the cosmos was leaking calamity into the universe; it was mine. "I just wish I could make the calamitrons disappear."

I stood holding the sweeper, not knowing what to do next. Well, for one thing, I had to figure out where I could hide it—it was way too big to carry around all day, and way too big for my locker. Maybe in the prop room? Mrs. Waked would let me, and people would think it was just another—

"Woah," said the entropy sweeper. I could literally hear it misspelling "whoa."

And now its screen was displaying an emoji with its mouth hanging open.

"What?" I asked.

"How'd you do that?"

"Do what?"

"Hang on," it said, turning blue. "Let me check something." It pulsed light and did whatever entropy sweepers do, its propellers spinning thoughtfully. "Yep, I was right," it said a few seconds later. Then a number appeared on its display.

Thirty-six.

"Huh. Are you saying one of the calamitrons went away?"

"Don't play coy with me, buster! I saw what you did there."

"Keep it down!" I said. I looked around for any sign of

Mr. Milagros, but I was still alone in the hallway. "I seriously don't know what you're talking about."

"Come off it!" the machine said, but at least at a low volume now. "You *ate* that calamitron!"

"What?!" I whatted. "No, I didn't."

"Well, okay, I guess since you stuck it up your nose, it isn't technically *eating*. I was being metaphoric."

"I am telling you," I said, getting harsher, if not louder, "I didn't eat, sniff, inhale, ingest, or do anything to any calamitron."

"Hey, I wouldn't have believed it, either, if I hadn't detected it with my own seventy-five distinct entropy sensors! You wished that you could get rid of the calamitrons, and the closest one in the hallway, like you had hypnotized it, drifted over to you, slowly, slowly, merrily, merrily, life is but a dream, and then, snort! You vacuumed it into your nose and out of this universe."

I stood there looking like that openmouthed emoji. It took ten seconds before I could even make sense of what the sweeper had said to me. Finally, I squeezed my brain like an orange to get a question out. "I snorted a calamitron?"

"Yep."

"And it's gone?"

"Yep."

"But where did it go?"

On the display the shrug emoji appeared. "You're the one who snarfed it. You tell me."

And of course, just then my alarm went off. Half hour to homeroom. I'd have to figure out if inhaling calamity was bad for your health later.

31

I BOOKED IT to the prop room. Mrs. Waked wasn't there, but I was sure she wouldn't mind if I stowed the entropy sweeper between, say, some poofy-skirt medieval costumes, which is exactly what I did. Then I headed downstairs for Culeco's courtyard.

Before school started, I needed to find all the girls Gabi wanted to take notes for her and deliver her messages to them, complete with bribes and/or veiled threats. As I made my rounds, I definitely saw some worried, Poultrygate!-inspired stolen glances. Whenever I caught someone's eye, I nodded at them, nice 'n' friendly, polite as a tipped cowboy hat. But for a few people, a nice 'n' friendly howdy-ho from a possible brujo is a reason to grab your bookbag and head to class early.

Great. And now I had to talk to Gladis.

Well, there she was, texting against a tree. Now or never.

She looked up from her phone and spotted me when I was twenty feet away. I waved weakly and, inside, braced for impact.

She waved back. Nicely. Like, one of those wiggle-finger waves. Her head dipped sideways as she smiled at me. And then, then—what the pants was happening?—she winked and waved me over.

Now I was even more scared. But I still walked up to her.

"Hola, Salvador Vidón," she said with a thicker Cuban accent than she'd had yesterday. She was smiling the way bank robbers do before a heist, all sly and excited. But then she became suddenly worried. "Oh, tha's you name, righ'?"

"Yeah," I said, my suspicion level rising fast. "We have a class together. Textile Arts?"

"Oh, we do? Here, too? Oh goo'. Maybe my whole eschedule will be the sa'e. Tha' woul' ma'e things heasy."

I had no idea what she was talking about. My face showed it, too.

"Oh, don' worry," she said. Then she stuck out her hand. "Me llamo Gladis. Gladis Machado."

"Um, I know?"

She laughed. She was having the time of her life. The more excited she got, the thicker her accent got. "No, Pipo. No' your Gladis. Ella está en el universo mío. And oh my Gah. She is *such* a san'weech. I' kinda gross' ou' tha' I' can even ha' sush a terrible personality."

"She's in my universe" this Gladis had said. The Gladis I knew had gone to another universe. Which could only mean . . . "Holy hot pants! You're the Gladis who knit the ojo turco scarf, aren't you?"

She tapped her nose.

I got as paranoid as a shoplifter pocketing hand grenades. I peered all around. No one seemed to be paying us much attention. But middle schoolers are experts at looking without looking.

I leaned in and whispered to Gladis, "What are you doing here? How did you get here?"

She fluttered her eyes at me, exactly the same way an evil fairy would, just before it stole your youth. "Why, you brough' me here, Sal." And when she saw the look of horror on my face, she added, "Well, no' *you* you, bu' *my* you. The you tha's in my universe? I was jus' texting you—I me' heem—to tell heem I an here, buena y sana y brinca la rana."

I just needed a little extra time to process her words. There were a million unbelievable things I wanted to ask her to explain to me.

But the one I couldn't believe the most was: "Your phone gets bars across universes?"

She nodded philosophically. "It pay' to buy the righ' plan, Pipo."

I shook my head clear. "But why are you here in the first place?"

She became even more excited. "Oh, fue mi eedea. I ask' Sal how he ma'e my escarf disappear, and he say I woul' not believe him, uh-un, and I say, 'Try me, Pipo!' An' thain he tell me, and I said '¡Qué mango!' and he said, 'You belief me?' and I said, '¡Quiero ir!' and he said, 'No way!' because you know how you get sometimes. But I was like, 'I wan' my escarf back, I' going!' And so he was like, 'Okay, I' eswitch you with the Gladis over there.' An' now I' here!"

I was noticing that, if I waited three seconds, her words

would kind of sink into my brain, like fish food sprinkled into a fishtank, and by the time they hit bottom, I understood what she had said. Well, as much as anybody can understand the multiverse. I was already used to the idea that there were a million billion different Sals out there, thanks to Papi. Here, I was feeling kind of "woah" and kind of competitive with that other Sal. He had switched two Gladises, from two different universes, just like that? *I* couldn't do that. Also, I probably wouldn't—not with what I knew about calamitrons now.

Except—this was just a feeling, but you know how I feel about feelings—I didn't think Gladis was leaking any calamitrons. Calamitrons make you feel like you're being watched by tiny sparkling eyeballs floating all around you: queasy and uneasy, like enemies are coming. I could feel them when I had cooked with Mami Muerta. I could feel them when I got near Yasmany's locker. But off this Gladis? Nothing.

Hmm. I'd have to check her with the entropy sweeper later.

When I finally replied to Gladis—she smiled and waited patiently; she was having a very good day—I asked, "And the other Gladis? How is she doing?"

She looked a little guilty and also very pleased with herself. "Well, she wa' acting li'e la última Coca-Cola en el desierto at first. Bu' then I yell a' her for beyee rude, an' she call' me a ghos' and casi se tenía que cambiar sus Pampers. Bu' maybe she better now. Le' me ask Sal."

Gladis took out her phone—people, it was clearly not from this universe!—and texted her Sal in perfect English. She even used punctuation. **Hey Sal, Sal wants to know how Gladis is doing.**

The reply, from someone named Sal in her message app who looked pretty much exactly like me (except my hair is better), came a few seconds later. **You tell me**

Very funny. The Gladis OVER THERE, you sandwich.

Yeah shes having like fifteen heart attacks

Gladis gave me an *oops-did-I-do-that?* giggle before she replied. **She going to be okay?**

That Sal didn't miss a beat. **Oh yeah definitely I think shes faking like six of them**

"She' fine," said Gladis, fooling not even herself.

Gladis and I checked her schedule online, even though I didn't think it would work. I mean, what were the chances that two Gladises from two different universes would have the same username and password?

Turns out, the chances are 100 percent.

She also had the exact same schedule in this universe as she had in her own. So she would happily take good notes and share them with Gabi—if I would get her mal de ojo scarf back from Principal Torres.

"Deal," I said. We shook on it.

Maybe if I were a better person—more like Gabi—I would have worried about all the chaos this Gladis could cause. I mean, I'd seen what my previous Mami Muertas had done. I knew Gladis had the potential to descend on Culeco like a cacanado. But to be honest, that would be interesting. I guess once you've broken the universe more than a half-dozen times, your tolerance for craziness goes way up.

And anyway, this Gladis seemed nice—way nicer than

my Gladis. Everything would be fine. "Ciao, pesca'o," she said, giving me another one of those wiggly-finger waves. I waved back.

One note taker down, two to go.

I found Teresita Tómas next. She panicked when I gently implied that the continued existence of her fashion column depended on the quality of her math and history notes. She quizzed me for five minutes about *exactly* what Gabi had said, and was she joking, and was she mad, and oh my God this was so unfair and, fine, she'd give Gabi her notes, but Gabi'd better hold up her end of the bargain.

I promised her she would. Just one more person to talk to.

Aventura Rios stood in the shade of palm trees with the cosplay contingent. There were a half-dozen kids wearing costumes that ranged from just begun to almost finished. Aventura was dressed up as a Latina Karin from Street Fighter, fake blond curls and everything. She and the other cosplayers stood around studying the stitching on their costumes and trading sewing tips.

When I told her Gabi would be absent today, she instantly jumped in with "Happy to share my notes with her." And before I could say anything else, she asked me, "Did Gabi tell you to browbeat me, the same way you manhandled Teresita?"

"You saw that?" I asked guiltily.

She laughed—"Oh, ho-ho-ho-ho!"—and shook her head. "Girlfriend needs to lighten up. She'll get her notes. But maybe I'll put them in code first or something."

I laughed. "Caesar cyphers are easy to code, and pretty easy to break, too," I offered. "It would be just enough to annoy her."

"Ooh, that sounds perfect! Will you be in detention again today? You can teach me."

We high-fived. The deal was done.

"You know," she added as I started to walk away, "any time you want to dress up, you just walk your pretty little self right back here."

"Um, sure?" Yeah, time to disappear. I waved good-bye and hustled off.

With my neck still blazing, I headed for the entrance. That's when I saw Principal Torres walk-stomping into the school entrance, unstoppable as a train. Behind her, walking hangdog slow, Yasmany followed.

"The last straw!" she yelled loudly, straight ahead. She and Yasmany disappeared inside.

I checked the time: five minutes to homeroom. Whatever Yasmany had done was none of my business. All I wanted was a nice, normal day of school. After the week I'd had, hadn't I earned it?

I sighed. And then I booked it over to the principal's office.

When I walked into administration, I saw Mr. Zacto standing, not sitting, at his desk. He wore a three-piece suit with creases so sharp it looked like it had been made in a lumberyard. He stared down at his desk like he knew something was off about it, but he couldn't figure out what. "Good morning, Mr. Vidón," he said to me, only reluctantly raising his eyes from his desktop. "May I help you?"

"Gabi's going to be absent today," I blurted.

"Yes, I know. She contacted the entire administrative staff early this morning. That girl is a true professional."

"Yes, well, since she's not here, I'm serving as Yasmany's lawyer today."

Mr. Zacto took off his glasses and shook his head as he polished them. "Yasmany has a team of lawyers now, does he? Well, the poor boy seems to need it, the amount of trouble he gets himself into. Go on in. See if you can be of help."

I considered knocking on Principal Torres's closed door before entering. But then I asked myself, "What would Gabi do?"

So I barged in. "Sorry I am late, but I only just realized my services would be needed," I said.

Yasmany sat in a chair in front of Principal Torres's desk, hunched like a gargoyle. He turned to look at me with a face that was half-stunned, and the other half more stunned. Principal Torres locked her high-beam glasses on me. "Sal! What are you doing here?"

I hustled over to the seat next to Yasmany and—*courage, Sal, courage!*—said, "Gabi cannot be at school today, so I am serving as Yasmany's representative in her place. Now, what seems to be the problem?"

"It's my mom," said Yasmany. "She—"

"This is between Yasmany and me, Sal," Principal Torres cut in, softly. She kept making fists and releasing them, but I didn't think she wanted to use them on either of us. I sensed she wanted to punch someone—someone who wasn't in the room. "You need to head to class, Mr. Vidón. You'll be late for homeroom."

"But—" I started.

"Now," Principal Torres finished.

Yasmany looked down. Principal Torres folded her hands

on the desk and waited. The mal de ojo scarf lay curled like a cobra on the corner of her desk.

But this was not the time to ask for it. "Sorry," I said, and got out of there as quickly and as quietly as possible.

I had trouble concentrating all day. At first I thought it might be low blood sugar, but nope. I guess I just had a lot on my mind, what with Iggy in danger, and my snuffling a calamitron, and a visitor from another dimension, and that scene with Yasmany in the principal's.

Whatever. Classes flew by. Gladis sat next to me at lunch and again at Textile Arts. Turns out she was not a cacanado at all. She wasn't having as much fun as she thought she would—her friends didn't seem as friendly to her in this universe—but she was making the best of it. And she was hilarious. People noticed us laughing and having fun together. I think I started getting fewer weirdo-brujo looks in the hallway for the rest of the day, thanks to her. Instead, I started getting *Sal and Gladis sitting in a tree!* looks.

Hey, a win is a win.

I made it to sixth period without any trouble. Just Health and Wellness, Intermediate Theater Workshop, and detention, and then I was home free for the weekend. And Health Science and the Practice of Wellness was just going to be fun. I was getting to the top of the red zone today, no matter what.

Except when I got there, the red zone wasn't the red zone anymore.

I mean, from a distance, I could see the green, yellow, and red zones of the climbing wall. But as I walked up to the crowd of kids lined up staring at it, I realized why they looked so disappointed, arms crossed, hands on hips. The green zone looked the same as it had yesterday, so full of handholds a sandwich could climb it. But now the yellow zone had just as many holds as the green. And so did the red.

As I joined the line, Octavio said, "Mr. Lynott noobed the wall. Now any filthy casual can climb it."

"Hey," said Mr. Lynott, jogging up to us, patting backs. "Why hasn't anyone gotten to the top of the red zone yet? I bet someone makes it today. Let's go, let's go, let's go!"

"It's too easy now," Octavio said.

He stopped. His smiling cheeks sank into expressionlessness. He somehow turned even whiter. "Oh. I just saw everybody struggling with it for the past few days. And a little bird told me that maybe it would be discouraging to kids to have a wall this hard."

He looked at me when he said that. And that told me everything I needed to know. Papi must have called Mr. Lynott and told him the wall was unfair. So Mr. Lynott had done his best to fix it.

"This class is so sandwich," said Octavio. "What are we supposed to do for fun now?"

Mr. Lynott's chin hit his chest in defeat.

I didn't think. I took a breath, relaxed. And I ran to the center of the room like the showman I am.

"I know exactly what we should do!" I exclaimed like a ringmaster, spinning with my arms wide to address the whole class. "I know an activity that's challenging, fun, and that promotes excellent health and wellness. You will love doing this activity. Especially you, Octavio."

"Yeah?" said Octavio, taking a step forward, big smile. I could see his yes-and instincts kicking in. "What is it?"

"We should try to get to the top of the red zone of the climbing wall!"

"What?"

I just needed a few more seconds. "Oh, I know, it's extremely difficult. No one has succeeded so far. But perhaps today one of us will have the combination of strength, flexibility, and grit to succeed. Are you up for the challenge?"

I could see Octavio wanting to play along, but he was too genuinely disappointed. "What are you talking about, chacho? Anybody could climb the red zone now."

I lowered my eyes like a murder clown. "Perhaps you should look again, Octavio."

He, and the rest of the class, turned to look at the red zone. And they saw it was back to being just as impossible to climb as it had been yesterday.

As the class went bonkers, I ran to the wall and on the way grabbed Mr. Lynott's hand. He, more bewildered than anyone, just kind of hop-ran with me. I turned us to the class with the wall behind us and, still holding Mr. Lynott's hand, took a big stage bow. When Mr. Lynott didn't bow with me, I elbowed him. "Oh, come on, Mr. Lynott, don't be modest! You were fabulous!"

"I was?" he asked.

"I never could have pulled off this magic trick without you."

"You couldn't?"

I gave a big vaudeville laugh. "Wow, Mr. Lynott, you are totally method, aren't you? But the trick is over. They loved it. Didn't you love it, class?"

Everyone applauded. Octavio started whooping and punching the air, and got the whole class doing it.

Covered by the cheering, I lowered my voice and said to Mr. Lynott, "It was a great magic trick that you and *my papi* and I set up. Thanks for playing along."

He thought. He blinked. He cocked his head at the happy class of kids. And then he got it. Like, I could almost hear his brain go *click*.

And now that he had it, he wasn't letting go. He took a stage bow of his own that seriously was better than mine, and the class clapped with double the strength.

Then he stood straight, begged with his hands for silence, and said, "Okay, okay. Magic is great, but it's not going to get you slugs in shape. Let's beat the red zone for real today. Octavio, you're first. Let's go, let's go, let's go!"

32

WHAT THE PANTS was I doing?

I didn't have the brains to think about the consequences of my actions for the rest of Health Science and the Practice of Wellness. All my thoughts had been rinsed clean by that sweet, sweet performer's high that actors know all too well. Octavio and Mr. Lynott and everybody else felt it, too, that goofy-happy-rompy nonstop rush that comes when a show goes perfectly and everybody loves it. No one made it to the top of the red zone, but that was the point! It was really hard! When someone did make it, they'd be a hero! We cursed the wall and made vows to one another like warriors and swore that we would be avenged, all of us, Mr. Lynott included. It was great.

I didn't use my critical-thinking skills on myself in Intermediate Theater Workshop, either. Mrs. Waked's class had worked its magic again. It always felt like playing instead of learning. I spent the whole period having a blast *learning* how to use masks, *learning* how to become someone else outside and then, slowly, on the inside, too. It's funny how the new face on the outside starts to soak you with its spooky new personality, and how eager your body is to sponge it up. It's almost like sometimes you wish you weren't stuck with yourself.

It's only when I left Mrs. Waked's class and was heading for detention that my brain started yelling at me. Since I'd just left Intermediate Theater Workshop, I imagined the conversation as a play.

ALL'S BAD THAT ENDS BAD
A Tragedy by Sal's Vidón's Brain

Starring Sal Vidón's Brain as the Voice of Reason,
& Sal Vidón as the Sandwich that Destroys All Life on Earth

SAL'S BRAIN: What the pants are you doing?

SAL: What?

SAL'S BRAIN: You traded climbing walls with a different universe!

SAL: Um, yeah. Mr. Lynott was feeling bad.

SAL'S BRAIN: [mocking] "Mr. Lynott was feeling bad. Mr. Lynott was feeling bad." Do you think Mr. Lynott is going to feel bad when the calamitrons you brought in destroy the universe?

SAL: We don't know that's going to happen.

SAL'S BRAIN: Is your papi a calamity physicist?

SAL: Yes.

SAL'S BRAIN: Did your papi tell you that even one calamitron was too much?

SAL: Papi said a lot of things. He doesn't even know what a calamitron is!

SAL'S BRAIN: Oh, and you know?

SAL: No.

SAL'S BRAIN: Are you a calamity physicist?

SAL: No.

SAL'S BRAIN: Then I ask you again, Salvador Vidón, what the pants are you doing?

SAL: [*In spotlight*] I don't know. I saw a chance to do a good thing. Mr. Lynott isn't perfect, but he means well. And Octavio wasn't wrong; he was just upset. Nobody was wrong, but everything was wrong. That's the worst. But I could fix it all. I saw the way. I have the power. So I went for it. And it worked! Everyone was happy!

SAL'S BRAIN: And all it cost was the whole universe.

SAL: The universe is fine!

SAL'S BRAIN: Is it, Sal? Is it?

END OF ACT I

I held the door handle to the library commons for a second. Act I wasn't looking so good for our hero. But Act II hadn't been written yet.

Teresita Tómas handed me her notes as soon as I walked into detention. She slapped them into my hand and told me to tell Gabi that her column was super popular and if she dropped it, well, it'd be the *Rotten Egg*'s loss, and anyway, she'd taken great notes, it wouldn't be her fault if Gabi failed, which, by the way, she totally deserved, the way she was acting, but don't tell her that part, Sal.

Then she walked away like a huffy supermodel. I did a patented American Stepmom "Phew, baby!" and tucked her notes into my bookbag.

I went over to Aventura next. She broke away from the cosplay clan, and we sat together for the next twenty minutes, creating a Caesar cipher out of her notes for Gabi. She told me what her notes said, and I rewrote them in code because, no joke, Aventura's handwriting looked like someone had dipped a mouse in ink, set it down on a piece of paper, and then set its tail on fire.

But they were really good notes. Just by talking with her, I knew she was smart, but now I knew *how* smart. Aventura was definitely someone I could work with.

I promised to text her all the juicy details of Gabi breaking her head against the code, maybe even sneak a pic or two.

I think I would have just hung out with Aventura for the rest of detention, but I got a text from Gladis, from the new app she gave to me to download during lunch. It was called AnyUni. Apparently I could use it to text from any uni. That sounded . . . promising.

Hey Sal, she wrote, **do you have the scarf? I have to, you know, BE LEAVING pretty soon**

Too many things going on. It was easy to lose track of stuff. *Focus, Sal!*

I went up to Daniel—he was walking around checking in with everybody, being helpful, and marking their progress on his tablet—and asked him if I could leave detention early. "I really need to talk to Principal Torres," I said.

Daniel was wearing a tuxedo. I mean, like, a real tuxedo, the kind you'd see on Oscar night a hundred years ago. His red cummerbund looked like the smile of a whale. He had his wavy hair parted down the center, and his fake bullhorn mustache was also parted down the center. He even had a monocle.

I didn't quite get why even the teachers at Culeco all dressed up. But I really liked it.

Just then, though, Daniel didn't look like he was having any fun. "Sal," he said, turning to me. "Have you seen Yasmany?"

Come to think of it, I hadn't. "He didn't show for detention?"

"No. When Gabi told me she was going to be absent, I promised her I would help Yasmany finish his report today. I thought I'd ask you to help, too. Was he absent?"

"I saw him this morning, in Principal Torres's office. But I haven't seen him since."

The monocle dropped out of his eye and swung like a dead man on the end of its chain. "Was he in trouble?"

"I don't know. Principal Torres wouldn't tell me anything."

Daniel nodded, thinking. "Tell you what. I'm sending you with a pass to ask Principal Torres if she sent Yasmany home. Tell her I'm happy to stay late if Yasmany's still around. I really want to help him. Text me what she tells you."

"Um, couldn't you just call her?"

"Probably. But then I wouldn't have a reason to let you leave detention early to talk to her."

"Riiight," I said. I gave him gun fingers and started for the door.

But the last glimpse of his sad smile stuck in my mind. I turned around for a second to say to Daniel, "Principal Torres probably just sent Yasmany home. I'm sure he's fine."

Daniel shook his head. "'Home' and 'fine' don't always go together." Then, with a stiff upper lip, he shoved his monocle into his eye and got back to work.

I texted Gladis as I walked. She met me in Mrs. Waked's classroom. No one else was there, but it was unlocked. Mrs. Waked said we could use the room anytime we wanted, to practice or whatever. Using an entropy sweeper to check Gladis for calamitrons definitely fell into the category of "whatever."

"I'm alive!" said the entropy sweeper the millisecond I stuck its battery pack back in the handle.

"Oh! Is Rafalito!" said Gladis, running over and hugging the entropy sweeper. "I so gla' you here, too, mi amorcito!"

"How do you know my real name?" the entropy sweeper asked her. It was nice to hear it caught off guard for a change.

I swept her up and down. Guess what? Not a single calamitron anywhere near her. "How in the name of ham-and-mayo sandwiches did that other Sal get you here without making a hole?" I muttered as I checked her a second time.

"Because is an even tra'e," said Gladis.

I hadn't really been talking to her, but now I was all ears. "What do you mean, an even trade?"

She shrugged. "Sal tell me. If he jus' put me here without trady—" She ended the sentence by making an explosion with her hands and puffed-out cheeks. "But if you ma'e an even tra', Gladis for Gladis, or escarf for escarf, then no trouble. And speaky of that, can we go get my escarf now?"

"Yeah," I said, thinking, lost in thought, too full of thoughts. I thoughtlessly went to yank out the battery pack when the entropy sweeper yelled, "Noooo! I want to live!"

"Be nice to it, Sal," said Gladis. "Rafalito is my frien'."

"Stop calling me that," the entropy sweeper muttered.

I checked the power level on its handle. It was at 91 percent, so I shrugged and left the battery pack in for now. Then Gladis and I headed for the principal's office to try to get her scarf back.

"So," I said, sounding like her dad, "how was your first day of school in a new universe?"

"Sal! I hlove it here. But is so weir'!"

"Why?"

"Because is jus' li' *my* universe!"

I don't think anybody really does a double take when they're confused. I think it's something actors invented so that people in the cheap seats could tell when a character is confused. But *I* do double takes, because I've trained myself to. I like them. They're funny.

So I did one now. "What? Really? Our universes are exactly alike?"

"¡No, Pipo, no todo! Pero, li', so mush! Culeco is, li', wa-hundre' percen' lo mismo. Gladis and I ha' all the same classes, all the same teeshers, everything. Is li' we're the same person!"

I shrugged. "I mean, you kind of are."

Her head wobbled back and forth, and she turned her hands into scales. "But tha's the weir' par', Sal. Everything is the same, e'cep' *me*! Some of my bes' frien's arren even my frien's here. They, li'e, were eshock' that I was bein' nize to them."

I patted her on the back. "Look on the bright side. At least you're not her."

She smiled weakly. "Is li'e you say before, Sal. I kine of am."

We walked the fifteen steps it took to get to administration from the staircase. It looked like pretty much everyone had gone home. Everyone except Mr. Zacto.

"Well, well, well," he said, looking up from cleaning his perfectly clean desk. "Can I take this as a sign that you two have patched up your differences?"

I didn't know what to say, but Gladis was all over it. "Oh,

sure," she said, with a *perfect* American accent. Well, it's Culeco. Everyone can do every kind of accent, I guess. But my eyes almost fell out of my head anyway. "It was all a silly little misunderstanding, Mr. Zacto. I mean, come on. Mal de ojo? I don't believe in that stuff for real."

"Is that so?" Mr. Zacto said, a lot like a detective would say, the sentence before he caught you in a lie. He pushed his glasses up his nose. "I see you're not wearing your charm."

Gladis looked at me. I thought fast. "Didn't you tell me," I asked her, "that you left your ojo turco at home by accident?"

But Gladis didn't miss a beat. "No, Sal, no, I didn't forget. Remember, I told you the reason I didn't wear it today is because I don't need it anymore? Because, remember, I don't really believe in that stuff?"

We both turned to face Mr. Zacto, smiling like idiots.

He laughed, and did the *oh well* thing with his eyes. Then he opened a drawer in his desk. "Well, Principal Torres did leave this for you, Sal. She told me to return it to you"—he pulled out the mal de ojo scarf!—"on the condition that you don't bring it to school again."

"Thank you," I said to Mr. Zacto, taking the scarf. I looked over to Principal Torres's office; the door was shut and the lights were out. "Did she leave?"

"She needed some air," he said, taking a seat. "Tough day at the office."

"Kids these days," said Gladis, tsk-tsking. "They're so bad, am I right?"

Mr. Zacto shook his head, smiling. "No. No such thing as

a bad kid, Gladis. Now adults, *those* are the people you have to worry about." He looked at the ceiling and decided that his glasses needed wiping. "Sometimes you wonder how people went so wrong with their lives."

He clearly had a particular adult in mind. I thought about the way Principal Torres had been making fists earlier, and what Daniel had said about Yasmany's home. I was starting to get the idea that things weren't so good for Yasmany in the parent department.

Mr. Zacto sighed, then tightened his tie and looked at me. "I bet you'll find Principal Torres in the cafeteria, Sal. And when you see her, do me a favor and tell her—" But he needed a second to find the right words. "Tell her that, if she needs to talk, she has my number."

"I will," I said. "Thank you."

"Ciao," said Gladis, wiggling her fingers.

Bellowing laughter chased us out of administration.

That made Gladis giggle. Even the way she laughed told me her Cuban accent was back. "Do jou theen' Mr. Zacto belief any of tha'?"

"Nope." We stopped walking in front of Culeco's double-door entrance. "So. Do you have to go back, like, now?"

"Yeah, I better. I' a leetle escare to fine ou' what Gladis say to my frien's. And I don' wan' her to talk to my paren's!" She frowned suddenly. "Oh! Now I feel ba' for her paren's!"

I kicked an imaginary pebble. "What about me? When Monday comes, I'll be stuck with mean-girl Gladis again."

"No es fácil," she said sympathetically. "Bu' you be okay. I know you, Sal. Is tha' other Gladis better be escare!"

Oh yeah. My Gladis would be coming back here now, too. That made me suddenly nervous. "What kind of day do you think my Gladis had in your universe?"

Gladis nodded sagely. "A twenny-Pampers day."

Yeah. This was not going to go well.

Both my phone and Gladis's dinged at the same time. My text was from Gabi. **You're coming to the hospital right after school, right? I have to do my homework right away, because I don't know how much my family is going to need me this weekend, and I have to be there for them, and Iggy. Oh, but don't worry. Iggy's doing better! That little bugger is as tough as an overcooked potato. But you can see for yourself when you come, so come quick! And, oh yeah, I've been meaning to ask, ARE YOU AND GLADIS MACHADO GOING OUT?!?! You sly dog. TELL ME EVERYTHING!**

I rolled my eyes—word gets around fast. I was about to answer Gabi, when Gladis said, "Tha' was Sal. He' coming in li'e ten seconds. He say, 'Get ready, girl!' Ha-ha-ha."

I double-took. "What, like, right here?"

"I guess so."

"He can't! Text him back, quick. The hallway's full of cameras!"

"Cameras? In Culeco?" She set a new text-writing record with her thumbs. "Tha's somet'ing differn' in this universe! Wha' shou' I say?"

"Tell him—" I looked around frantically. *No, no, no—yes!* "Tell him to use the all-gender bathroom!"

She gave me the cacaseca. "He can use the bathroom af'er he bring me back, Sal."

"Not *use* use the bathroom. Use it to make the switch."

But she'd already started texting him. "I know. I just messy wi' you."

We trotted over to the restroom. Gladis went first and held the door for me. But I pointed to the cameras. "Probably not a good idea if I go in with you."

"Oh yeah," she said. She looked at me sadly, but clown-funny-sadly. "Then thees is goo'bye. Oh, Sal, i' wa' so fun! I weesh you cou' come with me!"

I wiggled my phone at her. "We'll always have messaging."

She brightened. "Oh yeah! Tex' me to le' me know if Gladis is okay, okay, Pipo?"

I said yes, and in she went to the bathroom. The last thing I heard her say was, "¡Guao! Thees the cleanes' bathroom I ever see!"

I really wished I could have gone in with her. But with Mr. Zacto still in admin and Mr. Milagros prowling around some-where, I couldn't risk it. Which sucked. I had so many ques-tions for that other Sal. He seemed to be a lot better at relaxing than I was.

Yeah, maybe I was a little jelly, a little salty. I punched my hand with my fist.

My punch landed in a surprisingly soft cushion of yarn. Because *I was still holding the mal de ojo scarf that Gladis had come all the way from another universe to get!*

I lunged for the bathroom door and flung it open, saying "Gladis! You forgot your—"

And there, standing in the door, looking like she was a robot that had just gone online for the first time, was Gladis.

Same clothes as before, but this Gladis had one more accessory: an ojo turco necklace.

And when she spoke and I heard her American accent, I knew for sure I had my old Gladis back. "Sal. It's you. Is it you? Who are you?"

"It's Sal," I said.

"The brujo?" she asked.

I bit back the frustration on the tip of my tongue. "That's what you keep calling me."

She leaned toward me, squinted. "No. You're not the brujo. The brujo Sal is in the rainy place. He's a very scary boy." She turned to look out the open double doors of Culeco's entrance. "It's sunny here. So you must be a nice Sal. Are you a nice Sal?"

There is only one way to answer that question. "Yes. I am a nice Sal. The nicest Sal of all."

She nodded. "You made me the protection scarf. That was nice of you."

Protection scarf? Um. Sure. Yes-and, baby. "Yes, I did."

Her face clouded over. "But I didn't know it was a protection scarf. I wish I had known. I wish I'd had it with me when I went to the rainy place. That other Sal is a brujo, you know."

She took a woozy step into the hallway and discovered she knew how to walk. She nodded approvingly and looked around. "This is the Culeco Academy of the Arts."

"Yes."

"Is it time for school?"

Oh, dear. "School's over for the day."

"Oh," she said, pouting. "I was hoping that all had been a

dream. I guess there really is an evil Sal and a nice Sal, then. You're the nice Sal."

"Super nice."

She nodded in agreement before she added, "I think I would like to go home now."

"That's a good idea. How will you get home? Do you have a ride?"

Gladis thought. I could hear clocks ticking as I waited for her to answer. "My dad will pick me up. I will text him. Maybe I will wait outside for him. It would be nice to feel the sun on my face."

"Okay."

She grew briefly happier. "The sun is out here. It was raining in the other place. That is the place with the brujo Sal."

"Nothing but blue skies here, Gladis."

She went from glad to unreadable. "Good. Well. Thank you for my scarf," she said. Then she took it out of my hand—I just let her—and wrapped it three times around her neck, so that the words "Mal" and "de" and "ojo" were stacked perfectly, one on top of the other. "That's nice. I'm protected now. See you Monday, Sal."

And with that, she toddled to the exit and left Culeco.

I stood watching her leave for a few seconds when I got an AnyUni alert. Other Gladis had texted: **Don't keep me in suspense, Pipo! How is Gladis doing?**

I looked at the exit, then my phone, then the exit, then my phone. Then I texted back: **Youre gonna have to get your scarf back from Gladis yourself**

33

PRINCIPAL TORRES WAS sitting on the edge of the cafeteria's stage, kicking her feet like a kid. She had turned off most of the fluorescent lights, which made the tables look gray, the brown stage browner, and her blue suit black. Shadows blotted out whole chunks of the room, like a video game in which the whole scene wasn't rendered yet. To Principal Torres's left, a tiny red-and-white milk carton provided the only bright colors in the room. To her right, she'd set down her glasses so that they wouldn't get in the way as she rubbed the bridge of her nose.

I walked in and said, "Heard you could use a friend."

Principal Torres looked up, and once she squintingly realized which kid had interrupted her solitude, she smiled a little, blinked a little. "Shouldn't you be in detention, Mr. Vidón?"

I took out Daniel's note and waved it as I walked toward the stage. "Mr. Miranda Rivero sent me. He wanted me to ask you if you sent Yasmany home. He said he'd keep the commons open if Yasmany was going to show up. He wants to help him with his diabetes paper."

She sucked her lips and chose her words carefully. "Yasmany won't be at detention today. I'll let him know."

"I can do it." I boosted myself onto the stage next to her, the tiny, bright carton of milk between us. "He asked me to text him. If that's okay with you?"

She smiled, but she couldn't hold it for more than a second. "Thanks, Sal. I'd appreciate it."

I texted Daniel, then pocketed my phone and pulled out a bag of Skittles. I tore it open and shook the bag at Principal Torres, smiling like a devil. "Some sweet, delicious Skittles?"

She put up a hand. "Thanks, but I'm on a diet."

"Why?"

She smiled as if to say, *Really, chacho, you're going to make me say it out loud?* And then she did say it. "Because I'm fat."

I ate some Skittles. "My stepmom calls herself fat sometimes. And then my papi will hug her from behind and say, 'You're not fat. That's just American society brainwashing you. You're light as a feather!' And then he lifts her up and carries her around the house."

She stuck out her bottom lip and nodded approvingly. "Yeah? Does it make her feel better?"

"Yeah. But then she has to run away, quick."

"Why?"

I got up and started acting out the scene onstage. "Because once he puts her down, he goes, 'Okay, now, you carry me!' And Papi is the size of, like, three grizzly bears fighting over a ham. And my stepmom is all like, 'I can't lift you!' And he's like, 'Are you calling me fat?' And she's like, 'Yes, you are fat and beautiful, and I love you, and I am not picking you up!' And he starts chasing her around with his arms out wide and shaking his belly, going, 'Aw, c'mon, mi vida, just throw me over your shoulder and carry me to the kitchen, 'cause baby I'm soooo hungry!' And then they run all over the house for like twenty minutes."

One of the ways you know if an adult has been broken by life is if they never laugh anymore. Principal Torres? That woman *bellowed*. I mean, she laughed like the Loch Ness monster would, if it existed.

When she had wiped the last tear from her eye, Principal Torres picked up her milk and leaned it toward me. "Your papi is a proper caballero. Here's to him."

I clinked her milk with my bag of Skittles. She poured milk down her throat, and I poured Skittles into my mouth.

We sat quietly, kicking our legs and looking out at the abandoned cafeteria, watching the second hand of the huge clock on the far wall glide the time away. I broke the silence by saying, "Mr. Zacto says you can call him if you need to talk to someone."

She laughed away her surprise. "Mr. Miranda Rivero, Mr. Zacto—you've been busy. Got your fingers in a lot of pots, don't you? And it's only the first week of school." She smiled, brought her milk almost to her mouth for another swig. But before she drank, she added, "Can't wait to see what travesuras you've pulled by the end of the year."

I touched my hand to my chest. "Principal Torres! I am planning to pull no travesuras in your school. Zero travesuras. This will be"—and I gestured in a complete circle—"a no-travesuras zone."

Her glasses slipped down her nose. "Do you know what a travesura is?"

"No clue."

She bellowed again. *Of course* I knew what a travesura was. Back when Mami Muerta was Mami Viva, she used the word "travesura" on me more than she used my name. But I wasn't passing up a good punch line for anything.

Principal Torres took her time enjoying the laugh. But when it was over, her mood had gone back to a sad place. "I don't want to know how you do your tricks. Really, I don't. You keep your secrets, Sal. That's your privilege, as a magician. I actually love not knowing. I love magic."

"Cool, cool," I replied. Where was she going with this?

She slugged back more milk, then set her jaw. "Did you know, Sal, that the number one predictor for criminal behavior is abuse at home? Not video games, not movies, not music, not all the other cacaseca people try to blame it on. You want to know how kids get messed up? Look at their family life."

She was talking about Yasmany. Suddenly it felt like someone was wringing out my stomach like a dishcloth.

Kicking her legs again and looking at the fluorescent lights, she said, "I want this school to be a sanctuary. I want it to be a place that encourages all the students to make magic happen."

"It's a good school," I said.

She looked at me hopefully. "Yeah? You think so? Because, you know, you haven't had the easiest first week here."

Tell me about it. But to her I said, "I'm making friends. And I like my classes, too. I'm learning a lot."

"Now that is music to my ears, Mr. Vidón. Tell me something interesting you learned today."

I knew just the thing. I pulled out the two masks I had in my backpack and put one on. Each was a broad, white, mouthless face with a long chin that ended in a point. The eyes looked like sideways teardrops, the nose had huge, flaring nostrils, and mean-looking eyebrow bones jutted out of the forehead. "We started a unit on masks in Mrs. Waked's class today. She gave us these."

Principal Torres turned to face me full-on, sitting cross-legged and leaning forward. She instantly looked a thousand times happier. "That, Mr. Vidón, is no ordinary mask. That is a Venetian bauta mask. And it wasn't just for actors. People wore them all the time to disguise themselves."

I held the other one out to her. "Want to try it on?"

Smiling, she took it and slipped it on.

And changed. The way she cocked her head at me, she seemed like a totally different type of creature: still as smart as a human, but not really human anymore. Kind of a bird that was as smart as a monkey that liked hunting as much as a female lion. It was . . . unsettling.

I like unsettling.

Principal Torres popped up and started acting out her words as she spoke, using an excellent Italian accent. "You see, Mr. Vidón, back in the day in Venezia, anyone could disguise themselves in a bauta mask: ricco o povero, uomo o donna, it didn't matter. You had to treat everyone in a bauta mask with respect, because you never knew whose face was underneath. It was a way for everyone to play, to have fun together, to make everyone equal, for a little while, anyway. This mask, it was a tool for freedom."

I hopped to my feet. "That's like what Mrs. Waked said. She said that most of the time, people put on a mask to pretend they're something else. But before you can change into something else, first you have to become *everything*." I opened my arms to my nonexistent audience. "She said, 'The first thing you should do when you put on a mask is get rid of your boring little soul and become a sky god, and look down on all of Creation, and only, like, kind of care about it.'"

"She literally said 'become a sky god'?"

"Yeah." I switched my posture to impersonate Mrs. Waked. "Literally she said, 'You children are *practically* demigods already. I've never *seen* so many skilled and brilliant actors in one place. But today you must *ascend to the heavens* and throw off your *Earthly* concerns. Look down on this planet you *hath wrought*, ye sky gods, and decide Earth's very destiny!'"

Principal Torres leaned back and laughed. "I love that woman! Okay, then. I'll be a sky god, too. Gloria Torres is gone!" she announced. She moved behind me and spoke first in one of my ears, then the other, and her accent now became musical and otherworldly, the way you'd expect a friendly god to speak to humans. "Only I, Principalia, patron saint of principals' principles, remain! I look down from the heavens and answer the prayers of confused educators everywhere!" She reached over my shoulder and spread her fingers to the stars.

Inspired, I ran over to Principal Torres's glasses, still lying there on the stage, and put them on over my mask. "And I," I said, doing an over-the-top Cubana accent, "am Gloria Torres, principal of Culeco Academy of the Arts, the best middle school in America! And I have many questions, Principalia."

Principalia gripped its chin and nodded wisely. "Ah, yes, Principal Torres. I have been following the events of your school with great interest. Ask me your questions, mortal!"

I ran over to her and held my hands out to the empty tables and benches. "Great Principalia, my students hate the cafeteria lunches! They call it dog food!"

"On Monday, you must feed them real dog food! That way, they will truly know the difference!"

"Great Principalia, I have a power-hungry student council president who will stop at nothing before she takes over the school. What should I do?"

"Make her a mentor to other girls so they'll be more assertive and ambitious!"

We were having fun, jumping and dancing around the stage. But all the jumping and dancing was making the masks slip. Hers had gone disturbingly crooked on her face. But I made myself stare straight into her eyes when I asked Principalia, "What's going on with Yasmany?"

A bauta mask looks angry and beaky, like the skull of an eagle that died p.o.ed. But the way Principalia cocked its head at me was half mother and half priest. "I can't tell you that, Sal. I can't share private details about other students."

That's all she said. But the way she said it reminded me of a movie where a soldier belly flopped on top of a grenade to save the rest of her unit.

Principal Torres squatted down so our eyes were level. "But this much I know." She removed her mask, plucked her glasses off my mask and put them on, becoming fully herself again. "Yasmany needs all the friends he can get right now. Gabi's done so much for him, but he needs guys in his life, too. Maybe you could find it in your heart to be a friend like that."

She held out her mask to me, but I was reluctant to take it back. The problem with pretending is that eventually you have to stop. It never, ever, ever lasts long enough.

34

"WHY ARE YOU wearing that creepy mask, Sal?" asked Gabi from across the hospital cafeteria table.

I didn't answer. I kept my hands folded in my lap and looked at her with a chicken's one-eyed curiosity.

She went back to flattening with a fork—not eating—the piece of red velvet cake in front of her. "You're kind of freaking me out, dude."

As Google had taught me on the walk over to the hospital, chickens can't move their eyes. They have to move their whole heads to look at something. I snapped my whole head forward so I could focus both eyes on Gabi like a chicken.

"Fine. You don't want to talk? We don't have to talk. I can stare right back at you all day long."

She stared and I stared and she stared and I stared.

"Say something!" she yelled.

I didn't.

Her dimples filled with evil glee. "Vee have *vays* of making you talk," she said. And then she ducked beneath the cafeteria table.

I ignored her and passed the time looking around. This

place could seat two hundred people, easy. Each round white-top table was surrounded by eight cushionless yellow chairs. My guess is that the hospital didn't want to encourage people to stick around for long. Looked like it was working.

The cafeteria had exactly three people in it, besides Gabi and me: Three custodians, all sitting at different tables, clutched their mugs of coffee and tried not to fall asleep, even though it was only the afternoon. The cashier was a robot that didn't have legs. It looked like a woman from the waist up, and only one of its eyes still blinked. Its name badge said ALMA.

"I am coming to get you!" Gabi sang from beneath the table. "I am getting closer!" went the song. "I am almost upon you!" she tra-la-la'ed. "You'd better speak now, or you're gonna get it!"

I didn't.

And then Gabrielle Reál, straight-A student, student council president, and editor of the *Rotten Egg*, bit my leg.

As you might expect from a shark-girl, she bit to kill. She clamped her jaws on my calf and threw her head back and forth like a dog with its chew toy. *"Grrr!"* she said happily.

Lucky for me, I hadn't had a chance to update my wardrobe to Florida weather yet. I had on cargo pants (instead of, say, cargo shorts) that protected my drumstick. It turned Gabi's attempted mauling into a slightly uncomfortable but completely endurable gumming. The hardest part was not laughing.

But freaky dudes in bauta masks don't laugh. I sat there, unmoving, unperturbed. The three janitors sipped their coffees at the same time.

Gabi popped up from beneath the table so fast that all her fighter-jet barrettes flew a crisscross pattern in the air for a second before settling back into her puffball hair. She was frowning.

"Seriously, Sal, are you okay?" she asked. "Did something bad happen?"

Ploy to get me to talk, or genuine concern? I played it safe: I moved my head slowly closer to hers, turning it to study her from weird, inhuman angles, the way Principal Torres had. Then I ducked down beneath the table.

When I rose again, I had the other mask in my two hands. I held it out to her. In the wordless way of a loving animal, I gestured with my bauta beak that she should take it.

Gabi gave me an evil smile. She grabbed it and was just about to shove it on her face without thinking.

Nuh-uh. I interrupted her by handing her a note. Still holding the mask in one hand, she took the note, flapped it in the air until it was unfolded, and then read it out loud. "'Gabrielle Reál, girl with a thousand fathers, whose name means "reality," know this: Once you don this mask, you will cease to be a person. Your body will vanish, and all that will be left of you are the things you live for. All your past deeds, be they good or be they evil, shall define you. So before you replace your own face with that mask, ask thyself: Are you prepared to become what you believe?'"

"Sal!" she said, shocked and kind of thrilled. "Did you write that? That is so good! You must have written it, because I've never heard it before, and if it existed I would have heard of it. Oh my God! How did you come up with something so good?"

"You like it?" I asked. "I just wrote it on the way here. It's not bad, right? I read a lot of fantasy, so I'm pretty good at—"

"Ha!" she yelled in triumph. "Made you break character! All it took was a little flattery." She started dancing around the table. "Sal always wants to be the star, but vanity won't get him far, directors will say au revoir, if he can't share the cookie jar with other people, har-har-har!"

The left janitor snorted.

I wanted to laugh, too. Did she come up with all those rhymes on the spot? Gabi could lay down some bars.

But I wasn't going to tell her that right after she'd burned me. I wasn't going to say a thing. I was just going to stare at her. Like a one-eyed rooster.

"Aw, not this again!" said Gabi. "C'mon, Sal, cut the cacaseca."

I just tilted my head to the other shoulder, in pity for her. Rooster pity.

"Sal! Come on! You were telling me what the homework assignment was. So, what, we have to use the mask to invent a new character? Do we have to create a scene?" She tied on her mask.

That was my cue!

I flew out of my chair and swept over to Gabi, who'd gotten halfway around the table by then. "Beg you will, mortal, as all who came before you have, and all who come after you shall. For I am Life's End, I am Fin, I am Rot and Ruin and a pile of bones. You and I will walk you away from your body, arm in arm. We will journey together into the Great Hereafter. You will not want to come, but you *will* come with me. You have no choice. For I am—"

"Death!" she guessed, jumping up and down, clapping.

She already knew she was right, but I told her anyway.

"You are correct, m'lady!" I said, giving her a Renaissance Faire bow. "We have to create a scene. One of us plays Death, and the other one tries to bargain with Death. It's—"

"An Everyman play!" said Gabi.

"I love Everyman plays," said one of the janitors.

Of course Gabi knew what an Everyman play was. "I'd never even heard of an Everyman play until today," I admitted, taking my seat again.

She started dancing around the table at top speed. "Oh, they're so much fun! You're going to be all like, 'I am Death, and you have to die now!' And I'll be all like, 'Oh no, I am not ready, Death! Give me more time!' And you'll be like, 'No, there is no bargaining with Death!' And I'll be like, 'No, Death, have mercy!' And you'll be like, 'Too bad, mortal!' And I'll be like—"

"Why do I have to play Death?" I interrupted.

"Ha!" Gabi started creeping toward me from halfway around the table, wiggling her fingers. "What, are you scared of Death?"

"Um. Yes, actually. I've seen what Death can do."

I wish my voice hadn't cracked.

Gabi took off her mask, revealing the tragedy mask her face had become. "Sal, I'm so sorry. I didn't mean to trigger you. You're probably still suffering from post-traumatic stress disorder from the death of your beautiful mother, and here I am, making jokes. I'm just feeling so much better ever since I heard that Iggy's out of the woods. Now I'm all like 'Ha! Suck it, Death! My baby bro beat you again!' as if he'd defeated Death forever. But that's just plain ignorant of me, and insensitive. Please forgive me."

It's easier to forgive when you're wearing a mask, so I kept mine on for a little while longer. "S'all good. I wanted to play Death, anyway."

I texted the padres to ask for two favors. **Can I sleep at the hospital tonight? And could you bring some stuff from home? It's for a drama assignment.**

Yes and yes. It really helps to have great padres. I'm lucky, and I know it.

While we waited for them to arrive, Gabi and I knocked out all our non-theater homework for Monday. And PS, if you ever want to do the best homework of your life, partner with Gabi Reál. Seriously, by the time we'd finished, I felt like I'd grown an extra little brain in my left shoulder to hold all the new knowledge I had. I think it might be whispering to me still.

The padres walked into the cafeteria around dinnertime, horsing around, as usual. They each had a big box filled with props and costumes and toiletries and a few changes of underwear. They kept ramming into each other like bumper cars.

I had bought three espressos, one for each of them and one for Gabi (who, you guessed it, was already addicted to coffee), and had them waiting on our table. I kept smacking Gabi's hand away from hers so we could all drink espresso together.

Well, except me; I had water. I don't drink caffeine. Magicians need steady hands.

I'd also gotten them a thank-you flan for everyone (except me) to share. The padres sat down and were very grateful; they hadn't had anything to eat since lunch.

I told them it was important not to skip meals. "What," I said, "do you want to end up in the hospital or something?"

Trolling parents is fun.

The padres asked about Iggy, and Gabi cheerfully related how well he'd responded to a new drug regimen, and how she just couldn't wait for all this to be over and have her little brother safe at home. We toasted our drinks to that.

Once the flan was gone, Gabi sidled over to American Stepmom and chatted her up. She seemed especially interested in talking to her. I wondered why, paranoically.

Whatever. That gave Papi a chance to ask me the big question he had for me. "So. How was gym class today?"

"Health and Wellness," I corrected.

"Yes, right. Did anybody beat the red zone today?"

"Nope."

Cubans don't get shocked or stunned. They get asombrado—mysterious shadows cross their faces when they're confused. All sorts of shadows crossed Papi's face now. "Really? I mean, I thought after—" And then he shut his mouth fast enough that I heard his teeth clack.

Ha! He'd almost admitted he had called Mr. Lynott. I took the opportunity to torture him a little more. "After American Stepmom and I figured out how I could cheat to get to the top? Oh, I decided not to cheat after all. You seemed so opposed to the idea, Papi. I couldn't go against your wishes."

"I see," he said carefully. "And the red zone was . . . as hard as ever?"

"Oh yeah. I mean, Mr. Lynott had tried to make it easier for us. Everyone was so mad! Treating us like babies—how could he? We changed it back to the hard wall and made fun of him all period. I mean, how clueless can a chacho be?"

Papi sipped espresso. "Yeah. What a sandwich."

We both decided it was a good time to check in on Gabi and American Stepmom's conversation.

"What's it like being Sal's mom?" Gabi was asking. "I bet he's a real handful around the house."

American Stepmom turned her surprised mouth into a smile. "A handful? That's not what I would say. Sal is incredibly talented. I've never met anyone so driven to succeed."

"Well, you've only just met me," said Gabi.

American Stepmom laughed and blinked, and blinked a little more without laughing. "Sal is extraordinary. Has he shown you any magic tricks yet?"

Gabi gave her a look. "Oh yes. Have you seen the one where he throws a spider at your face?"

"We should head upstairs," I said, piling both boxes in my arms and heading for the elevator.

I led the way to the waiting room, where Gabi's mom and her many, many dads had set up camp. Reina Reál greeted us the second we walked in. She wore a parrot-bright outfit, but her hairdo fell around her shoulders in ruins. She should have sued her mascara company for claiming it was tearproof. She cried when she saw me, cried whenever one of Gabi's dads came or left, cried as she accepted good wishes from visitors, cried when doctors and nurses told her there had been no change in Ignacio's condition, cried as she prayed rosaries in groups, and cried to herself when she thought no one was looking.

But here's the thing. Her crying never kept her from smiling, laughing, joking, listening, thinking, or caring for anyone else. She just cried and did everything else she would normally do. When she met Papi and American Stepmom for the first time, she cried, and hugged them, and said "no es fácil" over and over.

She lavished praise on the padres, telling them how wonderful it was of them to come visit, how good-looking they were, and what a caballero of a son they had raised. They were most welcome. And now they must eat!

Before she knew what had happened, American Stepmom was balancing a heaping paper plate of steaming food in her hands, fresh from the infinite buffet of Cuban goodies against the left wall. She looked at me, panic in her eyes. I shrugged. *What can you do?* A Cuban mama's gonna feed you.

Papi, thoroughly trained in the ways of grieving Cubans, understood exactly what was happening and couldn't wait to get his plate. He didn't have to wait long.

I got to watch as Papi and American Stepmom introduced themselves to the five of Gabi's dads who were in the room for this shift. Papi kept waiting for American Stepmom to freak out when she shook hands with Dad: The Final Frontier, and American Stepmom kept waiting for Papi, who still seemed confused about even their own marriage sometimes, to freak out about this many people claiming to be Gabi's dads.

But no one freaked out. Everyone was nice. No one forgot that the reason we were all sitting in a hospital waiting room was because two floors down a little boy was fighting for his life.

I love it when adults remember to behave themselves. They forget all the time. Hard to blame them, though. They haven't been kids for a long while.

Gabi and I left the adults to their "networking," or whatever adults did when they were alone. We went to visit Iggy.

Well, first we went back to the cafeteria so I could pick up an espresso for Nurse Sotolongo. When I gave it to her at the NICU reception desk, she said, "You are officially my best friend in the entire world." Then, squinting hard at me, she asked, "You didn't put anything in it, did you?" She sniffed her cup like a squirrel.

"He didn't," chimed Gabi. "I watched him the whole time. You have to keep your eye on Sal, you know."

"Dime tú," she cacaseca'ed. "The second Chacumbele here walked in the hospital, I knew he'd be nothing but trouble."

What the heck was this? I opened my arms and told her what she should have said to me: "'Thank you, Sal, for bringing me coffee! That was so considerate of you, Sal! Of course I know you wouldn't try to poison my café, Sal!' Last time I buy you espresso."

Nurse Sotolongo shot out of her chair, ran around the reception desk, and enveloped me in a feet-off-the-floor embrace. "No, chacho, no! Don't say that! I need my cafecitos! I've worked more than sixty hours this week, and I still have to get through tonight before I can go to sleep until Monday. If you don't bring me coffee, who will?"

"You work sixty hours a week?" asked Gabi. "Sister, you need a union."

"Tell me about it. But it's never going to happen. The medical establishment thinks working nurses to death is good for their character."

"I did a report on unions last year. I know a lot about them now. If you want, I could help you start planning how to—"

"Um," I said. "Put me down?"

Nurse Sotolongo looked down and remembered that she'd been crushing me that whole time. "You bringing me a cafecito the next time you're here?"

"Yes."

"Prométalo."

"I promise."

She dropped me. "And that," she said, turning to Gabi, "is how you handle Chacumbeles."

"Pick them up and squeeze them until they give you what you want," Gabi replied. "Got it." They high-fived.

I was worried that, during the high five, one of them would notice that I'd stolen Nurse Sotlongo's Fitbit off her wrist. But they didn't. Gabi also didn't notice when I slipped it into her backpack as we walked to Iggy's room.

And that's how you handle getting double-teamed. I should high-five myself more often.

There was less space in Iggy's room for humans now, because it all had been taken up by tall, hot machines. They babbled to each other in the language of computer beeps. They muttered to themselves like old dogs. They talked in their sleep.

No room for chairs anymore, so Gabi and I had to stand. We stood on opposite sides of the incubator with our four hands on its lid, like we were healers trying to cast a Cure Disease spell. Iggy lay sleeping inside. He was in just a diaper and a little red hat today. They had tubes up his nose, and a tube in his mouth that went all the way down his throat. A fat IV was taped to his right wrist; another was taped to his right foot. The skin of his hands was peeling off.

"It's okay, Sal," said Gabi. "It's going to be okay."

At first, I felt embarrassed and angry that she'd caught me wiping my eye. But I've been in therapy long enough to know I just had to wait a second to let the feelings pass. Gabi was just being kind.

Therapy also taught me what to say next. "You don't have to tell me it's going to be okay, Gabi. I've been in hospitals a lot. When people lie to make you feel better, you feel worse."

"Yeah." She was almost crying. "Yeah, I know. I hate it when people lie to me."

I had been through a lot of the same feelings before, when Mami was in the hospital. My memories, all the confusion and helplessness I felt back then, rolled themselves into a ball and settled in my throat and made it hard to breathe.

So, time for some calming techniques. And time to express my feelings out loud.

I took deep, slow breaths. I closed my eyes, concentrated on the warmth of the incubator under my palms. And then I said, "None of this should be happening to Iggy. I feel sad, and angry, and powerless."

"Powerless," Gabi repeated. The way she said it made me open my eyes. She leaned her head back, breathing through her mouth, and the fighter-jet barrettes in her hair all did a nosedive toward the floor. "That's why I'm so wrecked inside. So"—and here she gritted her teeth—"pissed off. I want to fix this so bad."

"I know," I said. "I really, really know. In other universes, Mami is alive."

Gabi nodded for me to keep going.

I came around to stand next to her, put my hands again on the incubator. "There are other Sals out there who never lost their Mamis. Somewhere out there in the infinite reaches of space, there's a Mami who's alive and well and just waiting for me to find her."

"Does it help, knowing that?"

I shook my head. "It makes everything worse. The multiverse is *infinite*. I can't search all of infinity. I'd have to get so lucky to find the right Mami that Papi says it's a 'statistical impossibility.'"

Gabi nodded in sympathy. "'Statistical' is the worst kind of impossible, because it acts like there's a chance, when there isn't."

I wanted to cry, which always makes me want to hide. To fight the urge, I looked Gabi in the eye and said, "It's so hard to take. How am I supposed to take that?"

"How can I take it if Iggy—?" But she didn't finish. Instead, her face was lit from within by an idea. "Oh!" said Gabi, her hands dropping to her side. "This is how it happened."

I bunched my eyebrows. "How what happened?"

"How you broke the universe." I was about to complain, but she corrected herself. "No, not broke. Broke *through*. To other universes. To see your mami again."

I nodded. "And now I can't seem to stop."

The machines suddenly came alive, singing a choir song of *bleep-blep-bop*. We looked all around, scared something bad was happening. But the machines went back to their normal conversations in a few seconds, and Nurse Sotolongo didn't come charging in. Everything was okay for now.

Gabi stared hard at Iggy. Her fingers clawed at the top of the incubator. "I mean, what if you don't need to stop? What if you just have to learn the right way to do it?"

I thought of Other Gladis's Sal. "Maybe?" And then I added, "Today I snorted a calamitron."

"What?"

I laughed and then gave her a fifteen-minute lesson on calamity physics, which, trust me, covered pretty much everything anyone knows about it. Ask Papi if you don't believe me.

I could see why teachers liked Gabi. The longer I calamity-splained, the more excited she became. At the end of my lecture, Gabi gripped my arms. "Do you know what this means, Sal?"

I looked at each of her hands until, one by one, she let go. "No. But I am sure you're going to tell me."

"It means you *can* fix the universe!" She did a skip-twirl-dance around the incubator. Then, collecting herself, she stopped, and, putting both hands on the incubator and peering in, she became suddenly thoughtful. "We need to conduct more experiments immediately."

"I can show you on Monday, before first period." I suddenly remembered the entropy sweeper. I'd been so distracted by my conversation with Principal Torres that I'd forgotten all about it. I should probably try to get it from school before Papi missed it. "Or maybe sooner?"

"Maybe?!" Gabi said, the fighter jets in her hair scrambling wildly. "Are you kidding? We're going now! Right now! This very second!"

35

GABI HAD A WAY of making me feel like a seven-year-old.

I mean, *I* didn't have a MagicCarp.et app that I could use to call for a car anytime I wanted. I couldn't, because you need a credit card to make that app work, and the padres' response to my request for a credit card had gone pretty much like this:

SAL ASKS HIS PADRES FOR A CREDIT CARD
A Tragedy

Scene: Sal, a perfect son, asks his parents for a credit card.

AMERICAN STEPMOM: [snorts]

PAPI: No.

AMERICAN STEPMOM: [snorts]

FIN.

But it's also the way Gabi talked to her parents. We went back to the waiting room to ask if we could leave for a while. "Hey, adulting types," said Gabi. "Sal and I need to go back to Culeco for a few minutes."

"Back to Culeco?" American Stepmom started. "At this hour?"

"At *all* hours!" said Ms. Reál. "Gabi practically lives there. She's a very hands-on student council president."

"Oh," said American Stepmom. "But the school will be closed, won't it?"

"Principal Torres gave her keys so she can come and go as she pleases," said Lightning Dad. "Gabi practically runs that school."

"Gave her keys? Really?!" I don't know if the others got this, but American Stepmom, who was herself an assistant principal, had *I would never in a million years give keys to the school to one of my students!* written all over her face.

Cari-Dad smiled and sighed. "Kids today. They're so much more involved and active in their schools! Don't kids today seem smarter than we were?"

Grizzly Dad'ums nodded. "All I did was play soccer and video games back then."

"I got into lots of trouble when I was first being programmed," said Dad: The Final Frontier. She blinked as she remembered good times. "Oh, the humans I annihilated." When she saw everybody's face in the room, she added quickly, "What? Too soon?"

Ms. Reál looked dreamily at the ceiling. "All I did was fantasize about dating everybody," she said. "And I mean *everybody.*" She turned to Papi. "And what about you, Gustavo? What were you like as a child?"

"I was like Sal," said Papi. "A little too smart for my own good."

American Stepmom was looking around impatiently. "I don't know if it's a good idea to let the kids go to Culeco this late."

Ms. Reál laughed. She immediately regretted it and then, recovering fast, cleared her throat and put on a face that was six times more serious than it needed to be. "And why do you think that, Lucy?"

"Well," American Stepmom said carefully, "because it's nighttime. I don't think kids should be walking the streets of Miami at all hours."

Gabi raised her hand eagerly, waving it around like she was shipwrecked on an island and a ship was passing by.

American Stepmom, confused, wasn't sure what do to. She looked around, and all the Gabi dads signaled with their heads that she should call on Gabi. So she did. "Yes, Gabi?"

Gabi straightened her clothes and, as formally as if making a speech in English class, said, "We will not be walking the streets, as I will summon a car to convey us to and from our destination. I will pay for the car using my own money, so Sal need not ask you for any kind of bus fare or what have you. I promise that our business at Culeco will be completed by nine p.m., and that, barring any accident of fate, we will return to the hospital by nine-thirty. If any mishap occurs, I will send a group text to apprise you all of our situation and our new ETA. I hope you find these terms acceptable, and I remain open to discussing and negotiating any additional terms that would increase the comfort of all parties involved. Thank you very much for your time and consideration in this matter."

When Gabi finished, Reina and the Gabi dads burst into applause.

"Very convincing!" said Dada-ist.

"Who could say no to that?" asked Dada-dada-dada-dada Dadman!

Then everybody in the room turned to American Stepmom to see if she actually would say no.

"Um, well," said American Stepmom, "that's very thorough. I guess that's okay."

The room exploded into applause again.

"Thank you!" said Gabi, running up to American Stepmom and hugging her. American Stepmom hugged her back sincerely. I could see it happening in her face. She was falling under Gabi's spell now, too.

"Just one question," Papi added. "What are you actually going to be doing at school? You never told us."

I am so glad everyone was looking at Gabi and not me. I could feel my face start to glow with guilt. But Gabi? She had her answer ready.

"Science!"

More specifically, Gabi told Papi we were doing a science experiment, that it had to be done at Culeco, before Monday, and that the equipment we needed was at school.

"All true," Gabi added as she took out her Culeco keycard and unlocked the front doors to our school. Her fighter-jet barrettes caught moonbeams and turned to smears of blue-white light in her hair. She had also changed her shirt before we left. This one read: "WHEN I'M GOOD, I'M VERY GOOD, BUT WHEN I'M BAD, I'M BETTER."—MAE WEST.

"Totally," I agreed. "Those are the best kind of lies."

She turned around, her hand still on the door handle. "What? I didn't lie. Everything I said was the truth."

"Haven't your padres ever yelled at you for 'lies of omission'?"

"My parents don't yell at me," she sniffed.

"Yeah, well, if my papi finds out what we're really doing here, we're both gonna get yelled at."

Gabi, slightly offended, I think, stood as straight as she could. "We are about to conduct a scientific experiment, just like your dad does. Science is good, right? Plus, we're doing it for the best possible reason. We're trying to save the universe here, Sal! We are good people for doing this!"

"Don't have to convince me." I cut in front of her to grab the door handle and open the door for her. "After you, m'lady."

Gabi's British accent was terrible. "M'yes, a-thank you!" She started to walk in—

—when I thought of something. I grabbed her arm. "The cameras!"

Gabi looked at my hand like I'd just wiped all the slobber from a Saint Bernard's mouth on her sleeve. I let go.

Still using her *really bad* British accent, she said, "M'thar's nothing for you to be worried about, Sal. The cameras aren't on."

Blink. Blink. And one more blink. "What do you mean they're not on?"

She smiled proudly. "I, with the help of the student council, thought the cameras created an atmosphere of mistrust and unduly infringed on students' rights to privacy. We voted to have the cameras deactivated at the end of last year, and Principal Torres agreed to turn them off. She's a very reasonable woman, you know."

I quickly reviewed all the trouble those nonoperational cameras had caused me over my first week of school and, using yet another of my meditation techniques, popped the anger each memory brought with it like a balloon. Then, after a big juicy sigh, I said, "Great. No cameras. Makes our lives easier. After you, m'lady?" I bowed and gestured for her to go in already.

She started to, but then she took a step backward and, really seeing it for the first time, asked, "Why are you wearing that stupid hat, Sal?"

She was talking about my rainbow LED hat. I turned it on and tipped it toward her. "The better to see you with. And where we're going." And then, deciding that Gabi could hold her own door, I charged past her and went inside.

She followed right behind, trying hard not to giggle when she said, "You look like a unicorn and a Christmas tree had a baby." But she could barely finish without cracking herself up again.

Loudly. "Do you mind?" I shushed. "We're trying to carry out a secret operation here?"

"Sorry," she said, and capped her mouth with her hand. Which only made her start laughing again. "But it doesn't matter. It's not like anyone else is here."

Thanks to my hat, which was an excellent tool and a very smart investment, we didn't need to flip any light switches.

I glowed like a god through those hallways, thank you very much. We took the stairs up a floor and prowled over to Mrs. Waked's classroom. Gabi used her keycard to get us inside. I really needed to get me one of those.

Well, at least now it was my turn to surprise her. I pulled the entropy sweeper out from its hiding place in the costume rack.

As soon as it felt my hand on it, it cycled through colors like a baseball scoreboard. "I'm alive!" it proclaimed. "I'm alive!"

"Whoa!" said Gabi. "Are you really alive?"

"No," the sweeper said sadly. "I'm only a class-eight AI. That means I always *want* to cry at weddings, but I can't."

"Because you don't have human emotions?"

"No. Because I don't have a face." And it displayed an unhappy-face emoji on its handlebars.

I tried to tell Gabi that laughing at the sweeper's jokes would only encourage it, but did she listen?

After introductions—the entropy sweeper seemed to be half in love with Gabi already and insisted she be the one to carry it—we walked up another flight of stairs and down the hall to our target: Yasmany's locker. Zip-zip-zip and I opened it.

"I think the hole's a little smaller," said Gabi. "I mean, I think it is. Is it?"

I turned my head sideways. "Maybe a little? I can't really tell."

"I can! It's smaller!" said the entropy sweeper. "The dismembranation index of this space-time rupture was thirty-seven when I measured it this morning. Now it's thirty-six."

"Good machine!" said Gabi, petting the sweeper.

"Ahhhhhhhhhh," said the sweeper. Needy little thing.

"Thirty-six," I repeated. It took me a second to remember why that number was important. "That's how many calamitrons you said were left in the hallway today."

"Um, yeah," said the sweeper. "And thirty-six is less than thirty-seven. Very good, Sal." And then, whispering loudly, it added, "Geez, Gabi. This Sal kid isn't the sharpest cheddar in the dairy aisle, is he?"

I ignored it. "So all I have to do is snort up the rest of them, and the hole will close, right?"

"I don't know if that's a good idea," said the sweeper. All the sarcasm was gone from its voice. Now it sounded a heck of a lot like Papi. "We don't know what calamitrons will do to human tissue. They could act like radiation and make you sick, or worse."

"Or maybe they'll give me superpowers!"

"Dude," Gabi cacaseca'ed, "you can steal stuff from other universes. You're good on superpowers."

"The point is, we don't know what will happen. We have to be smart or brave. But which is the right one right now? To snort, or not to snort?"

Neither Gabi nor the entropy sweeper had a response to that. And neither of them thought my ingesting calamitrons was a good idea. The way they buzzed, changed colors, and slowly spun their propellers told me how worried they were for me. Well, that was mostly the entropy sweeper, but Gabi looked worried, too.

But I was the one who kept breaking the universe. I had to be the one to fix it. "Here goes nothing," I said. And then I sucked air with all my might.

"Thirty-five!" said the entropy sweeper.

"The hole's smaller!" said Gabi, peering into the locker. "I can definitely tell this time."

I inhaled again, bigly. "Thirty-three!" said the sweeper. "You got two that time!"

"It's working!" I said. "I can close the hole!" And I exhaled all the air in my lungs to get ready to fix everything with one mighty suck.

Just as I started to inhale, Gabi ran over to me and pinched my nose shut. I looked at her fingers cross-eyed.

"Not yet," she said. "We need to be scientific. You've popped four calamitrons so far today. How do you feel?"

I said with a pinched-nose voice, "Fine. I feel fine." And I really did. Maybe a little gassy, but that was from all the Cuban food I'd eaten back at the hospital. I really liked Reina Reál's black beans.

Gabi didn't all-the-way believe me. "Let's get Nurse Sotolongo to check you out before you pig out on any more calamitrons."

"Listen to her, Sal," said the machine, its voice shaky with worry.

I gave in with a sigh. "Fine," I said. "Now, can you let go of my nose?"

We had two more places to search for calamitrons before we headed back to the hospital: in the multipurpose room, where I'd switched the climbing wall, and in the first-floor restroom, where that other Sal had switched Gladises. The multipurpose room was closer, so, with Gabi carrying her new BFF, the entropy sweeper, we headed there first.

But when we arrived, we saw through the door's windows that a light was on inside.

We slowed down, and stopped in front of the door. Then we looked at each other.

"Are we there yet?" said the very loud entropy sweeper, letting every ax murderer and serial killer in the building know exactly where we were. Gabi and I both jumped in the air like cats.

"Shh!" said Gabi.

"Humans," the machine grumbled. "Even the nice ones turn on you."

I reached over and turned off the sweeper. Then, signaling to Gabi with my head, we both pressed our noses to the window to have a look.

Inside, someone had stacked the gym mats into a big pile and made a blanket out of the mats' canvas cover. A half-deflated football lay at one end like a pillow. And resting against the football pillow was a shaggy pink teddy bear with hearts for eyes.

"Oso Amoroso," gasped Gabi.

That means "Bear of Love." The name of the teddy, probably. But how the heck did Gabi know that? "What?" I asked her.

She didn't answer. Her face was volcanoing with blood, and she began to shake with rage. She walked a step away from the door and turned around. Then she pulled her phone out of her pocket and used voice-to-text to send someone a message. This is what she said:

"Guess where I am standing question mark I am standing in front of the all caps MULTIPURPOSE all caps ROOM comma and guess what I just saw through the window question mark I saw capital Oso capital Amoroso sleeping on a football pillow and a bed made of those gross gym mats period new line new line You are my friend period You are supposed to tell me when you need help period This is all caps COMPLETELY unacceptable period new line new line Write me back all caps THIS all caps INSTANT and tell me where you are period send."

Carefully, politely, I peeked over Gabi's shoulder to see whom she'd sent that message to. When I saw, I gasped.

But Gabi didn't respond. She just stared at her phone, trying to force it to send her a response. "Write me back," she said, her teeth clenched. "A curse upon your mother's head. Write me!"

And then, a second later, Yasmany did. **In bathroom dang how you find me**

36

YASMANY STOOD OUTSIDE the first-floor bathroom, brushing his teeth, as we walked toward him. He had on a Miami Heat tank top, a rolled towel draped over his shoulders, and striped old-man pajama bottoms that he'd rolled up to his calves. He was barefoot. His feet were as big as rakes.

He didn't look happy to see us. He scrubbed his molars and scowled as we approached.

I could feel Gabi tensing up. I walked a step behind her, my hands in my pockets, clutching trick props and ready for anything. She got right under Yasmany's chin and handed the entropy sweeper back to me. He stopped brushing but didn't take his fist off the toothbrush.

"Well," Gabi began. Her voice caught, though, so she had to swallow back a sob before she went on. "This isn't the gentlest way you could have let me know that you didn't want to be my friend anymore, Yasmany. But you've never been very gentle, have you? No, no one would ever accuse you of being a *gentleman*. But I suppose it's best to know these things, rather than wallow under misapprehensions. So, fine. I understand now. I won't bother you anymore."

"Gawah?!" exclaimed Yasmany. I think "Gawah?!" is how you say "What the pants are you talking about?!" when your mouth is full of toothpaste. Then he said, "Oou mah beff fren imba word!" and so much toothpaste juice dribbled out of his mouth I had to turn my head so I didn't barf on the spot.

Gabi took both of his hands into hers. "You ran away from home, Yasmany."

He became very still. Then he nodded, just once.

"And you didn't call me."

Yasmany didn't move.

"How could you not turn to *me* in your time of need? I am very good at solving problems, you know."

Yasmany stared at Gabi. Then, for two seconds, he glared at me. Then he looked at Gabi again.

"Who gave you Oso Amoroso, Yasmany?"

Finally he answered again. "Oou did."

"That's right. I gave you Oso Amoroso. In fourth grade, for Valentine's Day, back when I had a crush on you. I even gave him a name in Spanish, because I thought you would like that. Remember? I haven't seen him for years. But then, just a few minutes ago, boom, there he was, asleep on the terrible, horrible, lonely bed you made for yourself out of gym mats and a football. A football, Yasmany! In the multipurpose room. With no one to take care of you! How could you, Yasmany? How could you?"

Gabi started knocking on Yasmany's chest with both fists like he was a door she wanted open.

Yasmany, looking desperately at me, pointed at Gabi with both fingers and mouthed to me around his toothbrush, *Wha' do I do?*

I shrugged. I had no idea.

Help me! he pleaded soundlessly.

Sal to the rescue. I took a step and stood beside Gabi, put a kind hand on her shoulder. She stopped punching Yasmany and turned to me. Her look was begging me to find a way, somehow, to make everything better. So was Yasmany's.

So I did. I made everything better. By letting rip the fart of my life.

A word about farts.

They're overused as jokes. As someone who's serious about showmanship, I've learned that even the best-timed butt burp in the world won't get as many laughs as you think it will. It turns out a lot of people don't think farts are funny at all.

I know, I couldn't believe it either when I found this out. But it's true. It's smarter to find a more original joke whenever you can.

I know all this. But I have a confession: Pants bombs always make me laugh. Like, always. Can't help it.

And since Gabi giggled like a windup monkey whenever I said "cacaseca," I had a feeling they'd make her laugh, too. I decided to take the risk. And so I made my butt sing like an opera dude.

At first, no one said anything. Gabi's face was stuck somewhere between disbelief and disgust. Yasmany seemed to have swallowed some toothpaste, and he coughed a little.

Then Gabi, blinking, pulled out her phone. "Oh," she said. "I got a text."

"Who from?" I asked, looking for any way to change the subject away from my vulgar little performance.

"Your underwear," said Gabi, eyes wide. "It wants to die with dignity."

Yasmany's toothbrush flew like a missile out of his mouth and landed halfway down the hall, trailing a stream of toothpaste foam behind it. Gabi ducked and I dodged, both of us getting out of the way just in time.

And then we all fell on the floor and forgot who we were and cracked up for ten minutes. I laughed so hard it felt like I was being squeezed to death by an extremely funny boa constrictor.

Gabi and Yasmany, too. They kept begging for mercy, struggling to breathe, and then someone (me, for instance) would talk about my underwear on its deathbed, surrounded by its underwear family, pleading for someone to pull the plug so it didn't have to go back to work under my jeans ever again, and we'd all laugh some more.

And then, somehow—I honestly don't remember how it worked—Yasmany went to get his stuff from the multipurpose room, and Gabi went with him to "help" (really, to make sure he didn't bolt). He was going to come with us to the hospital, and Gabi's mami was going to feed him, and he'd have a place to sleep (because Ms. Reál had that whole hospital wrapped around her finger), and we'd figure out what to do in the morning.

Gabi and I didn't ask what had happened to him at home. We didn't ask him to share his feelings. Gabi started to, and

I cut her off, because I already knew he couldn't. Back when Mami was dying, I always got so angry and confused when people tried to make me tell them how I was feeling. My insides had felt like a tar pit, the kind that used to suck dinosaurs down to their deaths.

And then, one day when I was visiting Mami at the hospital, a clown volunteer tried to distract me by pulling a dove out of a newspaper. He fooled me *so bad*! It was a fake dove with plastic eyes, but when he started puppeting it, I couldn't believe how alive it looked. It was the first time I'd felt anything close to happiness since Mami had been admitted.

He taught me how magic can make something appear out of nothing, and make dead things more alive. He didn't tell me to feel better or to talk about the horrible blackness slushing around in my chest. He put on a show, and the good feelings came with it.

After that, I was hooked. I've been a showman ever since. Sometimes I do magic, and sometimes I endanger lives with a little thunder from down under, but the point is the same. Sometimes, when it's too hard, when it hurts too much, only silliness can save us. And I'm all about doing whatever it takes to help people make it to tomorrow.

Yasmany and Gabi left me alone in the hallway while they went to get his stuff. Alone with the entropy sweeper.

I turned it on.

"I'm alive!" it yelled, and put on its typical light show.

"Hey, buddy," I said, sweet as Splenda—which, to be

honest, has an aftertaste like medicine. "Maybe you could scan this hallway for calamitrons?"

"Already did," it replied, proud of itself. "I'm super good at my job!"

I waited for it to tell me. It just sat there changing colors like a multicolored sandwich.

"And?" I finally asked.

"Oh yeah." It turned red and serious. "Zero calamitrons on this entire floor."

"Even in the bathroom?"

It relaxed, started cycling through the rainbow again. "Yep, even in the bathroom. Which, by the way, is surprisingly clean. Your school should give your janitor a raise."

Man! How did that other Sal switch Gladises without any extra calamity? *I* needed to learn how to do that!

Which reminded me: There was still one more experiment to run.

I jogged up the nearest stairs to the second floor and into the multipurpose room. Gabi and Yasmany were stacking the mats back up. Near them, a duffel bag that didn't look very full had the head of Oso Amoroso sticking out of the zipper.

"We're almost done," said Gabi. "Sorry if you were bored downstairs."

Yasmany looked suspiciously at the entropy sweeper. "What the heck is that thing?"

I shrugged. "Long story, bro. I just need to—" And then I stopped talking.

Because I was looking at the climbing wall. Which was

back to being covered with handholds and footholds. The red zone was just as easy as the green and yellow zones. It was like I'd never changed a thing earlier that day.

"Zero calamitrons!" said the entropy sweeper.

"Okay, good! Zero calamitrons is good!" said Gabi, throwing the last mat on top of the pile. But she missed, and the mat rebounded off the pile, and a second later she was buried under it. Only her hands and feet stuck out from beneath it.

"Ow," she said. But it was a funny "ow," not an actual "ow." Yasmany, shaking his head, went to help her. "Girl, you got to grow *an inch!*"

I turned back to the wall. It had fixed itself, without me needing to snort anything. *Well,* I thought to myself, *most of the time, that's what the rips in the fabric of the universe do. Eventually. If you leave them alone.*

If I relaxed a little, I could start to see the climbing wall I'd stolen from another universe, kind of superimposed over the actual wall. But it was back in its own universe now, where it belonged. No harm done.

But here's what I didn't get: The climbing wall was way bigger than the chicken I'd put in Yasmany's locker. So why had the wall fixed itself already, while the hole in the locker remained? And there were lots more calamitrons still floating around at the Coral Castle. Why?

I felt like I could almost figure this out, like the answer was on the tip of my tongue. But it wouldn't come.

"You okay, Sal?" Gabi asked. She and Yasmany walked up to me. "You look a million miles away."

"Hey, Gabi," I said, pointing at the wall, "do you see what I see?"

She squinted. "What?"

"Don't stare. Relax."

She nodded. Her head fell on her left shoulder, and her eyes went sideways, like a drunk fish's. "Oh. Yeah. I see it now. A double wall! What does it mean?"

"I know!" screamed the entropy sweeper. "A dismembranation event happened earlier today that has since remembranated itself, resulting in—"

I flipped it off. And then I turned it off, too.

"I'm not sure," I said to Gabi. "But I know Mr. Lynott is going to be very confused on Monday."

"I don't see anything," said Yasmany, squinting.

"Oh!" said Gabi. She gave me a huge *Play along* wink. "It's 'cause you're doing it wrong, Yasmany. You have to relax first. Close your eyes."

He did and shook out his limbs like a boxer. "Okay."

"Good. Now, put your hands on your head."

He did that, too. "Yeah?"

"Okay, now take a deep breath and hold it," she singsonged.

Yasmany took a breath. He held his breath.

Gabi tiptoed around him and then, with zero warning, tried to give him a wedgie.

I mean, she grabbed the elastic band of his underwear, and she pulled and hopped around and flexed every muscle in her body trying to lift him.

Yasmany (who definitely had a bit of the showman in him, too), opened his eyes and looked left and right, trying to see what was causing him mild annoyance. Then, turning around, he looked at Gabi with his lower lip out, like a scientist discovering a new species of bug.

"This. Is. No. Fair!" said Gabi, still struggling to even budge him. "This. Is. Supposed. To. Work! I. Saw. A. Documentary!"

Yasmany shrugged, hooked two fingers through one of Gabi's belt loops and then started walking off with her like she was his purse. And not even a heavy purse.

Gabi, while hanging sideways from his hand, still tried to wedgie him. Got to give it to the girl: She doesn't give up.

But she couldn't even slow Yasmany down. He moseyed over to his duffel bag, scooped it up without breaking step, planted a kiss on the forehead of Oso Amoroso, and headed for the exit. "You coming, chacho?" he called over his shoulder to me. "I'm hungry. They got good food at the hospital?"

"My family set up a buffet," Gabi said, like it was totally normal to have a conversation when you were hanging from Yasmany's arm like a purse. "Cuban food. All your favorites. Even pernil."

The word "pernil" stopped Yasmany dead. He looked over his shoulder at me. And then he took off running, Gabi giggling and Oso Amoroso jiggling as he ran.

Yasmany was not all right. I had no idea how bad his day had really been. But jokes and food and attempted wedgies all helped. It would get us to tomorrow, anyway.

37

REINA SHOULD HAVE been Yasmany's mami.

She fed him. Oh, how she fed him. Then, after she had fed him, she fed him again. Then, when he said he was still a little hungry, she almost died of joy. And then she *really* fed him. I mean, that last plate she served him was so huge, someone could have carved four presidents' heads on it.

And Yasmany ate it all. He's pretty big for his age, but he looks more like a runner than a football player. I have no idea how he fit that much food in his body.

The Gabi dads all knew Yasmany and treated him like family—particularly, like the runt of the family. I'm not saying I loved it when Grizzly Dad'ums put Yasmany on his shoulders and helicopter-spun him like a pro wrestler, and then Yasmany almost barfed because he'd eaten like ten pounds of pernil, and then Grizzly Dad'ums got in trouble with Ms. Reál for playing too rough. But I'm not saying I *didn't* love it, either.

Dada-ist captured the helicopter in a sketch and gave it to Yasmany, who appreciated it as seriously as a child getting his first ever balloon. Daditarian dared him to eat a cheesy bug, and he refused and refused—until I ate a handful of them, crunching away. Then, making a pained face and scratching his tongue with his top teeth, he popped one in his mouth and chewed.

And almost barfed again. This time, Daditarian got in trouble with Ms. Reál.

Luckily, Cari-Dad was there. As a doctor, she knew exactly what would cure Yasmany's nausea: chocolate cake. She brought a slice over to him, and any chance of him getting sick before he vacuumed it off the paper plate vanished as quickly as the cake did.

I could see Cari-Dad doing a sneaky examination of Yasmany while he ate cake. She asked him a few questions: "Anywhere hurting right now? Where'd that bruise on your neck come from? Headache? Blurred vision? Did you feel dizzy at any point today?" And Yasmany answered them without thinking: "No. Fell. No. No. Only when chacho over there spun me around."

Grizzly Dad'ums shrugged.

Cari-Dad patted his back and left the waiting room. The walls were glass, so if I leaned back in my chair, I could follow her down the hallway. She stopped at the welcome station by the elevators, where two Miami-Dade police officers were standing. She shook their hands, and they spoke for a minute. Then Cari-Dad took out her phone and texted someone.

Ms. Reál's phone went off. She read the text, excused herself, and a few seconds later joined Cari-Dad and the cops in the hallway.

"Don't draw attention," Gabi whispered, sitting on the folding chair next to me.

I let my chair fall forward and land on all four legs. I didn't want to be nosy, but this was serious. So I wouldn't draw attention, I looked at the floor and whispered, "Is Yasmany's papi a bad guy?"

Gabi made one of those noises that sounded like a laugh but couldn't be a laugh because nothing about what she said was funny. "The bad guy is his mom."

"Oh," I said. And I didn't know what else to say for a long time afterward.

Luckily, Gabi has a lot of dads. They were hilarious and nice and liked to have fun. When one of them became sad—thinking about poor Iggy, maybe, or now Yasmany—another four kept the conversation going. Slowly, Gabi came out of her funk. Her dads really were magical.

I noticed there was at least one dad missing. "Where's Dad: The Final Frontier?" I asked Gabi.

"Recharging."

"That," said Papi, getting up, "sounds like a good idea. Time for all calamity physicists to go to bed."

"And assistant principals," added American Stepmom.

Like any proper Cuban gathering, it took the adults another forty-five minutes of conversation to actually say good-bye. The padres told me to obey Gabi's parents like they were my parents (which made me snort), go to bed soon, check my blood sugar, brush my teeth, etc. I said yes, yes, yesyesyesyesyes, and practically had to push them out the door to get them to leave.

But just as I had shoved them out, Ms. Reál and Cari-Dad came back in, and it took the padres another half hour of good-byes, this time with Ms. Reál thank-you-sobbing, before they left for good.

And actually, I did go to bed pretty soon after. Nurse Sotolongo came by the waiting room to get Yasmany and me, since we were sharing a room that night.

Nurse Sotolongo put out her hand to shake Yasmany's. "Hi!" she said. "It's good to meet you. Gabi's told me you're an old friend of the family."

Yasmany looked—I had no idea he had the ability to look this way—shy. "Hi," he said, and mostly looked away as he shook hands with Nurse Sotolongo.

Everyone in the room became suddenly interested in anything other than their handshake.

This wasn't a normal hospital room. I'm pretty sure it was a closet the hospital had converted into a room where doctors and nurses could catch a few hours' sleep. No machines, no monitors, no medicines, no medical supplies. No window, either. It was dark as a dragon's stomach.

Two small cots were wedged in there, side by side. The sheets smelled like disinfectant that was trying too hard to smell like a summer day. I only just fit in my bed. I couldn't see much, but Yasmany's Stonehenge feet had to be hanging off the edge of his.

I knew by our breathing we were both awake. But we didn't

speak for a long time. We just let the darkness pour into our eyes for a while.

"Sal?" said Yasmany.

"Yeah?"

But he went quiet again. I thought maybe he wouldn't say anything more for the rest of the night.

Then he did. "I don't know."

"You don't know what?"

He sighed. "Why I act like I do."

I turned on my side. I couldn't see a thing in the darkness, but I knew he could tell from my voice that I was facing him now, and that meant I was taking him seriously. "Don't you think about how you act?"

"Yeah. At night. When it's too late to fix anything." I heard him trying to fit himself better into the bed, which made both cots shake. "You always think before you say anything. How you do it?"

My turn to sigh. "I think too much, Yasmany. Way, way, way too much. And it gets me in trouble all the time."

He let my words hang in the air for a while. Then, sounding tired and quiet and like someone I could be friends with, he said, "Hey, Sal?"

Okay. Here it was. Yasmany was going to tell me all about his bad-guy mami. Things were going to get real sad real quick. But Principal Torres wanted me to be Yasmany's friend, and Gabi definitely wanted me to be Yasmany's friend. And you know what? Maybe I wanted to be Yasmany's friend at this point, too. Maybe. A little.

So let's go. "Yeah, man?"

He worked up his courage to speak. Then, squeaking more than speaking, he asked me, "Does Nurse Sotolongo have a boyfriend?"

I couldn't help it. I busted out laughing. When I heard him laughing, too, I knew I could joke with him about it. "Just you, Yasmango," I said, flipping onto my back again and gathering the blanket under my chin. "Just you." And with that, I went to sleep.

Well, actually, I faked being asleep. My mind was still running top-speed. It had been another busy day.

About twenty minutes later—I mean, I think it was twenty minutes? In that darkness, time was unknowable—but let's say twenty minutes later, Yasmany said one more thing that he didn't think I'd hear, because I am an expert at fake-sleeping.

"I'm sorry, Sal." And if he started quietly, carefully crying, I wouldn't tell you, because he didn't mean for anyone to hear it. I'll just say what I heard him whisper over and over: "I'm sorry."

38

SATURDAY, 5:30 A.M.: Gabi texts me to see if I'm awake.

I think the worst, ask her if Iggy's okay.

Oh yeah, he's fine. I just want to get started on the play, she writes back.

I roll my eyes and turn over.

Saturday, still 5:30 a.m.: Gabi texts me again to see if I'm awake. Yasmany makes annoyed piglet sounds from his bed. I silence my phone.

Saturday, 5:39 a.m.: I check my phone. Gabi has texted twelve more times. I text back, **Hi did you say something? Sorry WAS SLEEPING**

Also 5:39 a.m.: Gabi texts back. We're to meet in the cafeteria "posthaste."

5:40 a.m.: I write back, **Dont know that word goin to find dictionary might be a while start without me**

I know what "posthaste" means. I read a lot of fantasy. I'm just being annoying at this point.

Still 5:40 a.m.: Gabi writes back that I'm annoying.

Mission accomplished.

She also says I'd better come down, or she's going to send her "people" to come get me.

5:41 a.m.: I write back **Do ur worst cant get me outta bed its Saturday sleeping now gnight**

5:52 a.m.: Nurse Sotolongo opens the door to our closet. She puts a finger to her lips and gestures for me to come with her.

Also 5:52 a.m.: I roll over.

Also 5:52 a.m.: Nurse Sotolongo drags me out of bed. She enjoys it way too much. Yasmany complains with pig snorts but doesn't wake up.

5:59 a.m.: Gabi is waiting in the cafeteria. She and Nurse Sotolongo spend a few minutes making fun of my black silk pajamas that look exactly like the outfit Bruce Lee wears in *Fists of Fury*, which is one of my and American Stepmom's favorite movies. Gabi and Nurse Sotolongo start fake kung fu fighting all over the cafeteria, which, frankly, is insensitive to Chinese culture.

6:01 a.m.: I get my revenge by telling Nurse Sotolongo that Yasmany wants to know if she has a boyfriend.

Then she and Gabi get their revenge on me by making me repeat everything Yasmany said like twelve times. Lesson learned: Never try to outgossip these two again.

6:34 a.m.: Nurse Sotolongo uses her employee discount to buy us breakfast. She tells us to text her if we need anything and goes back to work. Gabi and I eat like garbage disposals.

6:48 a.m.: We clear our breakfast trays. Gabi takes out her tablet. We're ready to work on our Everyman play.

Also 6:48 a.m.: Gabi and I realize we're going to need a lot of help.

Also 6:48 a.m.: I text my parents.

Papi and American Stepmom showed up about an hour later, dressed in weekend shorts and sandals. They looked and smelled showered, but they sounded three coffees short of conscious when they asked Gabi how Iggy was doing.

I had espressos waiting for the padres at our table. They called me a very good son.

American Stepmom also hugged me and told me how proud she was of me, staying at the hospital to support a friend. Papi agreed and joined the hug, crushing American Stepmom and me with his love. Well, with his arms, but his arms were full of love.

"You're such a darling family!" Gabi explained. "And if you don't mind my saying, it's such a pleasure to see a man who is emotionally secure enough to display affection to his son in public. It's all too rare in machismo-stunted Miami."

"You talk just like your texts," said American Stepmom.

"Thank you," said Gabi.

We sat down. After coffee, I explained the Everyman play assignment to the padres. "Gabi says she'll write the script if I do the costumes and staging. But we need a story first. And we want it to be funny."

"Funny?" asked American Stepmom. "Aren't you worried that that will upset your family? I mean, your little brother . . ." She trailed off meaningfully.

"Iggy's doing better," said Gabi. "And anyway, I want to make something that will cheer them up. I want them to laugh at death. *I* want to laugh at death."

Papi, who always worried way too much about the rules, said, "But if it doesn't fit with the assignment, you won't get a good grade."

"I'd rather get a bad grade than make my family any sadder in this dark period in Reál history," said Gabi. She could be pretty scary when she wanted to be. The way she said "There's no way I can let Death win" would make me run the other way. If I was Death, I mean.

"And anyway," I added, "Mrs. Waked loves creativity. We can make it scary *and* funny. With great costumes and magic tricks. And for Gabi's parents, a happy ending. Everybody wins."

"That's a lot of work for a weekend," said Papi. "Is there enough time?"

"Of course there is," said American Stepmom. Gabi's speech had gripped her by the heart. Now she was fully on board. "We just need to think imaginatively."

American Stepmom has been my homework secret weapon ever since she and Papi started dating. And she didn't let me down today. With her leading the charge, Gabi asking all the right questions and taking furious notes on the tablet, and Papi and me sharing ideas as fast as we could think of them, we had a plan within half an hour.

Now we needed more stuff: tent poles, bungee cords, a ton of black fabric, and my jumping stilts. Our Death was going to jump around. Because the only thing scarier than Death is Death jumping around all over the place.

Papi drove back to the Coral Castle to gather the supplies. In the meantime, Ms. Reál walked into the cafeteria. She had on the same clothes she'd worn yesterday. She looked puffed and swollen, like a basketball someone had drawn a face on.

But she lit up when she saw us. She smiled as she hustled over to our table, gave us all our good-morning kisses, and took a seat.

"¡Buenas noticias!" she said. Iggy was doing even better. The doctors said he was in "stable" condition now, instead of "critical and we have no idea what's going on" condition.

American Stepmom got up and hugged the sitting Ms. Reál from behind. "That *is* good news!"

In American Stepmom's arms, while simultaneously weeping and smiling, Ms. Reál told us how she had spent most of the night awake, her body draped over the incubator as she prayed. Gabi's dads had taken turns bringing her food, trying to convince her to sleep, comforting her as much as they could. And she had cried, and cried and laughed, and cried and talked, and cried herself to sleep. But she'd woken up every few minutes to put her hands on the incubator and watch her son fight for his life.

Gabi went over and joined the hug. "He's going to make it, Mama. Iggy's going to beat this."

Ms. Reál used both hands to squeeze Gabi's arm. "We'll see, mija. That may not be Iggy's path. If it isn't, we're here to ease his passing, and to love him."

Gabi looked at the ceiling. The line of her bottom lip trembled like a sound wave. "But you've been praying. You pray all the time. Isn't this what prayer is for?"

Ms. Reál kissed her daughter's arm. "God isn't a genie, mija. He doesn't grant wishes. I pray to know Him better. To partake of divinity."

Gabi hugged her mami even more fiercely. But she aimed angry eyes at heaven.

"So," said Ms. Reál, taking a deep, tear-clearing breath, "what's going on here?"

American Stepmom released Ms. Reál so she could use her hands to help describe our idea for the Everyman play. American Stepmom talks with her hands when she gets excited. Sometimes she looks like two windmills fighting each other.

Gabi and I were excited, too. The three of us took turns spelling out our plan—Gabi right in her mama's ear, since she was still hugging her, and me from my seat. Explaining it to Ms. Reál made our idea even clearer and better.

When we'd finished, I was worried that Ms. Reál would be offended that we were treating Death so lightly, just like American Stepmom had said. And it looked for a second like my fear was becoming reality. Ms. Reál crossed her arms and stared at us like she was one second away from texting Satan with ideas about how we should be punished.

"What's wrong?" American Stepmom asked her.

With straight-backed dignity, Ms. Reál asked us, "And why, en el nombre de Dios, didn't you wake me?"

"Wake you?" I asked. "To help us do homework?"

Ms. Reál sniffed. "I love helping with homework. I *always* help you with your homework, Gabi. It's my *duty* to help you with your homework."

"But you hardly slept all night, Mama," said Gabi, intensi-fying her hug. "We wanted you to get a little rest."

In response, Ms. Reál bit Gabi's hand. Well, now I knew where Gabi got it from.

"Okay, okay!" said Gabi, giggling and pulling her hand away. "You can help. Geez. You left teeth marks, you know."

Ms. Reál smiled like she had just eaten Gabi's grand-mother. "Maybe next time you'll remember to call your mami when you need help."

And after Ms. Reál came the Gabi dads. She texted them in Spanglish to come down to help. Less than ten minutes later, they pushed the cafeteria's double doors open and strolled in like a slo-mo movie shot of Navy SEALs getting ready for action.

Dada-dada-dada-dada Dadman! swaggered front and center of the Gabi-dad formation, wearing cop sunglasses, a blue T-shirt with the collar ripped out of it, so that it kind of swam over his brolic chest, and gray drawstring sweatshorts with ragged leg holes, like the Hulk's.

On his left walked Dada-ist, wearing a barely buttoned linen guayabera, Hawaii-sunset swim trunks from fifty years ago, and flip-flops that he might have found on the street ear-lier today and just put on. He looked like a shorter, slimmer, blacker version of Papi, right down to the mismatched fashion, but instead of a scientific calculator, he carried a pad of artist paper in one hand and a box of colors in the other.

On Dada-dada-dada-dada Dadman!'s right came Daditarian, dressed like a telenovela actor trying not to be recognized: sunglasses; shoulder-length, product-perfect hair; blue T-shirt and white shorts, both expensive and brandless, and cut to show off biceps and glutes; a sailor-knot necklace; and wild dress shoes made of red-and-yellow fake rattlesnake skin, with no socks.

Two dads brought up the rear. Grizzly Dad'ums, his wild hair sprawling like an eagle's nest on his head, was dressed in serial-killer flannel, abused-to-death carpenter pants, and boots with crushed-in steel toes. Dad: The Final Frontier wore a dark blue version of the suit she'd had on when I'd last seen her. I imagined her opening her closet in the morning trying to decide which of her forty suits—all just slightly different shades of black, gray, and blue—she would wear that day.

"Our family has to work on making our entrance," American Stepmom said to me, sounding competitive.

"Daddies!" yelled Gabi, and threw herself at her dads. They hugged her and kissed her and passed her around, and she crawled all over their shoulders. Together, they walked over to us and said good morning, then lined up for their morning kisses from Ms. Reál, who told them each in turn how beautiful and special they were.

It turned out Dada-dada-dada-dada Dadman!, as Florida's favorite traveling-theme-park-superhero-slash-stuntman-for-hire, had worn, repaired, and helped to make costumes a hundred times more complicated than the one we were planning. He was voted lead costume designer for our production and couldn't have been happier.

"Okay," he said, looking around. "First, we need to see what we have to work with. Where's the sewing machine?"

Everybody looked at everyone else for the answer.

Dada-dada-dada-dada Dadman!'s face dropped. "No sewing machine?"

"I think I might have one," Ms. Reál volunteered. "At home, in the basement. Somewhere. Maybe."

"Can we just use needle and thread?" asked American Stepmom.

"Hand-stitching is really hard," said Dada-dada-dada-dada Dadman!

"How about we staple it?" asked Grizzly Dad'ums. "A hospital's got to have a . . . few . . . staples . . . lying around. . . ."

He trailed off because he realized what a dumb idea that was. Everyone sat quietly trying to figure out what to do next.

I got a text. It was from Aventura. It said:

Hey Sal I was gonna text Gabi but I thought maybe that wouldn't be a good idea

You know in case her brother isn't doing so hot

So do you think it's okay for me ask her how she's doing?

I wrote her back: **Lil bro still ill bro but hes a fighter** followed by **ya text her shell like that.**

She piled on something like twenty different heart emojis, then wrote: **How are you?**

Gud gud just hanging at the hospital were making a costume

This time the emoji pile was of the shocked-face variety. **You're at the hospital with Gabi? Right now?**

Ya her whole familys here were working on a death costume for school

And you were there yesterday too? To drop off my notes for her right?

Ya I spent the night here they put me in a closet lol

More Wow OMG Fireworks emojis. **That was so nice of you Sal!**

I try not to use emojis. Don't like 'em. But there's that weird one that's a red mask with a long nose and bushy eyebrows that is interesting. I sent that one. Hopefully, Aventura would get it.

I think maybe she did? **Lol** she wrote back.

And then, lightbulb. **Hey A you wouldnt have a sewing machine we could borrow would you**

The emojis took over my entire phone screen. I mean, smiley faces spinning and crying for joy, happy cats and clowns, hats and dresses and women in flowing gowns, more multicolored hearts, three full lines of scissors, and, for some reason at the end of it all, a cigarette.

I had no idea what all that meant. Luckily, at the end of the emoji storm, she wrote: **I'll be there in an hour.**

I looked up from my phone, smiling like an idiot. "Got us a sewing machine!" I announced.

Things started happening very fast.

I spread the boxes full of props that Papi and American Stepmom had brought last night over three tables. We sorted through them, brainstorming ideas on how we could use them in the show. Then Papi showed up with the cloth and the tent poles and everything, but I especially wanted the jumping stilts, because with them I could really show people what I wanted to do with the Death costume. I put them on and launched myself around the room, striding between tables like a giant, making some people cheer (like Daditarian and Grizzly Dad'ums) and others become a little worried for me (like Ms. Reál and Dada-ist). But American Stepmom assured the worriers that I was an expert on those stilts. Which I was.

Then Aventura arrived, carrying a sewing machine like nothing I'd ever seen before. It looked like R2-D2 and a jackhammer had a baby. Dad: The Final Frontier rushed up to help Aventura with that weird backward-knees walk of hers, and together they set it on a table. Then Aventura went over and hugged Gabi off the floor.

"Now we're cooking!" said Dada-dada-dada-dada Dadman! He rubbed his hands together greedily, looking at that sewing machine from the future.

After Gabi introduced Aventura around—as "a straight-A student and Culeco's premier cosplay artist"—we unanimously decided to make Aventura co–lead costume designer.

She and Dada-dada-dada-dada Dadman! were instant friends. Just a few minutes after they'd started working together, they'd created a bell-shaped frame for the Death costume out of tent poles and bungee cord. They had me get inside, stilts on, to make it the right height—so I could lift the frame just off the ground with the top of my head. Then they wrapped it in black cloth to measure how much they would need for the costume. A few expert twists and tucks, and they had made rough versions of the costume's hood and sleeves and hemline, marking the measurements with a piece of chalk.

The measuring was done. Now, it was time to sew.

Aventura, as the master seamstress, got started. The rest

of us, under the direction of Dada-dada-dada-dada Dadman!, had the job of hand-stitching 160 loops into the robe to hold all the tent poles in place.

He spread the robe-in-the-making out like a huge black flower on the floor and handed each of us black thread and a needle. He showed us how to cut loops out of the extra fabric and where and how to stitch them into the costume. Those loops had to be perfect, not too small and not too big, or else the costume wouldn't expand and shrink when it needed to.

Not exactly exciting work. But I liked it. When you do a slow, careful job like this one, the whole world seems to shrink and calm down, and suddenly life makes a simple kind of sense.

Gabi hated it. "Ugh!" she said about four million times. She kept stopping her work to complain. "This is going to take forever!"

"Gabi," said Daditarian, "maybe you'd rather work on the script for a while?"

"Oh my God yes I would good-bye!" said Gabi, running away before anyone could change their mind. She dug in her bookbag, fired up her tablet on a table far away from us, put in her earbuds, and, happy as a pop song, got to work writing.

Everyone laughed, except Dad: The Final Frontier, who opened her mouth to indicate laughter, like a muppet. Yeah. Her tongue really didn't move at all. Creepy.

We hadn't been working ten minutes when Lightning Dad joined us. He still had on a really expensive weatherman suit from his morning shift. He also had a thermos full of homemade espresso, which pulled everyone but Dad: The Final Frontier and me off the robe. The human adults stood around drinking espresso in tiny paper cups and catching up Lightning Dad, while the diabetic boy and the robot kept on working. It is so hard to find good help these days.

When the coffee break was over, finally, the adults resumed their sewing. All except Lightning Dad, that is. He took a moment to give my shoulder a strong thank-you grip. "This is a wonderful thing you are doing for us, Sal."

"What is?" I asked.

"Making us do your homework for you!" And before I could defend myself, he added, "Kidding, kidding! This is just what the doctor ordered. Well, not really, but they should have. I mean, here we are, in a hospital full of doctors, and not one of them recommended to us that we should distract ourselves by helping with our kids' homework. What were they thinking? Well, it's a good thing you're here, son, to take care of us. Thank you."

"Um, you're welcome?"

He put on the sincere face that must have charmed the AhoraMismo viewers at the end of every weather report. "Seriously, though, Sal, we appreciate the way you're giving of your time and your heart to bring us comfort in our time of need. We won't forget that. You're one of us, now, kid."

"You mean"—I brought both hands to my cheeks—"I'm a Gabi dad now, too?"

"You'll need a dad name," said Grizzly Dad'ums, never looking up from his sewing.

"He'll be Magic Dad, naturally," said Dad: The Final Frontier.

"I was going to vote for Hou-Dad-ni," said Daditarian.

"How about Ta-Da-d?" chimed in American Stepmom.

"All good suggestions," said Lightning Dad. "So, Sal, which will it be?"

"My name shall be . . . um, drumroll, please?" Everyone put down their needles to drum on their legs or the floor. "My name shall be . . . Presti-Dad-gitation!"

They cheered like Robin Hood's Merry Men. I bowed and got back to work.

Dada-ist, who was sketching us working from a nearby table, shook his head and said, "How do you even know a word like 'prestidigitation'? I could barely spell my name at your age."

"You can barely spell your name *now*," said Dada-dada-dada-dada Dadman! A crumpled ball of expensive art paper bounced off his head.

"He reads a lot," said Papi.

"Just like Gabi!" said Ms. Reál. "You are two of a kind."

"Two. Of. A. Kind," said Grizzly Dad'ums, paying careful attention to the loop he was finishing. The tiny little needle in his bear-size fingers looked funny to me. "Yep. That would explain why Gabi has been talking about you nonstop this week. 'Sal did this!' and 'Sal did that!' day after day."

"She has?" Aventura asked, still sewing, but looking over her shoulder at Gabi. And then, when she saw every dad looking at her, she added, "What? Did I sound jealous or something? 'Cause I'm not jealous. Nee nee nee. Nee nee nee."

She kept on nee nee nee–ing for a while.

"My point," said Grizzly Dad'ums, "is that Gabi's like her mother. Great judge of character. She can make a friend for life in ten minutes. But only if the other person wants to be friends, too." He snuck a glance at me. "So, Sal, you know . . . Do you want to be friends with Gabi?"

Papi snickered.

"They are clearly friends," said Dad: The Final Frontier. "Even I can tell that, and I often have difficulty gauging interpersonal human relations."

"You're having difficulties right now," Grizzly Dad'ums said, shooting Dad: The Final Frontier a look she was guaranteed to miss.

"Look who's talking," said Ms. Reál. "Stop terrorizing poor Sal, José."

"What? Can't a guy ask a friendly question about friendship between a boy who may be a friend and a girl who may be a friend, thereby making them boyfriend and girlfriend?"

Ah. Got it. Adults were as gossipy as middle schoolers. Well, then, I would deal with them the same way I dealt with annoying kids. Shock and awe.

"If you're asking if Gabi is my girlfriend, don't worry. I'm only thirteen. I'm not a sexual being yet."

Grizzly Dad'ums pricked his finger and sucked it. The sewing machine went quiet. Dad: The Final Frontier cocked her head like a confused but well-meaning Labrador. The other dads shut their mouths so quickly I heard their teeth clack. Papi took a break from stitching to rub his eyes.

And American Stepmom, quickly, and mostly under her breath, but loud enough for everyone to hear, said, "Well, there you go. I told Sal, 'Sal, you don't have to be a sexual being until you're ready, don't feel rushed just because some of your peers seem interested in the opposite sex or the same sex or sex in general, you do you, son, on your own schedule,' and I guess he heard me, because here he is, repeating my words, yep, good listener, that kid, and impeccable timing, don't you think?"

Once she finished, the only sound in the cafeteria was Gabi singing along to her headphones.

Lightning Dad knelt next to me and patted my shoulder. "Don't let the awkward silence fool you. Everybody here is behind you. You get to be whoever you want to be in your own time. You do you, just like your mom said." Then, as he took his place on the robe, he smacked Grizzly Dad'ums upside the head.

"What'd I do?" asked Grizzly Dad'ums, knowing exactly what he'd done, the sandwich.

"Yes, what did he do?" asked Dad: The Final Frontier.

39

YASMANY STUMBLED INTO the cafeteria a few minutes before noon, barely awake. He could only open one eye at a time, and only a thin little crack, before switching to the other or closing them both for a second. He was barefoot, still in the Heat tank top and pajama bottoms. He rubbed his face with his hand as he approached us.

The room had filled up with the lunch crowd of doctors and hospital staff and the families of patients. You could feel eyes locking on Yasmany—not that he noticed.

"Good morning, Yasmany!" we all said from our seats on the cloak.

Aventura turned around and bubbled with surprise. "Yasmany's here, too? I mean, is there anyone from Culeco not here?"

Ms. Reál swooped in, enveloping Yasmany in a hug, covering the top of his head with kisses. That made him laugh sleepily and say, "Stahp!" Ms. Reál then guided him toward the lunch buffet.

While the rest of us worked, Yasmany ate a heap of

empanadas and drank a bucket-size chocolate milk at the table where Dada-ist was sketching us. Yasmany didn't have much to say. One Gabi dad or another would occasionally mess with him, cracking a joke about his old-man jammies, or taking the long way to cut out a new loop so they could pass by and try to noogie him. Yasmany would laugh, and insult them back in a low, shy voice, and slap away any noogie attempts, promising them big payback later.

But mostly he just seemed quietly glad to be here. I got the feeling that Yasmany didn't have a life where he could wake up slowly, eat slowly, drink slowly, and just enjoy hanging out. Every once in a while, he'd turn his head suddenly and look over his shoulder, as if he kept expecting something to happen. Or some*one* to happen. And every time he didn't see anyone coming for him, he relaxed a little more.

After a while, he came over and crouched next to me. "I need your phone, chacho."

"Why?"

"My mom bricked my phone last night. I need to make a call."

I held out my phone. "To your mom?"

He looked at me like a roach was crawling out of my nose. "No, you sandwich. I ain't never calling her again. I need to talk to Principal Torres. Unlock it."

I typed in my passcode, and he went off with it to sit next to Gabi and make his call. Gabi, who hadn't even realized he was here until now, took out her earbuds and greeted him. When Yasmany made his call, they both talked to Principal Torres.

After the call was over, Yasmany walked the phone back to me. "Thank you," he said, his voice a little thick and formal. I don't think he was very used to saying those words.

"You're welcome," I replied. Also thick and formal. "You gonna be okay?"

He very kindly didn't notice me wiping my eyes. "Gonna try, chacho. Gonna try."

Suddenly I didn't care how big a sandwich it made me. I launched myself at him and hugged him.

And holy moly. Yasmany had abs like a brick wall. I mean, seriously, it was like hugging a crustacean. Dude had an exoskeleton.

Really glad we never ended up fighting.

Three seconds later, he hugged back. Three seconds is about how long it takes for machismo cacaseca to wear off. And he definitely could have used more practice hugging people. Like, even Dad: The Final Frontier could have given him pointers. But he tried. He patted my back and said, "Okay, chacho. You're a good little dude. Okay. Okay."

He went back over to Gabi, who'd already returned to writing our script. But when he sat down, she pulled a bud out of her ear and stuck it in his. His head moved just an itty-bitty bit to the beat of the music, just like Gabi's was. Maybe an hour later, four people entered the cafeteria. I knew two of them: Principal Torres and Cari-Dad. One of the others was a police officer. And the other, well, he had on a knit vest over a shirt and tie. There are only two kinds of people who would wear a knit vest over a shirt and tie in Miami weather. One was an earnest teacher with great fashion sense, like Daniel Miranda Rivero. The other was a social worker.

Principal Torres waved to Yasmany. He brightened when he saw her and nodded, then whacked Gabi's arm. She pulled the earbuds out of both ears; they spoke. Then Gabi hugged him and proceeded to bonk him on the head four times as she delivered a bunch of orders, pointing a serious finger at him. He just nodded, laughed at her, and cracked some kind of joke that made her laugh. Then he jogged over to Principal Torres and, maybe encouraged by all the practice Gabi and I had given him, hugged her.

Ms. Reál walked over to consult with Cari-Dad, the police officer, and Vest Man. Principal Torres crouched and talked to Yasmany eye-to-eye. He did a better job of listening than I had ever seen him do. Then Principal Torres guided Yasmany to Ms. Reál and the other adults standing there, and they all talked softly for a while.

Some of the diners were staring. That happens whenever a policeman is in the room, I know. But I still wished they would mind their own business.

After a little bit, Ms. Reál and Cari-Dad joined us around the cloak, and Principal Torres and Yasmany came over to talk to us. "Well," said Principal Torres, "I'm going to take Yasmany off your hands now. His aunt is making lunch for us even as we speak."

"But you're coming, too, right?" said Yasmany, looking at no one.

"You bet I am. I'm going to sit right next to you until you finish the paper on diabetes you owe me!"

"Aw man," Yasmany said sleepily. "I'll do it tomorrow."

"You'll do it today!" Gabi yelled from across the cafeteria.

"Anyway," said Principal Torres, "you have something to say, Yasmany?"

"Thank you, everybody," said Yasmany.

"You're welcome, Yasmany!" everybody said back. And then we all burst out laughing.

"And thank you from me, too," said Principal Torres. "Yasmany is lucky to have so many people caring for him. You are all such wonderful people."

Principal Torres was looking at me for that last sentence. Not gonna lie—I blushed.

She waved good-bye, and Yasmany waved good-bye, and the policeman and Vest Man waved good-bye, and we waved good-bye back, and they turned to leave. But Yasmany broke off from Principal Torres and crouched next to me. "Hey, yeah, um, do you know where Nurse Sotolongo is? I want to say thank you and good-bye."

I gave him the *Ooh, too bad!* shrug. "Sorry, man. Her shift ended at ten. She's home and asleep. She won't be back until the night shift tonight."

Yasmany popped to his feet. "Why didn't you wake me, man? Now I missed my chance to be a gentleman to her."

My dream, someday, is to be that deep guy who always says the right thing to everybody. I have my beard planned out and everything. So I stood slowly and, my voice dripping with wisdom, clapped a hand on his shoulder and said, "Being patient is the most important part of being a gentleman."

"You are a submarine sandwich," he said, and walked out of the cafeteria.

As he and the adults with him left, Gabi came up behind me. "I've got good news and bad news."

I turned to her. "What's the bad news?"

"My little brother is sick, and Yasmany isn't going to his own home, and the world is full of horrible things happening."

But she was smiling and waggling her eyebrows.

"Okay. So what's the good news?"

"My brother is stable, and Yasmany has a whole bunch of people including my family helping him, and I finished the script. It's pretty good, if I do say so myself!"

I gave her a cacaseca smirk and took her tablet out of her hands and read the script right where I stood.

She was wrong. Her script wasn't pretty good. It was freaking amazing.

40

SOME PEOPLE JUST got it. Nurse Sotolongo was a natural.

It was Sunday morning. Nurse Sotolongo stood smiling at the front of the cafeteria, which we had turned into our stage, wearing a black one-piece bathing suit, fishnet stockings, super-tall high heels she had brought from home, and a top hat she had borrowed from me. She twirled a white-tipped cane (also mine) as she pranced around a wooden easel that held up the poster Dada-ist had created for the show. It looked like one of those old-timey vaudeville signs, with skulls and tombstones and scythes and other Halloweeny symbols drawn all over it, and it read: DEATH ALWAYS WINS: A COMEDY!

The show was about to begin.

We had thought we'd perform our practice run of the play in the waiting room the Reáls had taken over to an audience of padres, Gabi dads, and Ms. Reál. But once rumor got around the hospital about it (thanks to Nurse Sotolongo), doctors and nurse practitioners and physician's assistants and custodians and admins and basically everyone who worked there (and wasn't otherwise occupied) wanted to see it, too. Minutes before showtime, the cafeteria was packed, standing-room only, and they shut down the registers so no as not to disturb the performance. The room sounded as happy as a barnyard.

The janitorial staff had rearranged the whole cafeteria to make it look like a dinner theater, with a big, broad space against the windows of the north wall to serve as our stage. They had pulled the floor-to-ceiling curtains over the windows, which made the room darker and different and perfect. Nurse Sotolongo strutted to center stage and, in a booming ringmaster's voice, brandishing her cane like the torch of freedom, started the show:

> *"Welcome, gentles, one and all,*
> *to this, our theater's curtain call!*
> *If you have to pee, there's time—*
> *at least until I end this rhyme!*
> *Go now, and make your number one,*
> *or wait until the show is done!*
> *And if you have to number two,*
> *you'll miss the play. But God bless you!"*

Gabi and I stood stage left, peeking out from behind the curtain. Gabi jumped up and down and whisper-cheered to me, "They love it! Yes! I was so scared to start with a poop joke. But thanks to you, now I'll always start with a poop joke."

"I don't think you always want to start with—"

She cut me off. "Oh! Sal, go, that's your cue! Go! Go!"

Gabi moved behind me so no one would spot her when I threw back the curtain and jumped forward.

What the audience saw was a black six-foot-tall robe that had a bleached-bone bauta mask for a face, holding a black-and-bloodred fake spear, lurch over to Nurse Sotolongo in three giant strides. I mean, she was twenty feet away from me, easy; I pretty much half flew over to her.

The audience gasped. Mrs. Waked had said that one of the keys to a good Everyman play was strong visuals. My Death-comes-at-you-fast costume seemed to deliver on that count.

Nurse Sotolongo's grin grew wicked as she proclaimed:

"A guest has joined us, dearest friends!
The one you'll meet when your life ends!
It comes alike for rich or poor,
for every gender, weight, height, or
whatever your ethnicity:
It's equal opportunity!
As you exhale your final breath,
you'll say its name. Its name is Death!"

I wore a modulator over my mouth from an old Halloween costume that made me sound like Optimus Prime with a head cold. I pointed my spear at audience members one at a time as I spoke my lines:

"My name is Death, and mortals be
indifferent to mortality!

But I will teach you to respect
how all your lives will soon be wrecked!
A single touch from my black dart
will stop at once your beating heart!
How long have you? A month? A year?
You do not know! So live in fear!
Yes, fear me always, last and first!
For soon I come to do my worst!"

The audience applauded and laughed, even while they booed and called out Spanglish insults to Death. I let them go on for a while, nodding grimly at their comments.

Then, in a gazelle burst of speed, I sprang over to Nurse Sotolongo and ever so gently touched her with my spear. *And she died.* With a whole lot of leg kicking and thrashing and excellent overacting.

The audience shrieked and gasped! They clutched their faces and protected their hearts!

I leaped into their midst. As I stalked around them, creaking and bouncing, staring at them from creepy stooped angles, they begged me to go away. I goat-hopped back to center stage and shouted:

"Did you not hear my words before?
One day, you'll die, forevermore!
So laugh no more. Prepare to cry.
For someday each of you must die."

And I laughed for all my evil worth.

Until I was rudely interrupted by a girl whose poofy hair gleamed with flags-of-the-world barrettes. She marched right up to me, stomped her foot, and said:

"You're such a jerk, Death. Get a life!
You're like my kitchen's dullest knife."

"I'm like a dull knife?" I said, sounding hurt and picking my way over to her. "I don't get it."

Gabi was all too happy to explain:

"A dull knife will not slice, but slip,
and cut you when you lose your grip!
You're using fear to make life dull,
to kill the brain inside the skull,
before we've died! That's premature.
Your words are, therefore, cow manure!"

Gabi had to take two bows to get the crowd to quiet down. I stood fuming and making threatening gestures with my spear, waiting for my chance to speak. Once I could be heard, I circled Gabi and delivered my lines:

"Ye haughty girl, thy clever tongue
means nothing when the day is done!
My victory is guaranteed!
You might as well, right now, concede!
For there's no power, trick, or art,
that can delay my poisoned dart!"

Boos from the audience. I hissed back.

"That's a nice spear you got there, Death," said Gabi.

"Oh, you think so? Yeah, I really like it. It's really good at killing!"

"But it looks so heavy! It must be a bummer to carry around all day."

"It's light as a feather," I said, handing the spear to Gabi. "See?"

"Oh!" she said, thrusting it a few times. "It *is* light!"

And then she stabbed Death in the face.

And Death's face *exploded.*

Specifically, the overinflated black balloon, over which I had put the bauta mask, and which had been floating in the hood of the cloak where a human head would normally go, popped. Gabi had pierced it with the tiny pin we had stuck at the end of the prop spear.

The crowd couldn't believe it when the bauta mask tumbled to the floor. The cloak's hood, now with nothing to hold it up, fell against the shoulders of Death and the top of my actual head.

I paused for effect, letting the audience digest what they had seen, as they laughed and tittered and whispered among themselves. Then, mockingly, I laid into Gabi.

"Ye foolish girl! I am not dead,
though you have murdered my own head!
At killing, only I am skilled.
Without my help, I can't be killed!"

"Really?" said Gabi, hand on her chin. "So, the dart doesn't do the actual killing? That's fascinating!"

"You think so?" I asked.

"Oh yes," said Gabi, making big eyes at Death. "You have such an interesting line of work, Death!"

"Well, it pays the bills . . ." I said modestly.

"It must take an extraordinary amount of talent, doing what you do."

I did an *aw shucks* kick. "Well, yes, it takes a little practice."

"How do you do it?"

"I have to say the name of the person who needs killing in a rhyme I make up myself."

"Oh," said Gabi, winking and tapping a finger against her temple. "So, let's say my name was, oh, I don't know, Death. How would you kill me?"

"Easy. I would say a rhyme like:

'Dear Death, you're life is done. Oh well!
It's time to send you down to'—hey, wait a minute!"

I waited for the audience to stop cracking up before I delivered my next lines.

"You can't fool me! I'm much too fast!
This little prank will be your last!"

I strode over to her in a frightening, galloping rush. Gabi covered her face with her hands melodramatically. Walking slowly now, I led her to the opening in the curtain, "faced" her (even though the Death costume had no head anymore) and said:

> *"Your time is ended on this Earth,*
> *And gone is all your worldly worth.*
> *I'll take you now beyond this veil,*
> *and leave the audience to wail."*

Meek, now, and defeated-looking, Gabi nodded assent, but quickly added,

> *"Oh Death, I know now I must die.*
> *But please, Death, let me say good-bye."*

"Make it quick," I answered grumpily.

Gabi turned toward the audience with a sad but brave smile on her face. This would definitely have been a spotlight moment if the cafeteria had owned one.

> *"Good people, sorry, I must go.*
> *Death is the end of every show.*
> *But here's the trick: We are not dead!*
> *Not yet. Don't act like it! Instead,*
> *enjoy each moment to the max!*
> *Someday you're gonna die? Relax!*
> *When that day comes, it comes. Till then,*
> *rejoice in life, time and again.*

For if you follow my advice,
not only will your days be nice,
but you'll discover all your fear
of dying—"

And here, Gabi grabbed Death's cloak and yanked it and tossed it to the ground. There was no boy beneath it wearing stilts. There was nothing in it at all.

"—will just disappear."

41

"THAT WAS A GREAT show," said American Stepmom. She was driving Papi and me home from the hospital as day changed to night. "I still can't believe how great a show that was."

Papi twisted around to address me from the shotgun seat. "Mijo, believe me when I tell you. You are going to be a star. If not today, if not tomorrow, someday very soon you are going to change the world. What a show!"

"What was your favorite part?" American Stepmom asked Papi.

"The ending, of course!" he said to me. "When you exited the costume—and you were so sneaky! No one saw anything! You exited the costume, and then Gabi threw Death to the floor, and that last line: 'will just disappear'! It was so perfect! I mean, I knew that's why the tent poles were there, to hold the costume up after you snuck out of it and hid behind the curtain, but, I mean, it was *so perfect*!"

"It's nice when a trick goes off the way you pictured it in your head," I agreed.

"Okay, mijo, you listen to me," said Papi. "You are very

good at picturing things in your head. You can work a problem out like no one I've ever seen before, and I've met some pretty smart people. You have a gift. And there are going to be a lot of people in this life who will try to hold you back because they won't have your imagination. But you don't listen to them, okay? You hear me? You trust that big beautiful brain of yours, okay?" And then he grabbed for me and scruffed my hair and kind of batted me around like a bear play-fighting with his cub.

"Okay, okay!" I said.

Papi faced forward again. We came to a red light. "What was your favorite part, Lucy?"

American Stepmom thought for a moment. I saw her smile through the rearview mirror. "My favorite part was how Gabi's family reacted. Did you see them?"

"Oh yes," said Papi, his voice suddenly a little hoarse. "Those poor people."

"Oh, the way they hoisted you and Gabi on their shoulders, Sal. And the way they cried with joy. Men, women, robots, everyone, just so happy for you."

"They kept telling me 'thank you!'" I said. "But they were the ones who helped me."

"You helped them more than you know, sweetheart. You gave them a story full of hope."

"And magic," added Papi.

"And something to hold on to, when their hearts are so broken they don't know what to think anymore. You gave them something beautiful to think about. It's just about the greatest gift you can give anybody." American Stepmom, crying now, said, "Petunia, take over."

Petunia is the name of her car. Petunia said, "Okay. I'm driving now. By the way, you have one new message. Shall I play it for you?"

"It's probably from Aventura," said American Stepmom, instantly cheered up by the idea.

"What a talented young woman she is, too," said Papi. "I think Culeco's cornered the market on all the bright young talent in Miami."

"When you and Gabi work up your act," added American Stepmom, "you should hire her as your costume designer. Okay, Petunia, play the message."

Petunia obeyed.

When the very short message had been played, American Stepmom said quietly, "I'm driving now, Petunia."

"Okay," said Petunia, "you're driving."

Then American Stepmom made an illegal U-turn and broke the speed limit all the way back to the hospital.

Once we got to the NICU, it didn't take us five minutes to put together the story, even though it came to us in broken pieces from one sniffling Gabi dad to the next. Ignacio's immune system was shutting down for good. It might take a day, several hours, or a few minutes. But definitely soon. This was it.

The Gabi dads stood around, mostly quietly, taking turns crying and comforting each other. I heard a little whispered Spanglish, an occasional sob, but the loudest noise in the NICU waiting room came out of the filter. It exhaled sanitized air like a grumpy giant.

Through the see-through walls of Ignacio's room, I watched

Ms. Reál, her eyes as pink as sick tomatoes, cradling tiny little Iggy in her arms. Her wet cheeks gleamed.

She wasn't wearing a mask or gloves. I guess, at the end, those things don't really matter anymore.

Ignacio was wrapped so snugly in a white sheet that only a little of his red-and-brown face was visible. He didn't move at all. His incubator gaped open like a treasure chest that had already been plundered.

Gabi was in the room, too. She sat on the bed, kicking her feet in a way that reminded me of Principal Torres on the stage. For the first time since I'd met her, she didn't have any barrettes in her hair. It puffed straight out in every direction. She looked like a brunette dandelion.

The second she saw me, she ran to the glass and impatiently waved for me to come in. I made *Okay, okay!* hands at her, and walked to the door. She opened it and shut it behind me.

As I passed her, I read her T-shirt. "OUR DEAD ARE NEVER DEAD TO US UNTIL WE HAVE FORGOTTEN THEM."—GEORGE ELIOT.

I kissed Ms. Reál on each wet cheek before sitting on the bed with Gabi. "Oh," Ms. Reál said, starting to cry again. "Thank you for coming back. I'm so sorry. You have school tomorrow! You're so kind. Oh, my son. Mi hijito, Sal. No es fácil, mijo. It's God's will, I know. Qué sea la voluntad de Dios."

"It's *not* God's will!" yelled Gabi. Her legs swung more fiercely.

Ms. Reál looked at her daughter with more kindness than I thought a face could show. Then she turned all that compassion onto me and said, "I lost my faith for a while, too. But I got it back. Do you know how I got it back?"

"How?"

She lowered her head and raised Ignacio until their noses touched. "I figured out the most important thing I've ever figured out. That God is just another word for 'goodness.' Every time we do a good thing, God grows. Inside us. Right here." She freed a hand long enough to beat her chest three times.

Gabi bunched the bedsheet in her fists. But then she let it go, smoothed it with both hands, and, all traces of anger gone now, hopped off the bed and approached her mama. "Mama," she said, with a cake-and-ice-cream smile, "would it be okay if I said good-bye to Ignacio now? Alone?"

Ms. Reál was so surprised by Gabi's question that she started to cry: just one fat, fast tear that fell off her face like an overripe orange.

But after a big breath, she said, "Oh, mijita, ¿cómo que no? Say good-bye to your hermanito."

She gently, slowly transferred Ignacio into his big sister's arms, laid a big kiss on both of her children's foreheads, and touched my head in blessing on the way out. I turned to follow her.

"Not you, Sal!" said Gabi with her patented whisper-yell. "You, I need. We have work to do."

I turned back to Gabi. She was staring fiercely at Ignacio, rocking him slowly, shaking her head, as if saying *No, no!* to some repeated question.

I waited until I heard the door shut behind me. "Work?" I asked.

"You know exactly what I mean. Do not play stupid with me at a time like this. Just do it!"

I stepped closer to her so we could speak more softly to each other. "Exactly what do you want me to do, Gabi?"

Gabi didn't feel like speaking softly just then. "Fix this!"

"How?"

She became confused. "You know. Do your . . . thing."

"That's just it. I have no idea what I'm doing. You *know* I have no idea what I'm doing."

Her face collapsed. "Just this one time, Sal. Just this once. This is too terrible. It can't be bad, to save a baby. Save my baby brother, Sal."

I wanted to yell, but I turned to look at the many moms and dads outside this see-through room to calm myself down. Several of them stared back.

I said to Gabi, as evenly as a teacher, "You're not getting it, Gabi. I can't even save my own mami. I have been trying for *years*. My own *mami*."

"But you're so much better now," she begged. "You know so much more. Remember how you switched the wall in the gym? No calamitrons!"

"So what do you want me to do, Gabi? Switch your brother for a healthy Iggy in another universe?"

She dropped her chin. "I don't know. Maybe."

"But they're two different people! All you'd be doing is sending your own flesh and blood to another universe, and bringing in a different baby to live with you."

I have never seen a thirteen-year-old with a scarier face than Gabi Reál at that moment. "But my parents wouldn't know that. They would think it was a miracle. They would think Iggy was cured. *They'd be happy*."

She was on the edge, beyond tears, her whole body shaking. But I'd been on that edge before, five years ago in a hospital with Mami. I knew what Gabi needed was a calm, sensible voice to remind her who she was. "Look at Iggy," I said softly. "The baby in your arms? He's one of a kind. There is no Iggy in the multiverse quite like him."

That's all it took. She looked at Iggy, and rocked him, and held him fiercely to her chest, and her resistance broke like a dam. She almost couldn't speak for weeping. "I know, Sal. I know. I know I know I know. *Rarrh!*"

"I know, too," I said. And then, the way a hot shower on a cold day can bring you back to life, an idea warmed me all over. "Wait a second. No, I don't. I don't know. What do I know? There is so much to know. We should go find out!"

Gabi, lovingly rocking her dying brother, watched me carefully. "What are you talking about?"

"We're looking for a solution to our problem, right? Maybe we can't find it here, Gabi. But maybe it's just in the next universe over."

"That—" She wanted to argue. But I could see her mind changing between sentences. "That's true, actually."

"It's a big multiverse out there," I urged.

"We can just look," said Gabi, getting excited. Iggy, maybe catching a little of her excitement, yawned and kicked a little. "There's no harm in looking, right? No rip, no calamitrons, right?"

"No calamitrons," I agreed. "Not if we just look."

"So let's look. Let's look!"

"But it might not work, Gabi." I chewed my tears and

swallowed them. No time to cry now. "You'll be so heartbroken if it doesn't work. I should know. I'm still heartbroken. My mami died, and my heart has never healed."

Gabi came close enough for Iggy's hand to touch my arm. "Sal, how much worse would you have felt if you hadn't done everything in your power to save your mama?"

She was right. I couldn't live with myself if I didn't at least try to find a way to save Iggy.

So I relaxed. All the way.

42

"WHAT'S HAPPENING?" ASKED Gabi.

"Everything," I answered, relaxing and relaxing. "Everything at once."

I wasn't trying to be mysterious. Everything that could happen really *was* happening, all around us, all at the same time. Ignacio died in Gabi's arms. And then he was fine, sleeping sweetly as Gabi cradled him, black hair peeking out from his swaddling. Then a different Gabi was cradling him, and then another and another, all with different barrettes: hot-air balloons, the entire periodic table, the word "love" in different languages, female superheroes. And then Ignacio was back in the incubator, and Ms. Reál and four Gabi dads watched him, sick with worry. Doctors and nurses appeared and disappeared, sticking Ignacio with syringes or more IVs in his tiny, bruised body. And then the room was lightless and empty, had been for a long time, no machines turned on, no sign of any of us.

Jump again: It was daytime, and the room had turned freezing cold, and sometimes I was in the room and sometimes I wasn't, and then a nurse I'd never met and would never see again noticed Gabi and me through the cling-wrap barrier between universes and was about to scream right before I moved us along. Transparent people vanished like ghosts and were replaced by others who burst to life in the room like a flame on a match. And then a baby girl was fighting for her life in the incubator, and the people in the room were her family—not Gabi's, not mine— and it was someone else's story altogether.

"I don't understand," said Gabi.

"Deep breath," I said. "Things will slow down if we relax."

Gabi sucked in air, let it out. The room started to change more slowly. We watched some Gabi dads weep when they received bad news then—*poof!*—laugh for joy at good news. Ms. Reál wailed and Ms. Reál rejoiced and Ms. Reál put on a brave face as she comforted other Gabi dads and Ms. Reál thanked God in heaven for saving her son. Some Gabis wept into their hands and other rejoiced, more grateful than they'd ever been in their entire lives. We saw all sorts of Sals, too, and Papis and American Stepmoms, and lots of people we would never know but who somewhere, sometime, were part of Ignacio's life and, sometimes, death.

"No one can see this but us?" asked Gabi, pointing to the people outside this little room.

I shook my head.

She walked around, putting her hands through ghosts. "All these things we're seeing," asked Gabi. "They're real?"

"Not in our universe. But somewhere, yeah."

"Okay. So, how do these other universes help us?"

I didn't say anything. Because *that was exactly my point,*

Gabi, remember I have no idea what I am doing, thanks for listening.

"Oh," she said, looking at me across the roomful of possibility between us. "That was what you were saying before, wasn't it?"

I gave her double thumbs up.

She walked over to me, passing right through a Gabi from somewhere else, who was screaming and crying at the unfairness of life. "Well, let's start with what we know. When Yasmany was being a jerk to you, how'd you find the chicken universe?"

"By relaxing."

"Okay," she said. If she was hoping saying "Okay" would help her understand, it didn't work. "But what does that mean, 'relax'?"

"We've been through this. Remember?"

"The screened-in porch. Yeah, I remember. But tell me again."

"Okay. It's the opposite of what you're doing now."

"Ugh!" She took a deep breath. "Okay. Okay. You're the kung fu master, Sal, and I'm the white belt. Please explain to me, Master, how to relax."

I could get used to being called Master. "Well, white belt, you can use meditation techniques, like I do. I learned a bunch from my psychologists back in the day."

"Fine. So teach me. How do I meditate?"

I moved so that we were standing side by side, looking out at the room. "Okay. Don't close your eyes. You have to use all your senses. Ready?"

"Ready."

"Okay, raise your hands in the air. It will help us concentrate."

"Um, Ignacio?"

I looked around. "Put him in the incubator."

She did, came back, and, copying me, raised her arms as high as they could go.

"Good. Okay. Now picture this. You are sleeping on the belly of a giant. He's a friendly giant. He—"

"Does it have to be a he?"

"Um, I guess not. I've always pictured a man giant."

"Typical boy. I'm picturing a fifty-foot woman."

"Picture a fifty-foot taco for all I care. But don't interrupt. You can't interrupt and meditate at the same time."

"Maybe *you* can't. I'm gifted."

I ignored that. "Breathe in, white belt, then breathe out. Listen to your master. Breathe in. Breathe out. Picture yourself sleeping, snug and safe inside your giant taco."

"Don't make me laugh!" she said with a laugh.

"Breathe in. Breathe out. Eyes open. Breathe out. You hear the giant taco's heartbeat."

"Tacos don't have hearts!"

"Silliness can save you, white belt. Breathe in. You feel warm and secure. Breathe out. The giant taco will protect you. The giant taco is your friend. Breathe in. The giant taco will help us choose. The giant taco is flying. It's like your own personal dragon mount, except it's a taco. Breathe out. Soar the skies on your giant taco, Gabi!"

The ghosts became smudges of color. Between blinks, furniture moved, monitors dissolved, equipment disappeared and reappeared in other parts of the room. The room lurched like a roller coaster, twisting and dipping. "I think it's working," I told her. "Keep breathing. Don't close your eyes."

"It's like watching my dreams and nightmares dance together," she said, openmouthed.

And then the room shook into focus, as if we'd slammed on the brakes. We had arrived. Somewhere.

The lights and lamps in the room had been turned off. On top of the incubator—sealed up tight in this place—seven candles of different sizes burned with yellow-brown light.

"Open flames in a hospital room?!" asked Gabi, her eyes bugging out of her head.

"Huh. You don't seem to be worried about it," I responded, pointing out to her the other Gabi Reál in the room.

That Gabi wore rainbow LED barrettes that slowly changed colors, and a shirt that read, NEVER GIVE IN, NEVER GIVE IN, NEVER, NEVER, NEVER, NEVER.—WINSTON CHURCHILL. She had taken over the nightstand in one corner of the room and was writing furiously in her journal.

Nobody seemed to know we were here. Everyone else sat on the floor in a circle around the incubator, holding hands, praying: Ms. Reál, and a half-dozen Gabi dads, and Papi, and another Sal, the only one with his eyes open, looking pouty and bratty, huffing like he didn't want to be there.

And leading them all in prayer was Mami Muerta.

Not muerta there. Oh no: very much alive. She and Papi sat next to each other, holding hands tightly, deep in concentration. She wore a red-and-white robe that matched the robe on the three-foot doll of Santa Bárbara in her lap. The doll's black hair flowed past its shoulders, just like Mami's.

As I looked around the circle, I saw other religious (and not so religious) stuff. Ms. Reál had a small Virgin Mary statue, the kind with a suction cup on the base so it can be stuck to a car dashboard, in the hand that held Lightning Dad's. Dada-ist, to Lightning Dad's left, clutched a rosary in the hand that held on to Cari-Dad's, and in his lap sat a laughing stone statue that looked African to me but probably, like him, came from the Dominican Republic: big face, big smile, little body, and a bowl for a hat. Grizzly Dad'ums held Cari-Dad's other hand, and he wore a paper bib that had written on it in red marker: I'LL BELIEVE ANYTHING IF IT MEANS SAVING MY SON. Dad: The Final Frontier sat between Grizzly Dad'ums and the Sal from there, and in her lap a bobblehead of Albert Einstein nodded yes forever. Papi had a coconut in his lap with shells for eyes and a mouth.

The Sal from there was the only one not participating. He had his cell phone in his lap. His eyes jumped from one face to the next, trying to find someone who agreed with him that sitting in a circle praying for a dying baby was the boringest thing in the world. But everyone else was being respectful. He was the only sandwich.

A sandwich *who wasn't diabetic.*

He couldn't be. He'd never act this way in a hospital, right in the middle of a medical emergency, if he had any clue about what being sick all the time was like. Plus, I didn't see a diabetes bag around, or any bulge in his clothing where his insulin pump might be.

I had to be sure. I walked over to him. Got real close. Stared in his eyes for a while. He had no idea I was there, breathing on him from another universe.

Right on cue, StupidSal whined into my face, "Why do I have to pray and Gabi doesn't? I want to play *Murder Fun Five*."

I really, really, really hated StupidSal.

"I am praying in my own way," the Gabi from that place retorted. She kept writing as she spoke. "I am composing a poem to celebrate Ignacio's recovery, to be read on the day we can finally bring him home. It's a song of hope and solace that imagines a future time when Ignacio will engage in all the winsome activities and pursuits of a growing boy: soccer, camping, reading about pirates and dinosaurs under a beach umbrella, and, eventually, graduating from college. It's written in heroic couplets, à la Alexander Pope."

"Oh. My. God," said my Gabi. "Please tell me I am not that extra."

ExtraGabi looked up from her journal and looked straight at my Gabi—without seeing her. "Did you hear something?" she asked the room.

"We are not alone," said Mami Not-Muerta. She was looking me in the eye. She *could* see us. "Two spirits are in the room."

"Liar," said StupidSal.

"Don't you call your mami a liar," said Papi, in a tone that told me they fought all the time. That made me feel a little sick.

StupidSal made an ugly face. "There's no such thing as ghosts. This is such—" And he said something a lot more vulgar than cacaseca.

Look, I know that, as a thirteen-year-old, I'm supposed to act all moody and independent and cool and whatever. Except that's not how I feel. Five years ago, losing Mami scared me— all the way down, and all the way up again. I would do anything to have her back. And I love Papi and American Stepmom so much. And here was StupidSal, treating his parents like garbage, acting like he was six years old.

I couldn't take it. Not for a second.

So I marched over to him, plucked his smartphone off his lap, and smashed it on the ground.

"Yeeee!" StupidSal wailed like a baby. He ran over to his mami's lap, knocking her Santa Bárbara statue out of the way. *Oh yeah,* now *you want your mami, after disrespecting her the way you did.* Stupid, stupid Sal.

Mami caught StupidSal and held him, but she never took her eyes off me. Everyone else crawled or scooted away from the exploding cell phone, screaming and clutching their statues in fear.

I held up my hands to signal I was done losing my temper. "I'm sorry," I said. "Can you hear me?"

"And me?" asked my Gabi.

Only Mami could. "I can hear you, espíritus. Tell me, are you espíritus buenos, or malos?"

"Oh," said Gabi, glancing at me, "we're good spirits."

"Yeah. We're totally awesome," I added.

Mami scanned us. "Then why do you look like Sal and Gabi? Pretending to be our children seems more like something duendes would do."

"One of them looks like me?" asked ExtraGabi. "I wanna see!"

"What are duendes?" asked my Gabi.

"They're like poltergeists," I answered. Then I turned back to Mami and said, "We're not duendes. We're nice."

Mami crossed her arms. "Don't lie to me. You broke Sal's cell phone."

I crossed my arms right back at her. "Yeah, well, maybe Sal should watch his mouth around you."

I didn't mean to sound as angry as I did. And I didn't mean to appear again. Everyone in the room sucked in their breath together.

"I heard it!" said ExtraGabi.

"*Him*—it's a him," said Dada-ist. At some point he'd put his statue down and he now had charcoal and paper in his hands. He started sketching. "Floramaria is right. He looks like Sal."

"Make it go away!" StupidSal cried into his mami's shoulder like a wussy mami's boy who should just go play in the traffic or something.

"How did they see you?" my Gabi asked me. She went over to the incubator and tried to pick up the candles. She couldn't. She put her hands into the flames and felt nothing. She looked back at me, fire jumping through her fingers, completely irritated. "I want them to see me, too! I want to do things! How did you grab the cell phone?"

"As usual," I replied, "I have no idea what I'm doing."

"Spirits!" Mami almost chanted. She was still patting and cradling StupidSal, but her voice had become as forceful as a priestess's. "We have called you here to help Ignacio. He is dying. We do not know how much longer he can survive. So, please, if you are kindly spirits, use your otherworldly powers to help him!"

Gabi and I looked at each other. Then, we peered into the incubator. By the shaky candlelight we saw *two* Iggys.

Well, kind of. They didn't look all the way real. They were superimposed over each other, like the gym wall had been.

"Holy frijoles," breathed Gabi. "They want us to save *their* Iggy, Sal!"

"I know."

"But we can't save their baby! We can't even save *our* baby!"

"I know!" I took a breath and calmed down. More quietly, I repeated, "I know." I walked toward Mami a step. "We can't cure your Ignacio, Mami. We came here looking for help for *our* Ignacio. He's dying, too."

"Can you see both Iggys, Mrs. Sal's mami?" Gabi asked. "Look in the incubator. You should see two babies in there."

Mami poured cowering StupidSal into Papi's lap, stood up, and padded on bare feet to the incubator. As her brown face entered the brown globe of light of the candles, she peered in. Her eyes slimmed, then grew startled. "I see them. I see them both." A tear hung from her eye like a fruit. "Is that Ignacio's soul? Is it leaving his body?"

"No!" said Ms. Reál, a denial, a wish. She stood up and walked over to the incubator but couldn't see what Mami saw, no matter how hard she squinted.

Papi poured StupidSal on the floor and came over to the incubator, too. "Two babies, you said?" He strained to look. "I only see one."

"Relax, mi vida," Mami told him, a hand, so gentle, on

his shoulder. They gazed at each other with the loving looks I remembered them exchanging. "Look less to see more."

Both Ms. Reál and Papi half closed their eyes and breathed deeply, trying to find our Iggy lying right on top of theirs.

But I started to feel my patience slipping. "It doesn't matter if you can see him or not," I told them, even though probably only Mami would hear me. "We can't help them."

"We came here looking for help," said Gabi.

"Our Iggy's sick, too."

"We just want to cure his immunodeficiency disease and let him have a normal life."

"We've traveled a long, long way."

"We have no idea how we got here."

"Or why."

"But we have to be here for a reason. Right?"

Mami tilted her head. She walked toward Gabi and me until she was standing right in front of us. "Did you say 'immunodeficiency disease'?"

"Yes," said Gabi. "Why?"

Mami traded looks with us. "Our Ignacio is suffering from neonatal meningitis. The doctors say it might have been caused by a staph infection."

"What?" said Gabi. She ran to the foot of the incubator and picked up Ignacio's chart, reading fast, flipping through pages.

The Reáls and StupidSal screamed and backed away from her.

"Gabi!" I said. "You picked up the chart! You're doing things!"

And just like that, the chart fell through her hands and clattered to the floor.

"Huh," she said. "It's like, when we really care about something, we become more real."

"Gustavo," Mami said to Papi, who hadn't yelled or even flinched, "there are two Ignacios from two different universes occupying the same space. Didn't you tell me something about your research a few years ago, about how things from two different universes could influence each other?"

"'Virtuous supermembranation theory,'" Papi quoted. "Bonita and I got a Tinsley Prize for that paper." He rubbed his mouth and mustache, thinking. "Bonita, come here, please. I need your help."

Dad: The Final Frontier backed into a wall and hugged Einstein. "But I'm scared of ghosts!"

"They're good spirits," Mami said to her gently. "They're here to help us. They're going to cure Ignacio."

"Mami, don't tell them that!" I said, not yelled, because I don't yell. "We can't help them, or ourselves. Now there are two dying babies in the incubator, and we can't do anything! It's not fair!"

Mami swooped over to me and tried to put her hands on my cheeks. They passed through my head. But she held them there as if she were touching my face. She smiled down at me like the sun and said, "Mijo, there are two babies in the incubator. They're both sick. But they're sick in different ways. And now they're occupying the same space, almost blended together, almost one."

"I wish we could give the healthy parts of each of them to the other," said Gabi.

"That's exactly what virtuous remembranation theory proposes," said Papi. Then he blinked. "Hey! I heard a little girl! She sounded like you, Gabi!"

ExtraGabi, though maybe a little scared, tiptoed over to the incubator. "Hello, Gabi!" she said, though she clearly couldn't see either Gabi or me. "I just want you to know you're really awesome! You can totally figure this out!"

"Thank you, Gabi!" said Gabi. "I think you're awesome, too!"

"Gabi thinks you're awesome, too," Papi told ExtraGabi. That seemed to make her night.

"I don't understand what Papi's theory means," I said, doing everything I could not to lose my gerbils. But we had to be running out of time. "What do we do?"

"Beats me," said Papi. "I just write the theories. I don't do practice. That's for engineers."

"How did you get here?" Mami asked me. "How did you find us?"

"We meditated," Gabi said.

Mami looked straight at me. She was so beautiful, not because she was beautiful, but because she was my mami, alive, and speaking perfect English like she never had before, and her eyes were full of love for me. "Exactly. You meditated, mijo. You dreamed about what you wanted to happen. You imagined what you wanted the world to be like. You imagined it so hard, you scoured whole universes until you found the answer. And now you're here, with the power to imagine two very sick little babies healthy again."

"You have to connect them," Papi added, picking up where Mami left off. "One Iggy is sick one way, but the other has a different sickness. You have to imagine that each Iggy is helping the other one. Meditate on connecting them. Like a circuit. Connect them across universes, and they'll keep each other healthy."

"Meditate on connecting them," said Gabi. "Got it. You got it, Sal?"

I was breathing hard. I felt confused and lost. I didn't understand half of what was happening. But *meditate on connecting them*? That I thought I could handle. "All we can do is relax and try," I said.

"I'll help," Mami added. "We all will."

For a second, I couldn't speak. Then I swallowed and said, "It was so good to see you."

Her loving hands couldn't touch me, but she tried. "Is your mami where you come from a lot like me?"

My eyes were suddenly underwater. "Not nearly enough."

Gabi patted my shoulder, like a coach telling his pitcher that he needs one more inning out of that arm.

I nodded to her and said, "Now the student is the master. Tell them what to do, Gabi."

"Me? But I don't—"

I cut her off. "Relax, white belt. Just tell the universe what you want. The universe loves us. It wants to help."

Gabi smiled. Then she nodded and, alive with confidence, she said, "All right, then. Mrs. Sal's mom, please tell everybody to imagine a giant taco."

EPILOGUE

(ONE WEEK LATER)

IT HAD BEEN a good second week at school.

Gabi and I got an A-plus-plus-plus on our Everyman play. "An A-plus-plus-plus," Mrs. Waked explained, "means that you'd be *nominated* for a Tony Award, but you wouldn't *win*, because winning a Tony is all *politics* and *corruption*. Being nominated is the *real* honor. Well *done*, children!"

She also gave Aventura, who was in her Advanced Theater Workshop class, extra credit for her work on the Death costume. Aventura texted me, **Tyty xtra cred!** and sent me so many thank-you emojis the whole world ran out of emojis for like ten minutes. I texted back, **Wat ty ur the one who did all this work on a Sat. just to help me and Gabi,** and she texted back, **Yeah sorry if i got a little weird in the hospital if im being honest i did get a little jealous of gabi still friends?**

What was she talking about? I had to show the text to American Stepmom to understand what the pants was going on. She, of course, ribbed me for twenty minutes before she made herself useful and helped me write back, **Ave ur da coolest of course were still friends IOU a BIG favor name ur price!**

Ooh! Aventura replied. **BIG favor huh lemme think bout that** Something about her reply made me gulp.

Gladis was absent from school on Monday but was back by Tuesday. She avoided me like I was radioactive. Ah, well. At least she wasn't spreading rumors about me. It seemed that the kids at Culeco still didn't know whether to call me a brujo, a mago, or just a boring old magician. But I didn't care anymore. The mystery would only enhance my mystique.

Yasmany returned to school on Wednesday. He didn't tell me about his life since I last saw him, and I didn't think it was my place to ask. If he wanted to tell me, he'd tell me. He was talking to Gabi, though, and she said he was in "a stable living situation for the time being."

Which was all that mattered, really.

Yasmany seemed to be having more fun at school, too. Instead of picking fights, he concentrated on beating the red zone of the climbing wall, which Mr. Lynott had returned to its previous impossible state. Not impossible for Yasmany, though. He got to the top on Thursday, after just one day of practice. Punk.

The hole in Yasmany's locker was getting smaller every day. I made sure of it. I'd pass by it on the way to my locker and take a big, calamitous snort. By Friday, the hole was so small, even a really skinny chicken worker would have had trouble fitting through it. Another week or two of deep breaths and it would be gone for good.

Every night that week, Gabi came over to check to see if I was carrying those calamitrons inside of me. Together, we'd sneak off with the entropy sweeper to some private part of the Coral Castle, and she'd scan me head to toe. "Zero calamitrons!" the sweeper always announced. I didn't know what happened to those calamitrons I was snarfing, but they didn't seem to be sticking around inside me. So that was good news.

If the news stayed good, once I'd closed the hole at school, I would clean up the Coral Castle and snort up all the calamitrons I'd brought here when I summoned Mami Muerta. Soon, our universe would be calamity-free. And maybe it would stay that way, now that Papi and Dad: The Final Frontier were spending day and night studying a paper called "Virtuous Supermembranation Theory: A Foundational Reimagining of Entropy in an Extramembraneous Multiverse," which apparently, to their great surprise, *they* had written. It said so right on the first page, even though they had never seen the paper before an anonymous person had left it on Papi's pillow one night.

But they liked it. A lot. They said it could be the next big breakthrough in calamity physics.

Finally, it seemed like everything was going according to plan. But the universe has a way of changing your plans. Or maybe it's not the universe. Maybe it's just Gabi.

Either way, Gabi definitely changed my plans when she texted me on Sunday night.

Sal! I need to COME OVER right now! Are your parents awake?

It was 11:00 p.m. **No but cannit wait fer tomorrow**, I texted back.

No it CANNOT wait until tomorrow. I am calling a car. I will be there in 20 minutes.

At exactly 11:20 p.m., Gabi's driver-for-hire parked the car at the curb in front of the Coral Castle. I watched from the living room window as her driver got out of the car and pulled a stroller out of the trunk.

Meanwhile, Gabi climbed out of the backseat. She was definitely trying to make herself as invisible as possible. She had tucked all her hair into a black cap, and wore black jeans and a black T-shirt with writing I couldn't read yet, since she was carrying Iggy's car seat in her arms.

Also, Iggy was swaddled in a black blanket. Even the baby was dressed for night ops.

Gabi put Iggy's car seat in the stroller, then reached into the backseat and pulled out a cat carrier. She waved to the driver as he pulled away. Five seconds later, she was standing at my front door, cat carrier in one hand, pushing the stroller with the other. Her T-shirt read: IF YOU WISH TO MAKE AN APPLE PIE FROM SCRATCH, YOU MUST FIRST INVENT THE UNIVERSE.—CARL SAGAN.

"Good evening, Bruce Lee," she said as she entered. She just couldn't go a second without making fun of my pajamas.

"Good evening, Call of Duty," I replied.

We went inside; I shut the door. I immediately made for Iggy. He looked—amazing. Just like a perfectly healthy baby boy.

Well, to be honest, he looked a little weird. Like, he was barely a month old, right? But he had smart, sharp eyes. Like he knew things. Like he could see into your soul.

But healthy! And that's all that matters, right? I gave Iggy a pinkie of mine to hold on to and asked Gabi, "So what's up?"

"We need privacy," she said. "And the entropy sweeper."

So we went to an unused bedroom all the way at the end

of the hallway. That room didn't even have carpet. But it had a door, which we closed.

Gabi pushed the stroller to the center of the room and put the cat carrier down next to it.

"You got a cat?" I asked.

"No," she corrected. "I didn't get a cat. And none of my many, many dads got a cat. *Iggy* got a cat."

"What do you mean?"

"Please allow me to demonstrate. You are going to *love* this." She pulled off the hat and fluffed her hair. Then she knelt and opened the cat carrier.

Out came an orange-and-white-striped cat so huge, it looked like a baby hippo dressed up as a cat for Halloween. It jogged over to Gabi and rubbed its face and head all over her knee. It purred like a motor revving.

"Aw," said Gabi, scritching the cat under its chin, "who's a good Meow-Dad? Who's the best Meow-Dad in the multiverse?"

I snickered. "Meow-Dad? Really?"

"That's just what I call him." She was still using her sweet, lovey talk-to-cats voice. "His tag says his name is 'Transub-Dad-tiation.' I bet ExtraGabi came up with that one after she noticed the Iggys fighting over him."

"What do you mean, the Iggys fighting over him?"

Meow-Dad suddenly tensed. He zoomed three feet one way, five feet the next, tearing through the room in short bursts and skidding to a stop on the carpetless cement. His eyes were huge and his ears were back, as if he were surrounded by dogs or ghosts or ghost dogs or whatever cats are most afraid of.

"Cat zoomies," said Gabi. "He gets them a lot when I let him out of his carrier."

"So this is normal?" I'd never owned a cat.

"This? Yeah. But keep watching."

Meow-Dad kept running around like he was nuts, zigging, zagging, dodging, sprinting, stopping, looking around like he was surrounded by enemies. I was afraid he was going to run smack into a wall and hurt himself.

But instead, with one last freaked-out look, Meow-Dad sprinted toward Iggy and, before I could react, launched himself into the baby stroller. Gabi, by the way, didn't try to stop him.

We looked inside the stroller. Iggy was happily looking around. And Meow-Dad? Meow-Dad was gone.

I blinked. "Did that cat just—?"

"Jump through my little brother like he's a wormhole to another universe so he could go hang out with his other Reál family and probably get a second dinner? That would be a yes."

I was thinking as fast as I could. "And you want to know—"

"If a cat using my brother as a portal to another dimension is leaking calamitrons into our universe, yes."

Well, okay, then. I grabbed the entropy sweeper, which was leaning on the wall, and turned it on.

"I'm alive," it whispered. "Hi, Sal. Hi, Gabi. I'm assuming we're using our indoor voices again?"

"Yes," I whispered back.

"May I use my lights to express my joy at being alive again?"

"Yes."

It rainbowed happily.

"Now," I said, "will you scan this baby for calamitrons?"

"I already have," said the entropy sweeper. "I am very good at my job."

"And?" Gabi asked.

"Zero calamitrons detected!"

Gabi and I both sighed. And then, because a sigh wasn't relief enough, I said, "Phew, baby."

Gabi scratched her head. "I don't get it, Sal. The cat just jumped into another universe. Right through my brother. It should have leaked at least a few calamitrons, right?"

I remembered how the Gladises got switched, calamitron-free. "Maybe. Not necessarily. But usually, yes. In my experience. You know what? I don't know." I pushed my hair off my face. "I have, like, no idea."

"No one does," said the entropy sweeper. "Science is like that. You finally figure out how something works, and twenty more questions pop up. It's enough to make me want to go to sleep." And when I didn't take the hint: "That means I'd like to be turned off now, thank you."

As requested, I pulled out the entropy sweeper's battery.

"Well," said Gabi, "it could be worse."

"Now you have a cat," I agreed.

"I've always wanted one. And Meow-Dad is so beautiful and fat! I love him!"

"And your baby brother is okay."

"Yeah." She scooped Iggy up in her arms. "There's no one in the multiverse quite like you, Biggie Iggy." She turned back to me, fighting to keep her face straight. "That's going to be his rapper name."

"It's perfect," I said.

What did Gabi hear in my voice? A single sob shot out of her mouth.

"Hey, you okay?" I asked, moving toward her.

She swallowed hard, flexed all the muscles in her face, and said, "Don't worry, Sal. We're just getting started. We're going to figure something out. We didn't know we could fix Iggy, but then we explored, and—*boom!*—we found the answer we were looking for. We're gonna do that for you, too. This, I vow." She looked at the ceiling and, through action-hero gritted teeth, added, "Watch out, multiverse. Here comes Gabi."

I blinked six times. It took me that long to figure out what she was talking about. "You mean my mami?"

She nodded, just once. Iggy stared into my soul and—I kid you not—nodded also, just once. Little chacho was scary.

But look. After the week I'd had, my feelings about bringing back Mami were . . . complicated. Of course, yes, my heart still wanted her back. But a heart is just an unthinking, selfish pump. I didn't want any calamitrons to come with her. And anyway, StupidSal's Mami was really nice. Maybe she wouldn't mind if I relaxed my way over to her universe every once in a while for a visit.

"We'll see," I said to Gabi. "We had to be brave for Iggy's sake. Maybe we should concentrate on being smart for a while."

"I'm always smart," said Gabi, cuddling Iggy closer, while smirking at me. "Can't help it."

"Oh yeah? Then why'd you let me stamp 'Gotcha!' on your right hand?"

Gabi turned to stone. "Oh my God, Salvador Alberto Dorado Vidón, I swear on the president's butt, if I look at my hand and see the word 'Gotcha!' there, I am going to scream so loud this whole universe is going to implode."

"Then I suggest you don't look at your hand," I advised.

She looked. She screamed. Iggy giggled. And, for a few seconds anyway, everything was right with the multiverse.

Acknowledgments

It's funny how, once you get down to writing a novel, you suddenly realize that *you know nothing*.

I mean, I am a first-generation Cuban American, so I should know a thing or two about my own experience, right? But here's the thing: I know exactly one thing. Me. What it's been like to be a Cuban American Carlos Hernandez. And let me tell you, mi gente, that's not nearly enough to capture the variety and complexity of my heritage. I needed help.

And that's my own heritage! Have you ever had to build your own middle school? Have you had to describe the daily life of someone with diabetes? Have you ever seen the inside of a NICU? Have you ever broken the universe?

Yeah, me neither. Not before this novel.

Luckily, I have tons of amazing people in my life who shared their knowledge, their genius, and their lives to help me write a better book. I basically need to spend the rest of my life thanking them.

To my family, Mami and Papi, Maria, Jesse, and Bárbii, I am the person I am because of you. Thanks for making me me.

Thanks for all the Spanish help, too. The Cubans I know have a pretty unique way of speaking—loud, fast, loving, and fierce, with words no other Spanish speakers use. Pronouncing the ends of words is totally optional, which always makes conversations, shall we say, exciting. With their help, I tried to capture that speech at a few points in the novel, because I love it so much. It's the accent with which my heart speaks.

When I started conducting research for this novel, I was shocked to discover the rising rates of type-1 and type-2 diabetes among the Latinx populations in the US, including Latinx children. Type "diabetes Latinos" into your favorite search engine and have a read. If you're as stunned as I was by those statistics, you'll know at least one reason why I wanted to draw attention to the issue. To Stephanie Shaw, who shared with me her experiences as a mother of a child with diabetes, a thousand thank-yous. As a writer, actor, and director, you knew how to help me think about diabetes both in terms of medical fact and how to portray it in fiction.

While we're on the subject of medicine, I needed a great deal of information about how newborns get help in hospitals. My source from the inside was D. T. Friedman, who, besides being a physician, advises writers on getting the medical details in their writing right. If I got anything wrong in the hospital scenes, it's my fault, because D.T. did her best to guide me. Thanks so much!

I consulted with fiber artist and fashion designer Betsie Withey for help in describing Death's costume (not to mention how it could be put together in the first place). Betsie is so inspiring and hilarious that I added the entire Textile Arts track at Culeco in honor of her and her art. My conversations with her reminded me of how many different types of geniuses there are in the world, and the huge variety of creativity that exists. Thanks for helping me dress up Death, Betsie!

Besides all the good people who helped me get my facts straight on the novel, I had loads of people who supported the actual writing of it. I've been studying how to write most of my life, and my number one lesson for all writers is this: Readers who know how to critique you and inspire you at the same time are worth their weight in saffron (and let me tell you, saffron is expensive!).

I had three readers who, only because they are unbelievably generous, read the entire manuscript and gave me blow-by-blow reactions, responses, and ideas for improving: Chris Kreuter, Julia Rios, and Jessica Wick. My dear friends, how many embarrassing errors and faux pas did you rescue me from? How many sentences did you improve? How many characters did you refine? I owe you each a life debt. Expect regular installments of thank-yous.

I belong to a writers' group full of literary luminaries: Ellen Kushner and Delia Sherman; Liz Duffy Adams and Joel Derfner; and my own beloved Claire. Dear comrades with pens, not only did you read and critique *Sal and Gabi*, but you provided the camaraderie, hilarity, and friendship that helped to make the long slog of getting words on the page possible. How many days have we spent spread like jacks over Delia and Ellen's living room floor, joking, critiquing, and raiding Ellen's stash of sweets and cheeses? The answer is: not enough. More days like those are required!

Delia and Ellen went a step further and invited Claire and me to spend a month—a *month*, people—with them in Paris—in *Paris*, people—as a combination writing retreat, honeymoon, and general opportunity to improve one's soul. Such wonders I saw! Such dinners! But best of all, mes amours, was having a month of flint-and-steel conversations with you about art, life, and the writing of books. It's a priceless gift you gave me. Thank you.

Like Delia and Ellen, many people helped me to write by providing space and time. As an editor, Erin Underwood has been an absolute champion of my work, and as one of the principal organizers of Boskone, she's put me on the program for three years running. Similarly, I'm endlessly grateful to the good folks at Readercon, and particularly my point person, Emily Wagner, for helping me grow as a writer by giving me a place at the table. Locally here in NYC, Jim Freund has generously had me several times on his radio show, *Hour of the Wolf*, and has featured me as a reader at the *New York Review of Science Fiction* reading series. Kenneth Schneyer invited me to join him and Edward Aubry, Annelisa Aubry-Walton, Anthony Cardno, Jeanne Kramer-Smyth, and Hope Erica on a writing retreat as valuable as it was companionable. To all of you, and to everyone else who has been so kind and encouraging to me as I applied fingers to keyboard, thank you.

The only reason Disney Hyperion approached me about the possibility of writing this book is because Bill Campbell, publisher of Rosarium Books, published a collection of my short stories (PS: Not a kids' collection!) a few years back. I was an unknown writer that he took a chance on, and that gamble led to Rick Riordan reading my collection, and abracadabra! Now I have this dream opportunity. Thank you, Bill, for helping my voice, and the voice of so many writers, be heard.

Once Disney Hyperion wanted to see a novel from me, I had to get professional, fast. I didn't have an agent, so Amal El-Mohtar—and, folks, go out and read everything Amal's ever written *right now*—put me in touch with her agent, DongWon Song, to see if we'd be a good fit for each other. To all of you writers out there, I bestow on you this blessing: *May your agent be half as good as DongWon Song.* DongWon is so great at contracts, and such a deep and thoughtful reader of literature (yet another great friend who critiqued my manuscript so helpfully), so good-humored, and such a joy to be around, that it's almost as if he burst into existence because I wished upon the right falling star. Thank you, DongWon.

And speaking of getting wishes granted, let me tell you a little about Stephanie Lurie, the indefatigable editor of Rick Riordan Presents. She's read and critiqued more than a half million of my words over the course of many drafts, and has taught me more about writing over the course of this process than six years of graduate school. She is relentlessly helpful, always (yes, seriously, no kidding, every single time, *always*) insightful, and, maybe most importantly, open to the wide range of approaches and writing styles different writers have. In other words, she pointed out issues and offered possible solutions but left me at the end of the day to find my own aesthetic way through the novel. Stephanie, I am so very, very grateful.

My second-biggest thank-you has to go to Rick Riordan. Talk about a writer who's doing everything right! Many years before *Sal and Gabi* would even be an idea, I'd read the first Percy Jackson series and was instantly smitten. Rick, to my mind, is one of the great contributors to the middle-grade literary renaissance we're living through right now.

But then, then, on top of consistently producing these utterly charming, humane novels of his, always rife with mythology and wonder, he starts his imprint, Rick Riordan Presents. His goal? Let writers from different cultures share their stories in their own voices and thereby enrich us all. He didn't have to spearhead the creation of a whole imprint. It's a ton of work, and he has books to write! But he did it because he feels so strongly in a chorus of cultural voices and using his success to help others succeed.

Rick, when I grow up, I want to be as big a champion for others as you have been. Thanks forever.

My biggest thanks goes to my love, my wife, C. S. E. Cooney. First, because she's a genius. Her glorious, ascendant prose inspires me to reach new heights as a writer. Second, because she could not be more supportive, carving out huge swaths of time for us to write together and listening to the book (we read aloud to each other constantly) as it was being written. I mean every. Last. Sentence. She is the single best critiquer of my work, both in terms of quality and quantity. Third, because she's hilarious, the absolute perfect playmate. And fourth, for, well, everything. What a life I have now, thanks to her.

Thanks to all of you, dear friends and colleagues. There are many more people who contributed to the completion of this novel than I can fit in here, but to everyone who has supported me, count on me to support you right back. And let me say this: Whatever flaws exist still in this novel are there because of me, since I had ten times more help and guidance than any one person deserves.

And no acknowledgments would be complete without thanking you, the reader. You made this book exist. It is literally nothing until you and I create it together, word by word. Thanks for helping me build and break a universe.

Now, what shall we cocreate next?

Coming in Spring 2020

SAL & GABI

FIX THE UNIVERSE

1

SAL COME QUICK I'M ABOUT TO FIX THE UNIVERSE

That's the text message that woke me up at still-dark o'clock in the morning. I read it like twelve times on my smart-watch until I was fully awake.

I didn't mind being woken up. Ever since Mami died, I've kept text notifications on because I'm scared of missing important messages. And I mean, this one seemed pretty important. Papi was about to "fix the universe," whatever that meant.

And hey, bonus: It had burst the nightmare I'd been having like a balloon. Glad to be free of it. Phew, baby.

Holding my smartwatch up to my mouth, I used speech-to-text to ask Papi, **"Where are you question mark"**

The response came a few seconds later: **REMEMBRANATION MACHINE HURRY**

If I'd been more awake, I would have known that the only place he could have been was inside the big computer that was the culmination of his life's work as a calamity physicist. Last I'd heard, it wasn't working very well. Sounded like maybe it was doing better now.

I sat up, flipped off the covers, planted my feet on the ground, and took a minute to try to Humpty Dumpty my brain back together again.

It'd been a rough night. You'd think that after having the same nightmare for five years I'd be used to it. Plus, most people wouldn't even consider it a nightmare. There's nothing scary about it. Most people who'd lost their mamis would welcome a dream in which she came back to life and was laughing and cooking in a kitchen, just talking about normal stuff, just being family.

But, see, the problem is then you wake up. Your mami vanishes along with your dream, and all that's left is the dark of night. Takes me forever to fall asleep again. I just stare at the ceiling for hours, feeling like I am my mami's grave.

Like you're your mami's grave?! I thought, making fun of myself. *Come on, Sal. Overreact much? Nightmares suck, but now it's morning. Time to reclaim your brain. The brain is the king of the body, remember?*

Whatever, brain. I'm moving, I'm moving.

Step one: Check in with myself. I felt groggy but fine. Nothing hurt. In fact, the more I woke up, the better I felt. Hungry? Yeah, a little. But I was absolutely parched. I smacked my lips: dry, dry, dry, dry, dry. I was as thirsty as a diabetic. Which makes sense, seeing as I *am* a type-1 diabetic.

Nothing to worry about, though. I had it under control. Mostly. Mostly mostly. A lot of the time?

This is why I had to use the smartwatch. It had all sorts

of apps and tools for diabetics—monitors and reminders and *Did You Know?* diabetes trivia pushing itself into your eyeballs at random intervals. After my blood sugar crash three weeks ago, which had earned me an overnight stay in the hospital, American Stepmom and Papi said it was either this smartwatch or a pump. I've tried the cgm thing before, and I know it's so great for so many people. But it made me feel like I was never allowed to forget for one second that I have a "condition." It kept waking me up at night. My smartwatch only does that when Papi texts me that he fixed the universe: And that has happened exactly once. With the smartwatch, diabetes doesn't feel like it's that big of a deal. It's just a pain in the pancreas, instead of being a 24/7 reminder that I have a disability with no cure and no chance of improvement.

Well, not in this universe, anyway. Not yet.

Well, no need to get depressed before I'd even gotten out of bed. I rose, stretched, and enjoyed the silky smoothness of my Bruce Lee pajamas. They never fail to make me feel powerful. If only they had pockets, they'd be perfect.

On my way to see Papi, I stopped in the kitchen for a bladder-busting, water-tower-size tumbler of water and chugged it. Ah. I refilled the tumbler again and headed for the living room.

Or what used to be the living room. The remembranation machine basically took up the whole space. (And let me tell you, that was an accomplishment. We didn't call our house the Coral Castle for nothing. It had a ton of rooms, and all of them were positively palatial.)

Turning the corner out of the kitchen, I basically ran into the massive black box of humming metal that was the machine's housing. It hummed because of all the internal fans that had to run constantly to keep its computer processors cool. It takes a lot of processors to repair holes in the fabric of spacetime, I guess.

"Papi?" I called out, and then sipped more water. Just couldn't get enough this morning.

"In here, Sal!" replied American Stepmom from inside the remembranation machine.

"Hurry, mijo, hurry!" said Papi. He was in there, too.

I walked over to the front, where the display monitor was mounted and one set of goggles (the ones that let you actually see calamitrons) hung from a peg. To the right of the monitor and goggles, the metal door into the machine lay open. I ducked my head and stepped inside.

This was exciting. I'd never been inside the remembranation machine before.

The interior had an eerie green glow thanks to the tiny lights on the black metal boxes stacked on my left and right. The processors were rattling and jumping on aluminum shelves and overclocking themselves so hard you could smell hot metal. It sounded like a low-key wind tunnel in there, thanks to all the fans running.

Straight ahead of me stood Papi, wearing his white bathrobe and poofy white slippers, big as a polar bear in this confined space. He had on a pair of calamity goggles, too, and in his hands he held a pile of papers from which he was reading out loud.

Listening to him read was my stepmom, American Stepmom. She had on her favorite sleepwear: flying-squirrel footie pajamas, complete with flying-squirrel skin flaps under the arms and a squirrel-head hoodie. I don't know how she could stand them. I mean, footie pajamas in Florida? She must have been a thousand degrees in that onesie.

". . . going to raise the calamity saturation value by two point four two times ten to the twelfth power and monitor the permeation valence," Papi was saying to her. "If PV rises more than point seven, Lucy"—he took a moment to whistle dramatically—"we'll know we succeeded."

"Oh," said American Stepmom, nodding fast, her flying-squirrel hoodie nodding one second slower than her head. "Yes, yes, of course. But what if the X factor starts to dance the electric bugaloo with my sonic screwdriver and I get sent back to ancient Egypt?"

Papi blinked. "What are you talking about?"

American Stepmom gripped his shoulders with her creepy squirrel mittens. "What are *you* talking about, Gustavo? I'm not a calamity physicist, remember? I am your darling wife, who is an elementary school assistant principal and a total hottie. Your science friends should be helping you with this!"

Papi laughed at himself. "I'm sorry, mi amor astronómica. I just couldn't wait. The inspiration hit me in a flash." He flicked the pages in his hands. "This paper has had Bonita and me stumped for two weeks now. I couldn't make any sense of it. But last night, as I was sleeping, I figured out the first page in a dream. Or at least I thought I had. I had to see if I was right."

"Buenos días, padres locos," I said.

Papi went nova with joy when he saw me. He handed American Stepmom the papers so he could run over and scoop me up. He's always been a scoop-you-up-and-hug-you-till-you-spit-up-your-guts-like-a-sea-cucumber kind of papi. "¡Mijo!" he yelled in my ear as he squished me. "¡Mijo, mijo, mijo!"

"Papi," I croaked. "Papi, papi, papi."

American Stepmom tapped Papi's shoulder to get him to release me before I lost consciousness. "Be careful, Gustavo! You don't want him to spill his water in here, do you?"

"I saw it," Papi said defensively, adding, "The machine is everything-proof." But still he put me down.

And that's just what American Stepmom wanted, because she took the opportunity to swoop in and give me a hug that wasn't nearly as deadly as Papi's. But it was, thanks to her squirrelly skin flaps, just as enveloping. "Good morning, Sal," she said, in a whisper so low and sincere you'd think I hadn't seen her for a year. "How are you feeling today?"

"Got to pee," I said, finishing my water. "Otherwise good."

She broke off the hug and rapped her smartwatch with the pages she still held in her other hand. "I didn't get a report yet this morning. You didn't test your blood sugar?"

"I would have," I said to her, sounding more like a

whiny kid than I wanted to, "except that Papi texted me to come right away. Something about fixing the universe?"

"I didn't want you to miss it, mijo," Papi said, high on life. "This could be the solution to all our problems. If my calamity calculations are correct, Sal, you're never going to have to worry about tearing holes in the universe ever again. Not to mention that this is scientific history in the making! Come, come!"

He didn't wait for us to come. He bulldozed American Stepmom and me deeper into the remembranation machine. By extending his hand, he asked for the pages American Stepmom had been holding. He visually scanned the first page one more time, then input some numbers on a touch screen on the back wall. He checked his math in the air, scribbling with his finger, and nodded.

"Okay," he said, taking two deep bear breaths. "Okay, it's right. I know it's right. So let's do this." Then, suddenly inspired, he said, "Wait! You do it, Sal. I want you to have the honors."

I generally enjoy having the honors. "Sure. What do I do?"

"Just press enter."

Easy enough. I pressed the key on the video screen.

And then Mami, whom I had felt living in my chest since the day she had become Mami Muerta, was gone. Instantly there was nothing of her soul left inside me.

I felt as empty as a grave without a ghost.

2

OUTSIDE THE REMEMBRANATION machine, I sat on the carpeted floor, looking out of the huge living room window in front of me and taking calming breaths. I had my knees up and my back against the remembranator's black-box housing.

To my right, also with her knees up, sat American Stepsquirrel.

She was watching me carefully. She wasn't crying, but her eyes were wet and ready. It was a little funny, seeing someone dressed like a furry being so concerned and adult. And also slightly disconcerting.

"I'm fine," I said. "It was just a dizzy spell. It's over now."

Which was true. I wasn't light-headed anymore. I still felt like I'd been grave-robbed harder than Tutankh-freaking-amun, but American Stepmom didn't need to hear that right now. It would just make her fret more.

"Sure, baby," she said, sharing one of those smiles that're meant to lend courage in times of trouble. "But let's be guided by the numbers, yeah? See exactly what we're working with?"

I find talking in a French accent a great way to lighten any mood. "Eet would be mah pleazhure," I said. Then—after showing her there was nothing up my right Bruce Lee sleeve, and nothing up my left Bruce Lee sleeve—I revealed a lancet and a test strip.

Where had they come from? It's magic! You've been a great audience! Don't forget to tip your server.

Even though she was eager for me to get on with the blood test, only someone who knew her as well as I did would ever know. American Stepmom's patience level is over 9000. "I never get tired of your magic tricks," she said, squeezing a little more love into my knee. "You're really, really good, you know."

"Bat of co-arse aye know!" I answered. "Aye am, how you zay, a zheen-yus!"

Then, making airplane noises (which you can still do with a French accent, by the way), I flew the lancet around us and buzzed her eyes a few times before I rammed the tiny needle into the side of my left index finger.

"Rammed" is an exaggeration. I barely felt it. Years of practice have taught me how to make finger sticks less painful than, say, sneezing while drinking Coke Zero.

I pressed the test strip against the little dot of blood that had formed on my finger. It lapped up the blood vampirically. Then I inserted the strip into a slot on the side of my smartwatch (told you it was smart). American

Stepmom brought her smartwatch up to her human and squirrel faces so she could see the results at the same time I did. (My smartwatch has WiFi and links automatically to the padres' watches.)

Results arrived almost instantly. My blood sugar number was pretty much where we expected it to be, given that I hadn't had breakfast or any insulin yet this morning.

"Phew," said American Stepmom. She has an almost magical ability to give the word "phew" an entire sentence's worth of meaning. This "phew" meant "When you almost fainted back there in the remembranation machine, I thought your levels might be off, but this reading has lessened, though not completely eliminated, my concerns."

"Phew news is good news," said Papi. He turned the corner to where we were sitting, bearing a tumbler of water he'd gotten from the kitchen for me—my third of the morning.

I took it greedily.

Now that his hand was tumbler-free, he looked at his own smartwatch and then exhaled his relief. "Oh, thank goodness. All normal. You're fine, Sal."

Glub, I confirmed. I had already started drinking and didn't see a need to stop to answer his question. Man, I just could not chug water down fast enough today.

"He is not fine," said American Stepmom. "He nearly fainted. And he's drinking a lot of water. Polydipsia is one of the warning signs for DKA."

"I'm not DKA-ing," I told her, sipping water sullenly. I hated even saying those three letters together. DKA had been Mami's official cause of death.

American Stepmom had more empathy than a mood ring. She backed off a little. "Okay, baby. But do you have any idea why you might have felt faint, Sal?"

"No," I said instantly. Like I was hiding something. Even though I wasn't. Was I?

American Stepmom turned to face Papi, and he was giving her one of those *Our child is not telling us the whole truth* looks. She faced me again, patted the air with both squirrel hands, and said, "Check in with yourself before you answer, baby."

Papi crawled toward us and put his head on American Stepmom's shoulder. "Do one of your meditation techniques, Sal."

I wanted to tell them I wasn't hiding anything, but to be honest, I wasn't sure I wasn't. I might have been hiding something even from myself. So I just said, "I can do that."

I crossed my legs, rested the backs of my hands on my knees, made beaks out of my fingers, and closed my eyes. Breathing is the most important part of meditating. You have to notice it, control it, lose yourself in it, and enjoy it, all at once. It's not easy, doing all of those contradictory things at the same time. But once you figure out how, you can truly relax. And when you relax, my chacho, the multiverse opens up to you.

Or at least it used to. Now, though, the opposite

happened. The urge to cry exploded inside me, billowing like a thunderhead. I opened my eyes and turned to my padres. I had trouble speaking. "I feel . . . less."

They looked at each other, then back at me. "Less what?" asked Papi.

"Just less."

Papi's face became serene, the way it did when he figured something out. "I wonder . . ." he began, raising himself off American Stepmom's shoulder.

"What, baby?" she asked.

Papi looked at me. "You say you're feeling, I don't know, smaller? Shrunken? Trapped inside your own body?"

"Yeah," I answered. "Something like that."

"Huh." Papi sat on his heels and looked at the ceiling. "You know, Sal, fainting may have been a good sign."

American Stepmom made a vicious face, like a mammal-mama protecting her young. "Explain."

Papi had never in his life turned down a chance to explain his thinking and wasn't about to start then. "For five years," he began, jumping up, "Sal has been able to peer into the multiverse. Sometimes he's even reached into other universes and brought other Floramarias here."

American Stepmom's voice had the slightest edge when she said, "Who could forget?"

"But now, thanks to this baby"—Papi lovingly patted the remembranation machine—"he can't do that anymore. It's natural that he would feel disoriented at first. Of course his world would feel smaller. But that's good.

That's how all the rest of us feel! None of us can kidnap people from other universes!"

"It's not kidnapping," I said, even though it was. Before anyone could correct me, I added, "Are you saying this is what it feels like to be normal?"

"Yes, exactly!"

Now maybe you were expecting me to say something like *But I don't want to be normal* or *Normalcy sucks!* Maybe you think it's a great gift I have, to be able to take a look around the multiverse, browse other possibilities for my life, and see how other Sals are getting along.

But when other Sals get to have a Mami and I don't, my relaxing doesn't end up being relaxing at all. It's the opposite. It's me picking the scab off a wound instead of letting it scar and heal. Every time I have ripped a hole in the fabric of spacetime, something inside me has ripped, too. And maybe I was getting a little tired of tearing myself apart.

So I just said, "Oh," and let my emotions—like, all of them, every single feeling I had in my body—dogpile onto my guts.

We all had a lot more to say, but sometimes it's hard to start talking. Before anyone could break the silence, it was broken by Papi's phone singing "Domo arigato, Mr. Roboto" on repeat.

"That's Bonita," said Papi, searching the pockets of his robe. "I asked her to come over early so we could go over this morning's results." Once he had pulled out the phone, he looked confusedly at the screen. "I wonder why she's video-calling me, though."

American Stepmom and I huddled behind him as he swiped his phone to answer the call.

We got an extreme close-up of Bonita's right nostril. It was the most beautiful nostril in the history of nostrils: booger-free, hairless, without a trace of chafing or blackheads—or even pores, for that matter. It's not really a fair competition with the rest of humanity, since her nostril was made of silicone. She was a robot, after all.

"Running over as fast as we can!" said Dad: The Final Frontier. That's Gabi's name for Bonita.

"Wait," said American Stepmom, "are you literally running?"

In reply, the camera pulled away from Dad: The Final Frontier and spun around, panning all the traffic that surrounded her. It wasn't a proper Miami morning rush hour yet, but even light Miami traffic is pretty heavy. The view rotated again to show us that Dad: The Final Frontier was running as fast as the cars around her were moving. She had no problem keeping up with traffic, even though she wore a skirt suit and two-inch heels. She beamed a big smile at the other drivers, waving and saying good morning to them as she used hand signals to change lanes.

Once she had stopped at a red light, it was a little easier for me to make out two really weird things about her:

1. She had a sphere attached to her torso by a harness. It was mounted by shoulder straps so she could carry it hands-free, and was frosted like a shower door, so

I couldn't see inside. On the front of the sphere, a small yellow caution sign hung from a suction cup, warning everyone that there was a Baby on Board.

2. Perched on top of Dad: The Final Frontier's head, strapped in what looked like a safety seat for a giant baby, was Gabi Reál. She had on a golden, glittering, double-sized motorcycle helmet—only a double-sized motorcycle helmet had a chance of holding her humungous hairball—and jeans, sneakers, and a red T-shirt with a message on it that wasn't in focus enough to read. She was making strange wizardy gestures with her hands. Each of her nails was painted a different color.

But when she made a *C'mere!* gesture and the camera zoomed in on her and Bonita, I figured out what she was doing. The camera filming all this was a flying drone, and she was controlling it with her two hands.

She and Dad: The Final Frontier waved to us—that made the drone move left and right dizzyingly fast. Bonita pressed her thumb to her phone screen. In response, the frosted glass of the sphere on her torso became transparent. Now I could see that, riding in a gyroscopic baby seat in the center of it and wearing a onesie that made him look like hugest, cutest empanada in the world, was Gabi's little brother, Iggy.

"See you in fourteen minutes!" Gabi yelled. And just like that, the call ended.